THE
SWORD
AND THE
DAGGER

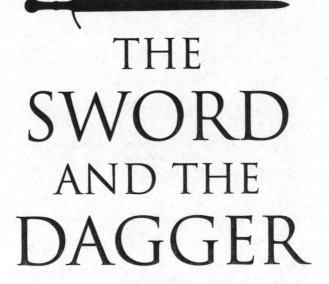

THE
SWORD
AND THE
DAGGER

ROBERT
COCHRAN

TOR
TEEN

A TOM DOHERTY ASSOCIATES BOOK
NEW YORK

THE SWORD AND THE DAGGER

Copyright © 2019 by Robert Cochran

All rights reserved.

Map by Jon Lansberg

A Tor Teen Book
Published by Tom Doherty Associates
175 Fifth Avenue
New York, NY 10010

www.tor-forge.com

Tor® is a registered trademark of Macmillan Publishing Group, LLC.

Library of Congress Cataloging-in-Publication Data

Names: Cochran, Robert, author.
Title: The sword and the dagger / Robert Cochran.
Description: First edition. | New York : Tor Teen, 2019. | "A Tom Doherty
  Associates Book." | Summary: From Tripoli in 1220, Elaine, a sixteen-year-old
  Christian princess, and Prince Conrad, her eighteen-year-old fiance, join Rashid, a
  seventeen-year-old Muslim assassin, on a quest to the court of Genghis Khan.
  Includes historical note.
Identifiers: LCCN 2018049284| ISBN 9780765383839 (hardcover) | ISBN
  9781466893450 (ebook)
Subjects: | CYAC: Adventure and adventures—Fiction. | Princesses—Fiction. |
  Princes—Fiction. | Assassins—Fiction. | Toleration—Fiction. | Betrayal—Fiction.
  | Genghis Khan, 1162-1227—Fiction.
Classification: LCC PZ7.1.C6317 Swo 2019 | DDC [Fic]—dc23
LC record available at https://lccn.loc.gov/2018049284

Our books may be purchased in bulk for promotional,
educational, or business use. Please contact your local bookseller
or the Macmillan Corporate and Premium Sales Department
at 1-800-221-7945, extension 5442, or by email at
MacmillanSpecialMarkets@macmillan.com.

First Edition: April 2019

Printed in the United States of America

0 9 8 7 6 5 4 3 2 1

For Laurie

The Journey from Tripoli to the Caspian Sea, 1220 A.D. [or C.E.]

Al-Jazirah

Antioch

Aleppo

Ar-Raqqah

The Eagle's Nest

The Crossing

Mediterranean Sea

The Garden

Bandit Attack

Tripoli

Syrian Desert

Black Sea

Caspian Sea

Turkey

Syria

Mediterranean Sea

Iraq

Iran

Egypt

Saudi Arabia

Persian Gulf

MODERN COUNTRY BORDERS

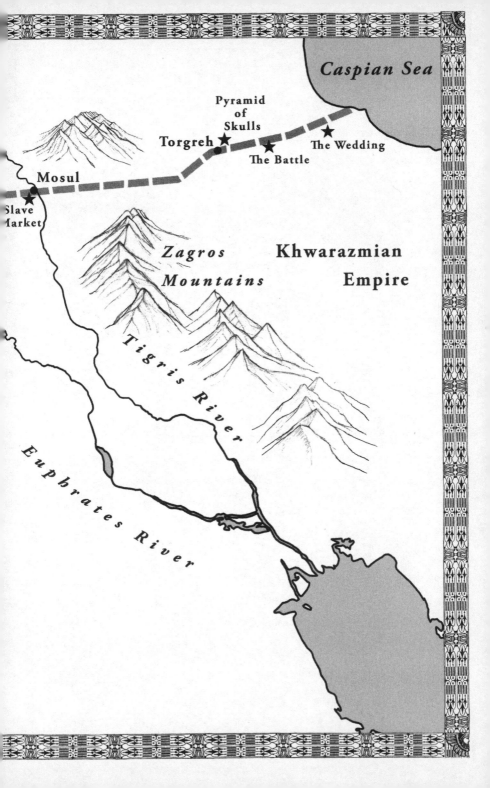

PART ONE

TRIPOLI

AD 1220

1

"What kind of an ass sends a lock of his own hair as a gift?" said Princess Elaine.

It was not a rhetorical question, though Bernard, Regent of Tripoli, seemed to think it was as he and Elaine strolled through the royal garden of the castle. Bernard pretended to be distracted by the lovely flowers that lined the path, sparkling with the dew of a bright spring morning. Dozens of species were present but only two hues—blue and white, the heraldic colors of the Kingdom of Tripoli. But Elaine wasn't to be put off. "Bernard?"

"You shouldn't speak that way of your betrothed," he said finally.

"But doesn't it seem vain?"

"I'm sure he meant well," Bernard said.

Elaine looked at him for a long moment and Bernard couldn't prevent the corners of his mouth from twitching upward in a reluctant smile. "It's a little vain, perhaps," he conceded. "But well intended." He smoothed his thin mustache with his thumb and forefinger, wiping the smile from his face. "The garden is looking quite beautiful, don't you think?"

Elaine nodded absently. The garden was indeed beautiful, and bustling with activity. Pageboys and maids were hanging lanterns and pennants from fruit trees, while gardeners clipped and trimmed juniper bushes into dragons, unicorns, and other fantastic shapes that defied description. Servants pushed barrows piled high with freshly picked vegetables headed for the kitchen and filling the air with the mingled scents of radishes, leeks, and garlic. Whenever anyone caught sight of Elaine they gave her a wide smile, usually accompanied by an annoying twinkle in their eyes, as if they knew how happy she must be. She smiled back, trying to seem genuine. Meanwhile, she pressed on: "As I remember, Conrad always was a little vain."

"That's not fair," said Bernard. "You haven't seen him for six years. He was just a boy! Suppose he judged you as a prospective bride based on his memories of you as a ten-year-old!"

"I suppose I should give him the benefit of the doubt, at least until I see him again."

"Oh, Bernard!" A high-pitched voice sounded from behind them. Bernard turned, thankful for the interruption. It was his wife, Margaret, always high-strung and now particularly anxious, her thin fingers waving nervously like leaves in the light breeze. "I'm worried about the sweetmeats. I mean, will there be enough?"

"Surely the cook has seen to that," Bernard said patiently.

"Well, I don't know," said Margaret vaguely. "I just . . . I just . . ."

"Would you like me to look into it?"

"Yes, if you don't mind."

"Of course."

Margaret nodded her appreciation, then turned to Elaine. "I'm so happy for you! This will be the most magnificent wedding since . . . since . . ."

"Thank you, Margaret," Elaine said. "And thank you for all the trouble you've gone to."

"Trouble? What trouble? You're the Princess, after all!"

Elaine watched as Margaret fluttered away. She didn't exactly dislike Margaret, but it was impossible to relax when she was around. And though Margaret had tried to be a mother figure to Elaine, she'd never been able to hide the fact that she found the task rather burdensome. Margaret's happiness over the wedding was no doubt sincere, for it meant that Elaine would soon be out of her hair.

Elaine looked down at the locket she held in her hand. It was made of silver and its design was simple and elegant, with a small clasp that opened easily. If it had contained something besides tangled strands of Prince Conrad's light brown hair, she would have admired it. She had an impulse to turn the locket over and let the hair fall to the ground, but that was impossible, certainly with Bernard watching; she was obliged to keep the gift intact and even appear grateful for it. She closed the locket and dropped it into the wide pocket of her dress.

"The locket is very beautiful," Bernard said. "At least your young man has taste."

"Assuming he picked it out himself."

From a nearby aisle came a peal of girlish laughter. Elaine glanced over to see several of her maids-in-waiting gathered around a large bush, which they were busily trimming. Their leader, Matilda, daughter of Lord Basil, one of the castle's nobles, saw Elaine watching and said something to the other girls, who stepped aside, giggling, revealing that the bush was now in the shape of a very large rooster. The rooster was a common fertility symbol and it was rather shocking that a group of young maidens would create it—at least they hoped it would be shocking. Elaine widened her eyes and threw up her hands in an exaggerated expression of horror that made the girls laugh, and they sent her on her way with cries of "Good luck!" and "May your marriage be a fruitful one!" and, of course, with big smiles and twinkling eyes. It occurred to Elaine that everyone in the castle was excited about the wedding except the bride. But she couldn't seem to help herself.

Then again, not quite everyone was excited. The castle's Constable, a tall, gaunt, stern-faced man named William Delancey, approached and spoke stiffly to Bernard. "My lord Regent, I'm told the Prince is about two hours away."

"All right. Everything seems ready," said Bernard.

"Evidently he's bringing quite a large retinue."

"Well, make sure we can accommodate them all."

"As you wish." Delancey gave Elaine a respectful but brief nod, then walked away. That he didn't smile was almost a relief, though it reminded Elaine that he disapproved of the coming marriage, claiming that he didn't trust Antioch to be a loyal ally. Of course, a constable was in charge of the castle defenses, and perhaps suspicion went along with the job. But these thoughts were quickly replaced by dismay at the thought of Conrad arriving in the next two hours.

As if reading her mind, Bernard said: "From all I hear, Conrad is a fine young man. Now, he may not quite be the man his brother was, not yet anyway. But of course Charles was extraordinary. When he died the burden fell on Conrad and he was too young to bear it. But I'm told the years in France have done him much good and there's every hope that he'll become another Charles. Something like him, anyway."

He doesn't even believe it himself, thought Elaine. Out loud she said, "It is possible for a woman to rule alone, you know." She'd had this conversation with Bernard before. It led nowhere but she felt she had nothing to lose.

"You've been reading your father's books again," Bernard said.

"Penthesilea, for example, Queen of the Amazons. And Boudica, who fought the Romans."

"Don't forget Cleopatra," Bernard said.

"And Eleanor of Aquitaine! She went on a Crusade, wore men's armor, ruled in her own name, married two kings, and gave birth to two more. Now that was a woman who *lived!*"

"I met her once," Bernard said suddenly.

Elaine couldn't have been more surprised if he'd sprouted antlers. *"You met Eleanor of Aquitaine?"*

"Indeed I did."

"Well, what was she like? Tell me!"

"It was many years ago, on a visit to France. I was quite young,

I don't remember much. She was old when I saw her, and quite thin, as I recall."

"Was she still beautiful?"

Bernard wrinkled his nose. "Not really."

"But she was wearing armor . . ." Elaine said hopefully.

"No, strangely enough she was wearing a dress, like a normal woman."

"But she wasn't a normal woman," Elaine insisted. "She'd seen the world!"

"It didn't do her much good, from what I could tell. She seemed rather sad."

"I don't believe she was sad, not after all she'd done and the places she'd been."

Bernard shrugged, not willing to argue the point.

"Sometimes I think her soul has been reincarnated in me," said Elaine.

Bernard stared at her blankly.

"That's when someone dies, and their soul comes back in another body. I think Eleanor's soul may be in mine."

"Where on earth did you get an outlandish idea like that?"

"I read it in a book, about all the different—"

"I should have known!" Bernard interrupted. "That was probably Eleanor's problem—she read too many books and they put crazy ideas in her head. In any event, this reincarnation business is blasphemy. Don't let the priests hear you talk such nonsense, and for God's sake, don't say anything like that to Conrad!"

This outburst silenced Elaine. After a moment, Bernard went on in a softer tone. "Elaine, I know you're a little nervous. It's only natural before a wedding, and, well, you probably feel a little bit alone. You never knew your mother, and I know you still miss your father—we all do—but I must say you spend too much time reading the books he left you. Some people thought I should have taken them away, but I felt they provided some consolation, yet they seem to have filled your head with . . ." He hesitated.

"Nonsense?"

"Let us say, with ideas that are not practical. And now the time has come when you must be practical. You must remind yourself that what you're doing is important."

"Yes, of course. Antioch and Tripoli must be united. I understand."

"I know you understand with your head. But do you understand with your heart?"

"I'm not sure what you mean."

"I mean you must find a way to give yourself to this marriage completely. It must last, it must produce children, it must be seen to be strong. Antioch and Tripoli are two islands surrounded by a vast sea of enemies. This wedding, this marriage, is not just about unity. It's about survival. Not only your survival, but that of everyone and everything you see around you. Our whole way of life! It's your duty as Princess and I tell you plainly, as I've told you before, it's what your father would have wanted."

Elaine fell silent again; there was no answer to this. Bernard went on. "Now the Prince will be here soon and you look like you're going to a funeral. Can you not manage a smile?"

In fact, she couldn't; but she tried, and the effort contorted her face and made Bernard smile and that finally brought a smile to her face as well, though a shaky one.

"Much better," said Bernard. "I have preparations to attend to so I'll leave you to gather your thoughts. But please be sure you're ready when Conrad arrives, all right?"

She nodded and Bernard walked briskly away. Elaine watched him for a moment, then her eyes fell on a nearby vegetable patch, where gardeners were gathering onions for the coming feast. Onions. No doubt they accounted for the sudden appearance of tears in her eyes.

Elaine continued along the path, rather aimlessly. Tripoli's royal garden had been designed to provide a glimpse of salvation, its paths laid out in the shape of interlocking crosses. Between the paths were groves of fruit trees, mainly apple and orange, which, after the long winter, were just coming into bloom even though the month of May was nearly over. An occasional cypress could also be seen, and here and there an acacia, with bright yellow blossoms that usually gave Elaine great pleasure.

No doubt Bernard was right in saying that her father, King Edmond, would have favored the marriage, and the reasons were plain enough. Three generations ago the Christians had stormed out of Europe and conquered the Holy Land. They'd taken much territory from the Saracens (as they sometimes called Muslims) and established four Crusader states: Jerusalem, Tripoli, Edessa, and Antioch. For a century they'd prospered, but eventually the Saracens had regrouped and retaken Jerusalem and Edessa. Now Tripoli and Antioch were all that remained, controlling their reduced dominions by means of a few strong castles like the one Elaine was in now. The marriage of Conrad and Elaine was intended to unite the last two Crusader states and halt further Saracen advances. All this Elaine knew, and she also knew that the marriage was inevitable.

She resumed her walk, which hadn't been so aimless after all, for she found herself in a familiar place—a narrow clearing that served as an archery range. Her spirits lifted. Archery had never appealed to her, but the range could be used for another purpose as well. She reached into the pocket of her dress—she had insisted that her dresses have pockets over the scandalized objections of Margaret ("so unladylike!")—and took out a length of flaxen string some five feet long; at one end of the string was a loop, at the other a small knot, and in the center a curved patch of leather. A simple device—and one of the oldest and deadliest weapons known to mankind: the sling.

Its use had become unfashionable in recent times, but a veteran knight, Sir Raymond, still had the skill and he had passed it on to Elaine. The sling was easy to make but difficult to use, so practice counted for more than strength; and, unlike a sword or lance or even a bow, it could be wielded as effectively by a woman as by a man, and it was Raymond's firm belief—unusual for a knight—that a woman should be able to protect herself if necessary.

It had been a while since she'd practiced—the wedding preparations kept getting in the way—but she felt confident nonetheless. She searched the ground until she found a stone the size of a robin's egg, and placed it in the leather patch. Then she put the loop of the string around the ring finger of her right hand, and held the knot between her thumb and forefinger of the same hand, letting the leather patch and the stone it contained dangle just above the ground.

For a target, she chose an orange tree fifty paces away—or rather, an orange on the end of one of its branches. She stood at an angle to the tree, her left foot slightly forward.

She took a breath, recalled Raymond's advice ("Speed means nothing if you miss. Take your time!"), then stepped toward the tree and swung the sling over her head twice. Then she whipped her hand forward in a throwing motion, letting the sling act as an extension of her arm. At the top of the arc she released the knot, and the stone flew, fast as any arrow, straight toward the target.

The orange spun and danced but remained on the branch; a glancing blow only. *Not good enough.* She found another stone, seated it in the pouch, and took her stance again. *Step, swing, throw, release*—this time the orange was catapulted from the tree and burst apart, spraying juice everywhere and landing twenty paces away.

Elaine laughed aloud, but this was followed by a pang of sorrow, for she realized what she was doing, what she had been doing since she'd awakened that morning. She was saying goodbye to her childhood, to the places she loved, to her life as she'd known it up to now. First she'd visited the grave of her mother, dead since Elaine was an infant, and next to it that of her father, dead for four years. Then she'd gone for a walk in the garden, where Bernard had found her, and now she was in the archery range where she'd spent so many carefree hours. She had one last place to visit.

The garden was located in the bailey, the open ground between the inner wall of the castle and the keep, a sturdy four-story building of wood and stone that provided living quarters for the royal family and its retainers. The keep was on high ground and as Elaine walked through the gate in the inner wall she could see the main courtyard spread out on the slope below and beyond that the crenellated stone curtain wall, twenty feet high, which enclosed the entire castle grounds. Just inside this curtain wall were the stables, which Elaine loved as much as the garden and the archery range.

She thought horses were the most splendid of God's creatures, beautiful and powerful and fast, and she had rarely encountered one that did not respond to kindness. There were more than a hundred in the stables at Tripoli: powerful destriers, trained for war; sleek coursers bred for speed and show; sturdy, dependable rouncies that worked in the fields alongside the peasants; and versatile palfreys that were used most often for travel.

The stables had something else she was fond of—old Walter, Tripoli's Master of Horse. He'd seen her coming and walked over to greet her.

"My lady," he said with a small bow.

"You're very formal this morning," she answered with a smile.

"It's a special day. And an even more special day tomorrow."

"I see you're only working the destriers."

"The others are being groomed. Isn't the Prince arriving soon?"

"So I'm told." Elaine tried to keep her tone light, but failed.

"Should you not be making ready?" he said gently, sensing her discomfort.

"I will, very soon. Have you seen Sir Raymond?"

"He's been away all week."

"I know. I was hoping he'd be back for the ceremony."

"There's still time. I'm sure he'll be here."

Walter was a sergeant-at-arms, a rank just below that of knight. Nearly sixty, he was still a formidable warrior, though he limped and was almost blind in one eye and his creased, leathery face made him look even older than he was. But around horses he had the energy of a boy, and Elaine had spent countless hours at the stables, especially after the death of her father, asking questions and learning to ride and generally, she later realized, making a nuisance of herself. But Walter never seemed to mind. "The Prince is well spoken of," he said.

"Yes, very well spoken of. How is Roland?"

Walter smiled. "See for yourself." He put two fingers in his mouth and gave a loud, distinctive whistle, which was answered immediately by a whinny from inside the stable's barn. A moment later a dappled gray palfrey cantered out of the barn and came straight over to Walter and Elaine. Elaine had several horses but Roland was her favorite—strong, gentle, with a touch of mischief that Elaine loved. Now he nuzzled her, pushing his nose toward her pocket.

"I'm sorry, Roland, I forgot to pick an apple for you!"

Roland tossed his head as if to show his displeasure, and Elaine and Walter both laughed. "He gets plenty to eat, this one," said Walter, then, to Roland: "Back inside now, let the stable boys finish grooming you." Walter accompanied the words with a broad gesture toward the barn, and Roland, with a soft whinny, trotted back toward his stall.

"Have him ready, I'm planning to take the Prince on a riding tour."

"Roland will be ready," said Walter. "The question is, will you?"

"You're right, I'm leaving now," she said.

Walter caught the note of sadness in her voice and touched her arm gently. "God be with you. I'm sure the meeting will be a happy one. And the marriage as well. And take courage from the fact that you're doing your duty."

She squeezed his hand but could not meet his gaze. She turned and walked quickly back toward the keep. She was beginning to hate the word "duty."

At the gate she turned for a last look at the stables. Walter was back inside the enclosure, working the horses alongside his stable boys, nearly all of whom were hired from the local Arab population.

Elaine had always enjoyed watching the stable boys work the horses and had learned much from doing so, but of course she had never become friendly with them. That wasn't allowed. In fact, the stable boys were forbidden to speak with her or even look at her except very fleetingly. So when she saw one of them staring at her intently she was quite surprised, and even more surprised when he didn't look away. He was lithe and taller than most of the others and was leading a coal-black stallion named Midnight. He held her gaze for a long moment, almost as if he were studying her face, and Elaine felt her cheeks flush with anger. Such insolence was inexcusable and she considered calling out to Walter to have the boy disciplined, but she really did have to prepare for the Prince's arrival.

She decided to let it go. After all, he was just a stable boy.

2

Rashid rode Midnight masterfully, guiding the powerful destrier in a series of tight figure eights using only the pressure of his knees and the shifting of his weight. It was a task that required his full attention, or should have, but at the same time he was cursing himself. He feared that he'd just let the chance of a lifetime slip through his fingers.

A few minutes earlier Rashid had taken Midnight out of his stall for a workout, barely noticing the Master of Horse, Walter, talking with some female by the corral fence, as the palfrey called Roland stood patiently next to them. Then, out of the corner of his eye, something about the girl got Rashid's attention. He risked a quick glance—and froze.

It was the Enemy. The one he'd been sent to assassinate.

Or was it? He'd been shown a portrait, not a very clear one, before leaving the Eagle's Nest six days ago. The hair and the eyes seemed right, but the rest of the face . . . he couldn't be certain. He hadn't seen many Christian women—hadn't seen many women at all—and he couldn't afford to make a mistake. Then Roland trotted back to the stable and the girl began walking back toward the castle keep, just as Ibram, a fellow stable boy, hissed at Rashid: "Stop staring at the Princess! You could be killed for less!"

The words hit Rashid like a blow. It had been the Enemy after all, not fifty paces from where he stood! For an instant he considered attacking anyway, but the Enemy was already nearing the gate to the keep, surrounded by servants preparing the grounds for the wedding, and there were guards with crossbows stationed on the wall. By the time he reached her, the alarm would have been raised and the guards alerted. He did not fear death, but failure was unthinkable.

He had let a golden opportunity—a miracle, in fact—go to waste. Now he was back where he started. He would have to find a way, this very night, to sneak through the castle grounds into the keep itself, past the guards and servants into the Enemy's chamber, and kill her there.

Yet even as he chastised himself, he had to admit that he'd been surprised that the Enemy seemed so . . . harmless. Kind, even. She'd been gentle with Roland, and when she'd noticed Rashid staring at her, she could easily have complained to Walter yet she hadn't. It was hard to imagine she was someone who had to die. But no matter. He had his mission and he would carry it out. If he failed, his whole life would become worse than meaningless.

That life, as far as Rashid was concerned, had begun twelve years ago when his father had brought him, at the age of five, to the castle called the Eagle's Nest, as an offering to God and to the Old Man of the Mountain. Rashid remembered the day well—the walk through the rugged mountain passes to reach the castle perched on a cliff, his own bewilderment at what was happening, the mixture of sorrow and pride in his father's eyes as he gave his only son to Hasan, the Old Man's chief servant. Rashid never saw his father again, but his tears were ignored for his training as an Assassin began that same hour.

His upbringing had been harsh but not cruel, provided he was obedient and worked hard. By the time he was twelve he could ride any horse, wield any dagger, remain motionless for hours, endure extreme cold or heat, live weeks without food and days without water. He was strong and fearless and utterly dedicated to the service of God and of the Old Man. The life had been a lonely one, for friendship among the trainees was discouraged, but when he turned sixteen there came an event that made all the hardships seem as nothing, an event that was almost too sacred to think about: a visit to Paradise. Not a dream, or a vision, or a hallucination, but a visit, which had lasted a day and a night. He still bore a mark from that visit, and to return to that blessed place and dwell there forever became the goal of his life. And now he was tantalizingly close to achieving that goal.

A week ago Hasan had come into his chamber. As always, Hasan wore a plain woolen robe and turban, for the Assassins despised ostentation. He had a grizzled beard streaked with gray and a nose that curved like the beak of a hawk. He had the eyes of a hawk as well, for no mistake, however trivial, escaped them. But on this day those eyes had an extra sparkle that Rashid had never seen before.

"You've been chosen," Hasan announced simply. Rashid had fairly trembled with happiness as Hasan explained the nature of the mission and showed him a portrait of the Enemy that was to be killed. Then Hasan had given him a *shabriyah*, a dagger with a hilt of antelope horn and a blade of gleaming Damascus steel, sharp as any razor. "This is your path back to Paradise, Rashid. Don't stray from it," Hasan had said, and Rashid had replied, "Never!"

The mission was to prevent the marriage of two Christians; Hasan said the killing must take place before the ceremony. Normally the Old Man dispatched Assassins for his own political or religious reasons, but occasionally he would sell his services to others, including Christians, and there was a rumor within the Eagle's Nest that a Christian had visited the castle recently and paid for the assassination. But the politics were not Rashid's concern, and he departed the next day, wearing simple cotton trousers and a loose cotton shirt with an inside pocket designed to hold—and conceal—the *shabriyah*. The journey was without incident, even after he entered the territory of Tripoli. The Christians, or Franks, as the Muslims often referred to them, might rule the land—for now—but the vast majority of the population was Muslim, so a poor Arab boy journeying along the road on foot attracted no attention, as long as he gave way and kept his eyes on the ground whenever he encountered a Christian.

He reached the northeastern outskirts of the city of Tripoli on the fourth day and, as Hasan had instructed, looked for a peddler selling dried fish under a palm tree at the very edge of town.

The peddler's name was Abu Adil. He was about fifty, and reminded Rashid of a squirrel, with a small nose and quick, precise movements. He took Rashid to his home, a small hut with two rooms, one for cooking and eating, the other for sleeping. Abu's wife received Rashid politely but asked no questions. She served a meal of dried fish and cornmeal baked with olive oil, then retired to the sleeping room, leaving Rashid alone with Abu.

"Your journey was uneventful?" said Abu.

"Yes."

"Did you speak with anyone?"

"No one."

"No one at all? You're certain?"

Rashid shifted nervously. "Just an old woman, in Tariq. She gave me water from a well there."

"What did you say to her?"

"I asked her for a drink, she gave me one, and I thanked her."

"Did she watch you as you walked away?"

"No."

"How do you know?"

"Why should she?"

"You were a stranger. People watch strangers. And gossip about them, too."

Rashid's heart sank. Had he made a mistake before his mission was even properly under way? "Did I do wrong?" he said.

"I ask you again, did the woman watch you as you left the well?"

"I don't know."

"Good. Now you're speaking the truth. It wasn't wrong to ask for water. But it was wrong not to take note of her behavior afterwards.

Then you could have informed me, and I could have taken the necessary steps."

"I'm sorry, Abu. I should have been more careful."

"As it happens, the woman was neither a spy nor a gossip and no harm was done. But do not forget the lesson."

"I won't." Inwardly, Rashid marveled that Abu knew about the woman. The Old Man must have spies who spied on his spies.

"Use your own name when you go to the castle," said Abu. "But you are my nephew, the son of my brother Ali, who lives in Ikrit." Rashid nodded; the deception was cleverly constructed. Ikrit was a small village about two days' journey from Tripoli, close enough to be known to the Christians, not so close that they would be overly familiar with it.

"Once you are in the castle," Abu said, "keep to yourself and speak to others as little as you can. Never forget the Franks have their spies, as we do."

Abu rose to his feet and with his sandal smoothed the surface of the dirt floor of the hut. Then he took a cooking knife from over the fireplace. With deft, efficient strokes, he began making marks in the dirt. When he was finished he looked up at Rashid.

"Do you know what this is?" he said.

Rashid stared at the marks. To his eyes they were nothing but a collection of lines and circles, arranged randomly, except that most of the marks were inside one large circle, and that circle was surrounded by an even larger circle.

"I'm sorry, Abu," said Rashid, shaking his head.

"Imagine you are a bird," said Abu.

"A bird?"

"An eagle, flying a little south of where we are right now. What would you see?"

Rashid forced himself to think. An eagle, flying a little south of Abu's hut . . .

"It's the castle!" he said. "The larger circle is the outer wall, the smaller one is the inner wall, and the other lines must be the towers and buildings near the keep!"

Abu smiled approvingly.

"But what good is it? I'm not an eagle."

"No, but you must think like one for now. It has been arranged for an opening to occur in the stables. You will be hired to fill the opening. You won't be allowed access to the rest of the castle, but to carry out your mission you must know it well." Abu pointed at various parts of the diagram as he spoke. "The main gate is here, in the north wall. There are two other gates, here and here. All are closed and guarded at night. The stables are here, and the gates to the inner wall are here, here, and here. And the keep is here. And the Enemy sleeps in one of the rooms in the keep, along the southern wall according to the information we've received. Do you see?"

"I see," said Rashid.

"Learn this well before I erase it. No trace can remain."

The next day Rashid had obtained the position as stable boy with no difficulty, for there were no other applicants—a circumstance that Rashid suspected the Old Man had helped bring about. Walter had kept a sharp eye on him for the first few hours but, satisfied that he could handle horses, seemed to accept him readily enough.

His mission had gone smoothly—almost too smoothly, for he had nearly lost track of time. Four days to reach Abu's hut, a fifth day to obtain the position of stable boy at Tripoli Castle. And now the Prince of Antioch was coming this very day, and tomorrow would bring the wedding, which must not take place.

An impatient chuffing sound from Midnight brought Rashid back to the present. The destrier thought he'd been worked enough and Rashid agreed. He slid off the animal's back and led him into the barn, where Ibram and other stable boys were busy rubbing down their horses. Ibram glanced up as Rashid entered. "What were you thinking, staring at the Princess like that?"

"I was just curious," said Rashid.

"That kind of curiosity will get your eyes put out."

Mizra, shorter than most of the others but powerfully built, came to Rashid's defense. "He's new. He'll learn."

Ibram grunted, then glanced at Rashid. "Where are you from, anyway? You never said."

"A small village called Ikrit," Rashid said. "I'm visiting relatives here in town."

"And what were you so curious about?"

"Just wondering what they'll all be doing tonight, before the wedding."

"Who cares? Drinking and fornicating like most Franks, I suppose."

Rashid joined in the laughter, but kept pressing. He knew the castle's layout from Abu, but he wanted an idea of tonight's activities. "Do you think the preparations inside the keep are complete or will people still be working?"

"How would I know?" said Ibram. "And what difference does it make to you?"

"The more we know about their customs and habits, the better chance we have of getting rid of them," said Rashid. This provoked a general murmur of assent from the others.

"They provide work," Ibram said with a shrug. "But yes. Someday we'll be rid of them, God willing."

"So, what do you think it will be like tonight inside the keep?" Rashid said, but he'd pressed too hard. Mizra stepped forward, eyeing him suspiciously.

"Are you thinking of sneaking into the keep? To steal something, perhaps?"

"The pickings will be fat," Rashid improvised. "Even one silver plate would fetch a fortune in the bazaar. I'll split it with you, with all of you."

"The only thing that will be split is your skull," said Mizra. "And then ours, for helping you." The others, including Ibram, nodded vigorously in agreement.

Rashid put up his hands. "I understand. I swear, I won't try to steal anything."

This defused the situation and Rashid went back to grooming Midnight, outwardly unconcerned but inwardly distressed that he was no closer to getting even a vague picture of what the inside of the keep might be like tonight. He'd have to take it one step at a time.

Or maybe, God willing, there would be another miracle.

3

Prince Conrad of Antioch rode a magnificent chestnut stallion along the coastal road that led from Antioch to Tripoli. Horse and rider were clad in their finest chain mail armor and surcoats, inlaid with silver and gold, and behind them rode a retinue of a dozen knights also in parade armor, followed by fifty squires and pages, all carrying lances sporting red-and-yellow pennants that danced and snapped in the early afternoon breeze. Sir Gilbert, a companion knight who had accompanied Conrad from France, rode side by side with the Prince.

"We're barely four leagues away now," Gilbert said. "Two hours, at most."

"There's no hurry," said Conrad. "It's pleasant enough."

It was indeed a lovely day. Fleecy clouds softened the sky, and sunlight sparkled on the rolling billows of the Mediterranean, creating a riot of gold and blue so bright Conrad's eyes ached when he glanced at it. The road was dotted with villages whose inhabitants lined the route, smiling and cheering and waving handkerchiefs of Tripoli's blue and white, or red and yellow as a courtesy to the visitors from Antioch. It was all very pleasant, or would have been, except for the horse. It was a beautiful courser, named Tranquil, with elegant lines and a rich, deep color, but young and high-strung. Like all knights, Conrad was an accomplished rider, but he was far more comfortable astride the big, powerful destriers that were bred and trained for battle. Tranquil, very badly named in Conrad's view, was a bundle of nerves, unsettled by the crowd and starting at every shadow. Once or twice Conrad thought he detected a trace of laughter from the crowd, but surely the people wouldn't dare laugh at the man who would soon be their ruler.

"Are you nervous?" Gilbert asked, watching him.

"What is there to be nervous about?"

"Come, now. A bridegroom, the day before the ceremony . . ."

"I told you, I know the girl already. Met her a few times, anyway."

"Yes, but you didn't tell me what you thought of her. What is she called again—Elaine?"

"Yes. She was just a child. Scrawny. Thick hair."

"Her face?"

"Sunburned, mainly."

"She sounds lovely."

"Yes, I fear she's not much to look at."

A lone seagull swooping overhead made a sudden dive across the road and Tranquil spooked once more and—Conrad was sure of it now—he heard laughter. He felt his face redden. At least the laughter was subdued; perhaps Gilbert hadn't heard it.

"Well, maybe she's improved over the past years," Gilbert said. "Besides, love isn't everything."

"Love isn't anything," Conrad corrected.

"You mustn't let one bad experience put you off love forever."

"I don't regard it as a bad experience at all. It was highly educational." A recently ended relationship in France had cured Conrad of any sentimental notions regarding love. So when his parents had informed him, the day he'd stepped off the ship ten days ago, that he was betrothed to Elaine of Tripoli, a girl he'd known slightly but had not seen in six years, and would be married to her in little more than a week, he had accepted the news without complaint. "One woman's as good as another," he said aloud.

"A very sensible attitude," Gilbert said. "Besides, you'll have other consolations. Ruling two kingdoms, for example, once your father—" He stopped abruptly. It was a tactless remark, for Conrad's father was seriously ill. "Of course, we all pray that day is a long way off," Gilbert finished hurriedly.

"Yes, of course," said Conrad.

Conrad tried not to let it show, but Gilbert's remark, inadvertent though it was, had stung. Ten days ago Conrad had returned to Antioch with high hopes. In France he had felt like an exile and not a day passed when he did not dream of home; yet on his return he found Antioch had greatly changed—or was it he who had changed?—and it had not felt like home at all. His father's ill health was one factor; most of the time he was too weak even to speak. And Conrad's mother was too preoccupied with caring for him to have much time for Conrad. The rest of the castle's retinue was respectful enough, but Gilbert, who had accompanied him from France, was his only friend. Oh, Conrad knew that Gilbert had other motives for coming, for the Crusader states afforded ambitious young nobles a chance for status and wealth that was not available back home. Still, Conrad was thankful for the companionship, though there were times when he wished Gilbert wouldn't talk quite so much.

"Have you given thought to your first official act?" Gilbert said.

"Official act?"

"Something bold, that will make an impression. Holding a tournament, perhaps. They must have tournaments here."

"Of course they have tournaments here," Conrad said. Gilbert's condescending attitude toward the "overseas" Christian kingdoms was typical of Europeans. Conrad himself, after six years in France, often felt the same way but it still rankled to hear someone else speak in that fashion. Yet he realized he himself had said "they" instead of "we."

"Then a tournament might be a good first step," Gilbert went on. "Or, perhaps you could pass a few new laws just to show you're in charge. Above all, you can't afford to show weakness. This laughter, for example . . ."

"Laughter?" Conrad said. So he had noticed!

"Yes, you must have heard it. It won't do to tolerate too much of it."

Conrad said nothing, but now he realized that the laughter had bothered him more than he cared to admit, for he'd had more than his fill of laughter in France. Even now, the memory was bitter. When he was twelve, he'd been sent, for the last stage of his knightly training, to his uncle's castle in Burgundy, a region of France known for its beautiful countryside and sophisticated inhabitants. Things had gone wrong from the start; he never quite knew why. Though a prince, he'd been treated like a country bumpkin, mocked for his manners and his accent, for the way he ate and dressed and danced. Even his appearance had been ridiculed; his tormentors had taken note of his unusually long arms. *Homme grand singe*, they'd called him. *Ape-man.*

But there was one thing he was good at: fighting. His brother, Charles, had taught him well. Conrad could still remember his first lesson, on his seventh birthday when his training for knighthood had formally begun. He'd stood timidly, wooden sword and shield in hand, facing another boy similarly equipped. Charles had whispered in his ear, "You look just as frightening to him as he does to you!" And so it had proved.

Over time, his muscles hardened and his long arms turned out to be an advantage and his loneliness and humiliation coalesced into a white-hot rage he could summon up at will. The turning point had been a tournament in neighboring Poitou, when the local champion, a seasoned warrior of thirty, had challenged Conrad, intending to put the bumpkin in his place. But a moment later the champion was sent hurtling from his horse and Conrad had triumphed.

He had imagined Charles smiling at his victory—Charles of the laughing eyes and strong right arm, the best brother and teacher on earth; Charles, who would have been the finest ruler in the Crusader territories had he not been killed in a freak accident in a tournament seven years ago. After that, the responsibilities and expectations that had rested on him had fallen to Conrad, and he'd been sent to France to make up for lost time.

He became aware that his hand had come to rest on the hilt of the sword that hung from his belt. The sword had once belonged to Charles. It was made of tempered steel, hard enough to hold an edge yet resilient enough not to shatter on impact. The blade was over three feet long and double-edged, three inches wide and tapering gracefully to a sharp point. The hilt was hardwood of a distinctive rose color, and set in the pommel was a brilliant sapphire, Charles's birthstone. The sword had helped him stop the laughter in France and, if necessary, he was confident it would help him stop it here as well.

"It's especially important since some opposition to the match has been expressed," Gilbert was saying.

"Opposition? Expressed by whom?" said Conrad sharply.

"Oh, nothing specific. For one thing, the Saracens can't be pleased to see two kingdoms united."

"The Saracens have nothing to say about it."

"No, of course not. But I have the impression some in Antioch think Tripoli is weak and will drag Antioch down. There may even be some in Tripoli who are less than pleased."

"How do you know all this? We've only been here ten days."

"I don't *know* anything. As I say, it's just an impression. But I do try to keep my ears and eyes open. I don't mean to alarm you. It's just—it's always best to be prudent."

"I can't see why anyone in Tripoli would be opposed to this marriage," Conrad said. "Surely they can see this is their best chance to survive."

"Yes, since their pathetic King couldn't produce a male heir."

"To be fair, his wife died."

"Then he should have taken another! Carried out his responsibility."

"Well, it's my responsibility now."

"Yes. And as I say, you must show strength. And you would do well to watch your back."

"You're too suspicious. That's what you get for growing up in French courts."

"I suspect courts are pretty much the same everywhere."

"I'll show strength, never fear. As for watching my back, I'll leave that to you."

"And I will do so, count on it. I just hope this Elaine has enough sense to be grateful for this marriage, or at least appreciative."

"I think she'll be easy enough to handle. I've already sent her a small gift."

"Excellent."

"A silver locket, with a lock of my hair. It's very fashionable in France."

"Very thoughtful."

"Yes," said Conrad confidently. "I'm sure it made a good impression."

He heard excited voices from the entourage behind him. He looked round to see what was causing the commotion and realized that the town of Tripoli was now in sight down the coast. Perched on the hillside over the town like a sentinel of stone was Tripoli Castle, where his bride was waiting.

4

"There they are!"

The exclamation came from Matilda, Elaine's maid-in-waiting. Her eyes shone with excitement as she looked out the window of the western tower. Elaine tried to remain unruffled, as befit a princess, but her curiosity triumphed and she went to the window.

"Where? I don't see anything."

"There! Just past the furthest pier."

Elaine looked at the spot indicated by Matilda's outstretched finger and saw the procession of horsemen, tiny at this distance, riding toward the castle along the coastal road.

"I wonder what he looks like?" Matilda said.

"We'll find out soon enough," said Elaine.

"Don't pretend you're not interested!"

"I'm interested, but I'm not going to fall out the window looking."

Matilda laughed and took a step back. "You're still upset about the locket of hair."

"You have to admit, it seems very conceited, which is mainly what I remember about him. That, and he was a bully."

"A bully?"

"I remember him picking on Richard—you remember, Sir

Reynald's son. He was much smaller and Conrad used to push him down. He pretended it was a game but Richard didn't seem to enjoy it very much."

Matilda shrugged. "Princes have to learn to assert themselves. That's how princes *should* behave."

"Maybe you should marry him," said Elaine.

Matilda gave her an exaggerated look from under her eyebrows. "That's an idea. Maybe I'll steal him from you!"

Elaine laughed. The two girls had been friends for many years, though they were very different: Matilda was obsessed with looks, clothes, dancing, and impressing young knights, while Elaine preferred reading, practicing with her sling, and imagining adventures in far-off places. They'd often joked that Matilda should have been the princess and Elaine the maid, but in recent years the joke had fallen away; it was too close to the truth. Matilda had the fair skin, flaxen hair, delicate features, and dimples that a princess ought to have, while Elaine had thick, unruly brown hair, a dark complexion from too much sun, a rather wide mouth, and not a dimple in sight. Such beauty as she possessed resided mainly in her eyes, pools of violet alive with intelligence and curiosity. In the last year she'd begun to sense that some men, under the gaze of those eyes, were willing to overlook her other shortcomings. What Conrad thought, she would find out soon enough.

"Here, let me look at you." Matilda turned Elaine around, examining the gown they'd chosen for the occasion. Silk, with alternating fields of lavender and rose trimmed with blue, it was formal yet understated, with a dignified charm. At least Elaine hoped so. Matilda straightened a pleat and adjusted the blue sash around the waist. "Perfect," she said. "But your hair . . ."

"What's wrong with it?"

"Oh, nothing, except it looks like a family of mice has been living in it. Here, turn back around."

Elaine turned and looked out the window again while Matilda fussed with the braids and pins that were intended to keep her hair in place, at least for a few hours. She looked away from the riders and out at the city and harbor of Tripoli—a magnificent sight and one she never tired of. Westward, just past the curtain wall, the aristocracy and wealthier merchants had built their homes of cedar and granite; next came the wood and mudbrick dwellings and workshops of the ordinary merchants and tradesmen; and finally, a mile or so distant, were the piers and wharves of the busy port, where ships from all over the Mediterranean came and went, loading and unloading their cargo.

Elaine felt her spirits lift. She looked again at the procession of horsemen, perceptibly closer now, and she dared to hope that Conrad might turn out to be a pleasant surprise. It was foolish to judge him based on half-formed childhood memories.

"There," Matilda was saying, giving Elaine's hair a final pat. "That'll do very nicely. Your father would be so proud!"

Elaine was suddenly overcome with a keen wish that her father were still alive, and here by her side. He would know just what to say and do to calm her worries. But she knew Matilda was doing her best, and she swallowed the lump in her throat and said, "Thank you, Matilda, I'd look a mess without you."

"You certainly would," Matilda teased, but she was pleased at the compliment.

The two girls stayed by the window and watched as the line of riders turned away from the coast and began to make its way up the hill to the castle. "They'll be inside the walls soon," said Matilda. "Shall we go down?"

"Not yet," said Elaine. "It's a warm day, I don't want to perspire and stain the dress."

"That's a terrible excuse," said Matilda.

"Give me a little time, I'll think of a better one."

Matilda smiled but didn't press the issue. The horsemen had entered the town and were winding their way along the narrow streets between the buildings. After another twenty minutes, the procession turned onto the road that led to the main gate of the castle, and the girls got their first real look at Prince Conrad.

His appearance was pleasing enough at first glance, but Elaine's gaze quickly shifted to his horse, a beautiful chestnut courser, young and high-strung. It tugged nervously on the reins, and when Conrad tugged back the horse skittered to the side, to the Prince's very evident displeasure.

"He's very handsome," said Matilda.

"Not much of a horseman," said Elaine.

"Who cares?"

"I do. You can tell a lot about a man from the way he handles a horse."

"I'm more interested in the way he handles a woman."

"You would be," said Elaine. "But the two things may be more closely related than you think."

"How would you know?"

"I just think it stands to reason."

Matilda gave a dismissive wave of her hand. "The horse is nervous, that's all. But look at his jaw, his hair, the way he holds himself."

"Conrad, or the horse?" said Elaine.

Matilda laughed then said mischievously, "He has long arms and long fingers as well. You know what they say about men with long fingers!" Elaine blushed but couldn't help laughing.

Conrad was nearing the barbican, the stone structure that protected the castle's iron gate. His horse shied again and Conrad jerked so hard on the reins that the horse made two full circles before Conrad could straighten him out. There was laughter from the crowd—Elaine could hear it even in the tower—and Conrad looked around angrily before digging his spurs into the horse's flanks and urging him onward.

Elaine shook her head. "Can't he see, the horse is afraid of the shadow."

"The shadow?"

"The shadow of the barbican!"

And indeed, the chestnut stallion became even more agitated as he came under the barbican's shadow. He balked, danced from side to side, and refused to continue. Conrad carried a heavy leather whip in his right hand, embossed with precious stones and meant for display rather than use; but he used it now, striking the horse sharply across its ears, twice.

Elaine recoiled in horror. Her stomach clenched as she imagined Conrad striking Roland the way he'd struck the unfortunate chestnut. "He's . . . he's a monster!"

Matilda looked at her sharply. "Be careful, Elaine. This time tomorrow he'll be your husband."

Elaine just shook her head. She'd only had a glimpse of the Prince but it had been enough to confirm her worst fears—and then it got still worse. The horse started to bolt; Conrad reined it in savagely; and when a groom reached out a helping hand, Conrad slashed his hand with the whip so hard it drew blood. He dug his spurs into the stallion again and finally managed to force it past the shadow, through the gate, and into the castle's courtyard.

Elaine, her eyes blazing, turned to Matilda. "What do you think now? Is that the way a prince should behave?"

Matilda wouldn't meet her gaze, and just said quietly, "We should go."

Elaine remained motionless. She suddenly seemed made of stone.

"Elaine, you have to greet him. The horse is anxious, and so is he. Don't judge him too harshly, you haven't even spoken to him yet."

"And I have no wish to, unless it's to tell him what I think of him," said Elaine.

"You'll do no such thing. And we have to go, now."

Impulsively Elaine took her sling out of the dress she'd worn that morning and put it in the pocket of the lavender-and-rose gown she had on. It made no sense, except perhaps as an attempt to carry something familiar into an unfamiliar situation, but it made her feel a little better.

Matilda said, with raised eyebrows: "Are you planning to sling a stone at the Prince?"

"I wouldn't rule it out," said Elaine, and finally allowed Matilda to lead her out the door and down the staircase to the courtyard.

By the time the girls came to the inner courtyard the castle's dignitaries were already assembled. Walter, Margaret, Constable Delancey, Matilda's father, Lord Basil, and a dozen other courtiers stood in a semicircle, with Bernard in the center. Conrad had already arrived and dismounted. Bernard was saying, "I'm sure she'll be here any moment, Your Grace. You know how women are, they want to look their very—" At that moment he caught sight of Elaine and turned back to Conrad.

"Here she is now."

Conrad turned and an expression of confusion crossed his face. Elaine could imagine why. *He's wondering which of us is the Princess. No doubt he hopes it's Matilda.* But Elaine was walking in front and Conrad realized his error soon enough.

"My lord Conrad," Elaine said, with a curtsy.

"Princess Elaine." His voice sounded a little hoarse. Or was it a note of disappointment? Up close, Elaine had to concede that Conrad was handsome enough in a conventional sort of way, with the square jaw Matilda had noted and thick brown hair cut rather short and light blue eyes that were not as cruel as Elaine had expected, but seemed somewhat arrogant.

"Allow me to present Sir Gilbert of Burgundy," said Conrad.

Elaine nodded to Gilbert. "And this is my maid-in-waiting, Lady Matilda."

Gilbert's eyes locked on to Matilda and she returned the favor. The two held the look for a long moment and Matilda produced a modest, dimpled smile Elaine had seen her employ often. Gilbert already looked half-smitten. If the occasion had not been such a serious one, Elaine would have been amused.

"You knew Conrad before he went to France, do you remember?" Bernard said to her.

"I remember."

"What would you say to giving him a tour of our castle grounds?" Bernard continued smoothly. "They've been enlarged, I think, since he was here last. The garden is especially lovely this time of year."

Elaine was expecting this—she and Bernard had rehearsed it—but she had decided to add a wrinkle Bernard wasn't expecting. "I would love to give the Prince a tour, but I wonder if we might do so on horseback? I haven't had my ride yet today, and I do so love to ride."

Bernard hesitated. He didn't like improvisation. "The horses are tired," he said. "They should be taken to the stables."

"We'll ride them to the stables," Elaine said. "Then walk to the garden from there."

Bernard glanced at Conrad, who said, "Certainly, if it would please the Princess."

"What would really please me," Elaine said, "would be if I might be permitted to ride your horse." She'd originally intended to ride Roland, but the chance to embarrass Conrad was too good to pass up. If she could control his horse better than he could, it might teach him a little humility.

Conrad smiled condescendingly. "You couldn't control him. He's quite excitable."

"May I not at least try? He's such a beautiful horse, it would mean so much to me! Please?"

Conrad shrugged. "If you insist. But don't blame me if he throws you."

Elaine approached the stallion and stroked him gently. "What's his name?"

"Tranquil," said Conrad. If he found any humor in the incongruity between the horse's name and his temperament, he gave no sign of it. Two grooms stepped forward and helped her into the saddle, making sure her skirts revealed no leg in the process. Another horse, a big steady gray, was brought forward for Conrad. The royal couple started off at a walk, while grooms, three from Antioch and three from Tripoli, followed at a respectful distance. Matilda and Gilbert trailed along as well. Elaine could hear Matilda giggling at something Gilbert had said.

For a while they rode in silence. There was a slight trembling from the stallion, and Elaine stroked his withers gently. If she stayed calm, so would the horse. They headed through the bailey gate into the courtyard and toward the stables, while Elaine tried to think of something to say. In the end it was Conrad who spoke first.

"You were late," he said.

"I was making preparations. I ask your forgiveness."

"Of course. But in the future please keep in mind the need to show proper respect."

"I shall endeavor to do so," she said coldly.

He gave a nod but did not seem completely satisfied, for he cleared his throat as if searching for the right words.

"Is there anything else?" Elaine asked.

"You received my gift?" he said.

"Your gift?"

"The locket."

"With your hair."

"That's right."

"Yes, I did receive it. Many thanks."

"You're not wearing it."

"It's far too precious to wear."

"Yes, you're right, of course it is," he said. She glanced at his face for some sign of irony but found none. He tried to meet her glance but she looked away. She was afraid if their eyes met she'd say something she'd regret.

"I remember you, from before I went to France," he said.

"Do you?" she said.

"Yes. You look different."

"How so?"

"You are . . . more pleasant to look at."

"Was I so unpleasant before?"

"No, not unpleasant, but . . ."

"Yes?"

"Well," he fumbled, "your legs were . . ."

"My legs were what?"

"Too long for the rest of you, somehow."

"Well," she said, "they had to reach all the way to the ground, you know."

He frowned. "Everyone's legs reach the ground."

"It was a joke."

"Oh," he said.

This was even worse than she'd feared. Would she really be spending the rest of her life with this vain, humorless prig? Despair settled around her like a cloak. She could tell that Conrad was aware of her disapproval but she didn't care. In fact, it only goaded her on.

"Tranquil doesn't seem so excitable as you predicted," she said sweetly. Conrad's face flushed and his jaw muscles tightened, but Elaine continued, "In fact, I would say he seems rather . . . tranquil."

"You mock me," Conrad said.

"Heaven forbid," said Elaine.

"Dismount," he said abruptly.

"I beg your pardon?"

"Get off the horse."

"You said I could ride it."

"You've ridden it."

"You want me to get off now?"

"That's right."

"We're not at the stables yet."

"I can see that. Dismount, if you please."

She stared at him; he was quite serious. She dismounted and he did the same. She refused his attempt to help her onto the gray and vaulted into the saddle, her skirts billowing. If he found that unladylike so much the better. He mounted Tranquil, and they resumed riding in silence.

The stables were in a state of confusion. The horses of the castle were being relocated to make room for the dozens more that had come with the Prince. Horses stamped and pawed, whinnying with excitement; stallions snorted threateningly. Stable boys and grooms, struggling to control their mounts, jostled, elbowed, and argued, their voices overlaid by the gruff shouted orders of knights and squires. Into this loud and dusty chaos Elaine and Conrad rode, and even Elaine, riding the gray, could sense the sudden tension in Conrad's chestnut stallion.

Conrad sensed it, too, and Elaine saw that he was more determined than ever to control the horse. Meanwhile, she could see Bernard and the others strolling toward the stables from the courtyard, eager to see how the first meeting between Prince and Princess had gone.

Tranquil jerked at the reins, and Conrad pulled back viciously. The contest of wills escalated and the stallion pawed and bucked. At that moment a stable boy passed by leading Midnight, and the chestnut crashed into it broadside. Both stallions reared, hooves flailing. Conrad tumbled from the saddle and fell heavily to the ground.

For a knight to be unhorsed, except by an opponent in the lists, was unheard of, and as Conrad scrambled to his feet there were cries of surprise—and laughter. He turned furiously on the Arab stable boy, who, Elaine now realized, was the tall one who had stared at her earlier that morning. He was staring at her now as well, with an expression of surprise and something else that Elaine couldn't quite decipher.

"You clumsy fool!" Conrad shouted. "I'll have you flogged! Seize him!"

Two large grooms grabbed hold of the boy's arms, holding him still, and while he was helpless Conrad struck him across the face with his riding crop. This was the last straw; loathing for Conrad rose inside Elaine like a flood. The grooms started to drag the stable boy off.

"Stop!" Elaine heard herself say. "The fault was not his."

The grooms stopped and Conrad turned on Elaine, white with anger. "Hold your tongue! I'll teach you your duty soon enough!" He turned back to the Arab and tried to strike him again but, despite being held, this time the boy somehow managed to duck under the blow, and Conrad's whip struck one of the grooms instead, which only enraged Conrad further.

"Do as I say, take him!" he said to the grooms. "I want him flogged to death!" Then he said to the Arab in a tone that made Elaine's blood freeze, "Not one inch of skin will remain on your flesh!"

"Let him be!" said Elaine to the grooms.

Conrad shot her a murderous glare but she met it squarely: "He's blameless."

"He attacked me!"

"He did nothing of the sort. The collision was caused by your poor horsemanship and nothing else. He will be dismissed, but he will certainly not be executed!"

Conrad shouted again to the grooms, "Take him, damn you!"

"Do not," said Elaine.

The grooms were from Tripoli, used to obeying Elaine; they didn't move. Conrad, livid and humiliated beyond endurance, turned back to Elaine. They spat the words at each other:

"By God, I will teach you to obey me!"

"I will never obey you!"

By now Bernard had arrived. "What's the trouble?" he asked anxiously.

"This Arab dog knocked me from my horse. I ordered him flogged but she defends him!"

"The fault was Conrad's," Elaine insisted.

"Elaine—" Bernard began, but she interrupted him.

"I saw it all, Bernard. The stable boy did nothing wrong. Nothing at all!"

Bernard hesitated, but only for a moment. Then he said, "Take him away and flog him as the Prince commanded."

But Bernard's hesitation had caused the confused grooms to relax their grip on the stable boy for an instant. He wrenched his arms free. Then, quick as lightning, he drew a dagger from his shirt, raised it high over his head, and charged toward Elaine.

5

Elaine was trapped in a nightmare, where things seemed to happen slowly yet she was unable to move. Or perhaps her mind simply refused to accept what her eyes saw: she was being attacked by a man whose life she had just saved. The Arab was three steps away, then two, then one, the dagger poised to strike . . .

Their eyes met, Elaine's wide and disbelieving, his determined. But then he hesitated, the knife poised to strike but not moving. Someone stepped forward and blocked his arm. Elaine, still in shock, dimly realized it was Conrad who had intervened.

The Arab yanked his arm free and turned toward Conrad, who was already drawing his sword. Then Walter stepped between her and the Arab and she heard him roar, "To arms! To arms!" Squires and knights were already reaching for their weapons amid incoherent cries of alarm and confusion.

Bernard's cry sounded above the tumult, "Seize him!" and the Arab turned and fled. A squire who tried to block his path had his belly slashed open for his trouble. The squire howled in pain while the Arab ran toward Tranquil, the nearest horse, and vaulted onto his back. He leaned over the stallion's neck, grasped the reins, and dug his heels into his side. Within a few strides the big chestnut was at full gallop, rapidly leaving the stables behind.

Bernard screamed, "He must not escape!"

Walter said in a calm but commanding voice, "Mount and pursue!" as he himself climbed on the closest horse. Conrad had already mounted the gray Elaine had been riding and was the first to give chase, with Walter close behind and a dozen others trailing after.

Elaine began to recover her poise. She saw that Margaret, Bernard's wife, had fainted dead away, and that Gilbert and Matilda were both standing motionless, wide-eyed and openmouthed. Then she saw the Arab ride through the gate that led to the bailey, and rein sharply to the right, leaning low on the horse's neck to present a smaller target for arrows. She realized he was making for the main gate, a logical choice, but she remembered—*the main gate would be closed.* Bernard had instructed the servants to close it once the Prince had passed through, lest too many commoners from the town crowd into the courtyard. She cried out, "The gate's closed, he'll have to turn back!" But Conrad and the others were already too far away to hear.

Elaine had a sudden vision of the Arab somehow evading his pursuers and doubling back to the stables and attacking her again. But this was impossible—the entire castle was on the alert and it was only a matter of time until he was killed—and Elaine, thinking more clearly by the moment, decided she couldn't allow that to happen. The attempt on her life demanded an explanation, and the Arab stable boy was the only one who could provide it. He must not die, at least not yet. She climbed onto a horse and, ignoring the startled looks of the squires still in the stables, started for the bailey gate. Bernard looked up from his just reviving wife and cried out, "Elaine! For God's sake!" but she ignored him and urged the horse on.

By the time she entered the bailey it was empty except for a few stragglers who were hurrying on foot toward the side gate that led to the garden. The Arab, finding the main gate closed, must have veered into the garden, hoping its orchards might provide some sort of cover. Elaine guided her horse past the stragglers and through the garden gate.

Armed riders were everywhere, brandishing their swords and heedlessly urging their horses forward, snapping off branches and trampling flowers. A tremendous shout arose near the garden's southern wall and Elaine rode toward the sound.

The Arab had dismounted and attempted to reach the southern wall on foot with the intention of climbing over it, but Conrad had managed to block his path and Elaine arrived just as the fight began.

The Arab faced the Knight, dagger at the ready. Conrad was still mounted, but it soon became evident that the Arab could move just as quickly on foot as Conrad could maneuver the horse at such close quarters, so he leaped to the ground, his sword raised. Walter and the other pursuers had gathered around but Conrad cried out:

"Hold off, he's mine!"

Conrad held a broadsword, a weapon so big some men needed two hands to wield it, yet as Elaine slid from her horse she saw that the contest was not wholly unequal. Compared to the dagger the sword was unwieldy; a blow was fatal if it landed, but if it missed, Conrad would be vulnerable to a counterattack and the Arab had already shown that he could move very quickly. Both combatants were cautious as they circled, trying to find an opening or provoke one.

Conrad feinted with his left foot as if to strike from that side, then swung his sword the opposite way. The Arab was fooled but pulled back as the blade sang past his face, missing by an inch. Now Conrad was slightly off balance and the Arab darted in for a thrust that Conrad avoided, though the dagger's point ripped his surcoat. They began circling again, breathing heavily and never taking their eyes off one another. Most of the men watching were armed and, despite Conrad's orders, Elaine knew if the Arab gained an advantage he would be killed instantly.

That was the very thing she could not allow. Quickly she

searched the ground until she found the right stone, then took the sling from the pocket of her dress and found a gap in the crowd large enough to give her a little room. She steadied herself and took a breath . . . *step, swing, throw, release* . . .

The stone flew straight and true and struck the Arab just behind his right ear. He dropped to the ground. A larger stone might have killed him, but Elaine had chosen well and he was stunned but alive.

Conrad turned on the crowd in a fury.

"Who did that?"

"I did," Elaine said.

"You?" He didn't believe it at first but then he saw the sling in her hand. "I said he was mine!"

"He must not be killed," Elaine said.

"Why the devil not?"

"Because he tried to kill me and I want to know why!"

Conrad was too angry to comprehend what she was saying. A gruff voice spoke from behind Elaine. "The Princess is right, Your Grace." It was Walter. He stepped past her toward Conrad and continued, "It would be well to know his reason."

"He was trying to stop the marriage. Is that not obvious?"

"It would also be well to know who sent him," Walter said.

Conrad said stubbornly, "How do you know he was sent by anyone?"

"The dagger," Walter said.

"What of it?"

Walter leaned over and took the dagger out of the Arab's hand and hefted it. "It's beautifully made, is it not? And perfectly balanced. See for yourself. The Saracens call it a *shabriyah*."

He handed the dagger to Conrad, who glanced at it and snapped, "And what of that?"

"How does a poor Arab stable boy afford such a weapon?" Walter asked, and there were murmurs of agreement from the crowd so that even Conrad couldn't argue the point further.

"Very well," he said. "Take him and do whatever you must. But don't kill him. Leave that for me."

"Of course, Your Grace," said Walter blandly, though Elaine caught the expression of contempt on his face.

She was aware that Conrad was looking at her and she turned to him. His expression had changed from hot anger to cold fury. She gave him a look she hoped was a match for his own.

"You must learn to do your duty, which is to obey me," said Conrad.

She lifted her chin. "We are not yet married, sir. I have no duty toward you at all."

"You take pleasure in defying me," he said.

"Nothing about you gives me pleasure," said Elaine, then turned on her heel and walked away. Now that the crisis had passed her knees were weak and her stride unsteady, but she tried her best to hide it and walked quickly toward the castle keep.

6

Elaine was alone in her chamber, where she'd been ever since she'd returned from the stables. Half-dazed from the attack, she'd fallen into a fitful sleep for a few hours, but now she was awake and aware of an unnatural silence that had fallen over the entire castle. No doubt everyone else was also stunned by the attack, but she felt the need for some human contact. No one had come to see her, not even Matilda.

She opened the door to her room and was startled to see three armed guards standing outside. Of course, it made sense that she would be assigned protection after what had happened.

"Your Grace," one of the guards said. "Is everything all right?"

"Where is everyone? Why is it so quiet?"

"Everyone has been told to remain in their rooms, Your Grace. No one is to be in the halls. As a precaution."

"Where is Bernard?"

"I believe in the council room, Your Grace. A meeting has been called."

"And I wasn't informed?"

"It was thought best not to disturb you."

"I'm fine. And I'd like to join the meeting. I'm sure it concerns what happened at the stables."

52

The guards exchanged uneasy looks. "No one is to be in the halls, Your Grace."

"The men used the halls to reach the council room, did they not? Well, so will I."

And she started off down the hall with a determined stride that left the guards scrambling to keep up.

The council room held a large rectangular table of oak, surrounded by a dozen chairs. When Elaine entered the meeting was just starting and the attendees—all men—looked up in surprise as she walked in. There were ten present, all familiar faces, but only four that mattered: Bernard, seated at the head, Walter, Lord Basil, and Constable William Delancey. Present as well were Conrad and his companion, Sir Gilbert. Evidently Sir Raymond had still not returned from his journey or he would surely have been there as well.

Bernard cleared his throat. "Your Grace—this is a council of war. It's not a place for you."

"I am Princess of Tripoli," Elaine said. "Someone wants me dead. It seems to me that this is exactly the place for me."

In the silence that followed she sensed surprise and irritation but also reluctant respect. It was Walter who spoke next. "This is a chance for the Princess to be further educated concerning affairs of state," he said, choosing his words carefully. "Perhaps it's not altogether improper that she remain."

Bernard puffed out his cheeks and blew the air out slowly. "All right. She may stay . . . to observe."

Elaine knew this was Bernard's way of telling her to keep quiet. Still, she felt she'd scored a victory. In truth, she was a little startled at her own boldness, but the day's events were changing her. She could feel it; she wasn't the same person now that she'd been this morning, and she might well be different again tomorrow. What she would ultimately become was probably out of her control, which she found frightening but also a little exhilarating.

After she sat down there was another silence, again broken by

Bernard. "If no one else will say it, I will. The attempt on the Princess's life was the work of the Old Man. It had to be."

Basil, who invariably agreed with Bernard, murmured, "Arab boy, suicide mission, *shabriyah*. The Old Man, without question."

Elaine had already reached the same conclusion, which was an obvious one, but still, to hear it said aloud was petrifying. She'd been taught from childhood that the Old Man was the nearest thing to the devil now walking the earth.

Sir Gilbert, Conrad's companion, leaned forward in his chair. "If a newcomer may be allowed a question . . . who is the Old Man?"

Delancey answered. "The Old Man of the Mountain. He's the leader of a sect of religious fanatics who call themselves the Nizaris. They're a band of assassins, highly trained, and eager to give their lives for the glory of their God and of the Old Man. They kill, and die, and then, so they believe, go to Paradise."

"Assassinations—to what end?" said Gilbert.

Delancey shrugged. "Politics, religion, revenge—whatever pleases the Old Man."

"I'm surprised you tolerate such a creature," Gilbert said.

"Nobody 'tolerates' him," Conrad spoke up sharply. "He dwells in a castle called the Eagle's Nest, deep in the mountains. Few people know the location, and his spies are everywhere. Long before any army could find the castle and besiege it, he'd be in a new stronghold. Many attacks have been launched, by Christians and Saracens alike. All have failed."

"Well spoken, Your Grace," Bernard said. "You remember your lessons well, even after all those years away."

"Once you learn about the Old Man, you don't forget him," said Conrad.

"You say Saracens have attacked him?" said Gilbert. "Is he not Muslim, as they are?"

"Yes, but most Muslims hate him as much as we do," said Bernard. "Their religious disputes are very bitter."

Gilbert sat back in his chair. "I see," he said.

But Elaine knew he didn't see, not really. No one could fathom the full horror of the Assassins in one short conversation. The Old Man would spend years training his killers, some of whom learned English and could pass for Europeans, and he might spend years more putting them in place to carry out his commands. Not only stable boys, but cooks, pageboys, gardeners, soldiers—anyone, even priests on occasion—could be hidden agents of the Old Man, waiting for the right moment to strike. And, it was said, once an Enemy had been selected, the Old Man never rested until that Enemy was dead. And now Elaine was an Enemy.

Walter said something that changed the course of the discussion drastically. "The Old Man invariably gives warnings before he strikes. He would have demanded that we call off the wedding."

"We would have refused!" Conrad said.

"Yes," Walter replied calmly. "But he would have made the demand, and no such demand was made. Then there's the fact that he hasn't attacked a Christian ruler for many years."

"He had no reason to," said Bernard. "This marriage gave him one."

"Perhaps, but there's another possibility. Gold."

The suggestion threw the meeting into an uproar. Conrad's voice rose above it. "Who would have hired him?"

"I was going to ask you the same thing," said Walter.

"Me? Explain yourself, sir!"

Conrad was always spoiling for a fight, thought Elaine. But she had to admit Walter's implication was very near the bone.

"I'm told some in Antioch opposed the match," said Walter.

Conrad looked startled, then turned to Gilbert. "You said something of the sort this morning, on the road."

Now all eyes were on Gilbert, whose customary air of smugness vanished. "Well, I . . . only rumors, as I said. . . ."

Instantly, questions erupted from all sides of the table. "What rumors?" "Who's spreading them?" "Who did you speak to?" "Give us names!"

Gilbert opened his mouth but no words came. It was clear to Elaine that whatever he had told Conrad earlier had been said for effect. He had no concrete information, or else was afraid to say what he knew. Cornered, he counterattacked. "I've also heard there are some here in Tripoli who opposed the match. . . ."

"That's true!" said Basil, and looked at William Delancey.

The Constable sprang to his feet. "If you're implying that I hired an Assassin you'd better be ready to answer with your sword!"

Basil, no fighter, shrank back in his chair.

"My lords, my lords!" Bernard brought his hand down hard on the table. "This is getting us nowhere. Calm yourselves, please."

"The stable boy's being tortured," Basil ventured. "Perhaps we'll learn something from him."

"I hardly think he's privy to the Old Man's private motivations," said Walter drily.

"Whatever the long term holds, some practical decisions need to be made now," said Bernard. "First and foremost, shall the wedding proceed?"

Elaine felt a sudden surge of hope. Now was not the time to obey Bernard and keep quiet. She said slowly, as if she'd given the matter a great deal of thought, "Perhaps it would be wise to postpone the ceremony until we've gathered more information—"

"That would be cowardly," Conrad broke in. "The wedding must proceed as planned."

"I agree," said Bernard, and the others nodded, crushing Elaine's hope as quickly as it had arisen. Bernard continued, "But the ceremony will be private. And the Princess must be closely guarded at all times, not only during the wedding but for the foreseeable future."

"Closely guarded?" said Elaine. "What does that mean exactly?"

"It means, Your Grace, that you don't take a step or make a move without three or four trusted, experienced soldiers within an arm's length!"

"Surely that's an exaggeration," said Elaine, with a smile that Bernard did not return.

"Not by much," he answered. "It's the only way to be certain of your safety."

"In fact I recommend she not leave the castle keep!" Basil said. There was a murmur of approval around the table.

Elaine could feel her future close around her like a tomb.

"My lords, surely I'm not to be a prisoner in my own castle!"

"Not a prisoner," said Bernard. "Guarded and protected, for your own safety."

"Just until all this gets sorted out," said Basil.

"And suppose it never does get 'sorted out'?" Elaine demanded. "Everyone knows the Old Man never gives up. Am I to be sequestered for the rest of my life? I cannot accept that."

"You must accept it," said Bernard. "It's your duty to accept it. You are the future Queen of Tripoli and Antioch, and it's our duty to do whatever is necessary to protect you, for as long as necessary."

Elaine's frustrations and fears came tumbling out all at once. "And I have nothing to say about it? Nothing to say about who I marry or when I marry, nothing to say about where or when I come or go, how I live or where I live, nothing to say about my life at all?"

"Naturally, we'll accommodate your wishes whenever possible," Bernard began, but Elaine cut him off.

"Will I be allowed to walk in the garden? Ride my horse? Visit my father's tomb? Venture outside the walls of this building?" She spoke so intensely that it took Bernard a moment to reply.

"We'll have to see," he said.

"I couldn't live like that. No one could!"

Bernard collected himself and said in a strained tone, "We'll accommodate your wishes whenever possible, as I said. But you will be protected how and when we see fit. Of course, when you reach majority, you can do whatever you like."

"That's five years from now," said Elaine.

"Even then," Bernard continued as if she hadn't spoken, "your actions will of course be subject to the approval and permission of your husband, to whom you will answer in all things." He glanced politely at Conrad, who nodded back graciously.

So there it was. The tomb was sealed. The men in this room had decided her fate and there was to be no further discussion. She looked at them, one by one. They looked back with expressions solemn or even disapproving—not even Walter showed any sign of sympathy. She wished Sir Raymond were there, then realized it would have made no difference; he would have agreed with the others. And then she looked at Conrad, whose eyes held an un-mistakable gleam of triumph. *How he must be relishing this moment.*

With as much dignity as she could muster, she stood and pushed back her chair. She willed her voice to remain steady. "My lords, please excuse me. I find I'm very tired."

The men stood and bowed respectfully, then she turned and walked out of the room.

Just outside the door the three guards were waiting to escort her back to her chamber. Her new life had already begun.

She entered her room and closed the door. The guards remained outside, talking in low tones—probably about how presumptuous she'd been to insist on joining the council meeting. Other guards were patrolling the courtyard below her window.

On the one hand, she was grateful for the protection. On the other, she realized that from this day forward she would be living in a prison with three circles. The first was the constant, suffocating presence of guards. The second, far worse, was marriage to Conrad—she honestly didn't see how she could go through with it. There wasn't a single thing about him that was likable or even tolerable. And not only would she have to share his bed and bear his children, she would have to seek his "approval and permission" for every move she made, for the rest of her life! How he would enjoy making her beg and plead for every scrap of freedom!

But the third circle of her prison was the worst of all: fear. The Old Man of the Mountain wouldn't rest as long as an Enemy still lived. Elaine knew there would be another attempt on her life, and another, and still another, until finally one succeeded. Regardless of what precautions were taken or how many guards surrounded her, someday another Assassin would find his way to her side—

perhaps even posing as one of her guards!—and that would be the end.

A sudden thrill of horror passed down her spine. She gathered herself and, feeling foolish and terrified in equal parts, slowly stooped down and looked under the bed. There was, of course, no Assassin there.

Yet.

But this was her future. A rigid, airless existence, marriage to a man she detested, all the while weighed down by crushing, paralyzing fear. She would be in a dungeon just as surely as the Arab stable boy was now, and her ultimate fate just as certain. Would it not be better to die than live such a life?

One faint hope occurred to her as she paced back and forth: if she could find out why the Old Man wanted her dead, it might provide a way out. If he wanted to kill her for reasons of his own, then her situation was hopeless. But if, as Walter had suggested, someone had hired him, and she could learn who that someone was, then maybe she could enlist enough support from that someone's enemies to survive. Maybe they could intervene with the Old Man somehow, by offering a higher price or providing some other service. He might be the devil but even the devil could be bargained with.

Or maybe not. But it was her only chance.

But who was the someone? She doubted that the stable boy would reveal the answer. Assassins were supposedly trained to withstand every known torture, and anyway, as Walter had said, he'd probably been sent to kill her without knowing why.

Her mind began racing again, and her heart along with it until her whole body was trembling. *Yes, far better to die than live like this.* And on the heels of that thought, deep in the night when all was still and the voices of the guards outside her door had faded away, it came to her suddenly. It was so simple it took her breath away, and she knew exactly how she would find out why the Old Man of the Mountain wanted her dead.

She would ask him.

7

Conrad lay in bed, staring at the ceiling. The day had been a disaster, to put it mildly. On an occasion that should have been a triumph, his dignity had been severely compromised. And to have so much of his humiliation take place at the hands of a girl was unbearable.

Of course, the political implications of the assassination attempt were troubling as well. But he felt they were under control. Elaine would be guarded, the wedding would take place, Antioch would be advised as to the increased danger from the Old Man, investigations into possible treasonous connections would be undertaken, and reprisals, if needed, would be carried out. In matters military and logistical—anything that could be addressed by drawing a sword—he felt quite comfortable.

But the behavior of Princess Elaine was a different matter.

He was far from inexperienced where women were concerned. At the age of fifteen, three years after he'd arrived in France, he'd been seduced by a widowed Countess, some years older but still quite energetic. For a year he had been her willing plaything, until she'd contracted a politically advantageous match and abruptly and coldly ended their liaison. Devastated, Conrad had wanted to challenge his rival to single combat, but a group of older knights had taken him in hand, plied him with copious amounts of wine, and brought him to a bordello, where he'd made the astonishing discovery that the Countess was not the only willing woman in the world.

Not that he had contempt for women. They provided pleasure and were necessary for the smooth running of castles and households and for bearing children. But he was a warrior, and after his escapade with the Countess he poured his time and energy into training and fighting. Women, including his wife when the time came to take one, would always be subordinate to those pursuits.

Well, now the time to take a wife had come. He was eighteen, a man of some experience, and his betrothed was two years younger and, he had been assured, a virgin besides. He was her superior in every respect and it was all the more baffling and infuriating to realize that for some reason he did not feel like her superior at all.

The problem had started with his very first glance at her. She wasn't beautiful, exactly—certainly not compared to the maid-in-waiting, whatever her name was, who had accompanied her—but for some reason she had thrown him off balance. It had taken a moment before he saw, in her large violet eyes and generous mouth, a resemblance to the awkward, ungainly girl he dimly remembered from years before. He should have said something clever, or gallant, but all he could manage was "Princess Elaine," in a sort of strangled croak. From that moment on, he felt, she'd held the upper hand.

And how could she have failed to support him in a quarrel with an Arab stable boy! In fact, she had sided against him and everyone in the castle knew it. He knew his own humiliation was of less importance than the boy's attack on Elaine, but this, too, Conrad felt, was somehow directed against him, for Elaine was his, or soon would be, and an attack on her was an attack on his authority and position.

At least he had been the one to capture the stable boy. But Elaine had ruined even this by preventing Conrad from killing him on the spot. Well, Conrad would remedy that oversight in the morning; the Arab most likely knew nothing useful and could be disposed of quickly. Would it be better to kill him in the dungeon, or give him back his dagger and kill him in a fair fight? It was the soothing effect of this pleasant choice that finally allowed Conrad to fall asleep.

He was awakened a short time later by a fearful pounding on his door.

"Your Grace! Your Grace! You're needed, at once!"

Conrad sat up sleepily. "What is it?"

But there was no answer, just more pounding, then nothing.

Sweet Jesus, this place was badly run! There would be changes when he took over, make no mistake. As he stumbled across the room he could hear the sound of running feet and excited voices on the other side of the door.

He yanked the door open. The corridor was in a state of chaos, with squires, pages, and nobles running every which way in various stages of getting dressed, speaking in half-coherent shouts with no one in charge. Gilbert, who supposedly was watching Conrad's back, was nowhere to be seen. Probably consorting with Lady What's-Her-Name.

"What's the trouble?" Conrad demanded loudly.

But everyone was too excited or too frightened of him to answer, so he finally grabbed a passing squire and slammed him against the wall.

"What the devil is happening?"

"Your Grace . . ." the boy stammered.

"Speak, man!"

"Your Grace . . . the stable boy has disappeared!"

"Stable boy? The one who . . ."

The squire nodded fearfully.

"How is that possible? He was in the dungeon!"

"He escaped, Your Grace."

"Escaped? How the devil could he escape?"

"No one knows, but he's gone, Your Grace!"

It took a moment for this to sink in.

"Surely he must be somewhere on the grounds. He can't have left the castle entirely!"

"The grounds have been searched, he's nowhere to be found. And . . ."

The boy stopped again, his face contorted with fear. Conrad shook him so hard it rattled his teeth.

"And *what?*" he demanded.

"Princess Elaine is also gone."

"Gone?" Conrad sputtered. "How do you mean, gone?"

"Vanished, sir. Vanished without a trace."

8

It took another hour after Conrad had been awakened, but order had finally been restored to the castle. Bernard decided that he and Constable Delancey would remain behind to secure the castle, while a search party rode out to find the Arab stable boy and Elaine and a dungeon guard who had disappeared at the same time.

The search party, two dozen strong, thundered out of Tripoli Castle into the streets of the city. They carried weapons, but rode swift coursers rather than warhorses used for jousting or battle. They were equipped not for war but for a hunt, and a hunt was what they were on. They moved rapidly through the upper part of the city and made their way into the narrow streets of the poorer section as the villagers scurried out of their way and watched apprehensively. They knew this hunt was not for wild boar or deer.

Conrad rode at the front, with Walter and Gilbert just behind him. Conrad hadn't wanted to bring Walter along—he blamed the old man for hiring the stable boy in the first place—but Walter spoke Arabic and he knew the surrounding area well. As for Gilbert, ever since the incident at the stable he had seemed to distance himself from Conrad, and even now was riding a few lengths behind as if seeking the company of the other knights. So much for friendship.

Conrad took some comfort from the Arab's *shabriyah*, which Walter had handed to him in the garden. Conrad had kept it and it was in his belt now, next to his sword, and he planned to use it on the Arab when he was recaptured. It was only fitting that the swine be killed with his own weapon.

A squire riding next to Walter said something and Walter stopped his horse in front of a small stone hut. "This is the place," he said to Conrad.

Conrad nodded and Walter dismounted and knocked sharply on the door. An old woman opened it, her eyes widening at the sight of the armed men.

"You are the wife of the Abu Adil?" Walter asked.

The woman shook her head uncomprehendingly. Walter gave her a blow across the face, open-handed but sharp.

"Please, sir, I'm coming, she doesn't speak your language," said a voice from within the hut, and Abu hurried over to the doorway and put a comforting arm around his wife. "Please, sir, don't hit her again, she's very old."

Walter struck the old man with his fist, knocking him over. The woman forgot her own hurt and knelt by Abu, wailing. Walter drew his sword and held it at the old man's neck. "Tell her to be quiet."

Abu said something in Arabic and the woman was quiet. He sat up slowly, wiping blood from a lower lip that was already start-ing to swell. "Why do you do this?" he said.

Walter ignored him and looked around the hut, lit by the rays of the early morning sun streaming through the door and windows. Except for a few sticks of furniture the hut was completely bare. A large, bulging sack was on the floor nearby. Walter slashed it with his sword. Blankets and clothes tumbled out onto the floor, along with various cooking utensils.

"You're leaving the village," Walter said.

"Yes, sir."

"Why?"

"There is better trade elsewhere."

"Why today?"

"We have planned it for some time."

"If it was planned you would have sold your furniture or hired a cart to take it with you."

"I sold the hut, and the furniture, too," said Abu.

"Of course," said Walter sarcastically. "Probably to your brother in Ikrit, the father of the stable boy you vouched for three days ago."

Abu didn't bother to answer. He'd wanted to leave as soon as the rumor of Rashid's capture had reached the village, but his wife had insisted on taking their meager possessions and Abu had allowed her a few minutes to fill the sack and now they would both die for some pots and pans.

Abu's eyes met Walter's for a long moment. The two old men were, each in his own way, warriors, and though they had never met before they understood each other well enough.

"*Spare my wife,*" Abu said quietly, in Arabic.

Walter studied him for a moment, then nodded.

"What did he say?" Conrad had dismounted and joined Walter inside the hut.

"He'll tell us the truth if we spare his wife."

"How will we know if he's telling the truth?"

"I'll know," said Walter. Then he looked back at Abu.

"What is the boy's real name?" he said in Frankish, so Conrad could understand.

"Rashid," said Abu.

"The Old Man in the Mountain sent him to kill the Princess."

"Yes."

"Why?"

"I don't know."

"He escaped this morning and took the Princess with him. Did you see him?"

"No. I did not know he had escaped."

"Liar!" Conrad interjected.

"His task was to kill the girl and he failed," Abu said calmly, still addressing Walter. "He would get no help from me and he knew it."

Walter considered this answer carefully and accepted it. But he needed something more to keep his part of the bargain.

"He left the castle just before daybreak and made his way through the city," he said. "Someone must have seen him."

"The city was still asleep," said Abu.

"Someone must have seen him," Walter insisted.

"There are certain beggars," said Abu. "Scavengers. They collect the refuse that's thrown from the castle gates and windows each morning and each evening. If Rashid left at daybreak one of them will know. This time of day you'll find them in the caves east of here."

Walter pursed his lips and considered this answer carefully as well. "I believe you," he said to Abu. Then he swung his sword in a short, powerful arc and cut off the old man's head.

At the caves to the east they found the scavengers, twenty or so in number, mostly Arab but some of mixed race. They were dressed in rags, and survived by competing with wild animals for the scraps from the castle tables, or collecting old trinkets discarded by the nobles and selling them for whatever they could get.

Walter ordered them to gather around himself and Conrad while the other soldiers waited to one side.

"An Arab boy and a young woman left the castle this morning just before dawn. Did any of you see them?"

There was no response from the scavengers. Walter reached into a small purse on his sword belt and took out a gold coin. A visible stir went through the crowd.

"Who speaks falsely will die. But who speaks the truth will have this." The scavengers stared at the coin greedily. "And another when we find the boy," Walter continued. "And protection afterwards."

At this a man stepped forward. He was missing one eye and his skin had a sickly gray hue and there were open sores on one leg, but his voice was firm. "I saw them at dawn. They were moving eastward, toward the mountains."

"They were on foot?" said Walter.

"Yes," said the man.

"Did you follow them?"

"No."

"Don't lie," Walter growled.

The man swallowed. "I followed them for two or three leagues."

"Why did you not rob them?"

"The boy looked strong. And . . ."

"And what?"

"The woman had a sling."

Walter nodded, satisfied that the man really had seen Rashid and Elaine.

Conrad stepped in. "The woman—did she go willingly, or was she coerced?"

Not sure what answer was safest, the man said, "I couldn't tell."

Before Conrad could press the question, another scavenger stepped forward. "I saw them, too," he said.

"Then you should have spoken up," said Walter, and flipped the gold coin to the one-eyed man. Then he called to the nearest soldier, "Take him to the castle and put him in a cell until we return. If he's lying he'll answer for it."

The soldier looked with disgust at the one-eyed man but allowed him to climb up behind him on his horse, which moved off at a trot.

"They can't have gone far," Walter said to Conrad. "We'll find them soon."

They rode for the rest of the morning and well into the afternoon, crossing the low-slung mountains east of the castle, without finding any sign of either Rashid or Elaine. Cultivated fields of barley and wheat gave way to rough pasture grazed by goats and cattle, which in turn gave way to wilderness, with its stubbly bushes and occasional juniper trees that became more scarce as the land became drier and more desolate. The horsemen spread out, casting a wide net, periodically regrouping to share what they had learned.

They'd learned nothing. They'd passed through villages and hamlets and farms, encountered hundreds of inhabitants—merchants, peddlers, farmers, tradesmen of every description—but throughout the long day neither threat nor offer of gold had elicited any information about a young Frankish woman or an Arab boy.

Frustrated, they prepared to camp for the night.

Conrad was still wondering how the Arab had managed to force Elaine to leave with him once he'd escaped; the possibility that she'd gone of her own free will was too humiliating to contemplate. Meanwhile, another idea had been forming in his mind. He'd kept pushing it away, hoping that Elaine and Rashid would be sighted at any moment, but now, as he watched the men-at-arms tend the horses and gather firewood, the thought captured his attention. Might not Rashid have started off in one direction, then doubled back and gone in another? He probably knew the scavengers had seen him, and he'd have realized they might betray his movements to a search party. So it stood to reason he would change course.

Which direction would he go, then, if not to the east? To the west lay the sea, to the south the desert. So he must have gone north. The more Conrad pondered the notion, the more certain he became.

Should he tell Walter? He looked around for the old Master of Horse, and spotted him across the newly lit fire, surrounded by a circle of men, including Gilbert, listening to him intently. Conrad was a prince and Walter wasn't even a knight, yet everyone looked to him as leader and Conrad knew the others would side with Walter if the old man disagreed with Conrad's opinion.

And suppose he, Conrad, insisted on veering north in the morning and turned out to be wrong? Then Elaine and Rashid would be gone forever and he would be blamed.

So he said nothing. But as the members of the search party fell asleep one by one Conrad stayed awake, and after an hour he rose and made his way to his horse and stole away silently in the dead of the night.

*   *   *

He rode alone in the darkness, using the stars to keep to a northerly course. The first two hours were all right, but as he grew weary the certainty began to drain out of him like sand from an hourglass. The terrain became more rugged and barren and it seemed to Conrad that the chance of finding any living creature, let alone two human beings, was diminishing rapidly.

If he was wrong about Rashid, he would look ridiculous, and even if he was right, he could never hope to cover as much territory by himself as all the horsemen had covered collectively. So most likely he would fail to find Rashid or Elaine and look ridiculous anyway. He should probably return to Walter and the others as quickly as possible, explain his absence, then face down their derision as best he could. He was about to turn his horse around when, on the horizon to the north, he saw the faint glow of a distant campfire.

9

Once she had made up her mind what had to be done, Elaine thought harder than she'd ever thought in her life. She had to plan carefully and there wasn't much time, for it was after midnight and the wedding was to take place at noon.

Getting to the dungeon undetected wouldn't be difficult. But afterward she would need to disguise herself, for traveling in a noblewoman's gown would invite robbery and worse. So she took one of her plainer dresses and ripped out the beads and embroidery and most of the puffing from the sleeves, then flung the dress to the floor and trampled it until it seemed sufficiently soiled and wrinkled. If she used one of the blankets on her bed as a sort of shawl she might pass for a commoner.

The real problem would be the guard in the dungeon; even at this time of night there would be at least one.

Elaine had a small dagger, a gift from her father, "in case I'm not around one of these days," he had said jokingly, but she knew it wasn't really a joke. Like Sir Raymond, her father thought a woman should be able to protect herself. He had even showed her how to sharpen the blade on a whetstone, though she hadn't done so for years and there was no time for it now. She took the knife from her bureau. It still seemed sharp enough to be lethal, but when she tried to imagine plunging it into the body of an unsuspecting guard her mind recoiled. Murder was a crime and a sin, and besides . . . well, she simply didn't think she could bring herself to do it. She would have think of another approach.

Her mother had died in childbirth, so Elaine knew little about her apart from a few things her father had told her; the subject caused him great pain, the same pain that kept him from remarrying, though as a monarch it was his duty to do so. Her mother, whose name was Catherine, had been beautiful, her father had said, tall and slender and elegant, and she'd had a fondness for horses that Elaine had clearly inherited. Apart from a few such details, Elaine had only two tangible links to her mother—the first was a small box of jewels; she'd taken them out from time to time over the years, examining each ring and ornament, hoping in some mystical way to gain a glimpse of the woman who had owned it.

Parting with the jewels would be difficult but it had to be done. She stepped out of her nightclothes and into the newly battered dress, arranged the blanket around her shoulders, slipped the dagger into the pocket of the dress, and put on the sturdiest pair of shoes she had. Then she picked up the box of jewels.

Next she searched her bureau to see what else might prove useful. Her sling, of course, and a few stones to go with it; a pair of flints for starting a fire; a few moldy figs and dates that might still be edible. She dropped the lot into her pocket next to the dagger and started to turn away, then hesitated. There was another item on the bureau, the second thing that connected her to her mother: a comb, once her mother's and now hers.

The comb was a work of art. Its spine was made of ivory, carved with a scene of courtly love—a knight knelt at the feet of his lady while another knight looked on, whether with approval or jealousy was not clear; the spine had teeth on both sides, coarse on one and fine on the other.

"Fifty strokes with the coarse, fifty with the fine every night, your mother used to say!" So her father had remarked once years ago, and since then Elaine had combed her hair faithfully one hundred times every evening. It had become part of a nighttime ritual before she went to bed: one hundred strokes with her mother's comb, a brief prayer for her mother's soul, another brief prayer for her father's, and sleep usually came fairly quickly. She added the comb to the pocket of her dress. If she had to part with the jewels she would still have something that had belonged to her mother.

She walked past her bed behind a stone partition to the garderobe, with its narrow shaft that carried waste to the ground three stories below. There was a torch burning in a sconce attached to the wall and Elaine removed it. Next to the garderobe was a small wooden door. It led to a compartment that was actually a landing for a winding stone staircase that led to the tunnels underneath the castle. Elaine opened the door and hesitated; she was suddenly seized with the conviction that her plan was insane, and she should close the door, go back to her bed, comb her hair, say her prayers, and go to sleep as she did every other night.

But this was not every other night, and the plan, insane or not, was her only hope. She said one prayer, not for her mother or father but for herself, that her courage would not fail her, then crawled through the small opening and, holding the torch before her, started down the narrow staircase.

The tunnels were not exactly a secret—many fortresses had them—but few people knew how to navigate them, and Elaine was one of those few. When she was a little girl, she and her father had spent many hours playing hide-and-seek, a game she loved. Only later had she realized it was her father's way of making sure that navigating the tunnels was second nature to her and thus protecting her, for the tunnels provided an escape route in the event the castle came under siege.

The stairs were narrow and she descended slowly, the torch flickering in the dank air. Six turns—two to each story—and she was at ground level, then two more and she was beneath the castle in a narrow corridor, black as night except for the little patch dimly illuminated by the torch. There were markings carved into the wall for those who knew how to read them and Elaine had little trouble finding the path she was seeking. Twenty minutes after leaving her bedchamber she found herself in front of a solid oak door and she lifted the latch and stepped across the threshold into the dungeon.

The dungeon was comparatively well lit, with torches placed at intervals around its walls. There was a pail of fresh water and a wooden bench, and unless you were a prisoner in one of the cells it was not a particularly frightening place. Still, the jailer sitting on the bench looked at Elaine as if she were an apparition from the underworld, his face rigid with shock.

"I am the Princess Elaine," she said helpfully.

He nodded and blinked once or twice but that was all.

"I came through the tunnels. They're just on the other side of the door here."

He managed another nod and got shakily to his feet, still gaping at her.

"I ask your pardon for startling you," Elaine said.

"Of course, my lady."

"What's your name?"

"Robert Frazier, my lady."

He was of medium height, about thirty, with sand-colored hair and an open, pleasant countenance. Not in a thousand years could she have brought herself to stab him.

"Robert Frazier, I have a favor to ask. I need to see the prisoner, the Arab stable boy."

"I'm afraid that's impossible, my lady."

"It's not impossible. He's in one of these cells and I want to see him. I think I'm entitled to a little revenge for what he tried to do."

Robert relaxed a little. It was strange for a woman to speak of revenge, but at least he understood what she was up to.

"My lady," he said earnestly, "I promise you, more revenge is being inflicted on him than you can imagine."

"It's not the same as doing it myself."

"I have orders not to grant access to anyone."

"I'm not anyone, I'm the Princess," she said with an edge.

He swallowed and glanced at the door that led to the keep and she knew he wanted to consult his superiors.

"Robert, I want to make an arrangement with you." She produced the box of jewels and opened it. He stared at it for a good long while. A necklace of pearls, another of diamonds, some earrings, two broaches—there wasn't a vast amount, but it was worth more than he could hope to earn in a lifetime as a castle guard.

"This will make you a wealthy man," she said. "You'll have to leave here tonight, right now, in fact, but you'll be able to go wherever you like and do whatever you please as long as you live. What is an Arab stable boy compared to that?"

His eyes darted from the box, to her, to the door, then back to the box.

"You'll never have another chance like this, Robert Frazier. Take it!"

He hesitated one last moment, then snatched the box out of her hand and closed the lid. "The keys to the cells are over the bench," he said, then hurried up the steps and out the door with an alacrity that was almost comical. She'd meant to send him out through the tunnels but didn't try to call him back. He probably wouldn't come and in any case she had more pressing things to attend to.

Rashid, wearing only a loincloth, hung from chains suspended from the ceiling of the dungeon, his feet barely touching the ground. His arms and shoulders ached terribly and the rest of his body was in even greater agony. He was alone, not because his torturers were merciful but because they needed rest. He knew they would return soon enough.

He had failed. He had failed the Old Man and he had failed God. The shame of failure was far worse than the pain; more bitter still was the knowledge that he would never again see Paradise.

How could he have been so weak?

He replayed the moment over and over in his mind. The opportunity was there, the element of surprise on his side, the Enemy vulnerable, the knife poised to strike, and then . . . he had hesitated. Why? Because earlier in the day he'd seen her be kind to a horse? Absurd!

Perhaps it was the look in her eyes at the moment of the attack—startled, of course, and baffled, but also . . . indignant. *I've just saved your life—and you repay me by taking mine?*

Or perhaps he'd only imagined that look, and it had been all his doing—from some place inside him he didn't know existed, a feeling had arisen that it was fundamentally wrong to kill someone who had just saved his life and so his hand had stopped.

But that was a terrible mistake, surely. What was wrong was failing in his mission, betraying the trust the Old Man had placed in him. Yes, that must be the right way to think about it . . . yet even now he was nagged by doubt. Whether the hesitation was of an instant only or would have stayed his hand completely he would never know, for the dog of a prince had stepped in and the chance was lost forever.

A key sounded in the lock and the heavy iron door began to move on its tired hinges. Now the torture would begin again, and he was almost glad of it, for it was no more than he deserved. He watched as the door swung open . . . and was astonished to see the Enemy standing in front of him.

Elaine knew the kinds of things that went on in dungeons but she had never actually observed the result. She had expressed curiosity on the subject once, years ago, and her father had taken her to a room just off the dungeon and showed her some of the instruments that were used on prisoners—knives, forceps, pliers, foot-long needles, and the larger devices such as the spiked chair, the rack, and the grill. One glimpse and a little imagination had told her all she wanted to know and she'd never asked again.

But now she could see the results for herself. The Arab's face was swollen and discolored, his body covered with gashes and bruises and burns and rivulets of dried blood. In places his skin had been peeled and raw flesh was exposed. She started to gag but controlled the impulse and forced herself to concentrate on what needed to be done.

"Can you hear me?" she asked. "Do you understand?" He didn't answer.

"I'm Princess Elaine, of Tripoli. Do you recognize me?"

He nodded almost imperceptibly.

"What's your name?" she said, and when he didn't answer she said, "Surely there's no harm in telling me your name."

"Rashid," he said finally, in a hoarse, pained whisper.

"I have the key to your shackles, Rashid, and I want to release you. Do you understand?"

His eyes narrowed with suspicion and she could hardly blame him. "I bribed the guard but another will be coming, I'm not sure when, but we need to hurry. Don't you want to leave this place?"

He still didn't answer and she continued, "They say you were sent by the Old Man of the Mountain. Is it true?" When he remained silent she added, "I want you to take me to him."

His eyes widened and he continued to stare at her. She had to make him understand.

"I spared your life this morning and you spared mine—at least it seemed that you did. I'll spare yours again now, and you spare mine again as well, at least long enough to take me to the Old Man. Will you agree to that?"

"He will kill you," Rashid rasped.

"Perhaps. But first I want to make him tell me why."

Rashid started to say that no one could "make" the Old Man do anything, but as he looked into her eyes he saw something—something he realized he'd already seen in the stables, though he hadn't realized what it was. She wasn't afraid; or, if she was, there was a spirit in her that overcame the fear. He didn't want to admire it but he couldn't help himself. How many times had Hasan told him: "The most important thing is to destroy fear; if you're not afraid, you cannot fail!"

The thought that he, a trained Assassin, might have something in common with this Christian Princess seemed ridiculous—but it flickered through his mind nonetheless. He wondered what Hasan would make of her.

"You have nothing to lose," Elaine was saying. "He can kill me if he wishes or for that matter you can kill me if he orders you to. All I ask is that you take me to him first. Will you do that?"

Their eyes met for a very long moment, then, almost imperceptibly, Rashid nodded.

"Swear by your God that you will bring me, alive, to the Old Man of the Mountain."

For a moment, nothing. Then: "I swear."

"Say the words. All of them."

"I swear by my God that I will bring you alive to the Old Man of the Mountain."

She unlocked his shackles and he collapsed to the floor with an involuntary moan of pain. His shirt and leggings had been thrown into a corner of the cell, and Elaine went over and picked them up. When she turned back around Rashid was already on his feet, watching her closely. Despite his bloody wounds and bruises, now that he was unchained he looked rather formidable and Elaine wondered if she'd been foolish to trust him.

She tossed his clothes to him from across the cell. He struggled into them then looked back at her. "My dagger," he said.

"It's not here," said Elaine.

"I've sworn by God," he said. "I will not break such an oath."

"I believe you, or I wouldn't have unlocked the shackles," said Elaine. "But the dagger isn't here. Look for yourself."

Rashid looked around the cell and it was obvious Elaine was right. His shoulders sagged—losing the dagger would add to his disgrace back at the Eagle's Nest.

"We need to go," said Elaine. She walked out the dungeon door and after a moment Rashid followed.

* * *

Elaine's original torch had burned out, so they each took one from the dungeon. Then, with Elaine in the lead, they entered into the tunnels, the last of which led eastward, on the opposite side of the castle from the harbor.

They emerged in a cemetery just outside the curtain wall: an eerie exit point but a clever one, for cemeteries were usually deserted. They made their way through the tombs and into the city. The streets were empty but wouldn't be for long because the first faint streaks of light were beginning to stain the eastern sky. Elaine started to tell Rashid to hurry, but despite the agony he must be in, he was already moving so fast she had trouble keeping pace.

"The hills, before sunrise," he said, and Elaine saw, about a mile ahead of them, a series of low-lying ridges that would shield them from the castle's line of sight.

Just before they reached the bottom of the first ridge they realized they were being followed. There were two men, beggars, and as they came closer Elaine could see that one of them was missing an eye. "Let them follow us," Rashid said calmly.

After a few minutes the beggars began to move closer and Rashid picked up a large stick from the ground and walked toward them. Elaine, following his example, took the sling from her pocket and picked up a rock from the ground. The beggars fled at once back the way they'd come and were soon out of sight.

After that Rashid and Elaine entered the foothills and turned abruptly to the north, and Elaine suddenly realized why Rashid had allowed the beggars to follow for so long. "If anyone asks them, they'll say we were traveling east," she said, but Rashid made no reply.

In daylight Rashid looked even worse than he'd appeared in the dungeon, and some of his wounds opened as they walked. She asked if he needed to rest but he only shook his head. He never complained or slackened his pace, and finally it was Elaine who needed to stop. They drank from a small stream, and found some wild pomegranates that were sour but edible. They talked hardly at all, saving their breath for their journey, and an hour after they started again they reached the crest line of the small range of hills and Elaine turned to look back toward the west. The city, dominated by the castle, looked very small in the distance, and there was no sign of pursuit.

They began to descend the eastward slope of the range, veering northward at every opportunity, stopping only when it was time for Rashid to pray, which he did five times in all during the day, facing Mecca and kneeling low to the ground. Elaine watched with interest. She knew Assassins were considered outcasts by most Muslims as well as by Christians, but in some respects at least they were apparently just as devout.

As they traveled on, the land grew more barren. There was an occasional stream to drink from but fewer and fewer trees, and Elaine felt worse than she'd ever felt in her life. Every muscle ached and every joint was stiff and her feet were on fire with newly forming blisters. She started to tell Rashid that she couldn't move another step but then she saw his face, swollen and battered, and his shirt and leggings stained with blood, and she stayed silent and walked on.

Finally, a little after sunset, they stopped near a small stand of juniper trees, beyond which lay wilderness as far as Elaine could see.

"A half day's walk," Rashid said, "and the country will start to grow fat again."

Elaine sat, or rather collapsed, on the ground with her back resting against a scraggly tree trunk, while Rashid gathered some dry sticks to start a fire.

"I have flints," said Elaine. She struggled to her feet and fished them out of her dress as Rashid gathered some twigs to start a fire. She handed him the flints and within moments a small flame had begun and they added larger pieces of wood. As the flames took hold Rashid sat down next to Elaine and they shared the figs and dates that she'd brought from her chamber.

"How did you get past the guard?" Rashid asked suddenly.

"I bribed him with some jewels I had from my mother."

Rashid nodded, then said, "Did you keep any?"

Suddenly Elaine felt sick with embarrassment. At first she couldn't even bring herself to answer, then she said, "We could have used them to buy food. I'm sorry."

"We'll pass some farms tomorrow," said Rashid. "I'll steal something." He didn't seem upset, which made Elaine feel even worse.

"It's an unnecessary risk," she said. "Or would have been, if I hadn't been so foolish."

He studied her for a moment. "You don't seem to mind unnecessary risks."

"You mean setting you free? If that was a risk, it was a necessary one."

"Why necessary?"

"My life would have been hell. Married to the Prince, always looking over my shoulder waiting for the next attack . . ."

"Better to risk death?"

"Yes. Far better."

She met his gaze steadily. His eyes betrayed nothing, but when he said, "We should get some rest, tomorrow will be another long day," she detected, or thought she detected, a measure of respect in his voice.

Rashid finished eating, then lay down next to the fire and closed his eyes. Elaine felt a profound weariness begin to envelop her and she had trouble keeping her eyes open, but first there was something that had to be done.

She took her comb from the pocket of her dress and ran it through her hair. Perhaps it was silly given the circumstances but she completed the task methodically, counting fifty strokes with the coarse teeth and fifty more with the fine. Then she put the comb back in her pocket, wrapped herself in her blanket, and prayed as she had every night since her father had died—that King Edmond and his Catherine might be together always, and that she herself might in due course join them, reuniting with her father and having the chance at last to know her mother.

She had hardly finished the prayer before falling into an exhausted sleep.

* * *

Just after dawn the next morning Rashid gave a sudden cry of alarm and scrambled hastily to his feet.

Elaine woke up abruptly. "What is it?" she said, then saw what Rashid had already seen.

Conrad stood not five strides away, on the other side of the dying embers of the fire. The rising sun at his back gave him the appearance of an avenging angel, and his sword was in his hand.

◈ 10 ◈

Conrad and Rashid bared their teeth like wild animals. "It's time to finish what we started, swine," Conrad snarled. "But answer one question truthfully and I'll show you the mercy of a quick death. Have you harmed her?"

"I haven't touched her," said Rashid.

"Threatened her, then."

"No," said Rashid.

"It's true," said Elaine firmly.

Conrad looked baffled. "Then why are you with him? How did he escape?"

"He escaped because I bribed the jailer," said Elaine. "He's taking me to see the Old Man of the Mountain. He gave me his word and, as you see, he's keeping it."

It took Conrad a moment to grasp what she was saying. "You must be mad. The Old Man tried to have you killed!"

"Don't you think I know that? But someone may have hired him. I want to find out who."

"We'll find out some other way."

"How?"

Conrad had no answer for this. Elaine went on: "I won't live my life in fear."

"You'll be protected."

"The way I was protected from Rashid?"

Conrad looked confused, then realized, "You call him by his name?"

"Yes, I call him by his name! I spared his life and he spared mine, but the next Assassin won't! And who will it be? A cook? A guard? A woman, perhaps, a sweep or a kitchen maid?"

"We'll keep you clear of Arabs."

"The Old Man has Assassins who can pass among us, you know that. I'll never be safe while he wants me dead. If I can learn who paid him maybe I can do something about it—pay a higher price, or provide a service . . ."

Conrad hesitated. Her point was beginning to sink in. "Come back to Tripoli. We'll send someone else to meet with the Old Man."

"How will I live in the meantime? Who will I be able to trust?"

"You'll be my wife," Conrad said. "You can trust me."

"I will never be your wife." The words escaped her before she had a chance to think. But she meant them, and she knew once she was back in Tripoli the men in charge would do what they wanted, regardless of her desires.

Conrad stared, panting as if suddenly short of breath. Finally he said, "Does your duty mean nothing to you? To me, to your country?"

"I tell you again, I will never be your wife." Her tone was calm but determined.

Conrad shook his head in disgust. "This Arab dog has poisoned your mind somehow. Perhaps when he's dead you'll come to your senses."

Sword in hand, he stepped toward Rashid, who said contemptuously, "What a coward you are."

"You talk of cowards! You who slit throats in the middle of the night!"

"You couldn't beat me in the garden, when I had my knife. Perhaps you can beat me now, when I have nothing."

Conrad smiled sourly. He realized Rashid had seen the *shabri-*

yah in his belt. He knew Rashid was taunting him, but he was also very aware that Elaine was watching. He couldn't appear afraid of an Arab stable boy, even one who had turned out to be an Assassin. He took the *shabriyah* out of his belt and tossed it on the ground.

Rashid picked it up and the two men circled each other as they had once before, probing and feinting. Conrad struck first, a straight thrust aimed at Rashid's belly. The Arab dodged to one side but not quite quickly enough and at the last instant had to deflect the blade with his dagger. He dared not do this too many times because eventually the heavier blade of the sword would break the dagger and Rashid would be helpless. Conrad knew it. His teeth were bared in a savage grin as he leveled his sword for another thrust.

Rashid gave ground, buying time, trying to make the Knight overconfident. He decided to parry the next thrust with his left hand. No doubt it would be badly slashed but he didn't care—in fact he didn't care if he lost it altogether provided it gave him an opening to kill the Knight.

Conrad stepped forward and Rashid stopped retreating. He raised his left hand and gripped his dagger more tightly with his right . . .

Suddenly something flew between them with the hissing sound of an insect, but far larger and swifter than any insect could possibly be. Startled, they turned—Elaine was already placing another sizable rock in her sling. She had backed ten paces away, enough distance to get off another shot should either of them think of attacking her.

"I will crack the skull of whoever strikes the next blow," she said.

"You threaten me?" Conrad said, outraged.

"I threaten whoever breaks the peace."

"There is no peace!"

"There was until you came. And there will be again after you leave."

"I'm not leaving."

"Well, you're not fighting either. Not on this day." Elaine fixed both men with an icy glare. She wasn't used to behaving like this; she decided she rather liked it.

For a long moment no one moved. Both men wanted to fight but neither could afford to strike first, for they'd seen what Elaine could do with a sling. And neither could afford to charge her, either—whichever one of them tried, even if he avoided the stone, would be vulnerable to an attack from behind by the other. Elaine waited until it was very clear that she was in charge of the situation, then she turned to Conrad.

"You speak to me of duty. What about yours? You need to know why the attack was made even more than I do, can't you see that? Whoever hired the Old Man was trying to stop our marriage. That someone is an enemy to Tripoli and to Antioch as well—the two countries you say you want to rule. It's your duty to find out who that enemy is, if you truly expect to be a king. Or would you rather stumble in the dark, not knowing your friends from your foes?"

After a moment Conrad said sullenly, "And you think the Old Man will tell us, all we have to do is ask. Far more likely he'll kill us both."

"It's quite possible," Elaine agreed. Then she landed the final blow, for she'd discerned Conrad's weakness: "Going on will certainly be quite dangerous, so if you're afraid, you must turn back at once. I won't judge you for it."

"I'm not afraid," said Conrad reflexively.

"Then perhaps you should come with us."

Both men's eyes widened in surprise. "You say you want to protect me," Elaine went on. "I may well need protection on this trip. I'm told there are bandits in this region and two blades are better than one." After another long silence she said, "There are three choices. We can stand here till we all starve, or you can go back to Tripoli alone, or we can all travel on together. Which is it to be?"

Conrad and Rashid exchanged a look. They were beginning to feel somewhat ridiculous, weapons in hand but not daring to move—yet there seemed to be no obvious way out of their predicament. For the briefest of moments, they were almost in sympathy with one another. What was to be done about a woman like this?

Elaine went on, "If we do continue together you will both have to swear in the name of the God you worship not to fight each other until we've spoken with the Old Man."

Rashid sighed. "I will if he will."

Conrad shook his head, as if unable to believe the dilemma he found himself in. Then he paused, took a final look at Rashid and Elaine—and nodded reluctantly.

Rashid lowered his dagger and looked at Conrad. "I swear by the God I worship not to fight you until we've spoken with the Old Man."

"As do I," said Conrad.

"Rashid has already proven that he keeps his oaths," Elaine said. "I trust you will as well."

"I can keep my word as well as any Assassin can," Conrad said stiffly.

"All right. Now I think we've wasted enough time already this morning. Let's be off." She put her sling back in her dress pocket and began walking.

Conrad sheathed his sword and turned to Rashid. "When this is over we still have business to finish."

"Gladly," said Rashid.

Rashid and Elaine began walking at once, while Conrad stayed behind to recover his horse, which had wandered a few yards away in search of forage. It was highly unlikely, Elaine reflected, that there were three more unsuited traveling companions in all the Holy Land. But no matter: bloodshed had been avoided—so far, at least. And with a little luck, in two or three days she would stand before the Old Man of the Mountain and learn her fate, whatever it might be.

PART TWO

THE EAGLE'S NEST

11

The three travelers continued on a northward course, with Rashid leading the way. They spoke little, each coming to terms with what had just taken place. Elaine wasn't happy to have Conrad along, but issuing the invitation was better than allowing a fight to the death between him and Rashid. Much as she disliked Conrad she had no desire to see him killed in front of her, and if Rashid had died instead, her hope of seeing the Old Man would have died with him.

Rashid, on reflection, was glad Conrad had joined them. He hoped that delivering two Christian rulers to the Eagle's Nest might win some favor, or at least some forgiveness, from the Old Man. As for Conrad, he knew he was already an object of derision back in Tripoli, and returning without Elaine would just make things worse. And telling the truth—that she had chosen to stay with Rashid—was unthinkable. Moreover, as her betrothed it was his duty to protect her at all costs; whatever she might say, he was determined that the marriage would take place eventually. It was his right to rule Antioch and Tripoli and he would do so. That is, assuming he somehow survived this trip to the Eagle's Nest.

By midmorning they had traversed the downslope of the small mountain range and the terrain began to flatten out. As the sun

91

rose higher Elaine's muscles began to ache a little less but the blisters on her feet became more painful than ever. She couldn't hide her discomfort and Conrad moved his horse abreast of her.

"Why don't you ride for a while?" he said in what he thought was a chivalrous tone.

"No, thank you," she said. She wanted no favors from Conrad.

"Why not? There's no reason you should walk all the way."

"I'll be all right."

Rashid turned around. "I think you should ride," he said to Elaine. "You're slowing us down. If you ride we'll move faster."

"If you insist," she said reluctantly.

"You do his bidding but refuse mine?" Conrad said.

"I do nobody's bidding. But what he said makes sense."

"Which is why I offered you my horse in the first place," Conrad said.

"Then why deny it to me now?"

Exasperated, Conrad dismounted, wondering how she always managed to put him in the wrong when he knew he was right. Elaine mounted the horse unaided, though pushing off her blistered foot almost made her scream with pain. "Thank you," she said coldly.

An hour later, they descended into the valley and the land finally began to get "fat," as Rashid had promised the night before. They crossed a few thin rivulets flowing down from the hills, and soon small shrubs and bushes began to appear and then, in the distance, farmland.

Even on horseback it was evident that Elaine was very tired; she nearly fell asleep in the saddle more than once. Still, she never complained. Rashid found himself wondering whether all infidel women were like her. The contempt he knew he should feel toward her kept getting elbowed aside by a nagging feeling of respect. Infidel or not, she'd earned a rest.

"Let's stop for a while," he said. "Let the horse drink." Elaine dismounted and led the horse to a nearby rivulet that had almost attained the status of a stream. The horse drank deeply and so did

Elaine. Conrad walked to the horse and reached into the saddle-bag, which contained some salted beef and dried fruit that he'd forgotten about until now. He offered some to Elaine. She hesitated but, overcome with hunger, finally accepted it. Conrad began eating but Elaine hesitated again. "What about Rashid?" she said.

"What about him?"

"He needs to eat, too."

"I'm not stopping him."

"You're the only one with food."

"And I share it with whom I please."

After a moment Elaine said, "This food is mine, then? You gave it to me?"

"That's right."

"Good." She walked over to Rashid, who'd been listening to the conversation in silence, and broke the morsels of fruit and beef apart, offering half to Rashid. "This is not from him," she said pointedly. "It's from me." Rashid took the food from Elaine with a nod of thanks and began eating. With an effort Conrad controlled himself and walked a few steps away, his jaw muscles working furiously as he chewed.

An hour after they set out again they saw a small farmhouse about a quarter mile in the distance. It was surrounded by a number of ragged fields, planted with barley and alfalfa, broken up by a ravine and two or three small stands of sycamore trees. All three were thinking the same thing: here was a chance for some real food. "Wait here," Rashid said, and went on alone.

A half hour passed, during which neither Conrad nor Elaine spoke a word, then Rashid reappeared carrying a dead hen, an expression of satisfaction on his usually impassive face.

"The people you stole from, were they Muslim or Christian?" Conrad said. The large majority of Arabs were Muslim but there were a few Christians among them.

"I didn't ask their religion," Rashid answered, and Elaine laughed.

"Let's build a fire," she said, eyeing the hen hungrily.

"Best to get away from here first," Rashid said.

Elaine climbed back on the horse and the three of them set out again to the north. Two hours later, as dusk settled over the countryside, they roasted the hen on a stick over a blazing fire. The aroma seemed to go through Elaine's nose straight to her taste buds and the bird's juices dripped into the fire with a satisfying crackle and it was all she could do to wait until it was cooked. Finally the meat was done and she and Rashid began pulling chunks off, heedless of the burns to their fingers and even to their mouths, barely bothering to chew before swallowing and reaching for more.

On the other side of the fire Conrad ate the beef and dried fruit from his saddlebag, unwilling to partake of anything that might possibly have been stolen from Christian farmers.

It was after they'd picked the hen so clean that its bones gleamed in the firelight that Elaine first noticed the scar on Rashid's arm, a thin angry line that seemed separate and apart from the marks he'd received in the dungeon. Somehow it looked old and fresh at the same time.

"Your arm—is it all right?" she asked.

"It's fine."

"You were scratched by the hen . . . ?" Rashid shook his head and provided no further explanation.

Later, after Elaine had combed her hair—ignoring the bemused looks from the two men—the three of them lay down to sleep, Elaine and Rashid on one side of the fire and Conrad on the other. Elaine stayed awake longer than she'd expected, gazing at the stars glittering in the inky blackness of the moonless sky. She said her nightly prayer, and afterward was aware of a feeling she hadn't experienced in a long time—since her father had died, in fact—and she wanted to pinpoint exactly what it was.

It certainly wasn't happiness. She was in the wilderness with two men she barely knew, one of whom she detested and who detested each other. Despite the hen, she could have used another meal. Also she was tired, achy, footsore, and unsure of the future, except that it was likely to be dangerous. So what was it she felt?

Her eyelids got heavier as she contemplated the mystery and she heard an owl calling in the darkness and the smell of burning wood was in her nostrils and the answer finally came to her just before she drifted off to sleep.

She felt alive.

The next morning they set out just after sunrise; it was warmer than the previous morning, a sign that summer was near. As they traveled, the farms became larger and there was an occasional village—a few mudbrick huts surrounded by fields of grain. They avoided these places and kept to the backcountry, staying out of sight as much as possible.

In the afternoon the villages became scarcer and then the farms, until they were once more in relatively barren terrain. Rashid had stolen another hen, and was wondering if it would be enough to sustain them for the rest of the trip, when he saw something on the ground a few hundred yards ahead. He motioned to the others to wait while he approached it cautiously, but they ignored him and came along close behind.

He needn't have worried, for the thing he had seen was quite harmless. It was a man, a Christian knight judging by his surcoat and chain mail armor. As they approached Elaine let out a cry of horror.

"You knew him?" Conrad said.

Elaine nodded numbly. She recalled her conversation with Walter about Sir Raymond, and when he would return to Tripoli. Now she knew the answer: Sir Raymond would never return, for he lay dead on the ground, an arrow through his heart.

◈ 12 ◈

Raymond's corpse had been there for several days. His eyes had been pecked out by crows and the worms had started to do their work on the rest of him, but enough remained to be recognizable.

"Who was he?" Conrad said.

"His name was Sir Raymond," said Elaine. "He was . . . my friend. . . ." Her throat tightened and no more words came.

"What would a knight of Tripoli be doing here?" Conrad asked, looking at the empty land around them.

Rashid started to say something but changed his mind. Elaine just shook her head. She thought of the many kindnesses Raymond had shown her over the years, his endless patience while teaching her how to use the sling, how he would always find ways to make her laugh when she failed, so that she was willing to try again.

"Look at this," said Rashid, who'd been studying Raymond's body.

Conrad crouched next to him. "Sweet Jesus," he said. The arrow had gone through Raymond's shield and chain mail hauberk and almost through his body as well.

Conrad and Rashid looked at one another and for the first time their glance was completely devoid of hostility. They'd stepped onto common ground: two fighting men facing a fighting man's problem.

"I've never seen a bow that could loose an arrow with such force," said Conrad.

"And the feathers," said Rashid, brushing them with his finger. They were unusually thick and had alternating stripes of black and bright orange.

"It's not a Christian arrow," Conrad said.

"Nor a Muslim one."

Their eyes met again, but neither had an explanation.

"One thing is certain," said Conrad. "The bow that did this can kill a man at two hundred yards. Perhaps farther."

They looked around uneasily. The land was rugged and barren, but until now had not seemed particularly threatening.

"There are two routes to the Eagle's Nest," said Rashid. "One lies further west, but there are bandits, so I thought it better to take the eastern route instead."

"Could this be the work of bandits?" said Conrad.

"They don't fight with bows and arrows," said Rashid. "Certainly not like this one."

"Then I think it might be wiser to take the western route after all."

Rashid nodded in agreement. Neither man relished the thought of being cut down by an adversary two hundred yards distant. It was no way for a warrior to die.

Rashid began walking and Conrad brought his horse to Elaine, but she remained motionless, looking down at Raymond's body.

"Come," Conrad said, not unkindly. "There's nothing we can do for him now."

"We can bury him," said Elaine.

"There's no time," said Conrad, now with a touch of impatience.

"He was my friend. I can't leave him like this."

Rashid had rejoined them. "The sooner we get away from this place, the better," he said.

"Then we'll do it quickly," Elaine said. "Let's start digging."

The two men still hesitated. Elaine's eyes blazed as she glared at Conrad. "He's a Christian knight, as you are!" she said. "He deserves a Christian burial. If you won't dig a proper grave, lend me your sword. I'll do it myself!"

Stung by her words, Conrad clenched his teeth in anger. But then he drew his sword and began scraping out the ground next to Raymond's body. Elaine knelt and helped as much as she could, using the small knife she'd brought from the castle.

For a long moment Rashid just watched. He cared nothing for burying Christian knights; on the other hand, the sooner this was done, the sooner they could move on. Finally he drew his *shabriyah* and helped them dig.

Half an hour later they'd hollowed out a depression large enough to hold Raymond's body. They placed the dead knight in the depression and covered him with dirt and whatever rocks they could find on the nearby ground. Then Elaine fashioned a small, crude cross from the branches of a bush and Conrad pushed it into the ground at the head of the grave.

I'm sorry, dear friend, you deserve a better funeral than this, Elaine thought. But it was the best they could do. She said a brief prayer for Sir Raymond's soul, then the three travelers resumed their journey.

On the new route food was less of a problem because there were farms and settlements along the way, the same farms and settlements that the brigands in the region preyed upon by robbery or extortion. But there were also stretches of wilderness perfect for ambushing travelers, and it was on one of these, only a few hours after they'd resumed their journey, that Elaine and her companions found their way blocked by five men on horseback.

Rashid cursed his own stupidity. Now that bandits had found them so quickly, it seemed foolish to have left the chosen path just because of a strange arrow and a single bow shot. The men must have been watching them for some time, for they drifted casually out of the woods from both sides of the rough road and came together as if by a prearranged plan. They were armed in the usual haphazard fashion of brigands, with swords and axes and various mismatched pieces of battered armor they'd stolen or scavenged. Their ragged appearance added to the air of menace that exuded from them like a stench.

The leader was a man with a prominent nose who smiled amiably as he approached, a little in front of the others. He addressed Rashid.

"Good day, friends," he said in Arabic. "A pleasant day, is it not? Too pleasant for fighting, I hope you agree. You have a horse, a woman, and, of course, your lives. We are reasonable men, and we propose a reasonable bargain. You will leave the horse and the woman with us, and walk away with your lives. That way nothing disagreeable will spoil so lovely an afternoon. What could be more fair?"

Conrad didn't understand the words but the situation spoke for itself and he didn't bother to ask Rashid for a translation. He gestured for Elaine to dismount. She did so immediately and Conrad climbed into the saddle. His sword made a whispering sound as he drew it from the leather scabbard. He was suffused with a great feeling of relief. For the first time in three days he knew exactly what he was doing and why. He'd been watching the five men closely, forming an opinion about each based on certain signs that Charles had taught him to look for. Besides Big Nose, the leader, there were four others.

The first had a scar on his face; he had seen combat and would bear watching.

The second was a giant of man who wielded a fearsome double-edged axe but seemed indolent, given to flesh rather than muscle.

The third wore an odd smile that never left his face. Such smiles were intended to hide fear and this man was unlikely to be dangerous, though he might attack from behind.

The fourth man had narrow eyes that shifted constantly. He

was cautious; not necessarily a coward but unlikely to be an aggressor when the fight began.

All this went through Conrad's mind so quickly and instinctively that he was hardly aware of it, and no sooner had he drawn his sword than he was urging his horse forward, straight toward Big Nose. If he could put the leader out of the fight first, then his task would be greatly eased.

Big Nose's eyes widened in surprise—he'd expected to do the attacking—but he recovered well, parrying Conrad's first blow with his own sword, a sturdy steel falchion. Conrad did not pause but drove straight past Big Nose toward Scar and raised his sword as if to strike a blow identical to the one he had just struck, but at the last instant he lowered the angle of attack and his blade slashed across the man's chest, drawing a gush of blood and a howl of pain.

Everything had happened so fast that Elaine was transfixed, rooted to the spot. But she saw Rashid draw his knife and this woke her up and she reached in her pocket for her sling. She quickly found a sharp-edged rock and seated it, but Conrad and his opponents were whirling and shifting so rapidly that she hesitated for fear of hitting Conrad.

Meanwhile Conrad had turned on the lethargic Giant, who just now was rousing himself to grasp what was happening. He raised his axe ponderously, but before he could strike Conrad drove his sword straight into the man's ample belly. Giant grunted with shock and pain and Conrad had already withdrawn the blade when the man looked down at the gaping hole in his body, then toppled off his horse.

Big Nose had followed Conrad, but the Knight had anticipated this and turned just in time to parry a direct thrust. He delivered a counterblow but Big Nose caught it squarely on his own blade and Conrad knew that the bandit had once been a soldier, and a good one.

Conrad reined his horse around, not daring to spend too much time on any one encounter, and found himself facing Scar, with a chest wound dripping blood and a face twisted in rage. He was game enough but disoriented by pain and Conrad was able to parry a blow and in the same motion land one of his own, opening a second wound on the man's chest next to the first. Scar cried out again and this time his cry sounded a note of fear and he tried to pull his horse away and thus opened himself up to a third wound to his chest and he fell off his horse, dead before he hit the ground.

Conrad now turned on Smiler, but he had no heart for a fight and backed his horse away. Watcher also was hanging back. Conrad wheeled back around just as Big Nose was coming at him again and the two swordsmen engaged in a quick, sharp series of blows and parries, the blades flashing in the sunlight. Conrad's superior reach—his arm and his sword were both longer than his opponent's—gave him the advantage, but now Smiler and Watcher both advanced on Conrad's unprotected back. Conrad could feel Big Nose start to wilt under the force of his attack and he was about to drive the final blow home when Elaine screamed something he didn't understand and he felt a sudden searing pain across his back. He spun around in time to see that Smiler had decided to fight after all and had slashed him from behind. The bandit raised his sword again, but now Elaine had a clear shot and let fly with deadly aim—the stone clanged off Smiler's steel cap helmet and he tumbled to the ground with a surprised cry. At the same moment Rashid leaped on Watcher and dragged him from his horse. He screamed and Rashid's knife rose and fell and the scream ceased abruptly. Then Rashid stepped over to Smiler, who was dazed but trying to rise. Rashid's knife flashed again and that was the end of Smiler.

Now Conrad could concentrate on Big Nose again, but the bandit leader had seen enough—he was already digging his heels into his horse for all he was worth. The mount was willing enough, but it was a workhorse, no doubt stolen from one of the farms in the area, and no match for Conrad's courser. In three strides the Knight overtook Big Nose, who turned just in time to receive a vicious blow that cut through his collarbone downward almost to his heart. He fell from his horse without a sound.

Conrad trotted back to where Rashid and Elaine were waiting.

He was breathing hard from the exertion, but otherwise seemed unperturbed, as though the whole business had been routine, and perhaps a trifle tedious. The other two just stared at him. He gave a little nod to Rashid by way of acknowledging his assistance, then looked at Elaine. "You used your sling?" he said.

"Yes," she said.

He nodded thoughtfully a few times, then said, "Well done." Then he added, "When these five don't return, others may come looking for them. We should keep moving."

Rashid nodded his agreement, but first searched the bodies of the brigands for anything that might be useful. Big Nose had a purse with a few coins in it, but otherwise there were only weapons, which the three travelers had no need for. Elaine started to walk on but Conrad said, "Take one of their horses." When she hesitated he added drily, "I'm sure these fellows won't mind." Elaine felt it was ghoulish to take the horses of men who had died so bloodily, but of course Conrad was right. They would make better time if they were all on horseback. So she chose one of the bandits' mounts, a sturdy mare with a dark gray coat, and Rashid chose another horse, and they set off again, Conrad riding a little behind as if to protect them from pursuit.

Elaine rode almost in a state of shock. She had seen tournaments and those were certainly dangerous affairs and most of the men she knew were good fighters. She had even witnessed one or two accidental deaths. But she'd never seen anything like this savage and bloody melee, or anyone who could wield a sword quite like Conrad. While she and Rashid had helped, it was mainly Conrad who had saved her from death and worse at the hands of the brigands. She would express her appreciation; she just needed a little time to collect herself. Her stone had stunned the bandit but Rashid had delivered the death blow; she wondered how she would have felt if her stone had actually done the killing. Knowing what would have happened to her had she been captured, she decided it was something she could have lived with, but at the same time she was glad it had been Rashid who had finished the man off. When she finally turned around to say something to Conrad, she was startled to see he seemed to be sitting a little unsteadily in the saddle.

"What's the matter?" she said. He stared straight ahead without answering.

"Conrad? What's wrong?"

This time he looked at her, but his eyes were glassy and uncomprehending and he slid from the saddle and fell to the ground.

"Rashid!" Elaine called. She dismounted and hurried to Conrad, and Rashid did the same. "I'm such a fool!" she said. She'd seen the blow that landed on Conrad's back, but he'd continued to fight so fiercely afterward that she'd assumed it must not be serious.

But it was. And now she understood why he had ridden behind; he hadn't wanted them to know how badly he was hurt. Looking back at the road, she could see a trail of crimson drops leading to where Conrad now lay. He was unconscious, and it was evident that he had already lost a great deal of blood.

13

Rashid and Elaine managed to lift Conrad back onto his horse, draping his body across the saddle, his arms hanging down one side and his legs down the other. He was still unconscious, but Elaine stopped the worst of the bleeding by tying a piece of her blanket tightly onto the wound.

They moved off the road into rougher country, where bushes and undergrowth provided cover, and they came to a gully partially concealed by a stand of juniper trees. It was by no means a perfect hiding place but it would have to do.

They took Conrad off the horse and laid him gently on the ground facedown to protect the wound, and covered him with Elaine's blanket. She took the flints out of the pocket of her dress and began to gather sticks.

"No fire," said Rashid.

"We have to keep him warm."

"The smoke might be seen."

"He saved our lives," she said, which made Rashid bristle a little, but he made no further objection. "He needs to eat as well," Elaine added, "to keep up his strength. We all do."

Rashid said, "I'll find something. But it may take a while. People may be watching for us."

Rashid mounted his horse and rode back in the direction of the road. Elaine dressed Conrad's wound as best she could with fragments of her dress and blanket. Then she used her flints to light a small fire very close to where he lay and settled down to wait for Rashid to return.

There were still about three hours of daylight remaining and though the fire was small it sent a thin wisp of smoke rising above the tree line and Elaine began to imagine what might happen if someone saw the smoke. She had her sling, of course, but she'd be overmatched by a gang such as the one they'd recently encountered, and Conrad was obviously in no condition to fight. And the smoke was rising higher . . . she wondered if Conrad really needed the warmth. She looked at him, breathing calmly, his expression peaceful—yet how ferocious he'd been during the fight! Why had he come along with them instead of returning to Tripoli? Pride, no doubt, but after today she couldn't doubt that he was determined to protect her at whatever cost to himself. *Because he thinks of me as a possession,* she reminded herself.

Still, she let the fire burn and added more sticks when it began to wane.

After an hour Conrad stirred and his eyes fluttered. He started to roll over but she stopped him gently.

"Stay off your back," she said.

He looked at her and blinked several times. Sweat on his forehead betokened a mild fever and he seemed very weak but he managed to say, "Where's Rashid?"

"He went to get food."

Conrad shook his head. "Risky."

"You need your strength and so do we."

"I'm all right."

"You fought well," she said.

"They were rabble. Charles would never have—" He stopped abruptly, staring tight-lipped into the fire, then closed his eyes and within a few seconds had fallen back to sleep.

Rashid returned just as darkness fell, carrying two rabbits. They roasted the animals immediately, and Elaine woke Conrad up just long enough to see that he ate a few bites and swallowed a little water, then let him rest again. Now that it was dark the gully hid the glow of the small fire and Rashid judged it was safe to keep it burning in order to keep Conrad from catching a chill.

"He fought well," Elaine said.

"I should have taken more than one," Rashid said. "Everything happened very quickly."

"He's certainly no coward," said Elaine.

After a moment Rashid said, "He's no coward."

In the three days since Elaine had freed Rashid from the dungeon the scars and marks of torture had begun to heal, but the scar on his arm remained as angry as ever and Elaine was curious.

"How did you come by that?" she asked, gesturing to it.

He shrugged. "It's not important."

"I'd like to know," she said, and the words surprised him. No one had ever taken an interest in the events of his life, or cared what he thought or felt. He and his fellow Assassins had spoken to one another only when their training required it. Like them, he was only a vessel for carrying out the will of God and of the Old Man and all else was a distraction. Why should this Christian Princess take any interest in him? And yet, he could not say that he found her interest unpleasant. So, to his own surprise, he found himself telling her something he had never spoken about to anyone. "A few months ago, I fell asleep one night and when I woke up . . . I was in Paradise."

"Paradise!"

"I had finished my training, and that was my reward—a miracle, performed by the Old Man in his holiness."

"What was it like?"

"It was a garden, it was so green . . . there were trees with figs and almonds and pomegranates, and vines with berries and grapes, and a stream, clear as glass, running through the middle of it all. And there were women—more than I could count, wearing clothes and veils that I could see through—not completely, but enough to know that they were beautiful, and they were smiling at me. All of them, smiling and laughing, and so beautiful. . . . I was there for, I don't know, a day and a night, perhaps, time passed differently there, it was so peaceful, and toward the end just before I fell asleep one of the women took my arm and with her fingernail gave me this scratch—just deep enough to draw blood. That's how I knew it was real, and not a dream—the scratch was still there when I woke up! I open it again, every so often, to make sure the scar remains, so I never forget and never doubt."

Elaine listened with rapt attention. She had never heard anything like this, but there was no doubting Rashid's sincerity. His face fairly glowed in the telling and it almost seemed that part of him had been transported back to Paradise even as he spoke of it. She had rarely seen such conviction, except perhaps from a few of the priests in Tripoli. As for herself, she believed in God and Christ and she prayed every night . . . but she had never attained the conviction she saw in Rashid's face. She didn't know what his visit to Paradise signified, and she didn't think she could ever believe the things he believed, yet at the same time she envied him. It was as if he didn't merely believe, he *knew*.

"You sound as if you want to go back," she said.

"Of course I want to go back, but . . ."

"But what? Perhaps you'll wake up there again one day."

"No. It's not possible," he said.

"Why not?" He didn't reply, but he avoided looking at her and she guessed the answer. "Because you didn't kill me! That's it, isn't it? You think you won't go to Paradise because you spared my life!" When he still didn't answer she said, "That's ridiculous. If you go to Paradise it will be *because* you spared me."

"You don't know what you're talking about."

"You showed mercy. Isn't your God a god of mercy?"

"Isn't yours?"

"Of course. That's exactly what I mean!"

He turned his gaze on her with sudden fury. "When the Christians took Jerusalem, knights waded in blood up to their ankles.

The blood of women and children! Don't speak to me about a God of mercy!"

"And how did the Muslims behave when they conquered Edessa?"

"We were merely taking back what was ours!"

"We were talking of mercy."

Rashid looked away and Elaine shrank back into herself. Whatever Rashid might think, she couldn't believe that God—any god—would punish someone for showing mercy, and Rashid's behavior at the stables had been an act of mercy, not to mention justice. And in her eyes (if not in his) it was all the more beautiful, for he had done what he had done believing it might cost him Paradise.

When Elaine arose the next morning Conrad was still asleep and Rashid was already mounting one of the horses.

"Where are you going?"

"Making sure we're not being followed. I won't be long."

Shortly after that Conrad awakened. His fever seemed better and his mind was clear, though he still seemed weak. He ate a few bites from the remnants of the previous night's meal and drank a good deal of water.

"You're feeling better?" Elaine said.

He nodded.

"Rashid has gone to see if we're being followed."

He nodded again. Elaine said, "You started to say something last night about Charles. Do you remember?"

"Charles was my brother."

"I know. I met him a few times before he . . ." She stopped, flustered.

"Yes, I'd forgotten, you must have known him."

"I don't recall him very clearly, I was too young, but from everything I've heard he was a very good man."

"That he was."

"He would have been proud of you yesterday," she said.

"No, he would have chided me for allowing an attack at my rear." He smiled slightly, as if imagining his brother's rebuke— unsparing but not unaffectionate and with a touch of humor. Elaine had never really found Conrad attractive, but when he spoke of his brother his expression softened and he looked almost agreeable.

"He must have been very fond of you," she said.

"Why do you say that?"

"The way you look when you talk about him. You must have been very fond of each other."

"You couldn't ask for a better brother or a better man. Some-times I think it would have been better if . . ."

"If what?"

"Nothing."

Elaine was sure he'd been about to say *if I had died instead of Charles*. To change the subject she said, "I don't know what's keep-ing Rashid."

"Maybe he paid another visit to Paradise," Conrad said.

Elaine looked at him sharply. "You heard?"

"A tale for children."

"He has the scar to prove it."

Conrad scoffed. "He gave himself the scar, he said as much."

"No. He keeps it fresh but the scar was given in Paradise."

"You don't seriously believe he went to Paradise?"

She shrugged noncommittally. "Every religion has its mystics."

"Not Christianity," Conrad answered stoutly.

"Of course it does," she said. "Saint Paul himself was a mystic. He even had a vision of going to heaven, it's in the Bible!"

Conrad, on shaky ground, having never read the Bible, just said, "It's not the same thing, Saint Paul was a believer."

"So is Rashid," she said, smiling a little.

"Not in the True Faith!" said Conrad. "Wherever Rashid thinks he went was a dream or a visitation by demons! He's going to hell along with every other Saracen."

"And they think the same of us!"

"Well, they're wrong."

Elaine didn't bother to answer. She was disappointed but not surprised. Conrad's mind was closed on the subject—on most subjects, she suspected. She was grateful for his strong right arm, but in the end that was about all he had to offer.

Rashid returned a few minutes later. He hadn't seen anyone, though he'd revisited the scene of the fight and the bodies had been removed, so the presence of the three travelers was certainly no secret. He thought it best to move along, provided Conrad was strong enough.

"I'm fine," Conrad said, and managed to climb on his horse unaided.

They stayed off the main road and kept to pathways in the sparsely wooded backlands. It was important to move quickly, but more important to remain undetected. At one point Elaine dismounted and went a little way off the path to answer nature's call. Conrad rode over to Rashid, who was surprised, now that he saw him close up, at how pale the Knight appeared.

"If I should become unable to ride," Conrad said, "travel on with Elaine. Get her to the Old Man safely."

"She won't agree. She feels beholden to you."

"You must make her agree," Conrad said. "Whatever the Old Man does to her can't be worse than what will happen if she falls into the hands of the scum in this place."

Conrad moved away again, and though he was obviously in considerable pain he took great care to hide it. *Truly*, thought Rashid grudgingly, *he is no coward.*

After another three hours Rashid said he doubted any brigands would pursue them this far, for they were near the border of the territory controlled by the Old Man.

An hour after that, they passed by a small rise and Rashid rode to the top of it, looked out over the land for a few moments, then beckoned the other two to join him. When they did, he pointed to the north, at a mountain range a few hours' ride from where they were, remarkable not for height but for the jagged, jumbled structure of its constituent hills. After a moment they finally saw what he was pointing at.

"The Eagle's Nest," said Rashid.

Through the haze, near the top of one of the jagged peaks, they could just make out the silhouette of a stone tower, which must be part of the Old Man's castle. If they rode steadily and Conrad's strength held out, they should arrive there just as darkness descended on the land.

14

Elaine paced back and forth in a small room in the north tower of the castle. It was bare save for a bed and a chamber pot, and it had a narrow window placed so high in the wall that she could not even catch a glimpse of the surrounding country.

She, Rashid, and a half-conscious Conrad had been met at the main gate of the Eagle's Nest by several of the Old Man's garrison, led by a grizzled-looking man, about forty, in a plain woolen robe and turban, with a scimitar hung from a leather belt. Rashid had called him Hasan and addressed him with a degree of respect that almost amounted to awe. Elaine had asked to see the Old Man of the Mountain, but Hasan hadn't even bothered to answer. Instead, over her protests and struggles, two burly henchmen had bundled her off down a hallway and up a staircase into the windowless room where she now found herself. That had been three days ago.

The first day hadn't been too terrible. She'd been given two plain but adequate meals of bread, cheese, and fruit, along with a cup of water, and her chamber pot had been emptied twice. These chores were performed by an elderly woman, who neither spoke nor answered when Elaine spoke to her, and avoided eye contact or any other form of communication. Still, Elaine had been grateful for the bed and slept in comparative comfort for the first time in a week.

When the second day came and went in exactly the same way, she tried to stop the woman from leaving the room without at least acknowledging her. But the woman proved much stronger than she looked, and had merely pushed Elaine away and closed the door firmly and locked it behind her.

When the third day came and went with no change in the routine and no sign that the Old Man had any intention of meeting with her, she flew into a rage and banged on the door with her fists for some minutes, which accomplished nothing but to make her feel more frustrated than ever and foolish besides.

She was seldom afraid. When her father had died she felt the very worst thing that could happen to her had occurred, and after that, what was there to be afraid of? But as the third day in the tower drew to a close she began to feel frightened. Not for anything the Old Man might do to her, but that he might not do anything at all; that for some perverse reason known only to himself he planned to keep her in this room, watered and fed twice a day like an animal, forever.

Rashid sat alone in his chamber, the same chamber where he'd spent most of his life—a stone ledge for a bed, a smoky candle, a prayer rug, walls of bare rock. Nevertheless everything was different.

Before, he'd been full of hope, aware that his future in this world would be short but meaningful, while anticipating an honorable death and the eternal reward that would follow. Now he was in near despair. He had been foolish to suppose that bringing the girl back would somehow excuse his failure to kill her as instructed.

As soon as they were alone Hasan had questioned him sharply about that failure. Rashid had tried to explain as best he could, but Hasan brushed his attempts aside. His eyes were hard with contempt and once or twice his hands twitched as if on the verge of delivering a blow—a blow that Rashid would have welcomed. He had begged Hasan tearfully for a chance to redeem himself—another mission, any mission!—but Hasan had just stared back at him coldly before leaving the room.

There was one saving grace—Hasan had not taken back the *shabriyah*. Perhaps it was a sign that the Old Man might decide to give him a second chance. Or so he told himself as he watched the candle cast its undulating shadows on the stark walls of his chamber.

Conrad was wide-awake for the first time in a while. He had only a dim memory of arriving at the castle, being taken from his horse and carried inside and laid in this small room on a stone bench that served as a bed.

Thereafter he slept for a long time, delirious for some of it, though he vaguely recalled hearing voices speaking in Arabic while someone spread a salve on his wound that stung at first but soon had a soothing effect. He also remembered being fed some broth, which, like the salve, was initially unpleasant but seemed to make him feel better.

Now the fever had broken and the danger was past. He sat up slowly. His back ached but not unbearably and he felt lucid and even reasonably strong. He looked around the room, seeing it clearly for the first time, or as clearly as the single candle allowed.

His clothes were laid out neatly in a corner and he realized he was dressed in a loose gown, like an Arab peasant. He stood up, waited a moment for his head to stop spinning, then shed the robe and put on his own clothes. Just one thing remained, and it was the most important thing of all. Where was his sword—Charles's sword? It was Conrad's most sacred possession and he must retrieve it, come what may.

There was a thin linen curtain covering the door to his chamber and he pulled it aside. There was a guard outside the door, a young man no older than Rashid. He had a scimitar strapped to his waist, was strongly built, and had the look of a man who could fight if called upon. He was also sound asleep.

It was the first bit of luck Conrad had had in some time, and he seized it at once, stepping noiselessly past the snoring guard. He was in a corridor, carved out of bedrock and lit by torches. There were many rooms like his, with openings covered by linen cloths. He walked to the first one, moved the edge of the cloth, and peered inside. It was occupied by a young Saracen, asleep on his stone bed. Conrad walked along the corridor, looking silently into each chamber. One or two were empty but most housed occupants who, like the guard, were asleep. It must be late night or early morning; there was no way to tell, since the only light was provided by torches.

This corridor ran into another that looked just like it and Conrad followed this for a while, with the same result. He realized he was in the very center of the den of the Assassins. These young men sleeping so peacefully were all, like Rashid, being trained to kill and to give their own lives in the process. He also realized that it was unlikely his sword had been given to one of these. It was too valuable and would have been given to someone higher up. He decided to return to his cell and wake up the guard.

But when he turned into the original corridor there was no guard to be seen. The man must have awakened, discovered Conrad's absence, and fled in a panic. Conrad walked to his cell, pushed aside the cloth—and stopped short. An Assassin was asleep on the stone bed. It took Conrad a moment to grasp the obvious truth: this wasn't his cell.

For the next half hour he wandered to and fro among the corridors, frequently certain that he recognized some indentation or other distinguishing mark in the rock walls only to be disappointed each time, until at last he had to admit that he'd become hopelessly lost.

He was also becoming tired. He thought about waking one of the Assassins, but the sight of a Christian might provoke a fight and he was not quite ready for that, not yet. He sank to the ground, his back against the wall, and rested.

That's when he heard voices—faint but distinct—and to his surprise they seemed to be female voices.

He stood and followed the sound to the end of the corridor, which opened into a room. The room was enormous compared to the cells, and the walls were hung with silken tapestries with lovely symmetrical designs, some woven with threads of gold. There were a dozen or more beds in the room, with wooden frames, mattresses of straw, and feather pillows and covers of brightly colored silk. The aroma of perfume was overwhelming, a delicious blend that seemed to combine every pleasing scent imaginable. He had never encountered anything like it, even in France.

The voices were louder now, and he crossed the room to a partially open wooden door and pushed through it into another world.

He was outside, in a magnificent garden lit by a hundred torches, full of lush trees and bushes with fruits and berries of every kind. The night sky was just beginning to yield to a rosy glow in the east and the gentle murmuring of a stream provided background music for the lilting, laughing voices. Conrad ventured a step into the garden and, through some vines, saw the women, a dozen in number, young, their forms and faces hidden by veils.

And in the midst of them was a boy of sixteen or seventeen, who received their teasing attentions with a deferential delight mixed by an occasional rush of desire that the women were careful to keep unfulfilled. At first Conrad didn't know what to make of it, but then he recalled Rashid's story and had to stop himself from laughing out loud. He had found Paradise!

A beautiful spot, to be sure, but located right here on earth, planted and tended not by angels but by the servants of the Old Man. Rashid, therefore, was not a liar but a fool, who'd been duped into believing he'd visited heaven. And Elaine had been duped as well. He could hardly wait to see both of them again and tell what he knew.

He left the garden and went through the perfumed room back into the torchlit corridors. His energy was restored by the discovery he'd made, but he still had no hope of finding his way back to his chamber. He could hear people beginning to stir behind the linen door hangings and was wondering what would happen when he was discovered when a voice spoke behind him: "Prince Conrad."

He turned to see an older man, hard-faced and stern, who had come up behind him without being heard.

"My name is Hasan," said the man in passable Frankish. "We met when you first arrived but perhaps you don't remember. I did not think to find you up so soon."

"The guard was asleep," Conrad said with a smirk. "I didn't want to disturb him."

"The guard will be dealt with as he deserves," said Hasan.

"Where is Princess Elaine?"

"She is well," said Hasan.

"I want to see her," said Conrad.

"All in good time."

"If any harm befalls her I will hold you accountable. And the Old Man as well."

"We tremble," sneered Hasan.

"If I had my sword you would not be so insolent."

"You will have your sword soon enough. And a horse as well."

Conrad stared, not sure he had heard correctly.

"But first," said Hasan, "you will have the great honor of an audience with the Sheikh."

"The Sheikh?" said Conrad.

"The Old Man of the Mountain, if you prefer. He wishes you to grant him a service."

"Why should I grant him a service?" said Conrad.

"Because he will grant you one in return."

"Such as?"

"The life of the Princess."

Conrad felt his fists clench. "I told you before, if any harm comes to her—"

Hasan interrupted with a wave of his hand. "Rest. You have a great task to fulfill, and you should have a clear head when the Sheikh tells you of it."

He turned and walked away. Conrad, not wishing to become lost again in the maze of tunnels, had little choice but to follow.

· 15 ·

Elaine, Conrad, and Rashid stood before the Old Man of the Mountain. He was frailer than Elaine had thought he'd be, but he held himself erect and had an unmistakable aura of authority. He had a white beard and skin wrinkled like ancient parchment. He wore a plain woolen robe and turban, but carried no sword. His glittering eyes seemed to fasten on Elaine like hooks when he turned his gaze upon her.

Hasan, off to one side, hands folded respectfully in front of him, watched the scene with great interest. He couldn't remember three such visitors in the Old Man's chamber, certainly not at the same time. Rashid's presence was rare enough, for few Assassins had done more than see the Old Man from a distance. For a Christian knight like Conrad to be present was even more unusual, and for a Christian woman to be granted an audience with the Sheikh—in his very chamber!—well, it was unheard of.

And all three at once? Unthinkable.

Yet here they were, Rashid nearly trembling with fear, Conrad rigid with prideful hostility, and the girl staring into the Old Man's eyes without even a trace of deference.

This last was the most galling to Hasan, but the Old Man himself didn't seem bothered by it. If anything, judging by the way his eyes rested on her in an almost fatherly fashion, he appeared to find Elaine the most interesting of the three, though he treated them all with his customary courtesy. "I lack for nothing and am surrounded by men who will carry out my every wish without the slightest hesitation," he had remarked once to Hasan. "In such circumstances, would not rudeness be an offense against God?"

There was a moment of silence, then the Old Man spoke to Conrad, in almost perfect Frankish.

"I trust you're feeling stronger."

"Strong enough," answered the Prince curtly.

"Are you in need of anything?"

"My sword."

The Old Man turned an inquiring look on Hasan, who growled, "I have told the Prince that his sword will be returned in due time."

"Return it to him now," said the Old Man.

Hasan stiffened with surprise, but he bowed respectfully and backed out of the room. Return the sword to the infidel? From what Rashid had said, if there was one thing the Christian lout could do passably well, it was wield a sword! What if he took it into his head to kill the Sheikh? There were many Christians who would gladly forfeit their own lives if they could kill the Old Man first.

Hasan retrieved Conrad's sword from a nearby storeroom and walked more slowly than usual as he returned to the chamber, trying to grasp the Old Man's purpose. Of course the Old Man did not fear death, but why hazard his life in such a cavalier fashion?

Then he understood. The Prince might be willing to sacrifice his own life to kill the Old Man; but that would mean sacrificing the girl's life as well, and that he would not do. The Old Man had discerned this weakness and thus had made an apparently generous gesture—one that might make the Prince a little more trusting.

Hasan returned to the chamber and handed the sword to Conrad, who fastened the belt and scabbard around his waist. Once the sword was in place the Prince did indeed seem to relax somewhat. Hasan managed to hide his own smile. The Old Man was very wise.

Hasan had been right in thinking that the Old Man found Elaine the most interesting of his three visitors. She was not modest in the way of most well-bred young women—Muslim and Christian alike—and if she was afraid she hid it well and without the compensating bravado that the Prince found it necessary to display. All this went through the Old Man's mind as he waited for Conrad to finish fastening his sword belt. Then he said politely, "Is there anything else?"

Conrad shook his head sullenly. The Old Man turned back to Elaine.

"And what of you? Are you in need of anything?"

"I have enough to eat and drink, if that's what you mean."

"What else do you need?"

"My freedom."

"In due course," said the Old Man.

Elaine reacted with visible surprise. "You're going to let me go?" she blurted.

"In due course," the Old Man repeated.

"I see." She paused, then added: "There's something else I require as well."

Hasan stiffened at this, and even the Old Man had a little trouble remaining unruffled and his eyes gleamed with something besides courtesy. "You *require?*"

Elaine swallowed hard, but managed: "Yes."

"And what is that?"

"You sent Rashid to kill me. I want to know why. That's the reason I came here."

"That I cannot tell you."

"Have I offended you in some way?" she asked.

"No," said the Old Man.

"Then someone must have hired you. Who was it?"

"It is a private matter."

"It concerns my life!"

"Nevertheless, it is a question I cannot answer."

"Then kill me now," said Elaine. "Have done with it!"

"You've been in my domain for four days and in my castle for three. If I wished you dead, why are you still alive?"

"That's not the point," Elaine answered. "You may no longer wish me dead, but whoever hired you presumably does. And if I don't know who that is I'm as good as defenseless."

"I may have some influence in the matter," said the Old Man. He let the words hang in the air to see if Elaine would grasp their true meaning. It didn't take her long to do so.

"But you want something in return," she said.

"Surely that is fair," said the Old Man.

"You admit I've done nothing to offend you, yet you threaten me with death unless I grant you a favor," Elaine said. "Do you call that fair?"

The Old Man was annoyed at her impertinence, but her point was not without merit. "I made no threats," he pointed out, and once more let the words linger until Elaine understood their import; threats were unnecessary because she had no choice but to accept his terms.

"What do you want?" she said.

"If it's something I can do, let her go free," Conrad said.

The Old Man turned his gaze away from Elaine. He'd almost forgotten that Conrad was in the room. "What I require," the Old Man said, "cannot be accomplished by the Princess alone, or indeed by any one of you. But it might be done by all three, if you work together."

The visitors, puzzled, remained silent as the Old Man walked to a shelf and took down a scroll of parchment. "Not long ago I wrote a letter, on a parchment such as this one," he said. "Before it could be delivered it was stolen and is now in the hands of those who have no right to it. Do you understand?"

"Who has it?" Conrad said.

The Old Man put the parchment back on the shelf and picked

up an arrow, with striped feathers of black and orange. The others recognized it at once.

"Have you seen such an arrow before?" he asked.

"Raymond, a knight of Tripoli, was killed by such an arrow," Elaine answered. "We passed his body two days' journey east of here."

It was evident from the Old Man's face that he already knew of Raymond's death.

"Was this letter you speak of stolen from Sir Raymond?" Elaine asked.

"That does not concern you," the Old Man said. "But it is certain that the people who made this arrow are now in possession of the letter. They come from a land far to the east. It's said they are a savage people, too numerous to count. It's said that they are very warlike, and that even their war arrows emit a death cry just before they strike home. Exaggerations, no doubt, but exaggerations sometimes contain a grain of truth. They are ruled by a man who calls himself the Great King."

"This letter," Elaine said. "What's in it, who is it to?"

"Again, that's not your concern," the Old Man replied. "You must travel east until you find the Arrow-makers. Tell no one your purpose except their Great King himself. I will provide gold— enough for your journey and enough to buy the letter back from the Great King."

"How do you know he wants gold?" Elaine asked.

"He's a king," said the Old Man.

"Even so, he'll want to know what's in the letter."

"Tell him it's a document sacred to the Nizaris. It's said that he respects God-fearing people, savage though he may be. He may part with the parchment if gold is offered."

"Or he may not," Conrad said. "You're sending us to die."

"I'm giving you a chance at life," said the Old Man. "If you're successful and return with the letter, both you and the Princess may leave in peace."

"Yet you refuse to tell us who wants to kill her."

"I have said, I will use my influence on her behalf. My influence is considerable."

Elaine said, "Why do you choose us? You have servants by the hundred."

"It is true, I have many servants." He hesitated—a rare moment of indecision. Elaine had the impression that the Old Man had given the question a great deal of thought and was trying to think of a way to explain it as simply and briefly as possible. Finally he continued: "God stayed Rashid's hand and spared your life, then led you to free him. Then He guided the three of you here through grave perils. It was for a purpose, and it may be that the purpose is that you recover the parchment from the Arrow-makers."

"Whose God?" Conrad asked. He meant it sarcastically but the Old Man found the question interesting. He would have liked to explain the truth to the callow young Prince, that there was one true God and one True Religion, the Nizari branch of the Shia sect of Islam, whom some called Assassins, and that even though non-believers such as the Prince were doomed, God might still use them occasionally for His own purposes before dispatching them to the fires of eternal damnation. But now was not the time for such a discussion.

He could have told them more, too, about his reasons for entrusting them with this mission. He could have told them how he had long heard stories of a wild people to the east who fought with deadly bows and strange arrows, a people who were fierce and inhumanly savage; how he had dismissed such stories at first but come to believe them over time, especially when unusual-looking arrows began to be found in his territory, indicating the likely presence of scouts or spies; how he had sent out spies of his own over the past year but most had returned with little useful information and others had not returned at all, for the Arrow-makers were said to be very good at catching spies and ruthless in dealing with them. So a different approach was required, and three travelers such as those who stood before him might be able to make the necessary journey without arousing suspicion and retrieve the letter before it was too late. He could have said all this, but they were struggling to take in what he had already told them, so he would remain silent and leave matters in the hands of the One who had brought them to the Eagle's Nest.

"I accept," Elaine said quietly. If it was the price of her freedom, she thought, she really had no choice. Besides, whatever this strange task might involve, it couldn't be worse than the life that awaited her back in Tripoli.

The Old Man nodded graciously. "Good," he said. "There is one further condition. It is said you can read and write."

"My father taught me," Elaine said proudly.

The Old Man took note of the light in Elaine's eyes as she said this. He was glad to see how much she revered her father, though he didn't think much of a man who would be so foolish as to teach his daughter letters. He said, "After you have recovered the parchment, you must swear that you will not read the words written on it. It is a private matter."

"I understand," said Elaine.

"Swear it," said the Old Man, "on the soul of your father."

Elaine hesitated—it seemed like such a solemn charge for so trivial a request. But she said, "I swear, on the soul of my father."

The Old Man nodded again, feeling that the business was now satisfactorily concluded. There was no point in extracting similar promises from Rashid and Conrad. The Old Man knew for a fact that Rashid couldn't read and neither could the vast majority of knights. He was startled to hear Elaine say:

"I have a condition as well."

The Old Man suppressed a sigh. "What condition?" he asked wearily.

"You said, should we succeed in recovering your parchment, that Conrad and I will be allowed to live. I want your assurance that Rashid will also be allowed to live."

"What is his life to you?"

"He spared mine. I want his to be spared as well."

"You know little of him if you think he values his life."

"I value it," Elaine said. "If we do all you ask, will you spare it?"

"I will consider it," said the Old Man.

"That's not good enough," said Elaine.

The air seemed to go out of the room. Then the Old Man said in a voice so soft it could scarcely be heard, "Your father was a ruler, as am I. Would he permit someone to stand in his castle, in his very chamber, and impose conditions?"

After a moment Elaine said, "No, he would not. I'm sorry." Everyone breathed again. "But you will consider it."

"I have said so," replied the Old Man.

"When shall we leave?" Elaine asked.

"When Prince Conrad is strong enough."

"I can leave today," Conrad said quickly.

"Bravely spoken," said the Old Man. "But you will serve your task better if you rest another day or two. It will take Hasan that long to make the necessary preparations in any case."

Though the Old Man had made no visible signal, a servant appeared at the door, indicating that the meeting was over.

"God be with you," said the Old Man, with a quick glance at Conrad to see if he would again ask, *Whose God?* But he did not, and the meeting ended. Elaine, Conrad, and Rashid followed the servant out of the room while Hasan stayed behind for a moment. He had a question for the Old Man.

"Lord," he said, "Rashid will do everything in his power to redeem himself. And the Christian Knight at least has a strong arm and sharp sword. But the girl. Will she not be a burden on such a journey?"

"Perhaps," said the Old Man. "But God spared her for a reason, too."

"What reason?"

"Perhaps to keep the other two from killing each other," the Old Man said, and his eyes crinkled at the edges in what might almost have been a smile.

* * *

The next day, in the castle's courtyard, Conrad found a few minutes alone with Elaine and told her the truth about Rashid's trip to Paradise. As he'd expected, she didn't believe him at first. "You were dreaming," she said, "or delirious, from your wound."

"It was no dream. Hasan saw me in the tunnels. Ask him if you don't believe me."

"How can you be certain this garden you saw was the place Rashid described?"

"Because the trees, the stream, the women, were all just as he said. But here in this castle, not in heaven."

He could see she was beginning to believe him, so he was all the more amazed when she said, "Don't tell Rashid."

"Why the devil not?"

"He won't believe you, for one thing."

"He'll have to believe me. I'll show him!"

"His visit to Paradise means everything to him. If you'd seen his face when he talked about it . . ."

"What's his face got to do with it?"

She remembered the light that had shone in Rashid's eyes as he talked about his visit to Paradise; she couldn't stand the idea of seeing that light extinguished. But of course Conrad would never understand that. So she just said, "If you tell him it might destroy him."

"Good."

"No, it's not good. Even from a selfish point of view we have a long and difficult journey ahead, and we need Rashid at his best."

"He'll just have to manage," said Conrad.

"Besides, it would prove nothing," Elaine added, surprising Conrad yet again.

"Of course it would. It would prove he never went to Paradise. It would prove his religion is nonsense!"

"It would do no such thing. Just because someone built a paradise on earth, doesn't mean there isn't a real Paradise."

"What?"

"Well, what do you think heaven is?"

"I don't know. It's . . . very high, I suppose."

"What else? Does it have clouds?"

"I suppose so," he said cautiously. He sensed a trap on the way.

"What about angels," she went on. "Does it have angels?"

"It must."

"And what are angels exactly? Do they have wings?"

"Yes."

"And is there music?"

"I suppose." He had a vague childhood memory of someone reading something from the Bible about harps.

"All right, then," Elaine said. "Suppose you found a place here on earth—on top of the mountain behind this castle, for example—where there were clouds, and music, and even people who look like they have wings. Would that mean there was no such place as heaven?"

"What are you babbling about?" Conrad said. "There are no clouds on the mountain, you can see that from here. And as for people with wings . . ."

"Don't be so thickheaded!"

"Don't talk rubbish!" he said, though he had to admit to himself that he often felt thickheaded around her.

Elaine said, "It would be common decency to say nothing to Rashid, that's all."

"I was taught that decency means telling the truth."

This struck home, because Elaine prided herself on being honest. "I'm not suggesting that you lie, only that you don't tell what you know. As I said, we have a long journey ahead, why begin it with something that's sure to cause trouble?"

"Because it's the truth," Conrad said stubbornly. He saw that her talk about the journey was a ploy; her real purpose was to protect Rashid. Her next words confirmed it.

"Then I ask you, I beg you, not to tell him," she said, looking earnestly into Conrad's eyes, "as a boon to me."

After a moment Conrad said, "I might consider it as a gift to my future bride."

She recoiled as if struck. "That's not fair," she said.

"It's as fair as what you're asking of me."

A long moment passed and then Elaine said, "No," and it was Conrad's turn to recoil. She went on quickly, "I know you think you have a claim on me, but—"

"It's not just my claim, it's your country's claim. It's your duty!"

Elaine forced herself to keep calm. "I believe that marriage must be, at least in part, an affair of the heart. I'm grateful for what you did when the bandits attacked. But I don't love you and I never will and I cannot be your wife. I'm sorry. Nevertheless, I beg you, don't tell Rashid what you know. Please."

She walked quickly away. Conrad stared after her, aware of anger and humiliation, which were to be expected, but surprised by a sudden stinging in his eyes.

After the meeting with the Old Man, Rashid spent most of his time with Hasan, preparing for the journey. Hasan made him memorize the details of the route they'd be taking, then drilled him on what he'd learned.

"What is the first river you'll come to?"

"The Euphrates, Hasan."

"How many days' journey is that river from here?"

"Four days, Hasan."

"What city provides the best crossing?"

"Ar-Raqqah."

"Who rules Ar-Raqqah?"

"Ali Jabar, a Sunni but a tolerant one."

"What lies beyond Ar-Raqqah?"

"The Al-Jazirah plain."

"And on the far side of the Al-Jazirah plain?"

"The Tigris River, Hasan, a week's journey."

"And the city that lies on the Tigris?"

A slight hesitation by Rashid; an impatient shake of the head from Hasan.

"You have not been listening!"

"I have, Hasan, I just forgot for a moment. The city is Mosul. I'm sorry, I'll try harder."

And so on, again and again, these questions and a hundred more, until three times running Rashid answered every one without error or hesitation. Only then did Hasan pronounce himself satisfied, and only then did Rashid dare broach the subject that had been tormenting him.

"Hasan, suppose we find the Arrow-makers and we retrieve the Old Man's letter and bring it safely back . . . might I, someday, possibly, be granted another chance to gain Paradise?"

"You'd be in Paradise now if you'd taken advantage of your last chance," Hasan said. "Why should you get another?"

"I shouldn't, of course, but . . . it seems the Old Man still finds me useful, so perhaps it was God's plan that—"

Hasan interrupted scornfully. "That God chose to use your unworthiness to work out His purpose does not make you any less unworthy. Nor does it make you any more useful to the Sheikh than the dust on his sandals."

"Yes, Hasan."

"And never again let any feelings for these infidels interfere with your mission."

"No, Hasan." But this was said with an almost imperceptible hesitation, which, slight though it was, did not escape Hasan's sharp eye. His expression darkened.

"It's just, they have done service to me, and I to them. . . ." The words were out before Rashid could stop them and he wished immediately that he had kept quiet.

"And what is that compared to your duty to the Sheikh and to God?" thundered Hasan.

"It is nothing, Hasan," Rashid answered, this time promptly.

Hasan glared at him for a long time and Rashid held his look, feeling that to look away might be interpreted as a fatal weakness. Finally Hasan, his expression still full of disapproval, turned on his heel and left. Rashid drew a breath and let it out slowly. Conrad might be courageous, and Elaine also, and she was kind besides, but he must remember that such things were not important. He was being given a second chance and he resolved that no weakness on his part would let it go to waste.

Three days after the meeting in his chamber, the Old Man watched as the three travelers, along with an escort of Assassins led by Hasan, left the Eagle's Nest. When they were out of sight he turned away from the window and knelt on his prayer rug and faced Mecca and prayed, even though the castle's muezzin had not issued a call.

Then he ate his usual meal of bread and dates and water and reflected on recent events. They had been interesting, mostly because of the girl, but also because of Rashid. Of course the Old Man knew that the "paradise" he had constructed in his castle was but a pale imitation of the glorious Paradise that awaited the faithful after death; it was not really a deception, but a promise, and one that had always been sufficient to motivate young Assassins to carry out their missions—until Rashid. Did that make him unusually strong or unusually weak? Time would tell. The Old Man truly believed that Rashid and the others had been chosen by God for the purpose, yet he also knew that no one, not even he himself, could be absolutely certain of God's will, and it was always possible for events to take an unexpected turn. The three were young, after all, and would be traveling through strange and distant lands about which little was known, looking for a people—the Arrow-makers—about whom even less was known.

It was not often that the Old Man prayed for the unworthy, but in this case he had made an exception. Though two of the three were infidels and the third a believer who had betrayed the trust that had been placed in him, the Old Man had asked God, in His mercy, to provide them with assistance and guidance on their journey.

He knew they would need it every step of the way.

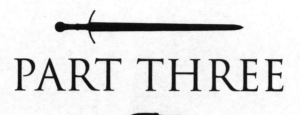

PART THREE

AL-JAZIRAH

· 16 ·

Elaine had expected the wilderness east of the Eagle's Nest to be barren, but the melting snows had sent gentle streams down the rolling hillsides, and blue hyacinth and white jasmine with an occasional splash of yellow bloomed in modest array. The lively colors and sweet scents added to her feeling of elation; uncertainty and danger might lie in the future, but so did the freedom and adventure she'd always dreamt of.

She, Rashid, and Conrad, along with Hasan, rode in the center of a loose cordon formed by a dozen mounted Assassins, all well armed and of stern visage; they were a formidable-looking company and any wayfarers who happened along gave them a very wide berth.

Hasan had explained the logistics of the expedition earlier. The travelers could not appear too poor, for peasants or beggars would not be on horseback, nor could they appear too prosperous, lest they become a target for thieves. Thus they wore clothes of no particular distinction—plain cotton trousers and shirts for Rashid and Conrad, and a plain but respectable cotton dress for Elaine—and their horses, one for each traveler plus a packhorse, were also nondescript, though Hasan had allowed Elaine to keep the gray she'd acquired from the dead bandits.

It was important that two things in particular be kept hidden. The first, of course, was the gold, a hundred coins in all, that the Old Man had given them. The coins had been sewn into the inside of the saddles of all four horses, so if one or more mounts were lost or stolen, some gold would be preserved.

The second thing that had to be hidden was Conrad's sword, which Conrad had refused to part with. It was unmistakably a knight's weapon and, while Frankish merchants sometimes journeyed through eastern lands, a knight was likely to be set upon and killed or held for ransom. Hasan had hidden the sword cunningly under the leather sacks carried by the packhorse. Conrad felt naked without it, and Elaine sensed that part of his mind always kept track of the horse that carried it.

Conrad and Elaine would pose as brother and sister, with Rashid as their hired servant. The three could not travel as friends, for a woman who associated with men not related to her would attract unwanted attention. Hasan had mentioned the possibility of Conrad and Elaine posing as a married couple, but even as Elaine started to object, he'd said: "But I think brother and sister is more fitting. In certain places that bond is more highly respected than the bond of matrimony." Elaine had breathed a sigh of relief.

Finally, because it was possible that reports of a missing prince and princess would be circulating even this far to the east, Conrad and Elaine would be traveling as "Edward" and "Elisabeth." Hasan did not deem it necessary to provide Rashid with an alias.

That night they made camp. The Assassins built a fire then withdrew to stand guard, leaving Elaine, Conrad, and Rashid alone with Hasan in the flickering circle of the fire's glow.

Hasan went over the details of the journey again, one last time. Then he said, "Concerning the region beyond the Zagros Mountains, little is known. Learn what you can as you approach them. But, God willing, you will find the Arrow-makers before you have to climb the Zagros, for their peaks are high and rugged. Spend as little gold as you can, so you have enough to buy back the letter.

And lose no time between here and the Euphrates, for this time of year it can make for a treacherous crossing."

When he had finished he stood and said, "God be with you," and without further ceremony left to join the other Assassins on the perimeter. Rashid, Elaine, and Conrad glanced at each other, but no one broke the silence and, each in his or her own time, they fell asleep.

They awoke the next morning to find that the Assassins, including Hasan, had slipped away during the night, leaving them with the three horses and the fourth to carry the supplies.

Now they were truly alone.

For the first hour they rode in silence, then Elaine found herself in the mood for conversation.

Since she and Conrad had barely spoken since the argument about Paradise, she turned to Rashid.

"How long have you known Hasan?" she said.

"Always," Rashid said.

"He was your teacher?"

"Yes."

"What did he teach you?"

"Everything."

"Such as?"

"How to fight, how to use the knife, how to hide, how to hunt, how to survive."

"Anything else?"

"Like what?"

"Well, I don't know, music, or poetry?"

Rashid looked puzzled and Conrad, riding a few paces behind, gave a derisive snort.

"There's beautiful poetry in Arabic," Elaine said loftily.

"How would you know?" Conrad said.

"I've read translations."

"Then it wasn't in Arabic, was it?" Conrad said. This silenced Elaine, but only for a moment.

"Is it true that Assassins use hashish?" she asked Rashid.

Rashid laughed. This was a widespread rumor which the Sheikh encouraged because it added to the Assassins' mystique, but hashish was the last thing a man needed whose work required a clear head and quick reactions. "No."

Elaine soldiered on. "What made you decide to become an Assassin in the first place?"

"It's not something you choose. My father took me to the Eagle's Nest when I was a boy. He wanted me to serve God and also . . ." He hesitated.

"Also what?"

"And also, take vengeance for my family."

"Vengeance against who?" said Elaine.

"Christians," Rashid said.

There was a moment of silence. Then Elaine asked, "Vengeance for what?" and Conrad, curious, nudged his horse a little closer.

"My father was crippled by Christians, and my mother and two sisters killed. It would be better to say massacred, since they had no way of fighting back. They were in the wrong place at the wrong time—a small village near a castle that was under siege."

After a moment Elaine said quietly, "That's terrible. I'm sorry." Then she felt bound to add, "But those who kill women and children are not true Christians."

"They were Templars," Rashid said bitterly. "Are not Templars true Christians?" Templars were warrior-monks, sworn to a life of celibacy and dedicated to fighting the infidel. In the eyes of most, there were no truer Christians alive. Elaine had met Templars from time to time, at tournaments; they had always treated her kindly, and it was difficult to imagine them killing children. Still, their eyes had been very hard.

Aloud she said, "There are no Templars at Tripoli. Yet you were going to kill me."

"The Old Man required it."

"But your quarrel is with Templars."

"The Old Man required it."

Conrad said in a casual tone, "How old were you when this massacre occurred?"

"Very young," said Rashid.

"Three? Four?" Conrad said.

"I don't know," said Rashid.

"Then you can't be sure it even happened."

"Hasan told me of it," Rashid said.

"He told you what he wanted you to believe," Conrad said. "So you'd become the Old Man's slave, which is what you are."

Rashid yanked his horse to a stop and turned on Conrad angrily. "I am proud to be his slave! But Hasan doesn't lie. He knew what happened and he told me!"

"He told you what he wanted you to believe," Conrad said again.

Elaine broke in quickly, "No one can remember things that happened when they were very young. That doesn't mean they didn't happen." Then she said to Rashid, "How old were you when your training began?"

It was a transparent attempt to distract Rashid from his anger, but Conrad, satisfied he'd made his point, said nothing more and Rashid and Elaine continued their conversation.

The afternoon shadows had begun to lengthen when Rashid suddenly pointed at something that had caught his attention. On a ridge in the distance a group of horsemen sat, motionless, evidently watching something below them on the far side of the ridge. After a moment the horsemen began trotting down the far slope and disappeared from sight.

Conrad glanced at Elaine. "Stay with the packhorse," he said, and Rashid nodded in agreement. It irritated Elaine to see how quickly Rashid and Conrad forgot their mutual hostility and shunted her aside when it suited them. Of course she ignored them. The two men rode quickly up the slope and she followed closely behind.

Rashid and Conrad reached the crest of the slope and looked down into the valley below, where a small caravan consisting of three riders on camels, plus four additional camels loaded with packs, was moving westward. As Rashid and Conrad watched, the horsemen began attacking the caravan, pulling the sacks from the side of the pack camels and ripping them open. The contents—a dark red flaky substance—began to scatter in the light breeze.

One of the camel riders, older than the other two, tried to intervene but was badly overmatched. The robbers pulled him from his camel and began beating and kicking him before he even hit the ground. The two younger men drove their camels a step closer as if to help the older man, but menacing looks from the attackers were enough to make them keep their distance.

Conrad and Rashid watched from the hill without much interest—a merchant was being robbed by a band of thieves, a not uncommon occurrence and no business of theirs.

"Do something!" Elaine had ridden up behind them, leading the packhorse behind her.

"I told you to stay back," Conrad said.

"That poor man. Look! Why don't those two help him?"

Conrad and Rashid remained motionless, but Elaine did not.

"*You* stay with the packhorse!" She flung the lead rope aside and spurred her mount down the slope. Rashid and Conrad exchanged a startled look, then—they could hardly allow a woman to go into battle while they watched—urged their own mounts forward. They caught up with Elaine as the ground leveled out, drawing their knives as they rode; Conrad didn't have time to retrieve his sword from the pack animal, but he knew how to use a knife, as he would soon prove.

The skirmish was short. These thieves were nothing like the bandits who had attacked them on the way to the Eagle's Nest; moreover they were taken completely by surprise, for neither

Conrad nor Rashid, both trained to be ruthless, had any interest in fair play.

Two of the thieves were dead—one by Conrad's knife, the other by Rashid's—before they even knew they were being attacked, and the remaining robbers scrambled on their horses and rode away. Neither Conrad nor Rashid thought it worth the trouble to chase them down.

Meanwhile Elaine had jumped from her horse and was bending over the merchant, who, despite being dazed from the beating he'd received, was trying to struggle to his feet.

"Stay still," Elaine said. "Lie back down."

The man, about fifty and slightly built but very determined to stand, ignored her and she realized he might not speak Frankish. "Rashid," she said. "Tell him he needs to be still."

Rashid, still on horseback, translated Elaine's words in Arabic, but the merchant only redoubled his efforts to stand, looking with an anguished expression at the dark red flakes from the torn sacks, continuing to disperse in the wind.

With a determined effort the man at last heaved himself to his feet, pushed past Elaine, and began screaming in Arabic to the two camel riders who had stood by passively during the attack. Hastily they dismounted and began putting the flaky substance back into the sacks. The merchant joined them on his hands and knees, salvaging what he could, tears streaming down his face as he realized how many of the fine, thin flakes had been lost. Finally he turned to Elaine and her two companions.

"You are Frankish," he said. He spoke Frankish after all, slowly and formally, and with a strong Arabic accent, but acceptably.

"Yes," said Elaine. "My name is Elisabeth. This is my brother, Edward, and our servant, Rashid."

"You are Christians, yet come to the aid of a Muslim."

The remark was addressed to both Elaine and Conrad, but Conrad didn't reply—if it had been up to him, no aid would have been given—so Elaine spoke up. "You were the victim of an injustice. And justice is a concern of Christian and Muslim alike, is it not?"

The merchant raised his eyebrows and smiled. "That is well spoken," he said. "You are a most gracious lady. My name is Yusuf bin Amin. I am greatly in your debt."

"Are you sure you're all right?" said Elaine.

"I am, thanks to you three," Yusuf answered. "You've done me a great service. You must allow me to repay it—with supper, at the very least. Then we can make camp near one another, in case the robbers decide to return."

This suggestion was a good one, with the sun so near setting, and the two small bands joined forces, left the bodies of the dead brigands where they lay, and resumed their journey.

"I am not quite so foolish as you must think me," Yusuf said, "to travel unprotected off the main caravan route. My nephew, Jamal, and two other servants are traveling with me but left some time ago to fill our waterskins at Lake Ramiyah. Do you know of it?"

"No, I don't," said Elaine.

"A lovely place," Yusuf said, "but frequented by all manner of men, and I thought it best to send two servants with Jamal for protection. He should have been back hours ago—I pray nothing has happened to them."

"Where are you traveling from?" Elaine asked.

"Aleppo," said Yusuf. "Bound for Ar-Raqqah."

"As are we," said Elaine.

"Excellent! Perhaps we can travel there together."

An hour later, as darkness fell and Yusuf's two servants set about preparing a meal, the three travelers conferred on the wisdom of accepting Yusuf's offer.

"This is a Muslim caravan," Conrad grumbled. "Besides, he's a merchant." Like most knights, he tended to look down on those who bought and sold for a living. "Best to keep to ourselves."

"We'll be less conspicuous traveling with Muslims," Elaine countered. "Plus, there's safety in numbers."

They turned to Rashid, who considered for a moment. "Yusuf knows the region. That might prove useful."

As they were talking, Yusuf's nephew, Jamal, returned with the waterskins and the other two servants. Jamal was no older than twenty, with a pudgy face and soft skin and a sullen expression that didn't change as Yusuf introduced him to Elaine and Conrad, but not to Rashid, supposedly a mere servant. Then Yusuf excused himself and took Jamal a little way from the camp to speak with him alone. He may have thought he was too far away to be overheard, but he was too angry to keep his voice down and he scolded Jamal harshly.

At dinner, Yusuf, Jamal, Conrad, and Elaine sat close to the fire while Yusuf's servants and Rashid arranged themselves a little to the rear. Bowls of water had been provided for the washing of hands, and after this was done, Yusuf spoke a brief blessing and ate the first morsel of bread, then the other three began eating as well. Conrad, after six years in Europe, and another ten days in a Frankish castle, wrinkled his nose at the food set before them, which he regarded as "Arab food" and therefore bound to be inferior. But he was hungry and forced himself to eat, and was surprised to find that it was quite good, consisting of full-bodied wheat-and-barley bread, pistachios, figs, wrapped grape leaves, and a pulpy dish that looked like porridge but was seasoned with an unusual spice. Yusuf smiled at their evident enjoyment of this last item.

"Tasty, is it not?" he asked.

"Very," said Elaine.

"It's seasoned with Aleppo pepper," he explained. "You've heard of it?"

"Yes, but never tasted it," Elaine said. "It's delicious."

"And valuable as well," Yusuf said with an accusing glance at Jamal.

Elaine said, "That's what you were trying to put back into the sacks. . . ."

Yusuf nodded. "Thank God I was able to save some of it."

"It's generous of you to share what you have left with us," Elaine said.

"If it weren't for you, I'd have none left at all!"

Elaine and Yusuf continued talking, as Conrad and Jamal listened. Yusuf spoke briefly of himself—a poor merchant, compared to some, but on the way up. He was fortunate to have contacts that allowed him to buy pepper on favorable terms. He was planning to cross the Euphrates at Ar-Raqqah, then press on across the Al-Jazirah plain to Mosul, where his pepper would fetch a higher price.

"But how rude I am," he said, "talking only of myself! Tell me about yourselves!'

After a slight hesitation Elaine said, "My brother and I are going to Mosul as well. We have family there, an uncle on my mother's side." This was the story they'd agreed to tell anyone who asked.

Yusuf looked surprised. "Franks, as far east as Mosul! Very unusual," he said.

"There are a few."

"Yes, a few," Yusuf said. "Have you visited Mosul before?"

"No, this is our first trip," Elaine said.

"May an experienced traveler offer a word of advice?"

"Please do."

"They say the snows in the Turkish mountains are melting late this year, which means the river is still rising. It might be wise to cross as soon as possible."

"I see," said Elaine. "It's about three days further . . . ?"

"It can be done in two," said Yusuf. "As I suggested before, we can journey together, if you don't mind rising early and traveling late."

"Perhaps that would be best," Elaine said. "What do you think, Edward?" She thought it would look well to ask Conrad's opinion; after all, he was supposed to be her brother. Conrad had just stuffed another grape leaf into his mouth, but managed to grunt and nod, and Elaine pretended that this settled things. The food must have overcome his earlier objection.

"Excellent," Yusuf pronounced.

* * *

Afterward, Rashid was unable to sleep. The reason was Yusuf's nephew Jamal.

Rashid had watched him carefully during supper. The young man had sulked, understandable given the tongue-lashing he'd received from his uncle, but there was something else as well—a certain furtiveness in the way he'd scrutinized Conrad and Elaine, studying them and drawing his own silent conclusions. Rashid knew that men who observed much and said little could be extremely dangerous, because it was the way he himself had been trained.

Jamal was trouble. Rashid was sure of it.

· 17 ·

Next morning, Conrad, Elaine, and Rashid found themselves alone around the breakfast fire. "We should ask Yusuf about the arrow," Elaine said.

"I don't trust him," said Conrad.

"Why? Because he's a Muslim? He's been very generous with us."

"He's a merchant," Conrad answered. "Merchants buy and sell. He may decide to sell us."

"I don't believe that. Besides, nobody knows who we really are— who would buy us? Rashid, what do you think?"

"Yusuf seems all right," said Rashid. "It's Jamal I wouldn't trust."

"We'll ask Yusuf, then," said Elaine. "He travels widely, he talks with other merchants who also travel. He might have heard something about the Arrow-makers."

"Ask Yusuf," said Rashid. "But the less Jamal knows, the better."

"All right. Yusuf only," Elaine said. Conrad looked away. She was always so quick to agree with whatever the Assassin said.

The opportunity came just after noon, when the travelers had stopped at a town situated near a small oasis. Jamal and the four servants had gone to the marketplace, and Elaine approached Yusuf with the arrow wrapped in a cloth. Rashid and Conrad followed closely behind her.

146

"We'd like to ask you a question," said Elaine. She unwrapped the arrow, its orange stripes standing out vividly in the bright sunlight. "Have you ever seen an arrow like this?"

Yusuf stared at the arrow for a moment in surprise. "Where did you get this?"

"We've had it for some time," said Elaine, evading the question. "We have business with those who made it."

Yusuf's expression turned very grave. "What business could you possibly have with the makers of this arrow?"

"It's a family matter," Elaine said. "It concerns the uncle in Mosul that I told you about before. I'm not free to discuss the details, I hope you understand."

Yusuf didn't answer right away. "I've never seen such an arrow as this. But I've heard them described."

"Have you seen the ones who make them?"

"No, and I have no wish to."

"We know they are from the east, ruled by a man they call the Great King, and that they've recently come west over the Zagros. We need to find them."

"They have not come over the Zagros," said Yusuf. "At least not yet."

Elaine frowned. "But this arrow . . ."

"Spies or scouts may have come over the mountains," Yusuf conceded. "But the main force remains on the far side, at war with the Khwarazmians. And I pray to God they stay there."

"Are you so frightened of them?" Conrad scoffed.

"I only know what I hear," Yusuf said calmly.

"And what do you hear?"

"That they are merciless, showing no pity to man, woman, or child. That to submit is to endure slavery, while to resist is certain death. That they are so swift in battle they seem to appear out of thin air, that their arrows have a death song, that when the battle is over they eat the hearts of their enemies and sacrifice their still-living children on the blazing altars of their gods."

"And you believe such stories?" said Conrad.

"I believe that men who inspire such stories are better left alone."

Elaine said, "Nevertheless, we have to find them."

"Then you must cross the Zagros Mountains," said Yusuf, "no easy task. And if you find the Arrow-makers, I fear your troubles will truly begin. But I see you're determined, so all I can do is wish you good fortune."

"These Arrow-makers," Conrad said. "What do they call themselves?"

"They call themselves Mongols," Yusuf said.

"Mongols? What does it mean?"

"No one knows. It may be a word that has no translation to other tongues. They're called by another name, too, by all who encounter them."

"What word?"

"Devils," said Yusuf.

The three travelers exchanged a quick glance. What was it the Old Man had said about the Arrow-makers? *A savage people, too numerous to count.* Probably an exaggeration, the Old Man had said, but Yusuf made it seem like an understatement. Elaine thanked Yusuf for his information, wrapped the arrow up again in the cloth, and turned quickly away before the merchant could see the troubled expression on her face.

Elaine had read about the Euphrates River in the books in her father's library, handwritten by monks and illustrated with maps. She knew the river began in the mountains of Anatolia to the north, was in some places nearly a quarter mile wide, and flowed in a southeasterly direction for well over a thousand miles until it emptied into the Persian Gulf. She knew that when the mountain snows melted in the spring, the river swelled and raced, sometimes violently, and that flooding was common.

But reading these things in a book and actually seeing the mighty river were very different things. It was muddy brown in color, and the apparent calm of its steadily flowing center was belied by its restless churning along the banks. Even as Elaine watched, small bits and clumps of earth were washed from the shore. She stood in wonder, sensing the power that lay beneath the surface.

Meanwhile, Yusuf was bargaining with a group of ferrymen. It was later than he would have liked—an hour before sunset—but the river was unpredictable and Yusuf thought it better to cross now than wait until morning, when conditions might be worse. He struck a satisfactory bargain and the process of loading the animals onto one of the ferries began.

At first Elaine thought there was no way the entire menagerie—seven camels and four horses—could be squeezed onto the ferry, which was nothing more than a large flat raft fitted with a crude tiller and a rickety wooden fence around the perimeter; not only the animals, but nine passengers plus the ferryman and his oarsman had to be accommodated. Yusuf, sensing her concern, gave her an avuncular wink and smile of reassurance, and the process began.

The ferry was moored to a pier that extended into the river, and the animals had to be led down one by one and induced to step onto the barge. Horses don't mind water and getting them on board was easy enough, but camels were a different matter. Stubborn creatures to begin with, they can swim if they must, but they don't take to water naturally, and being surrounded by it was distasteful to them. But eventually they, too, were in place, and then the humans stepped on board, squeezing into the gaps among the beasts as best they could.

By this time the sun was setting and the ferryman pushed the barge away from the pier. Elaine turned back to the east and smiled to see how the sun's rays, shining from behind her, bestowed their golden cloak even upon the muddy waters of the Euphrates. As often happened with her, the beauty of the landscape filled her with optimism. They had a long distance to travel yet but she was pleased with the progress they'd made so far.

When she turned back around she was surprised to see that by skillful use of the tiller to take advantage of the current, the ferryman and his oarsman had already guided them nearly halfway across. On the far side of the river, half a mile downstream, she could see the minarets and rooftops of Ar-Raqqah—she'd been too busy admiring the sunset to notice them before. It was at that moment she felt a slight tremor in the raft. Then it began to turn in a large, lazy circle.

When it came to water, Conrad sided with camels. He'd never been a strong swimmer and it had been years since he'd been in water over his waist. In his view the sooner they got off the river the better, so when the raft started turning he felt anxious. This feeling intensified as the circles became tighter and faster.

The animals began to stir. Rashid and Elaine kept the horses calm, while Conrad's attention was on one horse in particular—the roan packhorse near one railing of the raft. Conrad began moving unsteadily toward it and jostled against Elaine in the process.

"What are you doing?" she said irritably. She wasn't afraid of the water but didn't relish the thought of being knocked overboard.

"My sword," he said.

Conrad managed to reach the roan just as the ferry gave a sudden lurch and listed sharply to one side. The horse was thrown against Conrad, who in turn was pressed against the rail, which split with a sharp crack like the sound of a handclap.

"Edward, be careful!" Elaine called out.

The rail began to give, but then the raft, spinning faster now, listed in the opposite direction and Conrad was free of the rail. Elaine breathed a sigh of relief and exchanged a glance with Rashid. They both knew Conrad had had a close call. Rashid spoke soothingly in Arabic to the horses nearest him.

In the next moment the raft tilted back toward Conrad's side and he barely managed to avoid the roan as it crashed into the rail. This time a camel was hurled against the rail as well, and the combined weight broke the rail cleanly in half. The camel went into the water first, and Conrad, clinging to the part of the rail that remained fastened to the barge, watched helplessly as the roan, eyes rolling, slid into the river with a frightened whinny.

Elaine was holding to the rail on the side of the barge at right angles to Conrad's; the listing of the barge had not affected her directly. She saw the camel go overboard followed by the horse and for a moment she was afraid Conrad would fall in as well, but he managed to hold on to the rail as the ferry righted itself. Then, in the next instant, to her utter astonishment, Conrad dove into the river after the horse.

In her shock Elaine forgot to use his alias; she screamed, "Conrad, no!"

But it was too late. She stood on tiptoe, desperately trying to see Conrad, but every man and animal on board seemed to be in the way. Finally she glimpsed him, just for an instant, thrashing desperately in the current, already far from the raft and being swept farther away by the second. She thought she saw the horse as well, downstream beyond him, its head just above water, but she couldn't be sure. Then man and horse were both gone, too far away to be seen in the murky river and fading light.

18

They camped outside the town of Ar-Raqqah for two days, search-ing for some word or sign of Conrad, or "Edward," as Elaine again remembered to call him. Despite their considerable differences she must have grown used to his presence, for the idea that he might actually be dead seemed inconceivable. But Yusuf's servants combed both banks of the river for several miles downstream and no trace of Conrad or the horse was found.

At the end of the second day, Yusuf approached Elaine and Rashid, shaking his head sadly. "I'm sorry," he said.

"You've done everything in your power," Elaine said shakily.

"I should have waited to cross until the next morning, perhaps the river would have been calmer. Or hired two ferries instead of one. But why did he jump in? Was it the horse, or something it carried?"

"Edward was always very impulsive," said Elaine, and Yusuf sensed that she didn't want to discuss the subject further.

He said, "I know it's little enough, but let me pay you for the horse, at least. What was he worth, do you think?"

"I . . . I'm not sure," Elaine said, flustered as she realized how little she knew of the price of horses or of anything else. Rashid was no help either, for an Assassin was trained to steal what he needed.

"Well," said Yusuf, "let us say, two gold pieces. Is that fair?"

"Very," said Elaine. Yusuf handed her the coins and she thanked him and put them into the pocket of her dress and Yusuf withdrew discreetly to allow Rashid and Elaine some privacy.

The next day they resumed their journey. Yusuf maintained a tactful distance for the most part, while trying to anticipate Elaine's needs whenever possible. "Consider my servants to be yours," he said. Meanwhile, Jamal kept a close eye on Elaine and Rashid, while Rashid kept a close eye on Jamal.

Over the next few days a jumble of emotions swirled inside of Elaine, starting with something that felt very much like grief. Not the wrenching, devastating grief she'd felt when her father had died, of course, but still, a pang of sorrow so sharp it surprised her. Conrad, she realized now, had been so *reliable*. Yes, reliably stubborn at times and reliably obtuse at others, but nevertheless . . . reliable. Thank God he had been there during the bandit attack!

Remembering that fight made her mood veer suddenly into anger. He'd died *for a sword*. Not to think ill of the dead, but was that not foolish? She said as much to Rashid, whose answer surprised her.

"It was his brother's, was it not? It was a matter of honor."

"Rashid. Suppose your dagger—what is it called . . . ?"

"A *shabriyah*."

"Suppose your *shabriyah* had gone overboard—would you have risked your life for it?"

"Yes. It was a gift from Hasan." When Elaine just shook her head, he said, "What about you? The comb you use every night. I've seen the way you look at it. . . ."

"It belonged to my mother, who I never knew."

"Would you not risk your life for it?"

Elaine was momentarily at a loss. She hadn't made this connection. Then: "I don't know. Not if I knew people were depending on me."

The last sentence slipped out unbidden and sent her thoughts in yet another direction. Had she been depending on Conrad? Well, that's what you did with reliable people—depended on them. And after all, whether for pride or some other reason, he had come along to protect her—which meant, she realized, that she had indirectly caused his death. Suddenly she was ashamed of her anger, which was replaced by guilt, which in time morphed back into sorrow . . . and the emotions chased each other around until she longed for the relief of feeling nothing at all.

Rashid, too, was surprised at how affected he had been by Conrad's death. It was a very strange fact that in a certain way he'd gotten to know Conrad better than he'd ever known any other males of his own age. The other Assassins didn't really count, for training was a full-time occupation and friendships were discouraged. If any attachment seemed to be forming, pains were taken to separate the offenders at once, for nothing could interfere with absolute loyalty to the Old Man. There were many dozens of novitiates and Rashid had had no more than a passing acquaintance with any of them.

Did this mean that Conrad had been a friend? It was a word he knew but had never really understood the meaning of. On reflection, though, the answer must be *surely not!* Conrad was an infidel for one thing, and for another he'd sworn to kill Rashid and twice attempted to do so. Whatever friendship was, it couldn't be that. Still, he couldn't deny that he would have felt safer if Conrad were still alive and traveling beside them.

Besides coming to terms with the loss of Conrad, Rashid and Elaine had to decide whether to continue their journey or return to the Eagle's Nest. It was not an easy decision for Elaine.

"What do you think the Old Man would say if we came back?" she asked.

"He would not be pleased. And I will not stand before him, having failed again."

"I understand, but—"

"You can turn back if you wish. I'll stay with you until another caravan passes by heading west—one with Franks in it. They'll take you back to Tripoli or close enough—and you no longer have to concern yourself with marrying Conrad."

"That's true," Elaine said.

"And without the pending marriage, perhaps you will no longer be in danger."

"Perhaps not. Or perhaps I would. I alone was the target—you were not given a choice between myself and Conrad, correct?"

"Correct," Rashid admitted.

"So perhaps in the end maybe I, rather than the marriage, was the target."

Elaine thought for a long while. Continuing the journey would be perilous—but was it any more daunting than what awaited her back in Tripoli, even if she was no longer an Enemy? Five more years subjected to the whims of Bernard and the other men who ruled Tripoli—maybe the next arranged marriage would be with someone worse than Conrad! Then she had another thought, and in the end it was this that made the difference: for better or worse, she'd packed more life into the few weeks she'd been away from Tripoli than in the previous sixteen years. And that was not a thing to be thrown away. Having at long last started an adventure, she felt bound to finish it.

"If you're determined to go on," she said finally, "I'll go with you."

"So be it," said Rashid. He kept his face expressionless, but he was glad of her decision. He was slightly surprised to realize that traveling with her seemed better than going on alone.

So when Yusuf came to them the next morning after breakfast and said, "Surely you will not continue your journey now?" Elaine simply replied:

"We must."

Yusuf hesitated. A Christian girl and a young Arab man traveling together, whatever story they might choose to tell, were likely to encounter difficulties, and he felt an obligation to do what he could. "Perhaps you will honor me by continuing to ride in my caravan until we reach Mosul, which should take little more than a week. I'll provide food and drink and whatever else is necessary, it's the least I can do."

"You're very kind," said Elaine.

With a grave bow, Yusuf withdrew. Elaine tended to her gray while Rashid busied himself with the other horses and then Elaine went to her tent and, as always, swept her ivory comb through her hair one hundred times. But the rhythmic motion of her arm and the untangling of her hair did not have the calming effect they usually did.

That night she said her prayers, as usual, for the souls of King Edmond and Queen Catherine, and added one more soul to her prayers—that of the late Prince Conrad of Antioch.

The land between the Tigris and Euphrates, which Elaine knew from her father's books, had been called Mesopotamia by the ancients but which the Arabs called Al-Jazirah, was a broad, undulating plain, fertile and loamy, which nourished dates, figs, nuts, grains, and crops of all kinds, and provided pasture for goats, sheep, cattle, and camels. It was early summer and the land was lovely and the weather mild, but Elaine took little pleasure in it. As she encountered other travelers from time to time, she found herself glancing involuntarily at one or two who seemed to resemble Conrad, but she was always disappointed.

They continued eastward on the main route between Ar-Raqqah and Mosul. There were many merchants and other travelers along the way, as well as numerous small towns and markets, so there was little danger from thieves and little hardship in the traveling, for the land was level, though the temperature became hotter as summer began to settle in. As the days passed Elaine and Rashid spoke less of Conrad, and more about what lay ahead of them.

Even combining what Rashid had learned from Hasan with what Yusuf could tell them, they had little hard information to go on. The Zagros Mountains were very rugged and inhabited by a people called the Kurds, consisting of a number of fiercely territorial tribes. Beyond the Zagros lay the Khwarazmian Empire, ruled by the great Shah Ala al-Din Muhammad II, the son of a slave, who had forged a vast kingdom that, it was said, contained half a dozen cities even larger than Baghdad. It was the Khwarazmian Empire that the Mongols had invaded, and there were rumors of great battles with much slaughter. But such descriptions were vague, and Elaine and Rashid were acutely aware that once their journey took them beyond Mosul, they would essentially be traveling blind.

On the eighth day after they had given up the search for Conrad, the caravan stopped for the night and after dinner Elaine pitched her tent and fell into a deep sleep for the first time in a while. But she awakened suddenly a few hours later, her pulse racing.

Someone was outside her tent.

There was a faint scraping sound near the left side of the tent, as if someone were trying to dig their way in. One of Yusuf's servants? Or Jamal, who thought she didn't notice how he constantly stared at her? But why dig? Why not simply come through the flap?

Suddenly the side of the tent bulged violently and almost collapsed. Fully awake, her heart pounding, she remembered the dagger in her dress pocket and groped frantically to find the dress on the floor of the tent as the rustling outside grew louder and more intrusive.

She found the dress, fumbled for the pocket, then felt her hand close on the hilt of the dagger and she pulled it out. The wall of the tent was bulging again and there was a strange guttural noise that she couldn't identify. The feeling of being trapped in a small space in total darkness was unbearable and she burst through the flap and scrambled to her feet, extending the dagger in front of her.

Outside the tent were two animals from hell, or at least they appeared that way in the moonlight. They had four legs and dark splotchy fur and torsos that were massive and low to the ground.

They had thick skulls with enormous ears and small malevolent eyes and blunt muzzles in which sharp fangs gleamed as they snarled at Elaine.

One of them emitted a short, sharp cry and they came toward her, salivating and snapping their jaws. She was too petrified to cry out, let alone run, and very much aware of how useless her small dagger was against these hellhounds. When they were so close she could smell their foul breath a dark form glided in front of her and one of the animals yelped with pain and ran off, and the other loped after it with a whimper.

Rashid stood in front of Elaine, blood dripping from his dagger, which he used to dig deeper into a hole the two animals had been pawing at. He uncovered two bones, which he threw as far into the darkness as he could.

"Hyenas," he said. "It's all right, they won't come back. They left some bones here and returned to dig them up. They probably thought you were trying to take them away. You should have stayed in the tent, though it was brave to come out."

"I'm not brave. I was trembling like a coward."

"No," Rashid said. He hesitated briefly, then added, "Hasan says women are weak but he was not speaking of women like you." And he went back into his tent.

Late on the afternoon of the following day they approached another formidable river—the Tigris. The city of Mosul lay on the river's west bank and the travelers made camp on the outskirts, planning to cross the river the next morning.

Mosul was a larger city than Ar-Raqqah, lying somewhat closer to Baghdad, the great metropolis to the south where the two mighty rivers, the Tigris and the Euphrates, came together. Rashid marveled at the high, thick walls, and smiled as the evening call to prayer drifted over them to where he and the others had made camp.

After praying, he watched to see if the city's guards would close the heavy, iron-plated gates, but since there was no present threat to the city's security, the gates were left open. The eight travelers—Yusuf, Jamal, Rashid, Elaine, and Yusuf's four servants—ate supper. Conversation was cordial but restrained, for the shadow of Conrad's death still hovered over them. Afterward they retired to their respective tents for the night.

Two hours later, when all were asleep, or seemed to be, Jamal slipped out of his tent and made his way toward the south gate of Mosul. He did not notice another figure leave a tent nearby and follow him; and he could hardly be blamed because the other figure was silent and moved like a shadow within other shadows. Jamal entered the city and hurried down one side street and up another to a minaret, its tall form cutting a narrow slash in the stars overhead. He hadn't been there long when he was joined by a young man with a thin beard and nervous eyes.

"Nasir," said Jamal. "You got my message."

"This better be good," said Nasir.

"Your father still serves the Emir . . . ?"

"Yes. What of it?"

"You've probably heard the rumor that a Christian Prince and Princess are traveling east from Tripoli. The Prince is supposedly named Conrad."

"I hear a dozen rumors every day."

"This one is true. The Prince pretended to be a commoner named Edward but he drowned crossing the Euphrates and the Princess called his name. *Conrad.* I heard it plainly. She's asleep now, not ten paces from my tent."

Nasir blinked a few times, frowning. "You're certain of this."

"She'll bring a fine ransom from the Christians—or perhaps the Emir will take her into his harem until he tires of her, and then ransom her!"

Nasir smirked. "Yes, more likely."

"Either way, he'll pay a generous reward. We'll split it evenly."

Nasir licked his lips, thinking hard. "I'll need more than your word. I need to be able to say I've seen the girl myself."

"Come to my camp tomorrow morning. You'll see her then, I promise you."

"Where's your camp?"

"Meet me at the south gate, I'll take you there."

The two men exchanged a brief handshake, then Nasir hurried away. Neither of them had noticed a third presence, silent and still but close enough to hear every word they had spoken. Now that figure glided from its hiding place and followed Jamal through the streets of Mosul, back through the south gate, and into the fields outside the city. Jamal heard a soft footstep behind him and turned just in time to feel Rashid's blade plunge into his belly.

Rashid began digging into the earth with his dagger. The soil was soft but even so he didn't have enough time to dig a proper grave—but then he didn't need to. He only needed to bury Jamal's corpse deep enough so that it would be at least another day before it was discovered by hyenas or wild dogs, by which time, he hoped, he and Elaine would be many miles from the city.

19

Elaine awoke with a start to find Rashid in her tent. "We have to leave," he said.

She sat up, reached for her dress, and covered herself. "Now? It's not even daylight."

"Yes, now. Hurry."

"But . . . why, what's happened?"

"There's no time."

"Tell me."

"Jamal never believed our story," he said impatiently. "Somehow he found out the truth. He was going to sell you to the Emir of Mosul."

For a moment she was stunned. Then she said, "Where's Jamal now?"

"Dead."

"You killed him?" Realizing there could be only one answer, she continued, "My God, was it necessary?"

"Didn't you hear me? He was going to sell you to the Emir."

"Did anyone see you?"

"No. But we should go. Get moving!"

They worked quickly and silently, striking their tents and loading the horses. As they led the animals away the sun was coming up, though Yusuf and his servants were still in their tents. Elaine imagined how sad Yusuf would be when he realized his nephew was gone, but there seemed to be no help for it. When it had all finally sunk in, she said to Rashid, "Thank you, for keeping me from being sold."

Rashid barely nodded, his mind on what needed to be done. Elaine decided to follow his example and force herself to think ahead. "We should go to the market," she said. "We need food and extra blankets. Yusuf said the nights can be chilly in the mountains, even in summer."

"All right," said Rashid. "But quickly."

The marketplace at Mosul was by far the largest Elaine had ever seen. The city was on the Silk Road, that great web of interlocking paths and trails that carried trade between Europe and China, and the array of available goods was overwhelming and so was the resulting assault on the senses. The delicate aroma of rare spices from India mingled with the ripe smell of local produce and the stench of goats and sheep penned for slaughter; nearly translucent pastel silks from China rested in bins next to bright red wools from Cairo and rich purple linens from Genoa; above the wheedling calls of vendors and the haggling of customers could be heard the ceaseless buzzing of flies and the constant whisper of the large pheasant-feather fans wielded by servants of the more prosperous merchants. And so it went, for hundreds of yards in every direction, the jumble of carts and stalls and booths separated by narrow alleys through which buyers jostled and elbowed as they viewed the intoxicating array of goods.

It took the better part of an hour for Elaine and Rashid to conclude their business. They bought food to last for a week and were negotiating with a vendor of blankets when Elaine became aware of a stirring in the crowd. She turned to see what the commotion was about.

Two men were pushing their way through the marketplace, on their way toward the city center where Mosul's official buildings were located. The men had blue and yellow cockades in their turbans that marked them as magistrates of the city, and trailing behind like a swarm of bees was the murmur of gossip being passed from mouth to ear.

With a sinking feeling, Rashid knew what must have happened and the crowd's chatter soon confirmed it: a body had been discovered outside the city walls. It hadn't been hyenas or dogs that had unearthed the corpse but a farmer dragging a hand plow while taking a shortcut to his field.

Rashid turned to Elaine. "They found Jamal," he said tensely.

"It's all right," Elaine said with a confidence she didn't feel. "Yusuf has no reason to suspect us and neither will anyone else."

"We have to go now," Rashid said firmly, and Elaine didn't argue.

They purchased the blankets and started back to the stable where they'd left the horses. On the way Elaine saw something that shocked her, though she'd known such things existed: a slave auction. It was held in a clearing close\by the stalls and carts of other merchandise, and in that clearing slavers bought and sold human beings with no more compunction than if they were melons or cooking pots.

Elaine was repelled and fascinated at the same time. Serfs and peasants were often treated harshly in the European culture, but actual slavery was unknown. Most of the slaves were roped together by the neck, but a few—the most dangerous, no doubt—were chained and manacled. About fifty were to be auctioned off this morning, evenly divided between male and female, some of Arab lineage but quite a few from Africa and even some, judging by their appearance, from Europe. Some of the prettier women and younger boys had been set to one side—a special auction would be held for them—and Elaine winced remembering how close she had come to sharing their fate.

One slave had been so rebellious he'd been confined in a wooden cage. He was filthy and unkempt and naked except for a loincloth and many in the crowd jeered and taunted him. One man moved close to the cage to shout something and the slave's eyes blazed and he lunged at the man through the bars, causing the crowd to cry out, first in fear and then in amusement.

In that moment Elaine thought the man looked familiar, but surely that was impossible. Then she looked again and gasped and grabbed Rashid's arm and he followed her gaze and he, too, could not hide his astonishment.

The man in the cage was Conrad.

20

Conrad had been surprised to find that he was still alive after his battle with the river. He had awakened, exhausted, in the dark, lying in the mud, and at first he'd assumed he must be in the afterlife— heaven, perhaps, but more likely hell—and then, slowly, he began to remember.

He'd become separated from the horse almost at once; he'd hoped to latch on to the animal and let it carry him ashore but it was a far stronger swimmer and moved quickly out of reach, then out of sight.

The water was icy and the current swift and he could already feel his clothes becoming heavy, but his training came back to him and he tried to keep his lungs filled with air to help him remain buoyant. He thrust his arms forward and kicked his legs in a poor semblance of swimming, but it kept him moving. His last reserves of strength were giving out when he felt his feet touch solid ground. Even then it was a struggle to reach the shore but he managed, collapsing headlong on the muddy ground and falling into an exhausted sleep.

Now he was awake, and shivering, for though the night wasn't overly chilly his clothes were still soaked. There was no way to build a fire, so he took off his coat and wrung it out as thoroughly as he could, then sat down with his back against a tree and, wrapping the coat around him for whatever warmth it might provide, slept again.

When he awoke it was daylight. He came out from beneath the tree and let the sun warm his face. He was still tired, and his clothes were still damp, but they would dry out before long and he began to feel better. He turned back to the river and noted that it flowed from right to left, which meant that, by the grace of God, he had ended up on the northern bank—just like Elaine and the others, assuming they'd completed the crossing safely.

Encouraged, he began to walk upriver—he wasn't sure how far the current had dragged him, but it couldn't be much above two or three miles. If he kept up a brisk pace—

That was when he saw the horse.

He'd assumed it had drowned or was far away by now. But here it was, grazing peacefully not fifty yards away. The supply packs, and presumably Charles's sword as well, were still intact on its back. Mounted, he could quickly return to Ar-Raqqah, where Elaine and the others were no doubt searching for him.

But the horse moved away as he approached it.

It wasn't skittish. It moved calmly and deliberately and continued to graze, but it kept Conrad at a distance, with one eye always fixed on him. Conrad approached again, and again it moved away. He knew better than to run at it, so he forced himself to remain still. He didn't know its name or even if it had one. He suddenly remembered the horse he'd ridden to Tripoli—what was it called? Tranquil, that was it. What was it with him and horses? He could fight well enough on those that had been trained for warfare, but he'd never learned the art of reading the animals, sensing their moods, and adjusting his behavior accordingly.

"Stay," Conrad said to the horse soothingly. "Good boy. Stay."

He approached slowly and the horse didn't move and he succumbed to the temptation to lunge for the reins, but the horse was too quick and it jumped away. "Bastard!" Conrad shouted in frustration. The horse seemed to give him a reproachful look and moved a little farther off, maintaining a fifty-yard gap and leaving Conrad back where he started.

Maybe he should forget the horse. Even on foot it would take no more than an hour or two to reach Ar-Raqqah, where another horse could be purchased easily. But the horse had one-fourth of the gold the Old Man had given them to buy back his letter from the Mongols. More important, it had Charles's sword. No doubt Elaine and Rashid thought him foolish for diving in after it, but he'd seem even more foolish if he went back now without it. And anyway, it was Charles's sword; he could not abandon it.

He took another cautious step toward the horse—he'd catch the damned thing if it took all day.

"If it took all day" changed from a figure of speech to a distinct possibility as the morning wore on. The horse never ran away, nor did it ever allow Conrad to get near enough to make another attempt at the reins. Since he couldn't remember its name he gave it a new one, a more fitting name than "Tranquil" had been for the horse on the road to Tripoli: "Lucifer." He recalled some priest saying it was another name for the devil.

By noon, Lucifer had led Conrad several miles upland from the river. Whenever he got within earshot, Conrad would try to talk to the beast: "Good horse! Stay there now . . . no, stay put! When I catch you, damn you, I'm going to . . ." And then he'd catch himself and start over. "Lucifer want a carrot?" even though he didn't have one to give. But Lucifer remained unmoved by promise or threat, strolling from meadow to glen, up hill and down dale, enjoying the sunshine and the lush grass. Conrad's clothes became damp again with sweat and he was tired and his feet were beginning to ache. Furthermore, while there was water from the occasional stream, there was no food except a few wild figs that were all but inedible.

By late afternoon, Lucifer had finally gotten tired—or perhaps bored of making a fool of Conrad—and Conrad was finally able to make a try for the reins and succeeded in grabbing them. "I've got you!" he cried, but Lucifer just looked at him with a puzzled expression as if wondering why Conrad was so excited. Conrad resisted the temptation to smack the horse—it would be silly, and anyway he was too tired. Instead he rested for a moment, his forehead leaning against the saddle, then checked to make sure Charles's sword was in place; it was, and Conrad finally mounted Lucifer. There were still a few hours of daylight remaining and he should be able to get back to Ar-Raqqah before sunset if he pushed Lucifer hard enough, which he would certainly enjoy doing.

He rode for about an hour. The weather was warm and Lucifer kept a steady pace and Conrad almost felt inclined to forgive him, at least a little. It was then that he caught sight of a rider on the crest of a hill to the south. When he saw Conrad looking at him he disappeared behind the ridge, but fifteen minutes later he appeared again, this time joined by a second horseman. Both men had swords hanging from their saddles. They vanished once more behind the ridge.

Not long afterward he saw another rider on a beautiful white Arabian, this time to the north. Conrad loosened the strings, pulled out the scabbard that held Charles's sword, and turned Lucifer toward the rider, but he galloped away. There was no way Lucifer could catch the Arabian, but any hope Conrad had harbored that the first two riders had crossed his path by chance was gone. He was being followed. Over time he counted six riders in all—they were gradually drawing closer from both sides.

So this was how it would end. Spared by the river, he was nevertheless fated to die in obscurity in a distant land. He felt a pang of regret at the thought that people would assume he'd died by drowning instead of with sword in hand, but so be it. Fear rose within him but he had learned long ago how to push it back down so that he could no longer feel it. He would die fighting, and take as many with him as he might. There were worse ways to die. He drew Charles's sword from its scabbard.

The horsemen moved toward him from both sides and he could see they were trying to maneuver him toward a ragged stand of trees a hundred yards away. This was a mistake on their part, for he was well versed in fighting in woodlands and might be able to use the trees to his own advantage. He urged Lucifer toward the glade. Some of the horsemen followed, others circled around to enter the glade from the far side. Once among the trees Conrad turned to face his nearest adversaries and was suddenly aware of a flicker in the branches overhead, and an instant later a heavy net dropped on him from above.

He tried to cut his way free but the net tangled his arm and he lacked any room to swing his sword. Then they were on him, dragging him from his horse. He hit the ground hard and through the netting he saw a man brandishing a wooden club and then the club crashed down on his head and everything went dark.

· 21 ·

Conrad awoke with a throbbing headache and panicked feeling that he was paralyzed—he couldn't move his arms or legs. It took a moment for him to realize that he was tightly bound, hand and foot, with ropes. He began to struggle as much as he could, rolling from side to side and kicking out with his lashed feet, but it was hopeless.

Suddenly he was hauled upright, supported on each side by two burly men, and found himself staring at another man of about forty, tall and slender with delicate features, a neatly trimmed beard, and expensive clothing. His face and his bearing exuded authority and intelligence as he studied Conrad curiously.

"Untie me!" Conrad demanded. "By what right do you do this?"

"Speak only when spoken to," the slender man said in passable Frankish, and one of the guards thumped Conrad on the back of the head to emphasize the point.

"Who are you?" Conrad demanded, and got another blow to the head for his trouble.

After a moment the slender man said, "My name is Khaled al-Zahir. What is yours?" His tone was, if anything, rather pleasant.

"Untie me," Conrad repeated. One of the servants started to strike him again but Khaled raised a hand and the servant stopped.

"What are you doing in Al-Jazirah?" Khaled asked, receiving only a glare in response. Khaled made a gesture and a servant brought over Conrad's sword.

"Good sword," Khaled observed. "Yours? Or stolen?"

"Mine," said Conrad.

"Now it is mine," said Khaled, and Conrad spat in his face. This time the thugs were too shocked to react, and Khaled himself showed no outward signs of anger. He wiped the spittle from his face and said matter-of-factly, "Break him."

Khaled's servants were very good at inflicting pain without doing permanent damage, as Conrad quickly discovered. At first he didn't understand their failure to kill him outright, but, during the beating, he noticed a servant holding a set of irons of the sort that he had seen on slaves, and he realized the fate that was intended for him.

Horrified at the prospect, he struggled more desperately, but the cords that bound him were too tight. The hail of fists and feet continued to rain down on his ribs, kidneys, abdomen, testicles, and the back of his head (but not his face or his spine) until he was nearly unconscious again. Then one of the servants called out something in Arabic, and a moment later Khaled was standing over him.

"Kiss it," Khaled said, and placed his foot in front of Conrad's face. Conrad worked his mouth, trying to gather together enough saliva to spit again. He had difficulty doing so, but Khaled got the idea and spoke a word to his servants and the beating recommenced until Conrad lost consciousness.

He awoke on his back, manacled with slave-chains anchored in a thick wooden post and in greater pain than he'd ever experienced in his life. He'd known pain and wounds from tournaments and combat, but nothing like this; every move was agony. In addition the weather had turned hot and the sun beat down on his unprotected face, so with an effort he rose to a sitting position; the chains would not allow him to stand.

Even worse than the physical pain was the utter humiliation

and degradation of being chained and helpless. The possibility of dying in obscurity had been bad enough, but a lifetime of slavery was unimaginable—yet it was happening. He wondered what Elaine and Rashid would think if they could see him like this. Rashid would probably enjoy the spectacle, and Elaine, he supposed, would take pity on him. The thought irritated him—he didn't want her pity! At the same time he found himself wondering if she would be all right with only Rashid to protect her . . . assuming Rashid even cared to protect her. . . .

He shook his head angrily—if he went on like this his mind would become unmoored. He had to stay focused, and find some way to escape. Yes, of course, it was that or nothing. He would escape, or die trying.

He became aware of a man crouching in front of him, holding a plate that held a thin green gruel. The man was perhaps thirty-five, with dark eyes but light brown hair and a complexion that looked almost European. He offered the plate to Conrad, who found he had little appetite.

"You need to keep up your strength," the man said in Frankish. After a moment Conrad took a bite of the gruel, but it was bitter and he spat it out.

"I know," the man said. "But it's better than nothing and does provide nourishment." The man's Frankish was flawless.

"You're a Frank," Conrad said.

"By birth, yes," the man replied with a smile. "My name used to be Jean d'Acote. Now I'm called Hana."

"What are you doing here?" Conrad asked.

"I'm a slave, like you."

"I'm not a slave," Conrad said.

"You are the slave of Khaled al-Zahir," Hana replied. "And soon you'll be the slave of whomever he sells you to. But if you're wise you can live rather well."

Conrad gave him a look, and Hana said, "Well, you did spit in his face. He doesn't inflict pain for the fun of it."

"How long have you been a slave?"

"Nine years."

"And you call that living well."

"I'm living better than you are at the moment," Hana said, and held out a cup of water. Conrad was suddenly aware of an overwhelming thirst, and took the cup from Hana. Conrad's manacles allowed him just enough freedom to raise it to his mouth and drink.

"Thank you."

Hana took the cup back. "Now eat as well. You'll need your strength."

Conrad looked at the plate. Keeping up his strength would be the first step toward escaping. He took a bite of the food and forced it down.

"Good," said Hana. "As I said, food, and much else, will be better if you're sensible. I know what I'm talking about, for I was once as you are." Off Conrad's questioning look, he continued, "I was a soldier in the retinue of Count Bayard Gascoigne. You've heard of him?"

"Of course. His castle fell some years ago. You were captured . . . ?"

"That's right," Hana said. "Now think on what I've said. You have some important choices to make."

Someone spoke in Arabic. Hana left the food and water next to Conrad and walked a few paces away. Just when Conrad thought he was immune to further shocks he received another, for the hour of prayer had arrived, and Hana, formerly Jean d'Acote, faced toward Mecca and prayed with Khaled and the rest of his servants and slaves.

He's converted to Islam, Conrad realized. His first reaction was contempt and loathing, but underneath was a tremor of unease. What had Hana said? *I was once as you are. . . .*

No, Conrad told himself. *You have never been as I am, and I will never be as you are. Never.*

Conrad remained chained to the post all night, but was so exhausted that he actually managed a few hours of fitful sleep. After the morning prayer, Hana approached with food and water, and again began talking about how Conrad could avoid further suffering by being sensible, which might include begging for Khaled's forgiveness as well as taking a more expansive view of religion. Conrad drank the water and ate as much of the food as he could force down, then lunged at Hana and wrapped a length of chain around his neck and tried to strangle him. Other servants intervened before Conrad could finish the job.

Thus it was, an hour later, that Conrad found himself on top of a donkey cart, confined in a heavy wooden cage that had been constructed for that purpose. He was naked, save for a loincloth, and was given to understand that he would remain in the cage until he mended his ways.

That evening Khaled, Hana, and the rest of Khaled's immediate retinue joined a larger caravan, which included about a dozen camels and a line of at least three times as many slaves, men and women, roped together by the neck. The slaves were of various races, though most were either black or fair-skinned like Conrad. There were few Arabs, and Conrad remembered hearing that Muslims were not permitted to enslave anyone who had been born a Muslim.

Conrad's cage was placed near the other slaves, who were given reasonably large portions of food and water, while he himself was given neither, a living example of what lay in store for the rebellious. Conrad didn't mind; in fact he took pride in it, staring directly at the slaves. Some of them shamefacedly refused to meet his gaze, while others stared curiously, as if at a crazy man.

As the hours turned into days Conrad felt his resolve weakening. The hunger was tolerable; but under the now blazing sun his thirst was murderous. As the second full day wore on he began to regret his attack upon Hana, try as he might to push that thought aside as a sign of weakness.

At noon on the third day, one of Khaled's servants approached Conrad's cage with a cup of water and held it just out of Conrad's reach. "Please," the man said in Frankish, but with a heavy accent.

At first Conrad was confused, thinking the man was asking something of him, then he realized the man was saying, *I'll give you the water if you say "please."*

For three hours, off and on, as Conrad broiled in the afternoon sun, this was repeated until finally Conrad, hating himself, said the word. Or tried to. His throat was so dry and his lips so parched that he couldn't speak, but on the third or fourth try he managed to croak: "Please."

The man handed him the cup and Conrad drank—and instantly spat out the salty, bitter liquid. He'd been given a cup of urine.

The man laughed and so did the other servants who'd been watching. With a howl Conrad threw the cup at the man, which only caused more laughter. Conrad was on his hands and knees, head bowed, panting with humiliation and pain, and for the first time truly felt like an animal.

"My friend," said a gentle tone, and Conrad was surprised to see Hana holding out another cup, this one filled with water. The man must have forgiven Conrad for trying to kill him earlier, for his expression was placid. *In his own way, he's trying to break me just like Khaled is,* Conrad thought. But Conrad took the water and drew enough into his mouth to rinse out the foul taste, then spat it out. He stared at the rest of the water in the cup, hesitating. If he drank, might it not be the first step on the road to losing his very soul? He wasn't sure, and was ashamed to realize that at that moment he didn't much care. He drank.

It was the last water he was given for the next three days, though each day was hotter than the last. He remained in the cage lying in his own filth in a daze of humiliation and pain, hardly knowing whether he was awake or asleep. At times he tried to pray, but he could not make himself feel close to God in these conditions and his prayers went unanswered. Then, as time passed he began in effect to pray to Charles, or at least to try to speak with him. *Did I do wrong to dive into the river? Did I do wrong to follow the horse? I only thought to keep your sword!* But, like God, Charles was silent.

Three times Conrad was taken from the cage and given a severe beating and afterward Khaled presented his foot to be kissed. Conrad shook his head feebly. The foot was withdrawn, he was beaten some more and returned to the cage.

The second time he was taken from the cage and beaten he still had the strength to refuse to kiss Khaled's foot—but only just.

The third time Conrad was badly weakened by heat and thirst and the repeated beatings, and when Khaled put his foot out Conrad did not shake his head. Khaled seemed to sense weakness for he let his foot linger in front of Conrad's face for a long time.

Conrad knew it would be the first step down a path that had no end . . . yet what did it really matter? A few inches, a touch of his lips to a leather sandal, and the beatings would cease; he'd be given food . . . and water . . . and with sustenance, he told himself, would come strength—the strength to escape . . . yes, of course, kissing Khaled's foot was the key to escape!

This was seductive and Conrad knew it had to be wrong . . . yet, seemingly against his will, he felt his body take control . . . he began to lean forward . . . just a few more inches . . .

Suddenly there was an impatient word from Khaled, the foot was withdrawn, and the beating began again. Conrad wanted to cry out, *Wait, come back!* but his throat was too parched and he could only grunt wordlessly as the blows fell.

Toward the end of the third night since his last drink of water the caravan came within sight of a city and he knew that when the sun came up he, or what remained of him, would be sold to the highest bidder as a slave. He felt that nothing more could be added to his burden of despair, but he was wrong, for he caught sight of a cart being hauled past the cage, piled high with merchandise Khaled planned to sell along with his slaves. On top of the pile, destined to be purchased by some nameless buyer and thereafter to disappear forever from the Christian world, was the sword that had belonged to Charles, its lone sapphire blazing in the sun and glaring at Conrad like an accusing eye.

◈ 22 ◈

Khaled surveyed the marketplace with satisfaction. It was crowded and he had no doubt that his wares would bring a good price. He turned away with the intention of finding some breakfast but instead came face-to-face with a young woman, evidently a Frank, for she had violet eyes and skin paler than that of most Arabs. With commendable modesty she wore a headscarf that concealed her hair but not her face, which was an interesting one, with large eyes and a strong, determined expression. Next to her was a young Arab man, no doubt her servant. She spoke in Frankish.

"I'm told you are Khaled al-Zahir, and that you are the one offering these slaves for sale."

"That is true. May I know whom I have the pleasure of addressing?"

"My name is Elisabeth, and I would like to buy a slave."

"I have a fine collection, as you see."

"I'm interested in the one you have caged."

Khaled's eyebrows arched in surprise. "That one is to be auctioned later in the day."

"So I was told, but I would like to buy him now, without the trouble of an auction. I'll pay a fair price."

"Why that slave in particular? He is very difficult, I promise you."

"From his appearance, I believe him to be a countryman of mine. It saddens me to see him so ill-treated." Elaine tried to keep her tone casual. She didn't want to seem too eager, yet in the end she had to strike a bargain, fair or not, and quickly.

"He has earned his ill-treatment, I assure you."

"Then you should be glad to be rid of him," Elaine said promptly.

Khaled smiled. "You bargain well," he said. It occurred to him that the woman would make a fine addition to the harem slaves he would be selling later on. She would be a fetching sight with a silver chain around her neck, and it was unlikely that anyone in the marketplace would come to the aid of a Frankish woman, so there was nothing stopping him.

Except the Arab servant, whose eyes were boring into Khaled's as though the boy could read his thoughts. Khaled's servants could overpower the Arab, but he looked capable of inflicting considerable damage in the meantime. Khaled had made his fortune by knowing when to play and when to refrain from playing, and this game did not seem worth the candle.

"Five gold coins," he said abruptly.

"Three," she replied.

"Five. Accept at once, or the slave will be auctioned this afternoon."

"I accept."

"I will tell the auctioneer," said Khaled, and walked away.

Conrad was taken by surprise when he realized one of Khaled's servants was unlocking the door of his cage. But he gathered himself and prepared to attack as violently as his manacled hands would allow. The servant held him off with a long pointed spike.

"New owner! New owner!" he said in accented Frankish.

This had little effect, so the man added, "This lady. Nice lady!" and Conrad looked up and saw Elaine.

"It's all right, Conrad," she said. "You're free!"

Conrad blinked uncomprehendingly, but stopped fighting long enough so the servant was able to unlock his manacles before hastily backing away. Conrad climbed slowly and painfully out of the cage and stood upright for the first time in days. He looked like he was still afraid to believe this could really be happening, so Elaine said again, "You're free now."

She was even more shocked by his appearance now that she was close to him. He was gaunt and haggard and filthy and his body was covered with welts and bruises. His face was grimy and swollen and caked with blood. His breathing was shallow and raspy and she wondered if his ribs had been broken. And he reeked so badly that Elaine could barely keep herself from gagging at the stench. He seemed more like a wild animal than a human being. Yet Conrad was still there, inside this wreck of a man—she could see it in his eyes: the stubbornness, the defiance, the almost crazy courage that had kept him going. In that moment, whether she liked him or not, she couldn't help admiring him. He seemed calmer now, as if his mind had finally caught up with his new circumstances, and he blurted, "They made me a slave!" as if he still found the notion incredible.

"Yes, but they didn't do a very good job of it," Elaine said firmly. "They were so afraid of you they put you in a cage. Anyway, it's over now." At that moment Rashid appeared, with some clothing and sandals he'd purchased at a stall in the marketplace. Like Elaine, he was taken aback at Conrad's appearance.

"Is he all right?" Rashid said.

"Ask him," said Elaine. She felt the more they could engage Conrad in conversation, the sooner he would return to some semblance of normality.

"Can you walk?" Rashid asked.

"I can walk," Conrad said.

"Then put these on," said Rashid. "We need to leave here as soon as we can."

Rashid handed the clothing to Conrad, who began putting on

the loose linen trousers and shirt. It was a struggle, for he was un-steady on his feet and kept losing his balance while at the same time brushing off any attempt to help him, but he finally got into the clothes, then put on the leather sandals.

Rashid took him by the arm and said, "Let's go."

Conrad took one step then stopped.

"What's wrong?" said Elaine.

"My sword."

"What about it?" Rashid said impatiently.

"It's for sale, somewhere in this market."

"There's no time," said Elaine, but Conrad ignored this and started looking around. Elaine and Rashid exchanged a worried look.

Rashid said, "Conrad, there are thousands of swords for sale in this place. It would take hours to find yours and for all we know it might already have been sold—or perhaps it's being sold privately. We have to leave now."

Conrad started to object but Elaine said, speaking very slowly, "Listen to me. Rashid had to kill someone, he did it to protect me, but the body's been found and the trail leads back to us and we have very little time. It may already be too late. Do you under-stand?"

"Charles—" Conrad began, but Elaine cut him off again.

"I know, it belonged to your brother. And I'm sorry—truly sorry. But we can't delay any longer."

As the force of her argument registered with Conrad, tears sprang to his eyes and Elaine marveled at how much he cared about the sword even in his half-dead condition. Yet that condition was a blessing in a way, for if he'd felt stronger he never would have consented to leave the sword behind. As it was, she and Rashid had to tug at his arm to get him moving.

But after a few paces he stopped again. He straightened up, as if his body had received a sudden surge of strength. His eyes gleamed in a way that was truly frightening, and when Elaine followed his gaze she realized why—he had caught sight of Khaled. The slaver was only thirty paces away. Conrad glared at him like a man possessed and began to move toward him.

Rashid stepped in front of him. "No," he said.

Conrad tried to push past him, but Rashid used a wrestling move he'd learned from Hasan and sent Conrad to the ground. But Conrad had received training of his own and he caught Rashid's arm and yanked him down as well and the two men grappled in the dirt. Conrad was weakened but his craving for vengeance had strengthened him and the contest was equal. As Conrad started to pull free Rashid hissed in his ear, "Whatever you do to him, they will do to Elaine!"

Conrad continued to fight for an instant, but the Arab's words sank in. Rashid added, speaking urgently, "Don't you see? She freed you. If the slaver dies she'll be held to account. You'll be killed then she'll be killed—or end up in a harem."

Conrad had stopped struggling now and Elaine knelt beside the two men. She took Conrad's face in her hands. "Conrad, look at me. Look at me!"

Khaled was still visible through the crowd and unaware of the struggle taking place a few yards behind him—an easy target. But slowly, reluctantly, Conrad turned his attention from the slaver to Elaine. She waited until his eyes had locked on hers, then said in a quiet but urgent tone, "Conrad, you have to come with us, now. Please. *We need you.*"

For a long moment he stared at her without answering. Then the tears that had filled his eyes moments before came running down his face—tears of frustration and rage. Elaine understood she was asking him to forsake the two things in his life that he held most sacred—his brother's sword, and his sense of honor—in exchange for . . . what, exactly? Nothing, really, except her plea that she and Rashid needed him.

Yet it worked. The rage in his eyes diminished and was replaced by a kind of grief, and the strength seemed to drain out of him again. Elaine and Rashid helped him up and they began to walk out of the market, toward the stables. Conrad moved stiffly at first but kept pace, though Elaine knew he must still be in great pain. She glanced at him—the tears had stopped, their tracks still visible on his grimy cheeks. He didn't look at her or at Rashid but stared straight ahead, his face expressionless. She knew that, with Rashid's help, she'd saved Conrad's life by talking him down. But perhaps in his mind the price had been too high. Elaine wondered if he would ever forgive her for it.

They got their horses from the stable, paid the keeper, then rode out the city gates and through the outskirts to the Tigris River, forcing themselves to keep a deliberate pace, wanting to put Mosul behind them as quickly as possible without attracting attention.

The pier was a mile upstream from the main part of the city. It wasn't very crowded so they had to wait less than an hour for their turn to cross, but it was a nervous time and seemed much longer. But no magistrates from the city appeared and finally they paid the fare and boarded the ferry, a raft with railings much like the one that had proved so disastrous when crossing the Euphrates.

But the Tigris was kinder and the crossing was uneventful and they mounted their horses again and headed east toward the Zagros Mountains, leaving the river and the city of Mosul behind them.

With each step, Elaine felt safer but became more worried about Conrad. He was unsteady in the saddle, even more so than he had been when wounded in the fight against the brigands, and she feared he was again hurt far worse than he was admitting. They stopped long enough for him to bathe in a stream and get rid of the dirt and filth that had clung to him, but this made the bruises and scars on his body more visible. Elaine winced when she looked at him. But when she suggested a longer rest he just shook his head. His expression was haunted and his eyes fixed on some scene that no one but himself could see.

She thought of his behavior in the marketplace—how he had forsaken his sword and his thirst for revenge, for her sake, it seemed, though she knew she was little more than a possession in his eyes. She had to admit, his sense of duty was certainly stronger than hers. The urgency of her words had moved him and, in truth, had surprised even her, but the fact was they really did need him: his strength, his valor, his warrior's skill. It was very clear to her now that the Old Man had been right—the three of them were stronger together than any one of them, or even any two of them, was alone.

As for Conrad, the passing hours did nothing to allay his shame. To have been reduced to slavery was bad enough. But to be rescued from that condition by the woman he was supposed to be protecting! How could Elaine, after seeing him in that cage, ever think of him again as a man fit to be her husband?

The image of Khaled's sandaled foot, inches from his face, was stamped on his mind, along with the memory of how close he had come to kissing it. Yet in the end he hadn't kissed it, and that knowledge was all that allowed him—barely—to retain his sanity.

Every few hours, as they traveled, Rashid found a ridge or hillock and looked back over the path they had taken, watching for some sign of pursuit but seeing none. Still, as a precaution, they made camp that night without building a fire.

Rashid awoke first in the morning and once more climbed a hill to look for pursuers. It was only then that he allowed himself to face a question that had been nagging at him—why had he bothered to save Elaine? It would have been easy to leave her to her fate and slip away with the horses and the gold and carry out his mission for the Old Man alone. But the thought had never even occurred to him. The instant he'd heard Jamal betray her to the Emir's servant he'd formed the plan to kill Jamal and escape with Elaine. Why? Friendship? An infidel woman could never be a friend to an Assassin any more than Conrad could. He could imagine only too well how Hasan would react to such an idea!

Then why had he done it? Perhaps because the Old Man, back at the Eagle's Nest, had intended that they all stay together? But that was already impossible—as far as Rashid knew—when he saved Elaine from Jamal's scheme. Yet the three of them were together again, which wouldn't have happened had he not come to Elaine's aid.

So maybe it was God's will that the three of them not be separated and he, Rashid, had not really made a choice at all, but merely followed the path marked out for him by fate? It was a puzzle. He wasn't used to thinking such deep thoughts, and was relieved to have them interrupted by the sound of Conrad, slowly and laboriously making his way up the hill toward him.

"Elaine said you killed someone," Conrad said, panting, when he'd finally reached the top.

"Yes."

"Who?"

"You remember Yusuf's nephew Jamal?"

Conrad frowned. "You killed Jamal? Why?"

"He was making plans to sell Elaine to the Emir."

Conrad reacted, surprised. "He knew who she was, then?"

"Yes. He heard her call you by your real name when you went into the river."

"She should have been more careful."

"Yes."

"But Jamal certainly deserved to die."

Rashid was silent for a moment. "Yes," he said finally.

The men stared out over the landscape, reflecting on their brief conversation. Life could be complicated, but fortunately there were also times when it was quite simple. They turned and headed back down the hill to the campsite.

23

There are mountains, and then there are mountains.

So thought Elaine as the three travelers neared the foothills of the Zagros range.

There were mountains not far from her native Tripoli, the Lebanese range, but the Zagros Mountains were a different matter altogether. Not only were their peaks considerably higher, but there was a seemingly inexhaustible supply of them, standing like a vast army of rugged stone warriors each thousands of feet high, as far as the eye could see. Some ten miles to the west of those towering peaks the foothills began, and the travelers entered them on the fourth day after leaving Mosul.

Once they were certain they weren't being pursued they had slowed their pace, stopping at small towns along the way to replenish their supplies and also to allow Conrad time to recover. He was getting stronger, at least it seemed so to Elaine, but as they came closer to the mountains something seemed to be bothering him—something besides the ordeal he'd undergone at the hands of the slavers. It was a while before Elaine worked out what it was.

From time to time she noticed him looking up at the surrounding peaks with a strange expression on his face. Once, a stream of small rocks and pebbles came trickling down the hill to the west, dislodged by some animal, no doubt, and Conrad looked up with a start and then looked away again, almost shuddering, and suddenly she understood.

"You're afraid of heights!" she said before she could stop herself. Then she added hastily, "I am, too, I have been ever since I can remember!" *At last,* she thought, *we've found something in common—* but Conrad just clenched his jaw and looked straight ahead. He did not care to discuss a weakness, even one he shared with someone else.

As darkness fell, a thing that happened quickly in the mountains, the travelers made camp just outside a small village. The road they were on had narrowed into little more than a mountain path and they knew they would need a guide to lead them through the main range, which lay directly ahead.

"I'll try to hire one in the village tomorrow morning," said Rashid. "Meantime we should make camp and take turns keeping watch."

"Do you think it's really necessary? Keeping watch, I mean?" said Elaine.

"Best to be safe," Rashid said.

"I'll take the first watch," Elaine said. Conrad and Rashid said nothing but exchanged a look, which Elaine had no trouble interpreting.

"I'm just as capable of sounding a warning as either of you," she said. "Besides, what are you going to do? Force me to go to sleep?"

The two men exchanged another look, this of resignation.

After three hours, as nearly as she could judge, Elaine woke up Rashid, who, with a glance at the sleeping Conrad, whispered, "Shall I wake him when his turn comes, or let him sleep?"

"Wake him. He'll be insulted if you don't," Elaine said, yawning, and quickly went to sleep.

But she slept fitfully and awoke again just as Rashid was shaking Conrad awake. The Knight came around slowly, but stood without complaint and began to take his turn. Elaine waited for a little while, watching him, and suddenly he began walking into the trees near the campsite.

Probably just relieving himself, Elaine thought, but she stayed awake waiting for him to return and as the minutes slipped by she became concerned. She got up and walked over to the edge of the trees. The moonlight provided some visibility, but the woods looked nearly pitch black and she hesitated. "Conrad?" she called softly, but there was no answer.

Then she heard a faint noise from the hillside overlooking the trees. She stepped back into the clearing and looked up, straining her eyes, and saw the shape of a man, silhouetted against the stars, moving slowly along the ridge. She knew at once it was Conrad; even in the poor light the outline of his body and the way he moved were unmistakable.

Conrad walked slowly toward the highest point on the ridge, which ended in a ledge some fifty feet off the ground. There were no trees in the immediate vicinity to break the impact should he fall, but Conrad, after hesitating for some time, took one step out onto the ledge, then another . . . and a third, until he was on the lip of the overhang, standing stiffly upright and, judging from the position of his head, staring straight out in front of him.

Then he looked down.

Elaine held her breath. For one horrible moment she thought he was going to leap to his death, but he remained motionless. Elaine could sense the tension in his body, could feel the fear that must be trying to invade his mind. He remained still for a long while and then stepped back from the edge of the overhang. Then he turned and walked back along the ridge.

Elaine lay back down on her blanket. A few minutes later Conrad walked out of the trees and back into the campsite and began standing his watch, walking in a slow circle around the perimeter as Elaine thought about what she had just seen. There was only one explanation she could think of. Conrad, stung by her remark that he had a fear of heights or, more precisely, by the truth of that remark, had forced himself to climb the ridge and stand on the edge of the precipice for no other reason than to prove to himself that he could do it.

What a strange man, she thought, and finally fell back to sleep.

The next morning when Elaine awoke Rashid had already gone into the village in search of a guide. She and Conrad ate, saying little, and Rashid returned in less than an hour, accompanied by another man on horseback.

He was the first Kurd the travelers had ever seen and he was a striking sight. He wore baggy trousers with bright blue and yellow stripes, and a crimson sash over a white shirt with huge sleeves gathered at the elbows with strips of crimson cloth; on his head was an elaborate turban of royal-blue silk. He appeared to be about thirty, though it was hard to tell because his face was partially hidden by a magnificent black mustache that drooped a good six inches on either side of his lips.

The effect could have been comical but wasn't in the least. The man wore his finery with a natural grace and dignity, and a large scimitar hanging at his side also helped make the overall impression a serious one.

"This is Sangar, of the Bashuki tribe," Rashid said. "He has agreed to act as our guide."

Sangar nodded pleasantly enough, and Conrad and Elaine nodded back.

"These tribes have their own language," Rashid said. "But most speak Arabic as well."

"How long will the passage take?" Conrad asked.

"He says, about two weeks."

"Then we'd better get started," Elaine said. Rashid nodded to Sangar, who turned his horse and set off down the trail, the others close behind.

The price of Sangar's help had been five gold pieces, which seemed quite reasonable; but Rashid regretted letting Sangar know they had any gold at all. Yet it was unavoidable—the man wasn't going to guide them for free. They'd have to keep a close watch on him and on their saddles, into which the remaining coins, now down to sixty-two from the original one hundred, had been sewn.

Sangar led them by a northerly route, skirting the higher and even more rugged terrain to the south, and on the whole the journey was not unpleasant. For Elaine, the lasting impression from the trip would always be the rich and varied beauty of the landscape. They passed through the occasional village, nestled against some soaring peak, but for the most part they picked their way through the thick oak forests that, mingled with stands of pistachio and almond trees, covered the steep hillsides. Streams and waterfalls were plentiful, cascading down from the snow-capped peaks, and carving out narrow but lush valleys in which wildflowers of every imaginable shape and color flourished.

The wildlife was equally impressive. On the Al-Jazirah there had been animals aplenty, but mainly domesticated—chickens, geese, goats, cattle, and horses. In the Zagros, on the other hand, Elaine saw eagles, bears, deer, wild goats, wolves, foxes, and once she caught sight of a leopard, just before it slipped away into the shadows of the trees.

Of the native human population she saw frustratingly little. Several times she suggested mingling, but the deeper they went into the mountains, the more Sangar, speaking through Rashid, discouraged such notions.

"The tribes in these mountains have two traditions," Sangar explained cheerfully. "One is a strong tradition of hospitality to strangers, the other is an equally strong tradition of murdering and robbing anyone they take a disliking to. It is better to be prudent."

This was hard to argue with, and they stayed clear of the populated areas. Still, Elaine caught occasional glimpses of the towns, the men dressed as splendidly as Sangar, and the women, if anything, even more colorfully. At night the sounds of laughter and music often drifted to where the travelers were camped and Elaine thought it would be fascinating to at least observe the revelry; but caution prevailed, with one exception. Taking care that

Sangar wasn't observing him, Conrad took three gold coins out of his saddle and went into a village. He came back with a sword. It further depleted their gold, but they knew Conrad felt naked without a sword, and besides, he might well need it to defend himself and them. It was a beautiful weapon, very well made. But of course, in Conrad's mind, it couldn't compare with his brother's. But it would have to do.

One evening Rashid and Sangar were off discussing the next day's route and Elaine found herself alone with Conrad. He was practicing with the new sword, becoming accustomed to its heft and feel, and then he came and sat down next to her. She hesitated, then took the plunge.

"I have to tell you something," she said, "and I hope you won't take offense. That first night in the mountains, before Sangar, when you were standing watch, I wasn't asleep."

He realized at once what she meant. "You saw me on the cliff."

"Yes. And I admire you for it. That's what I wanted to say. In fact, I was thinking about doing the same thing myself."

"Don't bother," he said.

She bristled a little. "Why not?"

"It doesn't help. My knees still wobble if I so much as look at a mountain."

This sounded almost like a joke, and a self-deprecating one at that, but Elaine didn't really believe such a thing was possible from Conrad so she just said, "Still, you were brave to do it."

Conrad said, "I want to say something, too. I'm sorry for the loss of the gold you paid for me at the slave market. It was clumsy of me to let myself be captured."

Elaine was astonished. First a joke, now an apology! She couldn't help reflecting that being a slave had changed him for the better.

"It's all right," she said, and tried to think of something to add but couldn't. But the resulting silence, for a change, was not an uncomfortable one.

That night it began to rain. Weather in the Zagros was notoriously unpredictable, but even so, rain in July was very surprising.

"It means a short summer," Sangar said gloomily.

"Winter stayed late, summer should, too," Rashid said.

"But it won't," said Sangar. "Not in the mountains."

The weather cleared quickly, however, and they set out the next morning in good spirits and entered what proved to be the most rugged part of the journey. Often they rode single file through the defiles, and once or twice crossed narrow ledges with a sheer drop on one side. Sangar was used to such dangers and seemed hardly to notice them. Moreover, he kept up a steady patter of conversation the whole time, and Rashid passed on most of what he said to Conrad and Elaine.

Sangar was proud of his heritage and enjoyed expounding various aspects of Kurdish lore. "We are descended from an ancient people called the Medes, who are mentioned in the Holy Book of the Jews and Christians and who, along with the Persians, defeated the mighty Assyrian Empire. And even though the Medes did most of the fighting, the Persians received the glory, and to this day many believe that the Persians conquered alone, whereas in truth . . ." And so on. Gradually Elaine came to realize that the unending stream of talk was at least partly intended to help the travelers keep their mind off their own fear, and she was thankful for it.

On the morning of the twelfth day after entering the mountains, they reached the crest of a ridge beyond which lay a vast, uneven landscape, flat plains alternating with small and narrow but rugged mountain ranges, which stretched out before them all the way to the horizon. This was the Iranian Plateau, once part of Persia and now on the edge of the vast Khwarazmian Empire.

Sangar explained that the path they were on would take them down to the plateau and out of the Zagros. The travelers bade the talkative guide farewell, and with a final, courteous nod he turned and headed back up the trail.

It took them the rest of the day to descend the winding path, and an hour before sunset they found themselves at the outskirts of a town at the edge of the plateau.

"We should buy some food," said Rashid.

"It's late, the market will be closed," Conrad said.

"Someone will sell, if we have money."

"But what's the point?"

"We don't know what we'll find as we move further into the plateau," said Rashid. "Best to stock up now. And we'll be able to leave very early in the morning, without waiting for the market to open."

Rashid took out his knife and began to pry out one of the gold coins that had been sewn into the inside of his saddle. He looked at the coin for a long moment, then began prying out another.

"One will be more than enough," said Conrad.

Rashid ignored him, and pried out a third. Then he suddenly undid the girth and ripped the saddle off the horse. He flung it to the ground and began frantically loosening the threads that held the rest of the gold. That's when Conrad and Elaine noticed that the first three coins Rashid had uncovered weren't gold but pieces of brass, cut to roughly the same size as coins, but worthless. It didn't take long to verify that the rest of the gold had been removed from the saddle as well.

"Sangar took the coins from your saddle and you never noticed?" Conrad said.

Rashid looked at him grimly. "See to your own," he said.

Conrad took out his knife and went to work on his own saddle, but immediately he realized that Rashid was surely right. If Sangar had searched one saddle he would have searched all three. And so it proved. Within a few minutes there were fifty-nine pieces of brass scattered on the ground, instead of the fifty-nine gold coins they should have had. Rashid glared at Conrad.

"He must have seen you when you took the gold from your saddle to buy the sword!"

"He was nowhere around," Conrad insisted. "I was very careful."

"Not careful enough."

"Maybe you should have been more careful—you hired him!"

"There wasn't exactly a crowd of people begging to help us. I was lucky to find him."

"You mean, unlucky."

"Enough!" said Elaine. "What's done is done. We have to go back, find Sangar, and make him return the gold." As soon as she said it she felt foolish.

"We'd never find him again in those mountains and if we did he'd have plenty of friends to help him keep the gold," said Conrad.

"You're right," Elaine admitted. "But without the gold, we have nothing to offer the Mongols in return for the letter."

"I suppose we could go back to the Old Man, start over," said Conrad.

"I won't stand before him having failed again," Rashid said, for the second time since leaving the Eagle's Nest. Then he added, "Besides, how would we find our way back through the mountains?"

"Hire another guide," said Elaine.

"With what?" said Conrad. "We have no money, remember?"

For a long time no one spoke. Then Elaine said quietly, "Well, we can't go back and we can't stay here forever. So I suggest we go forward—we've got nothing to lose. We'll rest here tonight and go on in the morning. We'll find the Mongols and we'll get the letter back."

"How?" said Conrad.

"I don't know," Elaine answered. "We'll have to think of a way."

"It will take a miracle," said Conrad.

"It's a miracle we've gotten as far as we have," Rashid said suddenly.

"Wonderful," said Conrad. "Perhaps we should all lie down and pray for another miracle!"

He said it sarcastically but no one laughed. No one said anything. In the end, that's exactly what they did.

PART FOUR

KHWARAZM

24

The next morning Elaine reached deep into her pocket, hoping against hope to find a few crumbs of something to eat, and suddenly burst out laughing. Conrad and Rashid, who found little about their situation amusing, stared at her in astonishment.

"We prayed for a miracle," Elaine said, "and we got one!" And she held up two gold coins she'd found in her pocket.

"Where did you get those?" said Conrad.

"When you and the horse went into the river, Yusuf paid me two gold coins for the horse."

"That's right, I'd forgotten," said Rashid.

"So had I," said Elaine, "but they've been in the bottom of my pocket all this time and here they are."

"Hmph," Conrad grunted. "And how much did Yusuf pay for me?"

"Nothing," said Elaine. She decided to risk teasing him. "I guess he thought you were priceless."

"Or worthless," said Rashid, hiding a grin.

"Ha, ha," said Conrad grumpily, but he didn't really seem to mind the teasing. In fact, the discovery of the coins cheered all three of them up considerably, especially after they used some of it to buy a breakfast of freshly baked bread and oranges at the village market.

"North, south, or east?" said Elaine when they'd finished eating. She was talking about the three roads that intersected just outside the village.

"We should ask someone," said Conrad.

But it was soon clear that, though the villagers seemed friendly enough, none of them spoke Frankish or even Arabic, for they were in that part of the Khwarazmian Empire called Persia, and spoke only the language of that proud and ancient land.

"Maybe this will help," said Elaine, and she took the black-and-orange-feathered arrow from the supply sack and began asking, by gesture and sign, which direction might lead to more such arrows, or to those who made them.

The first few men they approached turned away, their friendliness suddenly gone. They wanted no part of the arrow or anything connected with it. Finally an old woman stepped out from behind the cart where they'd purchased their breakfast. She was short and squat, and stared at them from a face so full of creases it was almost crumpled. She looked at the arrow then pointed toward the road that led eastward.

"Thank you," said Elaine, but the old woman just shook her head and turned away.

The land east of the Zagros, while not nearly as high or rugged as that majestic range, remained uneven and the going was slow, though the road was well marked. The terrain was arid and dusty, cut by an occasional stream lined with oak and elm trees along with low-lying ferns and thorny shrubs.

The monotony of the landscape and the fact that they encountered no other travelers made the time pass slowly, and Elaine decided to start a conversation, though she had little hope of having a truly interesting one with Rashid and Conrad on her chosen subject, one she had contemplated from time to time.

"Do you believe in destiny?" she asked brightly.

Conrad and Rashid, as usual when Elaine said or did something they couldn't account for, looked at each other.

"Who are you talking to?" Conrad said.

"Both of you. Either of you. Do you believe in destiny?"

Rashid said, "I believe in the will of God."

"Isn't that the same thing as destiny?"

"I don't know," Rashid said equably. "If it is, then I believe in it, if not, then I don't."

Elaine thought for a while, then said, "Everything that happens is the will of God?"

"Yes, everything," said Rashid.

"Then why do you feel guilt for not killing me in the stables at Tripoli?"

Rashid frowned. "What do you mean?"

"Well, you do feel guilty, don't you?"

"Yes."

"Why?"

"Because I disobeyed the Old Man."

"But it must have been the will of God for you to disobey him, otherwise it couldn't have happened," she said.

Conrad smiled to himself, happy to see someone else fall into one of Elaine's little traps.

Rashid remembered something Hasan had said. "Just because God chose to use my unworthiness doesn't make me any less unworthy."

"It wasn't unworthiness that kept you from killing me," Elaine asserted briskly. "It must have been something else."

"The will of God," Conrad interjected, enjoying Rashid's discomfort.

"Exactly," said Elaine. "And if it was the will of God, why feel guilty about it?"

"You're playing with words," Rashid said.

"Not at all," Elaine said. "If destiny, or God's will, determines everything, then we have no choice about what we do and no reason to feel guilt or shame."

Rashid knew this couldn't be true, for Hasan had made it clear that he had every reason to feel ashamed, yet how to refute the argument wasn't obvious. "Perhaps God allows certain things to happen," he said slowly, "even though it isn't His will that they happen."

"That doesn't make sense," said Elaine.

"It could be God's will," Rashid said, "to allow certain things to happen or not, according to the choices we make. His will may be to allow us to make choices."

"Now you're playing with words," Elaine said, but actually she wasn't so sure. It was a subtle answer, one she would have to think about further. She turned to Conrad. "What do you think?"

Conrad groaned inwardly. "I think this whole conversation is foolish."

"How so?"

"We're talking about castles in the air," he said.

"We're talking about things philosophers have discussed for centuries," Elaine said.

"Then philosophers are fools. Why talk of things like God and destiny, when we know nothing about them?"

"You don't believe in God?" Rashid asked.

"Of course I believe in God," Conrad said. "And heaven and hell and angels. But what those things are really like, or what God is thinking, we can't know and therefore it's foolish to talk of them."

"Speak for yourself," Rashid said.

"What's that supposed to mean?"

"I know what heaven is like because I've seen it!"

Conrad gathered himself; this was the moment he'd been waiting for—the chance to destroy Rashid's foolish illusion once and for all.

"What you saw . . ." Conrad began, then became aware of Elaine out of the corner of his eye. She was rigid, as if anticipating a blow, and he remembered how she'd begged him not to tell Rashid.

". . . was a dream," he finished lamely, angry with himself for giving in to Elaine.

Elaine said quickly, "I think some people do have a destiny. And each of us must try to find that destiny and follow it." Whether she really believed this or not she wasn't entirely sure, but she liked the way the words rolled off her tongue.

"Provided it is the will of God," Rashid said, and Conrad rolled his eyes.

Whether they would have solved the ancient mystery of destiny had the conversation continued they would never know, for Rashid spotted something in the distance. It was on the road and coming their way, and soon they could make out a lone traveler riding a camel at a rapid pace. As he drew near they moved to one side to let him pass. The rider wore black robes and a black headscarf that covered his whole face except for his eyes. A scabbard, inlaid with gems, hung from the camel's saddle, but there was no sword, either in the scabbard or in the rider's hand.

The rider ignored them and the camel's large padded feet, broad as dinner plates, glided silently along the dusty road so that beast and man passed by more like an apparition than flesh and blood. Within a few moments they were gone from sight and there was once more nothing visible on the road, behind or ahead of the three travelers.

"What do you make of that?" said Elaine.

"A crazy man," said Rashid.

But that turned out not to be the case, or if it was, then they had entered a land filled with crazy men.

An hour later they saw four more riders coming toward them, one on a camel and three on horseback. Their robes and headscarves hung loosely about them and, like the previous rider, they seemed in a hurry. Nevertheless, Rashid fingered his knife and Conrad made sure his sword, concealed under the supply packs on his own horse, was within reach. But the four riders, though they looked at them with curiosity, did not slow their pace but rode quickly past.

"Soldiers?" Elaine wondered aloud.

"I saw no weapons," said Rashid.

"Well, I don't think they were merchants," said Elaine. "They carried no baggage."

"No, not merchants," Rashid agreed.

"What, then? Where are they going?" said Elaine, but neither Rashid nor Conrad had an answer.

Two hours later they encountered another group of travelers, twenty in number and mostly on foot, for the only animals among them—two mules—were harnessed to carts piled high with furniture and other belongings. It was an extended family, or perhaps two or three families traveling together. The very old and very young rode in the carts with tables, chairs, carpets, caged chickens or geese, and sacks of food; everyone else, male and female, walked.

One of the younger men said something in Persian, apparently directed to the three travelers, but, not understanding the language, they didn't answer. The man shrugged and said nothing more. On one of the carts was a wooden plow wedged in between two tables.

"Farmers," said Rashid, and it was only then that he realized something that he felt he should have seen much sooner. These people—the camel rider, the four men, the group of farmers—weren't going to anywhere in particular. They were refugees, fleeing from somewhere.

Or something.

Rashid, as he liked to do, found a hill and urged his horse to the top of it and surveyed the land ahead of them. Conrad and Elaine joined him.

The road ahead stretched out for several miles like a long dusty ribbon, and as far as their eyes could see it was full of people, some on foot, some on camels or horses, some with handcarts or mule carts full of possessions, and all heading west.

"They're running away," Elaine said. "From the Mongols, perhaps. Maybe there was some kind of battle."

"Which means the Mongols may not be far away," said Rashid.

"Good," said Elaine.

For the balance of the day they struggled their way upstream against a growing flood of refugees. Most were farmers and peasants, but some were wealthy, mounted on camels, surrounded by bodyguards, their women hidden in vans with wooden frames and curtains of silk. All, rich and poor alike, wore vacant expressions, their empty eyes focused on the road. Some took note of the three travelers moving against the grain but nobody tried to speak with them.

Conrad nudged his horse near Rashid's. "We should find out what we can from these people," he said.

"We don't speak their language," Rashid said.

"Some of them may speak yours," Conrad said.

"It will draw too much attention."

"We're the only ones traveling east," Conrad said. "I think we've already drawn attention."

Rashid had to admit this was true. He called out, "Does anyone speak Arabic?" Some people looked his way but no one answered.

Elaine moved her horse up to join the two men. "Offer money," she suggested. They'd received some silver coins as change from their purchase of breakfast and spending one of them for information wouldn't be a bad investment.

"A silver coin," Rashid called out, "for anyone who can speak to us in Arabic!"

But even this failed to produce a response.

As night fell, some refugees kept moving westward, but others, especially those with children or heavy loads, stopped to make camp. The three travelers decided to camp as well. They were eating supper when a voice spoke out of the darkness.

"You are seeking someone who speaks Arabic?"

The man was short and plump, about fifty, with a full beard and a turban wound about his head in the Persian manner.

"My name is Gaspar," said the man. "If it's information you seek, I'm willing to trade some for a little food." He spoke in a frank if weary tone and his eyes kept straying toward the scraps of food left over from dinner, spread out on a cloth next to the fire.

"What's he saying?" Conrad asked.

"He'll trade information for food," Rashid said.

"Ask him to join us," said Elaine, and Rashid gestured to a place near the fire. Gaspar sat down while Elaine produced some dates and a generous slice of bread.

Gaspar beamed. "Please tell the lady that she is as gracious as she is beautiful!" he said to Rashid.

"What did he say?" Elaine asked.

"He said thanks," Rashid answered.

They watched as Gaspar ate the bread and fruit, and washed it down with some water that Elaine supplied from a waterskin. When he had finished, he said, "I thank you. Your hospitality is like a small oasis in this desert of fear and pain."

Rashid translated this verbatim and Conrad frowned. "An oasis? What's he talking about?"

"It's the Persian way," said Rashid. He knew from Hasan that the language was rich in imagery and some of that flavor came through even though Gaspar was speaking Arabic.

"He's eaten," Conrad said curtly. "Find out what he knows."

Gaspar spoke in measured tones and Rashid was able to translate quickly enough so that at times it almost seemed they were all speaking the same language. Rashid began by asking Gaspar where he was from.

"From a city called Nishapur, some distance to the east of here," Gaspar replied. "I was a baker of bread and fine pastries. Nishapur is a lovely city. Or was."

"Was?" said Rashid.

"I do not know how much of it, if any, still remains. Its fate is in the hands of the Mongols. When they were two days away they sent messengers to the Emir demanding complete submission. He refused. I knew how the Mongols had dealt with other cities who had refused to submit—complete annihilation."

"So you fled," said Conrad.

Gaspar shrugged. "I have been fleeing for many days, for the Mongols keep advancing. And I am not the only one who prefers life to death, as you see." He gestured at the campfires, with their weary, huddled fugitives, scattered up and down the road.

"All these are from Nishapur?"

"By no means," Gaspar said. "There are many cities and towns whose inhabitants have no wish to trust themselves to the mercy of the Mongols. And yet, if I'm not mistaken, you are moving towards them, rather than away."

When this remark was met with silence, he continued quickly, "Forgive my discourtesy. I did not mean to pry. But you're young, your lives lie at your feet like an unrolled carpet. Would it not be better to allow the carpet a little time to reveal its pattern before throwing your lives away?"

"Do the Mongols kill everyone they meet, then?" said Elaine.

"They kill all who do not submit," Gaspar answered.

Rashid said, "Why do they attack the Khwarazmian Empire?"

"Ah," said Gaspar. "What can a simple man like myself know of the ways of kings? I can only repeat rumors, which float in the wind as easily as the feathers of a—"

"What rumors?" Rashid interrupted.

"Two years ago a caravan belonging to the Mongols passed through Khwarazmian lands. The Shah suspected that the true purpose of the caravan was to spy on his empire, and he ordered the caravan to be destroyed. The Great King of the Mongols, who calls himself Genghis Khan, sent three emissaries to demand restitution from the Shah for the loss of the caravan. The Shah not only refused restitution, he sent the emissaries back with their beards burned off. This was a special offense to Genghis Khan because emissaries and ambassadors are considered inviolable according to the customs of the Mongols."

"Where are the Mongols now?" said Rashid.

"God only knows," Gaspar said. "They are numerous as a plague of locusts, and like locusts they appear suddenly from nowhere, destroy and pillage and slaughter, then vanish only to reappear without warning in another place. But I've heard it said they were near a place called Torgreh."

"Where is Torgreh?" Rashid asked.

"A half day's journey to the east," said Gaspar. "A fine city, not so rich as Nishapur, but rich enough. You will go to Torgreh to find the Mongols?"

"Yes," said Rashid.

"I fear for you," said Gaspar. He climbed slowly to his feet. "I thank you again for your generosity, and now, as you must be as weary as I am, I will impose on you no more. May God go with you." With a final bow he walked slowly away.

"Well, that was a waste of food and water," said Conrad. "He was only repeating rumors, he said so himself."

"It's all we have to go on," Elaine said. "The Mongols can't be far away and Torgreh is as good a place to start looking for them as any." She started to say something else—that she felt Gaspar may have unwittingly given them the key to surviving their encounter with the Mongols—but they were tired and so was she. She would discuss it with them the next day.

In the morning they continued their journey, and just before noon, the river of humanity began to slacken. By the time the sun had reached its zenith they were once more the only travelers on the road in either direction.

Elaine found the solitude unsettling. The presence of other people, even frightened people who hurried past without a word, had provided a measure of comfort. Now in this vast landscape of barren, rolling hills, she felt diminished, like an ant crawling on the floor of some enormous castle. She shook the feeling off. Perhaps it was time to share her insight from the night before.

"I've been thinking about Gaspar," she said. "He said something very interesting. Namely, that the Mongols regard ambassadors as inviolate."

"So?" said Conrad.

"So that's how we'll present ourselves. When you think about it, that's what we really are—ambassadors, or emissaries, from the court of the Old Man of the Mountain."

"The Old Man doesn't have a court," Conrad said, "and I am certainly not his ambassador."

"Then Rashid and I can be the ambassadors and you can be our servant."

Conrad grunted and said, "Whoever heard of a female ambassador?"

Meanwhile, Rashid was staring into the distance with a perplexed expression. "We should be at Torgreh by now," he said. "Gaspar said it was half a day's journey, and it's well past noon." Stretched out ahead of them was a long, shallow depression, several miles in length. A city, if it existed, should be plain to see.

"Perhaps Gaspar was wrong about the distance," Elaine said.

"Wait," said Rashid. "There."

His sharp eyes had seen something five miles away and a little to the right of the road, where some sort of structure could be seen, rising from the ground.

"The mosque, I suppose," Rashid said.

"Anyway," said Elaine, "I think presenting ourselves as ambassadors is a good—"

"It doesn't look like a mosque," Conrad said. "And where are the walls, the minarets, the other buildings?"

The question hung in the air. There was no sign of civilization except for the mysterious structure Rashid had first seen. The feeling Elaine had dismissed earlier came back with renewed force. She felt a sense not merely of insignificance but of foreboding, as if the mystery they were seeing could only have a sinister explanation.

They traveled a while in silence, their eyes fixed on the structure ahead. Yet even when they had cut the distance in half they couldn't tell what they were looking at. It was perhaps a hundred feet high, shaped like a pyramid but with irregular edges, yet so symmetrical that it had certainly been made by men.

It took another twenty minutes for them to realize what they were seeing and twenty minutes after that to believe it. It was indeed man-made. But it was not a mosque.

That they had arrived at the site of Torgreh, or the former site, was plain enough, for the ground was strewn for a mile in every direction with the stones and bricks and wooden beams that had once made up the city. But the city itself had been torn down and the pieces scattered so that nothing remained standing.

Nothing, that is, except, in the center of the devastation, an enormous pyramid of human skulls.

Elaine couldn't bear to look at it yet she couldn't tear her eyes away either. Never in her worst nightmares had she imagined something like this—who could do such a thing? Who could even conceive of doing it?

She slid off her horse and sank to her knees in shock. What a fool she'd been, with her fatuous scheme of posing as "ambassadors" to the Mongols! It crumbled to nothing before this fragment of hell that had forced its way up to the surface of the world. The Mongols were devils, just as everyone said, and then she realized that some of the skulls on the pyramid were so tiny they must have belonged to infants. Speechless with horror, she groaned aloud and began to weep.

Conrad and Rashid also dismounted, needing to feel solid ground beneath their feet when confronting such a sight. Conrad had fought in two battles in France; he'd seen death and hideous wounds; he'd even seen helpless prisoners of war slaughtered like animals. But this surpassed all understanding.

"I've never seen its like," he said. Only when Rashid answered did he realize he'd spoken the words aloud.

"Nor I," said Rashid. Though he had no memory of it, in his mind's eye he had imagined the slaughter of his family many times over. It was, he felt, the very worst thing conceivable. But even that was not worse than this.

Conrad struggled to maintain, outwardly, at least, the calm detachment of a professional soldier. "The bones are picked clean," he said evenly, meaning by dogs and vultures.

"But not yet bleached by the sun," Rashid said.

Conrad nodded. "Two or three days old, then, most likely," he said. "Which means—"

"Be quiet!" Elaine screamed through her sobs. How could they speak of this horror as though they were discussing the weather or the merits of a horse?

Conrad and Rashid exchanged a glance, and dropped all pretense of being unaffected by the abomination that confronted them.

"What now?" Conrad said. "Do we go on?"

Rashid didn't answer immediately. It was the first sign of hesitation that Conrad had ever seen from him concerning the Old Man's mission.

Finally Rashid opened his mouth to reply, then stopped and grabbed Conrad's arm; he'd spotted something. Conrad followed his look and his pulse quickened. No more than two miles distant a dust cloud was forming. It was close to the ground but broad and growing as they watched. There was only one thing that could be causing it—a large group of riders racing directly toward them.

25

Conrad made a quick estimate of their chance of escaping and realized immediately that there was none. Their own horses had drifted a few paces away, grazing. It would take precious seconds to remount and spur them on, and in any case they weren't built for speed. They would be quickly overtaken by the onrushing cavalry. He had a sudden vision of three more skulls added to the pyramid. He looked at Elaine, who had risen to her feet by now. He grabbed her arm and pulled her toward her horse.

"Get on, hurry!"

"We'll never outrun all of them," Rashid said.

"You and I will slow them down, maybe she can get clear," said Conrad, and started to boost Elaine into her saddle, but she pushed him away.

"No! If we've learned anything it's that we should all stay together no matter what," she said.

"Elaine . . ."

But she'd already turned back to face the oncoming riders, and took the sling from her pocket, her expression both frightened and determined.

Damn her stubbornness! But at the same time Conrad had to admire her courage, which strengthened his own. He drew his sword.

At that moment Rashid said, "I don't think they're Mongols."

Since none of them had ever seen a Mongol, Conrad wondered how Rashid could know. But as the riders got closer he realized what he meant: whatever a Mongol might look like it would surely be something different and strange, yet the approaching riders didn't look very different from the Muslim warriors Conrad had seen on the other side of the Zagros Mountains.

"Persians, maybe," Rashid said. "Don't provoke them." He put his knife back inside his shirt and Elaine replaced her sling. Conrad, reluctantly, resheathed his sword.

A moment later the soldiers, two dozen in all, were at hand. They wheeled their horses and formed a circle around Conrad, Rashid, and Elaine, every rider holding a lance leveled directly at them. A sharp-eyed man with a crest on his helmet that apparently signified command barked an order in what sounded like Persian. Conrad and Rashid spread their hands to indicate that they didn't understand.

The commander pointed to the west, where the peaks of the Zagros Mountains could still be seen, then pointed at Rashid and Conrad. Then he pointed again at the mountains with a lift of his chin. Rashid and Conrad stared back in confusion. The commander repeated the gestures impatiently and spoke again.

Conrad shifted his feet and his sword hand twitched. Elaine noted the movement—he was always ready to fight, even if the odds were hopeless. The thought focused her mind and she suddenly guessed what the commander was getting at.

"I think he's asking if we come from beyond the mountains," she said. Rashid pointed to the west and nodded vigorously, hoping that this was the answer the commander wanted.

The man looked at the three of them for a long time, his gaze lingering a little longer on Elaine, then he issued commands to two subordinates, who brought the three travelers' horses over and indicated that they should climb on. This they did, and a moment later they found themselves thundering across the plain, surrounded by soldiers, bound for they knew not where but relieved to be leaving the pyramid of skulls behind.

Elaine had never seen anything quite like His Excellency, Shah Ala al-Din Muhammad II the Magnificent, Lord and Protector of the Khwarazmian Empire. The Shah sat on a throne of gold, inlaid with pearls and diamonds, and wore robes of purple silk lined with the mane of a lion and embroidered with gold and silver thread. On his head was a golden crown, with a sapphire as big as an eagle's egg. The Shah himself was about sixty, with a noble bearing, a graying beard, and bright eyes that studied the three travelers with great interest.

They had enough sense not to speak until spoken to. Instead they glanced around the room—which was really not a room but the inside of an enormous tent, the sides of which were hung with tapestries and curtains that would have done credit to a palace. The Shah's courtiers and advisers, fifty or so in number, stood by in silence.

Finally the Shah inclined his head slightly forward and the courtiers stirred in anticipation.

"Allow us to welcome you to our empire," said the Shah in perfect Arabic, and the courtiers nodded and murmured as if he'd spoken words of great wisdom.

"Thank you, Your Majesty," said Rashid.

The Shah smiled. "You're surprised that we speak your language," he said. "We speak several languages but not, alas, Frankish. Your companions are Frankish, are they not?"

"Yes, Majesty," said Rashid.

"Then you must translate for them as you find necessary," said the Shah. "We're told you come from west of the mountains."

"Yes, Majesty."

"We regret that you were subjected to such a sight as greeted you at Torgreh. These barbarians from the east—well, you saw for yourselves what they did. The Mongols are said to be fierce"—the

Shah's voice rose and his expression hardened—"but they slaughtered the helpless citizens of Torgreh and when we approached with our army they fled like dogs!"

A murmur of approval sounded in the tent and the Shah's voice rose above it. "But they shall not escape us again!" The murmurs changed to shouts with the words "The Shah! The Shah!" audible above the din. The Shah nodded graciously and the clamor gradually died away as everyone waited breathlessly for his next words.

"Now tell us," he said to Rashid, "what brings you and your companions to our empire?"

"I've come on behalf of my master to discover what lands lie beyond the mountains," Rashid improvised. "He knows little of these lands and wishes to know more."

"And who is your master?"

"Sheikh ad-Din as-Sinan, of the Nizaris," said Rashid.

An adviser standing behind the throne stepped forward and whispered something in the Shah's ear.

"He is also known as the Old Man of the Mountain, is he not?" the Shah asked.

"He is, sire. He is also called the Sheikh."

"And your companions—do they also serve this Sheikh?"

"They serve the Christian Kingdom of Tripoli," Rashid said. "But their purpose is the same—to learn as much as they might about the lands east of the mountains."

The Shah lifted an eyebrow. "They send a woman on such a mission?"

"The man is a nobleman, sire, and the woman his sister, of whom he is the sole guardian. They have been together since childhood and he did not wish to leave her to the care of others."

Not exactly an ironclad explanation, Rashid knew, but it was the best he could do on the spur of the moment. But the Shah accepted it, or perhaps didn't care enough to question it further. He leaned forward on his golden throne.

"Tell me, how are the Mongols regarded by those west of the mountains?"

"In truth, Majesty, we in the west know little about them."

"There are no armies, then, marching over the mountains to join us in our fight?"

"I do not believe so, Majesty," Rashid said.

"The west is asleep, then," said the Shah, almost to himself. Then he added in a loud voice, looking around the tent: "And we are most glad to hear it! For our glory will be all the greater when we defeat these barbarians unaided!" And the tent erupted with more cheers and shouts of "The Shah!"

When order was restored the Shah said, "I see that your companion carries a sword—he is no doubt a soldier."

"Yes, Majesty."

"And you, too, have seen fighting?"

"Yes, Majesty."

"Good. Then you shall both join our army, for we will engage the Mongols in battle and destroy them, and what better way for you to learn about our lands than to take part in such a victory? You will make your masters proud!"

Outside the tent, the commander with the crested helmet was waiting and led them through the encampment to their new quarters. Along the way Rashid explained what had happened.

"What are you saying?" Conrad demanded. "We're now part of the Shah's army?"

"Yes," Rashid said.

"You shouldn't have agreed."

Rashid gave him a sour look. "What should I have said, exactly?"

"Well, that we had pressing business with, uh, with . . ."

"With the people the Shah is fighting a war against?" said Elaine. "Brilliant idea!"

"I just wish there was some way to avoid this battle," Conrad said doggedly.

"Prince Conrad of Antioch actually wants to *avoid* a fight?" said Elaine.

"I've been in battles," said Conrad. "Anything can happen. It's chaos. It would be better to make contact with the Mongols before that happens." But then he noticed what was all around him and his opinion began to change.

Sprawled in all directions around the Shah's tent was the largest gathering of armed men that Conrad had ever encountered—not merely two or three times larger than what he was used to seeing in Europe or in Tripoli, but so much larger that his mind couldn't grasp it. He hadn't noticed on the way to the Shah's tent because he'd been surrounded by the escort, but now the vastness of the array was clear and Conrad's wonder only grew as they moved through the seemingly endless ranks. Persian cavalry armed with lances and scimitars, Turkish cavalry with their bows and short swords, Arab mercenaries who fought from camels—and beside all these there was an equally large number of infantry, including archers and slingers.

"Ask him how many men are in the army," Conrad said to Rashid, who relayed the question in Arabic to the commander.

"Over a hundred thousand," Rashid told Conrad. "And more coming every day."

"And how big is the Mongol army?" Conrad said.

Rashid spoke again to the commander, then translated: "Half as big at most."

Suddenly a cry sounded from a few yards away: "Sir Knight! Sir Knight!" No one had called Conrad "sir" since he'd left Tripoli, and even more surprising, the language was Frankish. He turned sharply toward the voice.

It was a woman, a few years older than Conrad, shabbily dressed and with a careworn face, but, for all that, not unattractive. She had tousled hair the color of wheat and her blue eyes widened with pleasure when he looked her way. "What's your name, where are you from?" she asked, again in Frankish. Before Conrad could answer the commander ran his horse at the woman, forcing her back, and said something in a harsh tone.

"She's unclean," Rashid told Conrad. "A whore."

The commander kept moving and soon the woman was well behind them. Elaine looked back—she knew what a whore was, of course, but had never seen one and she couldn't help being curious. She looked at the woman for some time and when she turned her head around she noticed that Conrad was still watching the prostitute. Elaine felt her mouth tighten disapprovingly. Men were men. Though, of course, in the end she could care less what Conrad chose to do or not do with other women.

The commander led them to a spot on the fringe of the encampment among other soldiers who had not been assigned to a military unit, then rode away without a backward glance. The three travelers tended to their horses, then held their own private council of war.

"I think it might be best to fight after all," Conrad said. "The Shah's army is twice the size of the Mongol army."

"Assuming the officer was telling the truth," said Elaine.

"I've never seen an army like this. I doubt there's ever been one."

"Suppose you're right," Elaine said. "Our task is to find the letter. How will defeating the Mongols help us do that?"

"Spoils of war," Conrad said. "We'll search for the letter after the battle."

"This entire army will be collecting spoils."

"Yes, gold and horses and weapons and other things they can sell. No one but us will care about a letter and no one will try to stop us from taking it."

"We won't be able to find it in the confusion. You said yourself, it'll be chaos. Maybe the letter will be destroyed before we even have a chance to locate it."

"What's your plan, then?" Conrad said. "You still want to play at being ambassadors?"

Elaine grimaced, remembering the pyramid of skulls. She turned to Rashid. "What do you think?"

The Arab took his time, looking thoughtfully at the vast number of soldiers all around them. "I know little of the Mongols," he said finally. "But unless they truly are devils I don't see how they could defeat this army. And as for being ambassadors, our gold is gone and we have no gifts to present. We should fight with the Shah."

After a moment Elaine nodded. "All right."

"Now it's all right," Conrad said.

"It's two to one," she said reasonably.

Conrad sprang quickly to his feet. "I'm going for a walk. I'll need a coin."

"For what?" Elaine said.

"For whatever I choose," Conrad replied. Elaine reached into her pocket and held out a silver coin without looking at him. He took it and left quickly.

"He's very childish sometimes," said Elaine.

To her astonishment Rashid replied, "He cares for you."

She stared at him, unsure if this was meant as a joke. "Perhaps as property—like a sword, or an acre of land."

"He nearly died for his sword," Rashid pointed out.

Elaine smiled. "A bad example, then—he valued that sword far more highly than he values me. But in the same way, as a possession. He's made it plain enough."

"Back at the marketplace in Mosul," Rashid said.

"What of it?"

"Why did he not kill the slaver?"

"It would have meant the death of all three of us."

"He cares nothing for my life," said Rashid. "Nor for his own at that moment, I think. So it must have been for your sake."

"He thinks he has a duty to protect me," Elaine said.

Rashid gave a little shrug, a sign that he had spoken his piece. "Night is coming," he observed. "I'll gather some wood for a fire."

As he started to leave Elaine said, "You're wrong about Conrad. I'll wager I know where he went on his so-called walk, and it has precious little to do with caring for me." She frowned, remembering the look on his face as he watched the prostitute who'd called his name. Not that it was any concern of Elaine's.

When Conrad returned early the next morning, the camp was buzzing with activity. Tents were being struck, animals groomed and saddled, supplies loaded onto wagons. Elaine was packing her own tent and looked up as Conrad approached but quickly looked down again.

"What's happening?" Conrad said.

"As you see," Elaine replied, still without looking up. "We're moving out."

"To where?"

"I don't know. Rashid is trying to find someone who speaks Arabic. He'll tell us when he gets back."

They stared at each other. Elaine knew he'd been with the prostitute and he knew that she knew. She wasn't jealous in the slightest, but she found his smugness annoying.

"I hope you got your money's worth," she said.

"Very much so," he answered, his expression, if anything, even more smug than before.

Elaine was trying to think of a suitably cutting remark when Rashid hurried up to them. "The Shah's scouts found the Mongol army, fifteen miles north of here," he said, his voice uncharacteristically tense. "There's going to be a battle, and soon."

"That settles it," said Conrad. "They'll be keeping a sharp eye out for deserters from this point on. We couldn't slip away even if we wanted to." His eyes rested again on Elaine. "The only problem is, what to do about you."

"What about me?" said Elaine.

"You can hardly fight in the battle. You need to be somewhere safe."

"She can stay with the baggage train," Rashid suggested.

"That was my thought as well," said Conrad.

"Why can't I fight in the battle?" Elaine demanded belligerently.

The two men looked at each other, and then at her, as if she were insane.

"I can fight with the slingers," she said. "This army has some, I saw them."

"Why would you want to?" Conrad asked.

"You saw the pyramid of skulls," said Elaine. "And you ask why I want to strike a blow against the creatures who built it?"

There was a moment of silence, then Rashid said, "The desire does you credit, but it would never be permitted."

"I can use the sling as well as most men, as you both have reason to know," said Elaine.

"Regardless, no woman would be allowed to fight in a Muslim army," said Rashid. "Or a Christian one either, I imagine," he added with a look at Conrad, who nodded firmly in agreement. The two men considered the subject closed.

Elaine didn't continue the argument, but not because she considered the subject closed. She just needed to think for a while. One thing was certain: she was through letting men dictate her fate. She began to feel much as she had that night in her chamber when she'd decided to visit the Old Man—a little frightened, and a little excited. She could sense that a plan was taking shape just below the surface of her mind, one that would seem obvious once she'd thought of it.

The army finished breaking camp and began to move out. The day became warmer as the sun rose higher in the sky. Elaine kept to herself, thinking, waiting . . . and then, finally, it came to her, and it was indeed so obvious, and so simple, that she almost laughed out loud.

26

As the day wore on Elaine began to realize that in military matters "soon" was a relative term. An army was like an animal with many legs, and could move only as fast as the slowest leg, and its slowest leg was of course the infantry. A distance that could be covered on horseback in a single day would take several for men on foot, and this didn't take into account any evasive maneuvers by the Mongols to avoid coming to grips with the Shah's enormous force.

Rashid had been mingling with other soldiers, learning what he could from those who spoke Arabic, and now he rode back to Elaine and Conrad.

"The Mongols are retreating," he said.

"The Shah must cut them off," said Conrad. "Force them into an open place, the larger the better."

"That's what he's trying to do," said Rashid. "There's a large plain five miles from here. . . ."

"Force them onto the plain and make a frontal assault," Conrad said in a knowing tone. "Let our superior numbers tell."

"You've fought in such a battle?" Rashid said, impressed despite himself.

"Once or twice," said Conrad, trying to seem modest.

"But with far smaller armies," Elaine said.

"The principle's the same," Conrad snapped.

Later in the day the news came that the Shah's maneuvers were having their intended effect, and a battle was sure to take place the next day. Elaine could sense the tension in the soldiers around her and glanced at Conrad and Rashid and knew they must be feeling it, too, though they were doing their best to give no outward sign of it.

That evening an armorer came by passing out weapons to those who needed them. When he saw Rashid with only a knife, he tendered a sword, but Rashid refused. The armorer said something in Persian, offering the sword again, and Rashid, conscious of others watching curiously, accepted it to avoid embarrassment. He and Conrad also accepted shields, small and round in the Turkish fashion.

"Why didn't you want to take the sword?" Elaine asked Rashid.

"Because he doesn't know how to use it," Conrad said. "He only knows how to sneak up on people and stab them with his dagger."

"I'll match my dagger against your sword any day," Rashid said.

"It will be useless in a battle like this one, I promise you," said Conrad.

Elaine sensed that neither man was really in a belligerent mood; it was mostly nerves talking. Still, she moved to head off any trouble.

"Then teach him," she said to Conrad.

"Teach him what?"

"How to fight with the sword."

Conrad and Rashid both reacted as if they'd been struck.

"I can't teach him swordsmanship in an evening," Conrad said.

"You can teach him something," Elaine said.

"I don't need any help from him," said Rashid.

"Yes, you do," Elaine countered. "And he needs help from you."

"What help do I need from him?" Conrad demanded.

"He can teach you to ride," Elaine said.

"I know how to ride!"

"Not as well as he does," Elaine said firmly, her hands on her hips. "Very soon you'll both be fighting in a battle unlike any you've ever seen before. You may need every bit of knowledge you can get just to stay alive, and you need to stay alive so you can help me find the Old Man's letter after the battle. So, teach each other now, while there's time."

"So we can 'help' you find the letter?" Conrad said. "Who put in you charge all of a sudden?"

"I didn't mean it like that," Elaine lied. "The point is, the horse you'll be riding hasn't been trained for battle, am I right?"

"I don't know," Conrad lied in turn. The plain fact was it was a palfrey—a travel horse. He tried to convince himself that Elaine's suggestion was silly, but failed. Instead his thoughts landed on a most unpleasant topic—the ongoing feud between himself and horses generally.

The memory of Tranquil still rankled, but far worse was the memory of the day he'd spent chasing down Lucifer. If he'd caught the horse sooner he probably wouldn't have been captured by Khaled and, more important, he'd still have Charles's sword—a loss that haunted him just as much as the humiliation of being enslaved. But he didn't have Charles's sword and, he realized reluctantly, this fact provided another reason why Elaine's suggestion made sense.

Conrad drew his sword, the one he had purchased from the Kurds, and stood facing Rashid. "The fact is, I could use some practice with this, I'm not accustomed to it yet. And you should get the feel of your sword if you're going to use it tomorrow."

"Then afterwards you can talk about horses," Elaine said.

Conrad clenched his jaw in irritation, but nodded.

"All right," said Rashid. He got to his feet and picked up the sword he'd been given earlier.

"You'll be mounted tomorrow," Conrad said, "but it'll be simpler if we begin on the ground. Hold the blade like this. It's called the guard position. Whenever you strike a blow, or parry one, bring the blade back to the guard position at once. If you remember nothing else, remember that. . . ."

And so the lesson began.

* * *

Elaine busied herself making camp and building a fire. She pretended not to be paying much attention to the two men, knowing they would be self-conscious, but she watched with interest as Conrad instructed Rashid. The Arab was an adept pupil, agile and strong and quick to appreciate the differences between using a sword and a dagger. What surprised Elaine was how good a teacher Conrad proved to be—patient, quick to spot a flaw, and equally quick to provide a remedy. *That must be the way he'd been taught by Charles,* thought Elaine, and she understood a little of why Conrad missed him so much.

After an hour, Rashid had learned at least a few rudiments of swordplay, and it was time for Conrad's lesson in horsemanship. Elaine took the opportunity to groom her own horse, watching the two men over the animal's back.

Rashid brought Conrad's horse over to him and stopped when the animal was about a yard away. "You can't be afraid," said Rashid.

"I'm not afraid," Conrad said.

"I know you're not afraid of being hurt," Rashid said. "But you can't be afraid of making a mistake, either."

"I feel . . ." Conrad began.

"You feel what?"

Conrad blurted, "Sometimes I feel that horses are laughing at me." He felt foolish as soon as he'd said it, but Rashid considered his words seriously.

"Horses don't laugh," he said finally, "but they play. You must play with them."

"What are you talking about?" said Conrad.

"Play builds trust, and if they trust you they won't fight against you."

"I don't understand."

"Watch."

Rashid stroked the horse gently for a moment, then gave its neck a push with both hands. Then he pushed again, harder, and the horse took a half step to the side. Rashid pushed a third time, really putting his weight into it, then stopped suddenly and backed away and when he did the horse stepped toward him.

It built from there. Rashid talked to the horse in Arabic, while running a few steps toward the horse, then away, while the horse kept pace—in effect, a game of tag between horse and man, so unexpected yet so natural that Conrad had to smile.

"Now you," said Rashid. "Go on."

"What were you saying to him?"

"It doesn't matter. Say whatever comes into your head, just let him know you're playing."

"Bet you can't catch me!" Conrad said, gave the horse a shove then backed away. Elaine covered her hand with her mouth to hide her smile. Conrad was clumsy, but at least he was making an effort. While the horse preferred Rashid, every so often it responded to Conrad, so that the game became a three-way affair. This went on for half an hour, then darkness fell and it was time to stop.

Elaine couldn't be certain, but she thought she caught the two men smiling at each other slightly as they lay down for the night.

With the first rays of dawn the encampment came alive with a current of urgency and anticipation. The Mongols were finally trapped on the plain. The mountain passes that might lead them to safety were too narrow for an army to traverse rapidly and they had no choice but to give battle. Conrad had saddled Elaine's horse as well as his own and led them both to where she was packing up the campsite. Rashid was with him.

"It's time to go," said Conrad.

"Where?"

"The baggage train. We discussed this."

"It wasn't really a discussion," Elaine said.

"We told you before, you can't fight in the battle," Rashid said.

"You'll be safe in the baggage train, I've made arrangements," said Conrad. "Now come, there's no time to argue." He reached for her arm but she pulled back.

"What kind of 'arrangements'?"

"You'll see. Hurry!"

Elaine hesitated, but only for effect, because now she had a plan of her own and the sooner she was free of Conrad and Rashid the sooner she could put it into effect. She turned to Rashid. "Good luck. Take care of yourself."

The Arab nodded. "You as well. We'll see you after the battle."

Elaine mounted her horse and followed Conrad through the forming ranks of warriors toward the rear of the army and, eventually, the baggage train. It was Elaine's first view of that part of the camp and she was surprised at its size. It seemed nearly as big as the army itself, and like the army it buzzed with activity. Carts and wagons piled high with arrows and other weapons were hurrying toward the front, while various craftsmen worked feverishly to make new weapons or repair old ones.

Just outside the camp an enormous herd of horses was being driven forward to provide spare mounts. The steeds neighed and whinnied with anticipation and their excitement transmitted itself to the domesticated animals crowded into the camp's many wooden pens. The cows and sheep stamped their feet and mooed and bleated as if anxious to join the fighting, unaware that their role in the coming battle was to be slaughtered for the victory feast.

Only at the very end of the journey did Elaine understand why Conrad had refused to disclose their destination. They had arrived at the brothels.

"You're leaving me with prostitutes?" she demanded furiously.

"Because it's where you'll be safest," he said.

"I'm of royal blood," she snapped. "These are whores!"

"Trust me, it's the safest place for you," he said again.

"If you insist," she said. But this was a mistake. Conrad reined in his horse and stared at her suspiciously.

"What?" she said.

"That was too easy."

"There's no pleasing you, is there?"

"I don't want any tricks."

She held his gaze steadily, and then he finally rode on, Elaine beside him. But it had been a close call. She'd have to be more careful.

Conrad stopped the horses before one of the smaller tents, in front of which stood a woman Elaine recognized as the blue-eyed prostitute who'd called out to Conrad a few days earlier. *I should have expected this,* she thought to herself. Conrad probably thought it was logical or efficient, but to Elaine it was adding insult to insult.

"Get down," Conrad said, and when Elaine hesitated he dismounted and forcibly pulled her off her horse and set her on her feet. She was amazed at how strong he was; it was as though she weighed nothing at all.

"This is Anna," he said.

"You must be Elaine," said Anna.

"You spoke of me to this . . . this woman?" said Elaine, scowling.

"Stay with her until it's over," said Conrad. "If Rashid and I survive we'll come back for you. If not, Anna will help you."

"Help me do what?"

"Stay alive," said Conrad, then mounted his horse and galloped back toward the army, taking Elaine's horse with him. She was angry with him but a moment later regretted not wishing him luck, as she had Rashid. But he had left so abruptly . . . besides, she told herself, when it came to fighting, Conrad didn't really need luck.

As she watched him disappear she became aware of a nervous fluttering in the pit of her stomach. Perhaps her plan was a little too daring. But whatever happened, it would be preferable to spending the next few hours in an outdoor brothel. She turned to Anna and said stiffly, "Thank you, but I assure you I don't need your help."

"If the battle is a victory, that's probably true," said Anna. "But if the army has to retreat there will be much confusion. You'll be glad of some guidance."

Elaine's expression softened a little. She could see that Anna was trying to be helpful, but she was also aware that Anna was treating her almost as an equal, rather than with the respect due a princess. When she saw Conrad again she'd let him know in no uncertain terms that she did not appreciate being placed on equal terms with a prostitute, even a well-meaning one.

"Come into my tent, before you begin attracting attention," Anna said. "You don't exactly look like one of us."

"Thank you, no. I won't be coming into your tent. In fact, I won't be staying."

Anna gave a puzzled frown. "What do you mean? Conrad told you to stay with me."

"I don't take orders from Conrad."

"I promised to look after you and I don't want to break that promise. He cares for you."

"He cares for you, too," Elaine said, and startled herself by adding caustically, "At least, he did for one night." The words were ungracious and she wasn't quite sure where they had come from. "I'm sorry," she said, shaking her head. "I didn't mean that the way it sounded."

Anna smiled slightly. "You're jealous that Conrad and I were together."

"Certainly not. That's absurd!"

Anna started to answer but Elaine cut her off. "I don't care to continue this conversation, if it's all the same to you—and even if it isn't. All I need, if you really want to help, is for you to tell me where I can buy some clothes. There must be a place around here somewhere."

"Clothes? Why on earth do you need clothes?"

"That's my concern," said Elaine. "If you could just point me in the right direction . . ."

"I don't understand what the point—"

"Please. It would be a big help."

Anna shrugged. "Back the way you came, about two hundred yards, there's a cattle pen. Turn left and keep going and you'll come to the clothing stalls."

"Thank you."

"Afterwards, please come back here right away. You never know how—"

"Thank you," Elaine called back again over her shoulder. She was already hurrying along the path Anna had described.

Things went even more smoothly than Elaine had hoped. At the stalls she purchased a shirt, a pair of trousers, and a long turban. From earlier transactions she knew roughly what they should cost and she didn't bargain—she couldn't anyway since she didn't speak Persian. The woman running the stall looked at her a little strangely but probably assumed she was making the purchase for some man. Elaine found a spot behind a large oak tree and within moments had shed her dress and put on the trousers and shirt instead. If a woman couldn't fight in a battle, then she would become a man, at least for a few hours.

The turban was slightly trickier. She had seen men wind it not only around their heads but around their faces to keep out the sun and sand, but exactly how the winding was done she had no idea, and of course she had no mirror to help her. Eventually she managed to arrange the strip of cloth so that only her eyes were uncovered. Then she took her sling from the pocket of her discarded dress, and her comb as well for good luck, and stepped back into the bustling camp.

As she'd hoped, no one paid her any particular attention. She was small, but some men were just as small. There were a few Persians with blue or violet eyes, and her hands, after many weeks in the sun, were only slightly paler than those of most of the people around her. As for any language problems, the air was heavy with tension and no one was in the mood for small talk. And probably no one would have cared even if they'd discovered she was a foreigner. All that mattered was what the sling in her hand clearly proclaimed—she was willing to fight.

Her final task was to find the battlefield, and this proved to be an easy matter. There were dozens of horse-drawn wagons, loaded with arrows and swords and other armaments, all moving in the same direction, and Elaine fell in with them. There were a few soldiers walking nearby, most carrying bows and quivers but a few with slings. One or two glanced casually in her direction but none tried to start a conversation. Then she noticed that some of the wagons were piled high with rounded stones of various sizes, perfect for slinging, and she smiled. Of course—this was an army! She'd imagined having to scrounge around in the dirt to find appropriate projectiles, but even that detail had been taken care of.

An hour passed, then another, with Elaine trudging along among the wagons. She tried to imagine what the coming battle would be like, but she had little to go on. She'd read about battles in books and heard knights like Conrad describe them but she knew the real thing would be much different. She wondered what Conrad and Rashid would think when they found out that, in her own way, she'd fought in the battle, too; she smiled, imagining the looks on their faces when she told them.

In the end it was the horses who first sensed that the battlefield was near. They tossed their heads and chuffed and whinnied and, despite their heavy loads, began to quicken the pace. Soon Elaine heard shouting from up ahead, then became aware of beating drums and sounding trumpets in the distance—but not too far in the distance. A jolt of nervous energy shot up her spine and for a moment she wondered if she was making a mistake. Perhaps Conrad and Rashid were right and she didn't belong in a battle or anywhere near one.

Then she remembered Torgreh and the skulls of women and children as well as men piled halfway to the sky, and knew she would never forgive herself if she turned away from this chance to help avenge them. Above all, she would not wait passively while others decided her fate.

Her nervousness disappeared and she walked with firm strides toward the battlefield.

27

When Conrad left Elaine in the baggage train and rejoined Rashid the army was ready to march, but there was a delay—something was causing a commotion in the ranks. There was a strange, rhythmic, undulating motion in the mass of soldiers—men parting briefly then coming together again as though something were moving through them. Meantime men were yelling and shouting furiously in languages foreign to both Conrad and Rashid.

"What is it?" Conrad asked. "Can you see?"

Rashid stood in his stirrups but shook his head. "Some kind of animal. . . ."

But as the turbulence came nearer they could see that it wasn't an animal moving through the ranks, but a man—or what was left of one. It was a moment before they realized that the creature they were looking at was a Mongol prisoner.

His skin hung in shreds from his raw flesh. One eye had been gouged out and most of his nose was missing along with both ears. He was being pulled along by a chain fastened around his neck and when he fell he was prodded to his feet by the tip of a spear. As the Mongol was dragged past them he was struck, kicked, and spat upon. The watching soldiers cried out in hatred and delight at his agony.

Conrad understood the purpose of this spectacle well enough—to instill bloodlust in the troops and prove that Mongols could suffer and die like anyone else. Remembering the pyramid of skulls, he felt little sympathy for the Mongol, but he didn't share in the general frenzy, for Charles had taught him that it was best to fight with a clear head, and from the distaste on Rashid's face he sensed that the Arab agreed. The two men half-consciously moved their horses a little closer to one another. The ways of the men around them were not their ways and whatever happened from this point on they would face together.

The trumpets, stationed throughout the host, sounded the march and the troops began moving forward, cavalry in the front, infantry and archers in the rear. The urgency of the early morning was still present and the pace was quick. From various points came the sound of beating drums, and the steady pounding gave energy to men and animals alike. Competing with the drums were the sonorous, chanting war-songs raised by various tribes and units interlaced with the piercing battle cries of single warriors. And under it all could be heard the constant neighs and whinnies of nervous horses along with the strange, guttural drone distinctive to camels. It was a terrific din, chaotic and intoxicating, and Conrad could feel his own blood starting to rise, eager for battle. And then, without warning, the army ground to a halt.

Animals stamped their feet, men shook their heads and cursed, exchanging looks of frustration but also of relief, for they were soldiers who wanted to fight but they were also men who wanted to live. The smell of fear mingled with that of sweat and excrement, not all of it from the animals, for fear made some men lose control of their bowels. The minutes stretched out and Conrad could feel the energy begin to drain out of the army.

"Perhaps there will be no battle after all," said Rashid, sounding disappointed and relieved at the same time.

"This happens sometimes," Conrad said. "The calm before the storm. Stay ready."

Even as he spoke, a surge of renewed energy flowed through the army, and shouts from the vanguard were heard and relayed through the ranks. Conrad and Rashid didn't have to understand the words to sense their meaning: *"The enemy is in sight!"*

The din started up again—the drums, the battle songs, the cries of men and animals, louder than before—and a hundred trumpets together sounded the charge. Like a great ravenous beast the army gathered itself and surged forward to devour its prey.

As the army galloped farther into the plain it began to spread out, and through the gaps Conrad caught his first glimpse of the Mongols and he felt his blood rise further. He drew his sword and noticed that Rashid had forgotten to draw his.

"Rashid. *Rashid!*" The Arab heard him above the din and looked over. Conrad brandished his sword and Rashid, understanding, drew his own.

The Mongol force was a half mile distant, all on horseback and, as had been reported, considerably smaller than the Khwarazmian army. But they were arrayed in ranks drawn up in a more regular formation than Conrad had expected, which made him a little uneasy. He'd imagined the Mongols as a pack of wild animals, but evidently there was more to them than that. Armed mainly with bows, they began to move forward at a disciplined trot.

In unison the Mongol ranks took arrows from their quivers and drew their bows and loosed a volley—a volley so thick that for a moment it blotted out the sun. Along with the volley came an eerie wailing sound that Conrad realized must be the infamous "death cry" of the arrows. He had been expecting it, but it was so unnerving, like the collective screech of ten thousand war-birds from hell, that he barely remembered to raise his shield. He felt the shock of an arrow striking it and the point pierced the shield and stopped a few inches from his left eye. At the same time from all around him came the screams of hundreds of men who hadn't been so fortunate. He knew he had to remain in the saddle even if hit; if he fell he would be trampled to death.

The Mongols loosed another volley. There came again the sudden darkness and the banshee shrieks of the arrows, and Conrad understood why some called the Mongols devils. He had trained all his life for such moments and there wasn't a cowardly bone in his body, but he was human and deep inside him the worm of fear gave a little twitch. But he spurred his horse onward. If Charles was looking down from heaven, Conrad was determined to make him proud. Perhaps Charles would even forgive him for losing his sword to infidels.

The charge was now a deadly race between two different types of speed—that of horses and camels on the one hand, and that of archers loosing arrows on the other. If the Khwarazmians could reach the Mongol line before being shredded by the deadly barrage that continued to rain down on them, they would smash the Mongol center.

The attackers closed within two hundred yards, then a hundred. From the Mongol ranks a line of soldiers appeared on foot and their arms heaved forward and thousands of sleek, barbed javelins flashed through the air alongside the arrows, their impact just as deadly, for though they moved more slowly they were far heavier and even a glancing blow would knock a man out of the saddle.

Conrad was near the front line of the attack now, shield high and head low behind his horse's neck. A quick glance reassured him that Rashid was still nearby. The Mongols were very close and Conrad could see them in some detail. They wore armor of leather and strange-looking caps of thick cloth; their faces were broad and their noses rather flat and most seemed to have mustaches; and as Conrad took in these trivialities the Mongols loosed one last volley at close range so that the arrows were level with the ground when released. Arrows shrieked past Conrad, missing by inches, and he remembered Raymond of Tripoli's corpse and braced himself for the impact that would rip open his body and hurl him from his horse. But it didn't come.

The volley took a terrible toll. The attacking line wavered and a number of gaps appeared, but the bulk of the riders still came on and then at last they were among the Mongols. No arrows now, just a desperate, thrashing melee of flesh and bone and blood and steel and grunts and screams and curses. Very quickly Conrad realized that however capable they were with bows and javelins, the Mongols were not particularly formidable at close quarters. They tended to be of slightly smaller stature, and their horses—ponies really—were proportionately smaller as well, giving the Khwarazmians an advantage in size. Moreover the Mongols' swordsmanship was indifferent and their armor offered limited protection. Conrad brought his sword down viciously on the head of a Mongol warrior and the blade cut through the padded cap easily and split the man's skull. Conrad yanked the sword free and took on the next enemy, blocking a javelin thrust with his shield, then stabbing his sword into the man's exposed side. With a hoarse scream the Mongol disappeared from view.

Rashid, wielding a sword for the first time, managed to survive mainly on instinct. The "guard position" was mostly a fantasy, because the need to parry and counter was constant, with little time to recover. And yet even as he fought desperately to stay alive he could see the sense of Conrad's instruction—the closer he could come to centering the blade after making one movement, the better position he was in to make another, since there was no telling where the next attack might come from.

While fighting, Conrad kept aware of what was happening up and down the line of battle. The greatest danger in a cavalry charge is that one group of warriors might penetrate too far into the mass of enemy troops, only to be cut off and destroyed. The Shah's army had not been drilled on this tactic, or any other, for that matter, at least since Conrad and Rashid had joined it, but by luck or instinct the Khwarazmians maintained a relatively even front as they pushed forward.

Every battle has a turning point, a decisive moment that is a test of will more than of weaponry or skill. In that moment one side refuses to relent while the other gives way. It is a phenomenon of mind and spirit more than body, and Conrad sensed it before he saw it. The Mongols began to give ground, almost imperceptibly at first, keeping their mounts facing the enemy, still thrusting vig-

orously with sword and lance, but nevertheless yielding to the in-
exorable pressure of the Khwarazmian army's superior numbers.
And then, like a dam bursting before a river, the Mongols broke.
A few wheeled their ponies around, showing their backs to the
enemy, then others followed suit, and suddenly the entire line was
in headlong retreat.

A great cry of exultation went up from the Khwarazmians and
Conrad realized he was shouting along with everyone else. He
looked for Rashid, saw him nearby—the Arab was also shouting
and he and Conrad exchanged a look of triumph. They, with the
rest of the army, urged their mounts forward in pursuit of the enemy.

The Mongol ponies were very fast and the Khwarazmians
gained little ground in the chase. But it was important to keep the
enemy from re-forming so they pressed on. Occasionally a retreating Mongol would turn in the saddle and loose an arrow at his pursuers, but these volleys were ragged and sporadic and had little
effect.

Then something caught Conrad's attention. On a hilltop about
a half mile distant, beyond the retreating Mongols, was a small
group of Mongol horsemen, perhaps twenty in number. They were
holding huge flags, some white and some black, which they raised
and lowered as if transmitting a signal. It almost seemed comical—
what was the point of signaling an army that was retreating wildly
from the field of battle, all semblance of discipline lost? But as the
flagmen continued to raise and lower their flags in calm and me-
thodical patterns, Conrad began to conceive of another possibility, which made him feel suddenly sick. Maybe the men on the hill
knew something he and the rest of the Khwarazmian army did not.

Conrad looked to his left and grunted as if struck by a blow.
The Khwarazmians on that wing were breaking off the chase and
wheeling their horses at right angles to the line of pursuit, which
must mean they were being attacked from the flank. He looked to
his right and saw the same thing happening on that wing and his
stomach clenched as he realized the Mongol "retreat" had been
feigned—a carefully orchestrated maneuver designed to draw the

Khwarazmian army into a trap. The ploy had worked perfectly and now, vulnerable and in disarray, the army was being enveloped on both flanks.

"Rashid! Slow down, it's a trap!"

He couldn't tell if Rashid had heard him, but others had begun to notice and cries of alarm sounded throughout the ranks and the impetus went out of the charge as men dealt with the assaults on their exposed flanks.

When Conrad looked back to the front the Mongols had stopped retreating and, with perfect discipline, had turned and were again facing their pursuers, bows at the ready. In unison the Mongol battle line notched their arrows and let them fly. The volley ripped into the army like a hurricane. Hundreds of riders and animals fell in an instant and in that same instant all semblance of order ceased completely.

A Persian lancer directly in front of Conrad had been killed by an arrow and in dying had shielded Conrad. Rashid was unhurt as well, but Conrad knew another volley would be coming within seconds and arrows were beginning to rain down from both flanks. The army was starting to collapse in on itself. The air was filled with the cries of dying, maimed, and panicked men and animals.

Conrad tried to keep a cool head. The battle was lost, in fact it was a disaster, and all he could hope for now was to save himself and Rashid and then get back to the baggage train where Elaine was waiting. He saw a small gap in the Mongol line, perhaps two hundred yards wide at most, at the hinge between the troops of the front line and those that were attacking the Khwarazmian right wing. It wasn't much of a chance, but it was better than nothing.

He looked for Rashid and for one horrible instant thought they'd become separated. But then he saw him, deftly guiding his horse through the panicked swirl of soldiers.

"*This way!*" Conrad called, then dug his spurs into his horse's side and rode for the gap, which was already beginning to narrow. Rashid was close behind him and a few others were trying the same thing. Most of the Mongols were concentrating on the main body of Khwarazmians, but some noticed the small band of fleeing riders and began shooting at them. The arrows came screaming past and a Persian a yard from Conrad dropped off his horse with a horrible cry. Conrad dug his spurs in harder. He felt a blow to his left shoulder and knew an arrow had found its mark. He reeled in the saddle but stayed aboard and kept riding.

Then he was through the gap, Rashid riding abreast of him along with a half dozen others. Another shower of arrows rained down and two more riders were hit but Conrad and Rashid were spared. Now the arrows were fewer and farther apart, and when they ceased altogether Conrad risked a look back. There was no pursuit and he reined his horse in a little to conserve its strength. They were off the plain now, in a series of foothills that provided a screen from the ongoing slaughter, the sounds of which they could still hear in the distance.

An arrow was in his shoulder and another embedded in his saddle close by his leg. Rashid was unhit, but two arrows protruded from his horse's left flank and blood was streaming from the wounds. Conrad and Rashid were both too tired to talk. By some miracle they were both alive but they knew their day's work still wasn't finished.

Keeping behind the cover of the hills, Conrad began to head south to where the Khwarazmian army had begun the day.

"Wait," Rashid said.

"We have to get back to the camp," said Conrad.

"First, the arrow," Rashid said, and Conrad, knowing he was right, reluctantly stopped his horse and dismounted. Rashid dismounted as well, took hold of the arrow, and shook it gently. Conrad winced but did not cry out.

"It didn't enter bone," Rashid said. "It might be better to pull it through."

"Go ahead," said Conrad.

Rashid broke off the back half of the arrow and tossed it aside, then took hold of the front half, sticking out of Conrad's upper arm just below the shoulder, and pulled. Conrad gave a muffled groan but the arrow came through cleanly and though the pain was sharp it did not go very deep. Rashid tore a strip off his shirt and quickly bandaged the wound.

"Let's go," said Conrad.

"My horse," said Rashid, and began examining the arrow wounds in the horse's side, gently probing to see how deep the heads had gone in.

"Rashid, we have to hurry," said Conrad. They had to get back to the baggage train, and Elaine, before the Mongols did—yet Rashid's horse badly needed tending.

"Go on," Rashid said. "I'll catch up."

There was a time when Conrad would have left at once—or left without even waiting for Rashid to suggest it—but after what they'd just been through together he found himself hesitating.

"It's all right," said Rashid. "Go."

"How will you find us?"

"We'll meet at the pyramid of skulls," said Rashid.

"The skulls," Conrad agreed, and urged his horse forward.

Conrad found the line of march the army had taken to the battle and followed it in reverse for two hours. He was relieved not to encounter any Mongols, but apart from a few wounded stragglers from the Khwarazmian army, he didn't encounter anyone else either, and he began to feel sense of foreboding. The feeling was justified, for when he reached the place where the baggage train had been he found nothing but a vast smoking ruin.

How was it possible? Could the Mongols have completed the destruction of the Khwarazmian army, found the baggage train and destroyed it, and then left without a trace all in the time it had taken Conrad to ride back here? No, more likely the Mongols had sent a separate detachment to raid the baggage train before the battle was even over, while the Khwarazmian army charged blindly forward, unaware of what was happening a few miles behind it.

While these thoughts flashed through his mind, he looked around frantically. *Where was Elaine?*

The Mongols had carried away everything of value, including, presumably, those human beings who might serve as slaves, and burned or killed everything and everyone else. The ground was littered with the charred remains of wagons and tents, as well as hundreds of corpses. He reached the spot where, as best as he could tell in the carnage, Anna's tent had stood. The tent had collapsed and was partly burned. A human foot protruded from one of its charred edges. Conrad groaned and slipped off his horse and, his heart pounding, pulled back the fabric of the tent. . . . Anna, or what remained of her, lay underneath. He stared at the mutilated body and he was filled with a renewed hatred of the Mongols. Anna had been a good woman and he prayed she might rest in peace. Still, he thanked God it wasn't Elaine. But where was she?

After that, he rode desperately back and forth over the whole area, holding his sleeve over his nose against the smell of charred flesh. It was impossible to tell for certain amid the rubble and human remains, but he didn't think Elaine was here. If she'd been killed he would have expected to find her at or near the site of Anna's tent.

Either she had been taken by the Mongols as a spoil of war—something Conrad couldn't even bear to think about—or she had managed to escape. He knew this was a forlorn hope but he pushed his weary horse into a canter, riding in widening circles around the remains of the camp, calling out Elaine's name. The sun dropped below the horizon and Conrad kept riding until well after dusk. The horse began to stumble and he reined the animal in and gave one last despairing cry: *"Elaine!"* But the word was swallowed up by the silence and the darkness.

He dismounted and unsaddled his horse and was overcome by such a powerful wave of fatigue that he just threw the horse's blanket on the ground and collapsed on top of it. Despite the pain in his shoulder and his worry about Elaine he was asleep almost at once.

When he awoke it was midmorning and the sun was already well up in the sky. His shoulder hurt like the devil, but at least the wound hadn't opened up during the night, and fortunately the horse was no Lucifer. He was grazing quietly a few yards away and stayed put when Conrad approached.

He rode back to the devastation that had been the baggage train. The stench of death was even stronger now as the bodies decayed and hundreds of vultures were settling down to the feast of a lifetime. Hyenas and wild dogs could already be seen on the periphery of the camp, and the horse shifted its hooves nervously. There was no point in waiting for Elaine to return to this hellish place.

He turned south, toward Torgreh, where he would join Rashid at the pyramid of skulls. The two of them together would decide what to do next.

◈ 28 ◈

Rashid waited uneasily. The proximity of the skulls made his skin crawl and he kept a healthy distance between himself and the pyramid. Adding to his discomfort was the fact that there wasn't a living creature to be seen, human or animal. The desolation wreaked by the Mongols was total.

When Conrad finally appeared on the road from the east, Rashid rode to meet him with a feeling of relief, tempered by the fact that Conrad was alone. As he came closer Rashid saw Conrad's expression and feared the worst.

"Is she dead?"

"No sign of her."

"Then maybe she's alive," Rashid said hopefully.

"If so, she's been taken by the Mongols," Conrad answered, with an involuntary glance at the pyramid of skulls. "God knows what they'll do to her."

"It's possible she escaped," said Rashid without much conviction.

"Perhaps she went west, back towards the mountains," Conrad said.

"I doubt it," said Rashid. "The land westward has been stripped clean by refugees." Conrad looked so miserable that Rashid added, "But I'll help you look for a day or two, if you like."

Conrad stared at him. "A day or two? Then what?"

"Then I need to find the Mongol camp. The Old Man's letter . . ." He stopped, for Conrad's stare had turned to a glare and his face was coloring.

"Sweet Jesus!" the Knight exploded. "After all this time you still care about nothing but the Old Man's letter!"

"I said, I'll help you for—"

"Never mind! I'll find Elaine myself. You can go to hell and take the Old Man's letter with you—it's where you're going to end up anyway!" He yanked his horse's reins sharply and began riding toward the west at a fast trot.

Rashid thought this profoundly unfair. He wanted to find Elaine, certainly, but he didn't want to be disloyal to the Old Man. He knew Hasan would have severely disapproved of the concession he was willing to make. Nevertheless, he urged his horse westward after Conrad, though remaining at a safe remove. After a half hour or so Conrad slowed his pace and Rashid allowed his horse to edge closer.

"Conrad . . ."

"Get away! I told you, you're not needed."

A few minutes later Rashid tried again. "I do care about finding Elaine," he said. "But if we don't find her in two days chances are she's with the Mongols. We'll find her and the letter at the same time."

Conrad just kept riding. But his horse gradually came to a stop and he sat motionless in the saddle, his head bowed. Rashid approached cautiously and was surprised to see tears in Conrad's eyes. The Knight brushed them away quickly. "I've no cause to be angry with you," Conrad said, in a shaky voice. "It's my fault, I should never have taken her to the baggage train."

"It seemed right," said Rashid. "I thought so as well."

"Do what you must," said Conrad. "Find the letter. I'll look for Elaine."

"I'll search westward with you for two days, as I promised. But I truly don't think there's much point."

Conrad raised his head and surveyed the vast, rugged wilderness they were riding into. Then he heaved a long, sad sigh. "I suppose you're right."

"As I said before, she may be with the Mongols. Then we can find her and the letter together."

"Even supposing that's true," Conrad said gloomily, "how do we get them back?"

"I don't know," Rashid admitted. "But we have to find them first."

Rashid was suddenly aware how natural it seemed to be using the word "we," as if, when all was said and done, there really was no question of the two of them going their separate ways. It was surprising how easily it had slipped off his tongue, and how quickly Conrad had replied in kind.

"All right," Conrad said. "Let's find the Mongols."

They turned their horses eastward, once more passing the hideous mound of gape-mouthed skulls and leaving it behind, hopefully for good.

They rode for hours, then made camp for the night. The land was barren of trees or even shrubs of any size, and building a fire seemed more trouble than it was worth. So after tending to the horses Rashid unpacked some stale bread and dried fruit and offered some to Conrad, who took it though he didn't feel very hungry.

"If anyone is at fault for all this, it's me," said Rashid. "We never should have joined the Shah's army in the first place."

"I was at fault as well. The army was so big, I didn't see how we could lose."

"Big, but badly trained," said Rashid.

"And badly led. We should have kept Elaine with us and stayed clear of the fighting."

"I still say you did what you should have done, taking her to the baggage train."

"I doubt she even stayed there," Conrad said, staring into the fire. "She probably went her own way as she always does. She's stubborn and headstrong and arrogant, and . . . everything a woman shouldn't be."

"You're angry with her," said Rashid.

"Do you blame me?"

"That means you're probably in love with her."

"That's ridiculous," Conrad snapped. "I have a duty to her as her betrothed, but love . . . why would you say such a foolish thing?"

"She gives you pain," said Rashid.

"And that means I love her?"

Rashid nodded. "Hasan says that women give pleasure until you love one, then they give pain."

Conrad opened his mouth to answer but nothing came out, for he wondered if the statement might actually be true. Finally he said, "Then why do men look for a woman to love?"

"I don't know," Rashid admitted. "Hasan says it is a great mystery."

After a moment Conrad said, "Have you ever loved?"

Rashid shook his head, but something in his expression caught Conrad's attention. "Desired, then," he said, and Rashid nodded slightly.

"In Paradise," Conrad said, and Rashid nodded again. Conrad was tempted to tell Rashid the truth about Paradise—Elaine wasn't around to interfere—but, despite his fatigue and his worry about Elaine, he was curious.

"What was she like?" he said.

"Very beautiful," Rashid said. "Her eyes . . ." He stopped, searching for words, but none seemed adequate. "She was very beautiful," he said helplessly.

"Did you take her?" Conrad asked.

"It wasn't permitted," Rashid answered. "That's for later, when I return."

Rashid had no more to say on the subject, and now was the perfect opportunity to disabuse him once and for all of the foolish notion that he had actually visited Paradise. But Conrad found that the urge to do so had faded. True, the visit was an illusion, but Conrad had begun to wonder if perhaps most men lived under illusions. The one he himself had lived under—his own invincibility—survived by a slender thread, or more precisely, by the exceedingly narrow space that had separated his lips from the foot of Khaled al-Zahir. Perhaps he should not be too eager to shatter another's illusions when his own were so fragile. Conrad was in no position to judge; he decided to hold his peace.

They rose at dawn, wolfed down a little food and a mouthful of water, and pushed on. Their plan was straightforward: find the battlefield, and from there follow the path of the Mongol army until they overtook it. After this, things were less clear. They would try to present themselves as emissaries from the Old Man, as Elaine had suggested before the battle, but how the Mongols would react to emissaries who bore no gifts or gold was an open question. It was, as the Old Man had said, in the hands of God.

At midday they came again to the site of the baggage train. The vultures and the hyenas had already done their work. The site was now a valley of bones to go along with the mountain of skulls back at Torgreh, and Conrad wondered again what manner of creatures the Mongols truly were. Then he remembered the battle and how several of them had fallen beneath his sword. Demons or not, they bled and screamed and died like men.

"Look!" said Rashid, pointing to a small dust cloud a quarter mile to the north, which they both watched until they were sure it had been caused by nothing more than the wind. Later Conrad looked sharply to the south as a sudden movement caught his eye, and they saw a wild dog loping wearily along, its tan coat almost a perfect match for the dry and dusty ground.

It had been so long since they'd seen another living human that the sight of a group of horsemen a mile in the distance almost came as a shock. Rashid and Conrad reined in their horses and watched as the group came closer.

"They're not Mongols," said Conrad.

"No," said Rashid.

"What, then?"

"The remains of the Khwarazmian army," Rashid suggested, and this seemed the most likely explanation. But as the horsemen approached, Conrad and Rashid exchanged a puzzled look. The riders, perhaps a dozen in number, looked like beggars, covered with dust and grime and dressed in little more than rags. A few had weapons but made no move to employ them as they approached.

When the group got within fifty paces they stopped and a lone rider came closer and said something in a language neither Conrad nor Rashid understood.

"Do you speak Arabic?" Rashid asked.

The man nodded and spoke again, his Arabic fluent: "We only wish to pass in peace."

"As do we," Rashid said.

"We would also buy food," said the man.

"We have none to spare," Rashid said.

The man stared at Rashid and Conrad for a moment, then wheeled his horse around and returned to his companions. Meanwhile Rashid translated the conversation for Conrad.

"They don't look like they have money," said Conrad.

"Yet he spoke very well, for a beggar," Rashid said, "and his Arabic was excellent."

Conrad looked at the horsemen, who were talking things over and casting frequent glances toward him and Rashid. Conrad's eyes narrowed. "I've seen some of these men before . . ." he said. The truth struck both of them at the same time.

"The Shah!" Rashid said.

And it was true. In the center of the group was the Khwarazmian Shah, disguised as a beggar. No wonder they hadn't recognized him! His magnificent robes and splendid crown, the aloof and condescending air, were gone, replaced not only by the guise of a beggar, but the fear and shame of one as well.

"Fleeing the Mongols," Rashid said.

"They won't flee from us," said Conrad, and he was right, for the horsemen began to approach and those that had swords—six horsemen in all—drew them. The lead rider brandished his weapon and rode toward Conrad. There was a blur and a sound like a melon being sliced and two holes appeared in the man's neck, one on each side. Blood gushed out in twin fountains and the man had just enough time to look surprised before all expression vanished from his eyes and he fell from the saddle.

It took Conrad another instant to realize what had happened—an arrow had passed cleanly through the man's throat—and that could mean only one thing: Mongols. All thought of fighting ceased and the combatants on both sides looked around wildly for the source of the arrow. A hundred yards away, twenty Mongols were galloping toward them on their sturdy ponies, closing the gap rapidly.

With cries of alarm the Shah and his remaining horsemen dug their spurs into the sides of their horses. The startled animals broke into a run as the Mongols, silent and still as statues in their saddles, surged after them.

Conrad and Rashid watched as the deadly chase unfolded. The Mongols ignored them—all but one, who glanced in their direction as he rode past, then plucked an arrow from his quiver and, still riding at a dead run, shot it straight up into the air. A strip of bright red cloth had been fastened to the arrow near the head, and as the arrow rose the cloth unfurled like a pennant, fluttering brilliantly against the powder-blue sky.

"What was that about?" Conrad said.

"I don't know," said Rashid.

"We're near the battlefield," said Conrad. "We should push on." They were about to do so when another party of Mongols made a sudden appearance, from the opposite direction as the first. This group was riding directly toward Conrad and Rashid, and Conrad realized the arrow had been a signal.

"Shall we ride?" said Rashid. They had only an instant to decide.

"No," said Conrad. "We've been trying to find them, now they've found us. Let's stand our ground."

"Then sheathe your sword," said Rashid, and put away his own knife. Conrad returned his sword to its scabbard and waited.

The Mongols rode up to within a few yards and formed two perfectly even ranks. They wore the same leather armor that Conrad had noticed in the battle. All carried bows and a quiver of arrows, and the front rank already had arrows in the ready position. Two of the Mongols rode slowly in a circle around Rashid and Conrad, examining them carefully front and back. Then one of them spoke.

To Conrad's ears the language was harsh, and of course unintelligible, far stranger than the Persian dialects he had heard spoken among the Khwarazmians. He could only shake his head and indicate, by gesture, that he could not understand. Rashid did the same. The Mongol quickly became impatient and snapped out an order. The front rank raised their bows and notched their arrows.

Rashid said in Arabic, "We are ambassadors, envoys, emissaries! We have business with the Great King!"

The Mongols did not look impressed. Conrad suddenly half remembered a term Gaspar the Persian had used to describe the Mongol King. He searched his memory desperately, then it came to him. "The Khan!" he said. "We have business with Genghis Khan!"

The words caused a stir. The leader spoke again and the front rank lowered their bows. Another order, and the horsemen wheeled as one and began moving northward at a fast trot. The leader gestured to Rashid and Conrad to follow, and they did.

At first the two men did not look at each other—they hardly dared breathe—but after a few minutes they exchanged a glance of relief, with a touch of triumph. They were among the Mongols and still alive and, they had reason to believe, on their way to see the Great King himself.

After which, Conrad fervently hoped, they would find Elaine, alive and well.

PART FIVE

THE CASPIAN SEA

◧ 29 ◨

Temujin, also known as Genghis Khan, a term translated variously as Great King, Universal Ruler, and Supreme Lord, was the most powerful man alive, and he knew it very well as he sat on his throne, receiving the homage of ambassadors from various parts of the newly conquered Khwarazmian Empire.

He was wealthy beyond imagining, possessed of eight wives and five hundred concubines, and was the absolute master of every city, village, farm, forest, man, woman, child, and beast that his eyes fell upon, yet he felt himself in danger of succumbing to the one enemy in life he truly feared.

Boredom.

It had been his curse since childhood, the dark side of the restless, prodigious energy that had driven him to unite the squabbling Mongol tribes and then conquer a domain that stretched from the Yellow Sea in the east to the Zagros Mountains in the west, an area of six million square miles, a number so large that few men even knew how to calculate it. His scholars had informed him that the world had never seen an empire to match it, and it was still growing.

Yet he was not really interested in conquest for its own sake, enjoyable as that was. His mission, which burned inside him like a hot coal, was to unite the entire world under his rule so that there would be order on earth instead of chaos. This was the will of heaven, as had been revealed to him in a vision that he had received years ago directly from the Spirit of the Eternal Blue Sky. In obedience to this vision he had authored a legal code that every person in his empire, rich or poor, was bound to obey; ordered his scribes to create a system of writing for the Mongol language so those laws could be recorded for all his subjects; and created a postal system of roads and pony stations, so that messages could be carried rapidly over enormous distances.

Of course, much fighting remained before the entire world submitted to him, but this too must be the will of the Eternal Blue Sky. Though Temujin had no regrets about the enormous slaughter his conquests had inflicted, he took no pleasure in it either. It was his destiny.

Evidently it was also his destiny to be bored.

Boredom was absent only during times of struggle. He had been a slave for a time when a young man and that had been soul-crushing but not boring because he had been ever alert for a chance to escape, which he had eventually done; battle wasn't boring, when it was kill or be killed and the bloodlust raged within him like a storm; and lying with his wives and concubines wasn't boring, either.

But there was only so much time a ruler could spend in bed or in battle, and when, as now, he was engaged in affairs of state, he could feel boredom poised at the edge of his mind like fog rolling into a meadow, and he had to force himself to pay attention to the task at hand.

An envoy from Tabriz begs the privilege of submitting to the mercy of the Great Khan in exchange for which he hopes the city will be spared the fate of Torgreh.

The Khan wishes to know how much the city of Tabriz is willing to pay in tribute.

The envoy begs to reply, One thousand gold coins.

The Khan demands, Double that amount.

The envoy looks alarmed, but the look is a little too practiced—an imitation of alarm rather than the real thing—and the Khan realizes he should have demanded more.

After this the Khan decreed harsher terms from the other cities whose envoys stood passively in line like sheep waiting to be fleeced. How right he was to annihilate any city that dared offer resistance! For every one he razed and decorated with a pile of skulls, ten more surrendered unconditionally, so that in the long run lives were saved—not only the lives of his Mongol soldiers, but the lives of peasants and tradesmen and merchants, all of whom would pay taxes to fund his future conquests, a cycle that would end only when the entire world lay at his feet.

But the diplomatic aspects of conquest, however necessary, were dull. He was about to call an end to the session when his eye fell upon two envoys who seemed different from the others. They were not bearded, middle-aged men with fine clothes and frightened eyes. They were very young, and plainly dressed, which the Khan approved of, and they made a rather odd pair: a dark-eyed Arab, tall and slender, and a European, nearly as tall but more heavily built. Suddenly the Khan recalled hearing them mentioned when his courtiers had briefed him earlier that morning. They came from beyond the mountains and he seemed to remember that one of them had, for a time, been a slave, as he himself had been. He also remembered something about a hundred gold coins. He decided to let the session continue a while longer.

Conrad and Rashid had spent two days in the Mongol camp and had been treated far better than they had any reason to expect. They were given their own tent, a small but comfortable structure made of felt, which the Mongols called a *ger*. They were fed twice a day, the meals consisting of a sort of stew with chunks of beef or lamb, followed by cheese and yogurt and accompanied by a drink the Mongols called *airag*, which was made from fermented mare's milk. Conrad's shoulder was sore, but mending well and in no need of attention.

They were not restrained, but neither were they permitted to stray more than a few yards away from their *ger*. Even so they caught enough glimpses of the encampment to see how organized and disciplined it was. In contrast to the haphazard jumble of the Khwarazmian camp, the Mongol camp was laid out like a town, with broad, straight roads running at right angles so that navigation was simple. The troops were organized in units of ten, and each of those units was part of a larger group of ten, and so on, with each group living, eating, and training together. Seeing this, Conrad realized how inevitable the result of the recent battle had been. The Shah's disorganized and undisciplined army had never stood a chance.

During the second day, two Mongol officers appeared outside the *ger* along with a translator. The translator, whose name was Bataar, was about forty and his hair was arranged in the distinctive fashion typical of Mongols: bald on top but long in back and braided into a scalplock; a large drooping mustache; and on the forehead a fringe of hair sprouting a short forelock that came to the bridge of the nose. The effect was an expression of perpetual rage, though Bataar was in fact quite mild mannered. He said, in passable Frankish, that the officers wanted to ask a few questions and he would translate. The "few questions" ended up taking most of the day.

"What are your names?"

"Conrad, Prince of Antioch, acting as envoy for the Regent of Tripoli, an ally of Antioch."

"Rashid, envoy for Sheikh ad-Din as-Sinan. We wish to see the Great Khan."

"What is the nature of your business with the Khan?"

"We are sworn to discuss that only with the Khan himself," Conrad said.

"This Antioch you speak of, it is far to the west?"

"Yes."

"How large is its army?"

"That's of no matter, for we come in peace," Conrad said.

So it continued, as Bataar alternated questions about the journey, which Conrad and Rashid answered forthrightly, with questions about military matters, which they evaded. One thing, of course, had to be concealed completely—that they had fought in the recent battle on the side of the Khwarazmians.

At times it was obvious that Bataar, or the officers he was translating for, knew more than they pretended to—for example, when Bataar remarked that the time taken to cross the Al-Jazirah seemed surprisingly long.

"You are familiar, then, with the Al-Jazirah?" said Conrad.

"Not as familiar as we would like to be one day," Bataar said.

Conrad felt a chill go down his spine as he remembered the pyramid of skulls, but he just said, "We were delayed. I was taken by an enemy who tried to enslave me, but he did not succeed."

"Then you are to be congratulated on your good fortune," said Bataar.

The session went on until Conrad and Rashid were exhausted, but they knew it was coming to an end when Bataar brought up the matter of tribute. "It is customary for envoys to bring gifts when they come before the Great Khan. Yet we do not see any gift or tribute."

"An unfortunate occurrence," said Conrad. "Our gift was stolen."

"That is extremely unfortunate," Bataar said. "What was the gift?"

"One hundred gold coins. They were stolen in the Zagros Mountains," Rashid said.

"A great pity," said Bataar, "but I will make the Khan aware of your request."

"There is one more thing," Conrad said. "We were traveling with a companion—my sister, called Elaine. We entered this region right after the battle and in the confusion she became separated from us. She may be here in the camp."

"The camp is very large," Bataar said.

"Nevertheless, will you make inquiries? There cannot be many Frankish women here."

"I will look into it," Bataar said, then nodded courteously and left the tent with the two officers. Conrad doubted his plea had made much of an impression.

Rashid and Conrad spent a sleepless night, thinking of all the things they should have said or would say if they were granted an audience with the Khan.

"We shouldn't have mentioned the gold coins," said Conrad.

"We had to. We're supposed to be envoys."

"Then we should have a better story than 'they were stolen.'"

"It's the truth."

"It makes us look foolish. Another thing—Bataar was asking military questions."

"You did a good job avoiding them."

"But what if the Khan asks? He might not be so easy to get around."

"I think we have to tell the truth."

"About our military situation?" Conrad was indignant.

"The Mongols have spies west of the Zagros. If we're caught lying it could be fatal."

"Then we should plead ignorance."

"Ignorant envoys? He won't take us seriously. . . ."

And so it went, with no clear resolution, and they became more pessimistic as the night wore on. When Bataar appeared in the morning they feared the worst. But he said, in a friendly tone at odds with his apparently fierce demeanor, "The Great Khan will meet with you within the hour."

They had been escorted through the camp and placed with a large crowd of other envoys, and now had ample time to observe the Great King at close range.

Though well into his fifties, the Khan was imposing, with a deep chest and powerful arms. His face was large and square and his skin smooth, for he had spent a lifetime masking his emotions. He sat with dignified stillness on the throne, yet underneath that stillness there seemed to be an almost volcanic energy ready to be released. A beard consisting of few long strands of dark hair hung like a wispy waterfall straight down from his chin, and he had intelligent and piercing eyes of green.

The Khan's court was a clearing in the center of the Mongol camp, his throne a wooden chair. He was dressed in the simple cloth trousers and robes worn by all the Mongols, and wore no crown or ornamentation of any kind. Rashid reflected on the contrast to the Shah of Khwarazm. The Shah, in silks and jewels, had looked like a monarch; in rags he had looked like a beggar. Rashid felt that Genghis Khan, however clothed, could never be mistaken for anything other than a king.

At last they found themselves near the front of the line. The envoy ahead of them made his plea, the Khan pronounced his decision, and the man bowed humbly and moved away. Now Rashid and Conrad stood directly in front of the throne. Bataar appeared next to them, ready to translate the Khan's words into Frankish and the responses back into Mongolian.

The Khan looked at the two men for a moment, then said, in a deep voice that was not unfriendly, "You come from west of the mountains."

"Yes, Your Majesty."

"Tell me of your country." His eyes fell on Rashid, indicating that he wished to hear from the Arab first.

"It is called the Eagle's Nest," said Rashid, "and is ruled by Sheikh ad-Din as-Sinan, a just and wise man in whose name I speak today, and his subjects are known as the Nizaris."

"I'm told they are also known as Assassins," said the Khan.

"They are called that by some," Rashid said.

"Do they carry out assassinations or not?" asked the Khan.

"At times."

"What times?"

"When there has been an offense against God," Rashid said. He felt that the discussion was taking an unfortunate turn, but there was little he could do about it.

The Khan turned his gaze on Conrad. "And you?"

"I am Prince of Antioch," Conrad said, "a great city on the shore of the Mediterranean Sea, and will someday be King there."

"Are you not Christian?"

"I am."

"And you, Muslim?" This to Rashid.

"Yes," said the Arab.

"Are not the Christians and Muslims at war?"

Conrad answered smoothly, "It is often so, but our mission here is of such importance that we have made peace with each other, even as we wish to make peace with Your Majesty."

The Khan nodded approvingly, for there were few things he detested more than religious conflict. For that reason he had decreed freedom of worship throughout his empire. He himself worshiped the Spirit of the Eternal Blue Sky—was it not obvious that God must be infinite and could dwell only in the infinite reaches of the sky?—but he had no interest in forcing others to believe as he did. Each man would find the truth or he would not, and would be dealt with as the Eternal Spirit saw fit.

"You were a slave for a time," he said to Conrad.

"For a time, yes." Conrad felt his face turn red. Even now, it was difficult to speak of.

"But you escaped?"

"Rashid purchased my freedom."

"You spoke to my men of a sister," the Khan said.

"Yes," said Conrad eagerly. He'd been wondering how to bring the subject up and was relieved that the Khan had saved him the trouble. "We became separated in the aftermath of the battle with the Khwarazmians. Is there any word of her?"

"Did you fight in the battle?"

"No, Your Majesty. As I said, we come in peace."

Before Conrad answered he had hesitated slightly, but not so slightly as to escape the notice of the Khan, who had a great ability to read men. The Khan's instincts told him that these two were warriors at heart, for their eyes were the eyes of men who had killed, and when there was a battle such men would naturally fight in it. He knew they had not fought for him, so they must have fought against him. All this he had surmised before they had spoken a word, and the Christian's hesitation had removed all doubt. The Khan was disappointed. He hated lying, especially lying born of cowardice. These two envoys were not very interesting after all.

"What is your mission?" he said briskly.

"There is an important letter," Rashid said quickly, sensing that the Khan's attention was starting to wander, "written by my master to the lord of Tripoli. We believe that this letter is in Your Majesty's hands—"

"Why important?" the Khan interrupted.

"It contains a discussion of sacred matters that can, according to our faith, only be read by the one it was intended for."

"How did it come to be in my camp?"

"A traveler from your army came west of the Zagros Mountains some time ago," Rashid said, careful not to use the word "spy." "It appears that he took the letter, no doubt by mistake, for it can be of no interest to anyone except my master and the man to whom it was written."

"So," said the Khan. "You wish to purchase the letter and were given one hundred gold coins for the purpose."

"Yes," said Rashid.

"But the coins were stolen."

"Yes, Your Majesty."

"What have you to offer in their stead?"

"The friendship of the Sheikh of the Eagle's Nest," said Rashid. When the answer was translated there was laughter among the Mongol courtiers.

"I have many friends," said the Khan. "What else?"

"I offer you my friendship as well," Conrad said. "I will one day be King not only of Antioch but Tripoli also. You will then have three allies west of the Zagros, should they ever be of use to you."

This provoked no laughter, though no one seemed particularly impressed either. The Khan preferred allies, but he knew very well how to deal with enemies, as the Khwarazmian Empire had just learned.

"I will consider it," he said. "And I will make inquiries about your sister, who became separated from you in the aftermath of the battle."

The Khan stood abruptly. Rashid and Conrad realized the audience was over and that they had failed, for it was obvious that he had little interest in the letter and less in Conrad's sister.

Conrad sensed what had gone wrong. It had been revealed in the Khan's tone as he said "your sister, who became separated from you in the aftermath of the battle." Even without translation Conrad caught the hint of sarcasm that means the same in any language: *I don't believe you.* He realized he was on the verge of never seeing Elaine again and fought down a feeling of panic. He had to think of something.

"That was a falsehood," he said loudly.

The Khan sat back down and frowned at Conrad as the remark was translated. Conrad went on, "She is not my sister but my betrothed. I called her my sister because in certain places that bond is more respected than that of husband and wife. Furthermore we did not become separated in the aftermath of the battle."

"How, then?" said the Khan.

Conrad took a breath. "Rashid and I fought with the Khwarazmian army. After the battle she had disappeared."

The Khan looked at Conrad for a long while, his expression hard. "You tell me to my face that you fought on the side of my enemies."

"Yes, Your Majesty," Conrad said.

"That you killed my soldiers," said the Khan.

"Yes, Your Majesty," said Conrad.

"That you would have tried to kill me had we met on the battle-field."

"That is a soldier's duty, Your Majesty."

"Then why did you lie?" said the Khan.

"We did not wish to give offense," Conrad said. "But it is a greater offense to lie to a king than to fight honorably against him, and so we now speak the truth." He was aware that the clearing had become extremely quiet.

The Khan's eyes narrowed slightly but he said nothing. He stood again and walked away, his aides scurrying after him. Bataar guided Rashid and Conrad back to their tent and left quickly. Conrad felt he'd taken a reckless gamble that had failed.

"I didn't know what else to do," he said.

"There's no blame," said Rashid. "We had nothing to lose."

"Except our lives," Conrad said drily, but Rashid just shrugged. As far as he was concerned, death was preferable to failure.

But at that moment Bataar fairly burst back into their tent. "The Great Khan is giving a banquet in three days' time," he said. "He has invited you both!"

The two men looked at each other in surprise and Bataar continued proudly, as if he were responsible for the sudden upturn in their fortunes: "It is an honor. You have found favor in the eyes of the Great Khan!"

· 30 ·

Three days later Conrad and Rashid were awakened early in the morning by Bataar, who gave them a breakfast of cheese and bread and then escorted them to their horses, which were waiting, groomed and saddled.

"Where are we going?" Conrad asked suspiciously.

"As I told you, to a banquet," Bataar said. "Come!"

Soon they had joined a group of a hundred riders, with more coming from every direction. The Khan himself was there, with a number of his generals and court officials. Among the other riders Conrad recognized a few envoys who had stood in line with him and Rashid three days before.

"You will ride with the other dignitaries to the banquet site," Bataar explained.

Conrad turned to Rashid. "Sit up straight, we're dignitaries now!" he said.

Rashid smiled. Both men were in a cautiously optimistic mood. They were hardly in the Khan's inner circle, but they had been included in the day's festivities and they dared imagine that the Old Man's letter would soon be in their grasp and that Elaine would be found as well—unharmed, they hoped, though they both knew this might be wishful thinking. But anything was better than uncertainty, and the sooner they learned the truth the better—tomorrow, perhaps, or today even, before the banquet. . . .

This hope faded as time passed and it began to seem that a long day's journey might lie ahead of them. "How far are we going?" Conrad asked, and Bataar confirmed his worst fears:

"We will be riding for most of the day."

"And the destination?"

"The Khan wishes to surprise his guests," Bataar said coyly, "so I dare not say. But it will be worth the trip."

In another hour, the dry rolling hills of the plateau began to give way to more mountainous country. As the road wound higher greener vegetation and more trees began to appear, and the terrain resembled that of the Zagros Mountains some miles to the west.

At noon the party stopped for another meal and to let the horses rest.

"This will be a wasted day," Rashid said.

Conrad nodded gloomily. "Maybe we should ask Bataar if he's heard anything about the letter, or Elaine."

"He'd have told us," said Rashid, but nevertheless asked Bataar if he had any news.

"Inquiries are being made," the translator said.

The assemblage remounted and started off again. The road narrowed as it followed the crest of the mountain and their progress was slow, but eventually the road broadened again and began to descend, and they broke through some trees onto a large promontory and Conrad saw a sight that took his breath away. At the foot of the mountain was a narrow plain and on the other side of that plain was an ocean—a vast expanse of rolling blue, sparkling and dancing in the sun from horizon to horizon. Rashid and Conrad were both struck by the same thought: in some bizarre way they must have come full circle to the Mediterranean; yet that was impossible, for the Mediterranean was hundreds of miles away to the west, far beyond the Zagros Mountains. Speechless, they turned to Bataar for an explanation.

"The largest lake known to man," he said with a smile.

"Lake!" Conrad said incredulously.

"Fed by many rivers but landlocked. So, yes, a lake, but some call it a sea because of its size."

"By what name?" Rashid asked.

"It's called the Caspian Sea," said Bataar. "And now we must move on, it's farther away than it looks."

The descent took another three hours, then they emerged from the mountains and onto a fertile plain a few miles wide; beyond that, just as the sun was setting, they reached the shore, a stretch of lovely white sand against which the blue waves lapped soothingly. They also saw something they hadn't noticed earlier: along the shoreline, partly in the water and partly on sand, lay long strips of something black and viscous.

"Tar?" said Conrad.

Bataar nodded and said, "Remarkable, isn't it?" and Conrad had to agree, for he had seen tar deposits before, but they were small and mostly underground, while these lay on the surface and stretched out for hundreds of yards.

"Some of it is quite thin," Bataar said. "It can be poured, like a liquid."

"What's it good for?" Conrad asked.

"Lighting lamps"—Bataar shrugged—"and one or two other things, as you'll see."

They continued along the coast, away from the tar, for another half mile until they came to a pavilion evidently intended to serve as a sort of banquet hall. It consisted of a round wooden platform, fifty feet across, raised two feet off the ground, and surrounded by poles on top of which a makeshift ceiling of cloth had been stretched, though a large opening remained in the center. On the platform were several long tables and benches for the Khan and his retinue, while dozens of additional tables had been placed on the beach around the platform for everyone else. Nearby, cattle and sheep and chickens were being roasted in sand pits and the pungent smell reminded Conrad and Rashid that they'd had only two light meals since they woke up that morning.

Smiling, Bataar said, "The banquet will begin soon, but first the Khan has prepared some entertainment." He nodded back down the beach, where a Mongol on horseback had just been handed a flaming torch. The rider spurred his pony down the beach toward the strands of tar and when he reached the edge of the nearest deposit he hurled his torch onto it, then wheeled around and galloped back up the beach.

The flames began instantly, first racing along the line of the tar, then, as the fire grew more intense, leaping higher and higher into the sky, mostly yellow but some white-hot. The light from the fire was so bright it was as if the setting sun had changed its mind and climbed back up over the horizon. Conrad and Rashid could feel warmth on their faces even though the fire was a half mile away.

Then, towering above the flames, huge billows of black smoke began to appear, fortunately carried out to sea by the wind, but adding to the awful majesty of the scene.

"How long will it burn?" Conrad asked.

"Months," said Bataar.

"This must be what hell is like," Rashid whispered, and Conrad, not normally given to religious gestures, crossed himself.

Nor was the Khan's entertainment finished. When the banquet guests had been given time to marvel at the fire, they noticed a procession approaching—a dozen men in chains, led by Mongol guards. Conrad and Rashid soon recognized the prisoners: the Khwarazmian Shah and his followers. The unfortunate captives were led to the platform and, one by one, forced to lie on the ground underneath it and chained hand and foot in that position. There were only a few inches between their chests and the bottom of the heavy wooden floor.

It was then that Conrad realized the floor had been suspended by a system of pulleys and ropes so that it would gradually descend as weight was placed on top of it.

The Khan stepped up onto the platform, followed by some three dozen of his closest advisers and officials, and the platform sagged visibly, pressing down on the Shah and his companions. Then the waiters came, bearing the heavy iron platters of food, and the wooden floor sagged even more, and it was obvious that it would sag more and more as the ropes stretched.

Conrad and Rashid looked at each other uneasily. They'd seen suffering and torture before, but nothing quite so elaborate as this.

"What's the point?" Conrad whispered.

"I don't know, but let's not ask," Rashid answered, and Conrad didn't argue. It seemed safer to avert their eyes and pretend it wasn't happening.

The rest of the banquet party found places at the tables surrounding the platform. Rashid and Conrad managed to secure seats not far from the Khan's location—perhaps he would glance down and remember who they were. Conrad watched the Great King, who seemed to be enjoying himself, and if he gave any thought to the men chained underneath the platform he gave no sign of it.

In fact the Khan was very much aware of the prisoners underneath the platform. He'd devoted considerable thought to them ever since the Shah had been captured five days ago. The Shah, however contemptible, was a king, and the Mongols had a strong tradition of respect for royalty, even that of other nations. Whenever possible they strove to avoid shedding royal blood. They also had a strong tradition that forbade torture. Slaughter was one thing, but the infliction of pain on helpless victims was beneath the dignity of warriors.

So, after due deliberation, the Khan had decided on suffocation, since no blood would be shed. He did not consider the arrangement to be torture, properly speaking, for under the weight of the heavy platform the Shah and his followers would likely survive no more than a few minutes. And if they did—well, the Khan had seen the remains of Mongol prisoners in the Khwarazmian camp after the battle. They had been subjected to every atrocity imaginable.

If the Shah lingered, let him spend his last few struggling breaths contemplating the fate of those prisoners.

Meanwhile the Khan was enjoying the tar fire, which he had heard described but never seen until now, and he also felt the evening's spectacle might have an edifying effect on the envoys and diplomats who had been invited to the banquet. The Eternal Blue Sky was above his head, his enemies were being crushed under his feet, and nearby burned the fires of hell. Let any man who might be tempted to resist the Great King observe and take heed.

The food was served and Conrad and Rashid, careful not to glance under the platform lest it ruin their appetite, ate heartily. The roasted meat was excellent, the *airag* flowed freely and was supplemented by wines and liquors from the various provinces of Khwarazm. The mood on the beach soon became very festive.

The Khan himself, Conrad observed, did not indulge in much *airag* and was certainly not drunk. But many Mongols drank freely, and this was especially true at an adjacent table with a dozen army officers who talked and laughed and sang ever more loudly as the night wore on.

One of them, shorter than average but with broad shoulders and a swagger made more pronounced by a slight limp, walked to another table to talk with someone and on the way back spilled some wine on a man sitting near Conrad. Instead of apologizing, the officer sneered at the man and made some joke that provoked laughter at the officers's table. The man, an older diplomat, pretended to be amused, though he was clearly humiliated. Conrad pursed his lips in disapproval. He himself had been prone to bullying when very young, but Charles had cured him of it. There was no honor in lording it over someone weaker.

"Who's that?" Conrad asked Bataar, nodding at the Mongol officer.

"Chormaghun," Bataar said. "A general." Seeing the expression on Conrad's face, he added, "He can be forgiven for celebrating as he is getting married soon."

"Married!" Conrad said. "To who?" It was of no real interest to him, it just seemed odd that a warrior, especially a general, could find the time to marry while campaigning in a foreign land.

"A captive he took a fancy to. A princess, they say."

Conrad sat bolt upright. "A princess? Captured when?"

Bataar realized what Conrad was thinking. "I'm sure it has nothing to do with the woman you're seeking," he said quickly.

"Find out when she was captured—and her name!" Conrad said.

"I don't—"

"Do it, or I will!" said Conrad. He wasn't sure how he'd carry out this threat since he didn't speak Mongolian, but Bataar was anxious to avoid trouble. He approached someone at the other table and exchanged a few words in Mongolian.

Rashid put a hand on Conrad's arm. "Be careful," he said.

Bataar came back and sat down slowly, with a frightened expression that spoke volumes. Rashid's grip tightened on Conrad's arm.

"Well?" said Conrad.

"I wasn't able to find anything out," Bataar said, averting his eyes. "They're all too drunk!"

Conrad jerked his arm free of Rashid's hand and grabbed Bataar by the throat. "Who's he marrying?"

"Please . . ." Bataar gasped, but Conrad shook him fiercely.

"Tell me!"

"A Frankish princess, captured after the battle, but . . ."

That was as far as he got before Conrad leaped to his feet. Rashid made a grab for Conrad but it was too late—he'd already stepped over to the General's table, dragging the hapless Bataar with him.

"What's her name?" Conrad said. "Ask him!"

Bataar asked. The General looked at Conrad coldly, but answered readily enough. His accent was thick but the name was unmistakable: "Elaine."

"That's my betrothed!" Conrad said. "Elaine. My betrothed! Tell him. *Tell him!* And ask him where she is!" A terrified Bataar managed to stammer out the words to Chormaghun, who gave a short contemptuous laugh and spat out a reply.

"He says she is his betrothed and she is in his camp, where she belongs."

"She's mine!" Conrad thundered. "She was promised to me long ago! Tell him!"

But no translation was needed because Chormaghun understood the gist perfectly well. He stood, leaned over the table toward Conrad, and snarled a few sentences in Mongolian.

"What did he say?"

"I really think it would be better if we—"

"What did he say?"

"He says he will marry her in two days and if you don't like it you can suck his—"

Conrad leaped across the table and knocked Chormaghun to the ground. They began fighting like enraged animals. They were both strong and angry and drunk and it took several men to separate them.

Mongols enjoyed a good fight and normally would not have interfered, but this was a diplomatic banquet and such behavior was highly disrespectful. When Conrad finally stopped struggling against the men who held him, he looked up to see Genghis Khan himself looming above him from the edge of the platform, his normally impassive face contorted with rage.

· 31 ·

Elaine, her disguise still shielding her from any unwanted attention, had continued following the supply wagons until she found
herself on a promontory above the battlefield, sheltered on both
sides by rocky terrain and protected from frontal assault by a
steep slope that led down to the plain where the main battle was
taking place. There was a loosely organized regiment of slingers,
several hundred strong, flanked on each side by regiments of archers. She had arrived just as the Khwarazmian army began its
charge, and a thrill went through her as she watched the stirring
spectacle. The drums and bugles, the fearsome war cries, the hundreds of colorful banners snapping in the breeze, the glint of sunlight from thousands of polished weapons, the reckless, headlong
charge of horses and camels, combined to create a breathtaking and
glorious scene.

A steady stream of arrows and stones was already pouring down
from the promontory onto the nearest part of the Mongol army,
while runners from the wagons kept the slingers and archers supplied with projectiles. Elaine took a pouch of stones from a runner
and found a position among the other slingers.

On the plain below, the two armies were about to collide. Elaine
looked for some sign of Conrad and Rashid, but it was impossible

to pick them out in the crush of horses and camels—the battle line stretched for nearly a mile across the plain.

She said a brief prayer for their safety, placed a stone in her sling, and let it fly. It disappeared into the blizzard of stones and arrows overhead and there was no way to tell what effect if any it might have had—a disappointment, for she wanted to see some Mongol skulls cracked by stones from her sling. She had never killed before, nor had any desire to, but the ghastly pyramid at Torgreh was still fresh in her mind.

As she took a second stone from the pouch, the two armies came together with a terrific crash of metal on metal and flesh on flesh. Within seconds the screams of wounded and dying men were added to the fearful tumult. For a moment Elaine stood aghast at the sight—men toppled from their mounts, limbs and heads hacked off and sent flying, spurts of bright red blood gushing everywhere. An involuntary groan of horror escaped her lips and any notion that war could be glorious vanished in that instant.

She took a step back—she had an urge to get away from this carnage as fast as her legs could carry her—but she forced herself to stand firm. The battle was being fought, Rashid and Conrad were in the thick of it, and she was determined to do her part however small. She took a deep breath and slung the second stone into the melee. After that she used up her remaining stones quickly, took another pouch from a runner, then another and another, until she lost count and her arm began to ache.

A great shout went up from the Khwarazmian army, echoed by the archers and slingers on the promontory. The enemy line had broken—the Mongols were fleeing and the Khwarazmians were in close pursuit! For an instant she thought she saw Conrad in the front line—of course he would be in front—brandishing his sword high above his head, but she couldn't be sure. No matter—the Mongols were in full retreat and she felt a wave of elation. Surely Rashid and Conrad would survive and rejoin her and together, somehow, they would find the Old Man's letter in the ruins of the Mongol camp.

When things went wrong it happened quickly. The Mongols stopped retreating and there seemed to be confusion in the Khwarazmian ranks. Elaine didn't completely understand what was happening but suddenly the Mongols seemed to be gaining the upper hand. She felt a stab of fear for Conrad and Rashid. She was starting to pray again for their safety when the man next to her screamed. She looked at him just in time to see an arrow bury itself in his chest so deeply that only the orange and black feathers remained visible. Then she looked around and gave a terrified scream of her own.

Strange-looking men on horseback were everywhere, thrusting with lance and sword and firing arrows at point-blank range. The promontory had seemed impregnable because of the slope in front and the rocky hills on the flanks, but somehow the Mongols had managed to maneuver their agile ponies around and through the rocks. A slaughter was under way. The archers and slingers didn't have time to use their weapons and most were too panicked to try. They fled in all directions, trampling each other in a frantic attempt to find safety, but there was none to be found, for more Mongols were appearing by the second.

Elaine didn't run so much as she was swept along in the press of desperate men, first in one direction, then in another. There were shouts in languages she didn't understand but she knew they were pleas for mercy. But the Mongols were merciless. A man near Elaine was stabbed by a spear and tumbled to the ground, taking her with him. As she tried to scramble to her feet her turban came undone. A moment later she was lifted up violently by her hair and thrown over the front of a horse. She screamed in pain and fear and struggled with all her strength until a blow to the back of her head turned everything dark.

A few minutes later she woke up in hell.

She was still draped over the front of a moving horse, held in place by an inhumanly strong grip, and surrounded by flames and smoke and death. It took her a moment to realize she was back in the baggage train where Conrad had taken her a few hours ago—or, rather, in the charred rubble that the Mongols had made of it. Shattered and burning tents and wagons were everywhere, along with corpses whose gaping wounds and sightless eyes seemed a reproach to anyone who had managed to still be alive. She'd barely taken this in when she was thrown to the ground as abruptly as she'd been lifted. She landed hard but sprang to her feet, ready to begin running again.

But there was no place to run. She was with dozens of other women, trapped in a pen whose walls were formed by mounted Mongols who taunted and leered at them. Elaine couldn't understand the words, but their meaning was plain enough. The women in the pen had one thing in common: they were young and at least passably attractive. The older and plainer women had been slaughtered with the men. Elaine realized that her turban coming off had revealed that she was a young woman and thus saved her life. Whether that was a good thing or a bad thing remained to be seen.

In the next few minutes more women were herded or dumped into the pen, while the sounds of looting and destruction gradually faded away. One Mongol, a general, perhaps, was maintaining order, ensuring that the spoils from the camp were arranged in an orderly fashion for later division. His men obeyed him for now, but Elaine knew he would soon turn them loose on the women. Elaine looked around for Anna—a familiar face, even one she barely knew, would provide at least some comfort—but Anna was nowhere to be seen.

A girl standing near Elaine suddenly panicked and tried to escape. She was stopped by one of the horsemen, who yanked her up across his saddle and began to rip off her dress as the other Mongols laughed. The girl appeared even younger than Elaine, but she had courage, for she bit the Mongol's arm as hard as she could. The soldier yelped in pain and knocked the girl to the ground with his fist. Then he got off his horse and unbuckled his belt and began to beat her with it as his comrades cheered.

Elaine suddenly realized her sling was still clutched tightly in her hand—she hadn't let go even when she'd been knocked unconscious. Elaine's hatred of the Mongols and her pity for the girl overrode her fear. She found a stone and seated it in the pouch. *Step, swing, throw, release.* The stone flew straight and true and struck the Mongol squarely in the forehead. He went down in a heap and lay motionless on the ground.

There was a sudden silence. The Mongol General began riding toward Elaine and she suddenly felt that a quick death would be preferable to the looming alternative. She found another stone and loaded the sling and let fly, but the General was either very agile or very lucky, for he jerked his head to one side just in time and the stone flew by harmlessly. Before Elaine could reach for another stone, several soldiers dismounted and threw her to the ground and began tearing at her clothes. Then the General said something in a loud voice and the attacking soldiers released her.

The General dismounted and walked toward her. He was bowlegged and walked with a limp. A thin trickle of blood on his cheek showed that the stone hadn't missed completely after all. He ignored the blood and stood over Elaine, studying her with what almost seemed to be a glint of admiration in his eyes. After a long moment he snapped out another order and the soldiers pulled Elaine to her feet and began leading her away. Behind her she could hear the screams of the other women as the soldiers began to claim their reward for the victory.

It was several hours before General Chormaghun returned to the Mongol camp. He had given his men ample time to pillage the baggage train and slake their lust on the captive women and carry off such booty and slaves as might please them. For himself, he had claimed a twentieth part of any gold found in the camp, which was his right as a general, and, of course, the woman with the sling. She should already be here in the camp waiting for him, a thought that pleased him very much.

A group of fellow officers was gathered nearby, celebrating the victory. Chormaghun joined them for the sake of protocol but left quickly, knowing he wasn't popular and never would be. For one thing, though he was Mongolian in appearance he was not full-blooded, being a quarter Turkic on his mother's side. For another, except for his unusually broad shoulders he was physically unimpressive, below average in height and with a face that had never been called handsome. And then there was his limp, the result of a fall from a horse when a young boy.

Fortunately, in the army of Genghis Khan birth and appearance were of little import. What mattered were courage, skill, and ambition and Chormaghun had those in abundance, especially ambition. There were many like himself, undistinguished by background or appearance, who had succeeded on merit, but very few who had attained general rank by the age of thirty as he had done. If he was a little arrogant, he had a right to be.

He entered his tent, bigger than those of his subordinates but not overly so, for the Khan discouraged ostentation. There was a small table and chair, and several wooden chests, some holding weapons or clothing and some containing booty Chormaghun had accumulated during the current campaign. He removed his armor and drank a little *airag* from a jug and sat down for a moment to rest.

He thought again of the woman. He had seen very few Franks in his life and her eyes, hair, and complexion struck him as exotic. Not beautiful, exactly, but desirable—all the more so because of her fighting spirit. Mongol women were strong and fearless, but this Frankish woman was like a warrior! She had nearly killed one of his officers, and him as well, and the thought aroused him. Maybe she was a common whore—she had been in the baggage train, after all—but something about her was different. He wanted to find out what that something was.

Elaine had been treated well enough since her capture. To replace her torn clothes she'd been given Mongol garb—a loose blouse and trousers, and a sort of jacket to wear over them—and she'd also been given a decent enough meal of stew and yogurt.

She was attended by two sturdy Mongol women who treated her respectfully but were clearly under orders not to let her leave the tent. They spoke no Frankish, responding to her questions with shrugs or blank-faced indifference.

She knew she'd been extremely fortunate so far, but she wasn't sure why and she worried that things might change at any moment. She was also deeply troubled about Conrad and Rashid. She tried to convince herself that they could have found a way to survive the disaster, but in her heart she feared they hadn't, for she'd seen too much of the way of the Mongols to deceive herself.

The tent opened and the General from the camp entered. The two Mongol women bowed and stepped back, but Elaine raised her chin a little and looked him straight in the eye. However afraid she might feel, this was no time to show it.

The man pointed to himself and said, "Chormaghun."

She nodded and said, "Elaine."

He repeated the name once and she nodded again and then he said something to the two women. They hurried out of the tent, and another woman entered. She was slender and young, only a little older than Elaine, and she said in quite good Frankish, "I am Noyon. I will interpret."

"Good," said Elaine. "Ask him if I am a prisoner."

"General Chormaghun will ask questions first," said Noyon. The rest of the conversation took place through the translations of Noyon.

"Where do you come from?" Chormaghun began.

"A place called Tripoli." She'd expected a blank look, but Chormaghun's eyebrows went up as if he'd heard the name before. "You know of it?" said Elaine.

"We know it. Beyond the Zagros, by the Mediterranean Sea."

"Yes. I am a princess there."

"A princess!" He laughed.

"Yes. A princess," Elaine said in a way that seemed to impress him, though she wasn't sure he really believed it.

"Then why are you in Khwarazm?"

"I came here with my brother and a servant, as envoys to the Khan. I demand an audience as soon as possible."

Chormaghun smiled to himself. A captive who made demands! Truly, an unusual woman. He said, "Where are they now—your brother and servant?"

"I—" For the first time Elaine faltered. Suddenly her eyes were moist and she was unable to continue.

Chormaghun guessed the truth. "They were killed in the battle," he said.

"I don't know," said Elaine. "Maybe they survived."

"That is highly unlikely," Chormaghun said flatly. "And if they were envoys, as you claim, why did they fight against the Khan?"

Elaine had no answer for this—in fact there was no answer. She'd fallen into a trap of her own making. She drew herself up and said with firmness and dignity, "Whatever the fate of my brother and servant, I am Princess Elaine of Tripoli, and I demand to be treated as a princess!"

Chormaghun should have found this amusing but somehow he didn't. The woman was either deluded or a skilled impostor or . . . Surely she couldn't be telling the truth?

"Where did you learn to use the sling?" he asked.

"A warrior taught me."

"Not your husband?"

"I have no husband."

Chormaghun looked at her for a long time. He saw she was not quite as fearless as she pretended, for her bosom rose and fell more than it should if she were truly calm. He reached out and placed his hand on her breast. She knocked it away angrily. He slapped her across the face—the motion was almost casual, but quick and powerful, and it sent her sprawling to the ground. She stared at him, shocked, then her shock turned to anger as she got quickly back to her feet.

"*How dare you!*" she said. "Tell him he's a coward! And tell him not to touch me again, I am Princess of Tripoli!"

Noyon licked her lips nervously, trying to decide how much of this to translate, but Chormaghun held up his hand and she remained silent. He stared at Elaine thoughtfully for a long moment, then turned and left the tent. Elaine turned to Noyon, who was looking at her without a trace of sympathy. If anything, she seemed envious. "You are fortunate," the translator said.

"Fortunate!" Elaine sputtered. "Fortunate . . . !"

"Yes, fortunate. Fortunate that you're a princess, if you truly are one, for we Mongols have great respect for royalty. But God help you if he thinks you're lying." Then she too left the tent.

Elaine watched her go, still angry but aware that, bad as this had been, it could have been far worse. She wanted to call Noyon back and demand a fuller explanation of what exactly was going on, but she was too proud. Besides, she wasn't sure she really wanted to know.

As a general, Chormaghun had access to all the information possessed by the Mongol army, and the Mongol army gathered a great deal of information. Dozens of scouts and spies had ventured west of the Zagros during the past year and he ordered his aides to question all of them. Meanwhile, he sat in his tent and thought.

He had met many women in his life, but none quite like this Elaine. Judging by the way she carried herself, he didn't believe she was a peasant or a commoner. Her reason for being in Khwarazm was still unclear to him, but if she had no husband and her brother and her servant were dead—and Chormaghun knew that virtually no enemy soldiers had survived the battle—then she was without a protector. Men and women of noble birth were a breed apart and must be treated with care. The proprieties had to be observed. The Khan insisted on it, and on the whole Chormaghun agreed with him. An idea began to take shape in his mind, but he wanted to be sure of his ground before proceeding.

The next day his aides reported back. The scouts had confirmed that Tripoli had a princess named Elaine, and, while it couldn't be said with absolutely certainty, there were rumors that this princess had mysteriously vanished some eight or ten weeks before, perhaps in the company of a prince and also, possibly, an Arab. For some reason they had all run away together and their current whereabouts were unknown.

Chormaghun dismissed his aides and thought some more. It now seemed quite likely that, against all odds, the girl he had captured was indeed Princess Elaine of Tripoli, just as she claimed. The idea that had crossed his mind now came into sharp focus, and he did something that was very rare for him. He allowed himself to smile.

32

Night fell but Elaine was wide-awake, her mind churning. She badly needed a plan, but the situation was too uncertain and no plan came to mind. She should have been more friendly toward Noyon, tried to find out more about Chormaghun, or at the very least persuaded the translator to make inquiries about Conrad and Rashid.

Whether she'd actually seen it or only imagined it, the sight of Conrad brandishing his sword while leading the Khwarazmian charge was burned into her mind, and it seemed impossible that she might never see him, or Rashid, again. If the Mongols really respected royalty as Noyon had claimed, perhaps they'd taken Conrad prisoner . . . but given the chaos that prevailed on the battlefield, how would they even know he was a prince?

She remembered the trouble he'd taken before the battle to ensure her safety, despite the danger he himself would soon be facing. And she hadn't even wished him luck before he rode away! He wasn't perfect, certainly, but he was a courageous man and, despite his faults, a good one. His loss would not be an easy thing to forget.

Elaine must have drifted off eventually because she awoke just after dawn with a start as she realized someone was entering the tent. It was Noyon, whose expression managed to convey excitement and annoyance at the same time.

"I have news," the translator said. "General Chormaghun now believes that you are indeed Princess of Tripoli."

Elaine wanted to weep with relief. "Thank God. And thank you, if you helped convince him."

This was an attempt to flatter Noyon, which proved partly successful. "I did nothing but translate," Noyon said, but her manner softened.

"I was wondering," said Elaine, "if you could find a way to make inquiries about my brother and my servant. I mentioned them yesterday. . . ."

"Yes, I remember."

"Perhaps they've been taken prisoner."

"The army doesn't usually take prisoners."

Elaine swallowed a sudden lump in her throat. "I know. But if you could ask . . ."

"I'll see what I can do."

"Thank you. Now, you say the General believes me?"

"Yes."

"When do you think I can start back?"

Noyon stared at her blankly. "Back?"

"Home, to Tripoli."

"You will not go back. You will stay here."

"What do you mean, stay here?"

"You are the most fortunate of women!"

"I don't know what you—"

"General Chormaghun intends to marry you!"

At first the words didn't seem to make sense—Elaine couldn't comprehend them. When she did, she had a wild impulse to laugh, but when she opened her mouth all that came out was something between a gasp and a sob. After a moment she managed, "You can't be serious!"

"He's a general in the army of the Great Khan," Noyon said. "It is an honor to be his wife."

"I can't marry him—it's impossible!"

"You can and you will."

"I'll die first!"

"He could give you as a plaything to the entire army. Would you prefer that?"

"He can't force me to marry him. He can't!" Elaine said, clenching her fists, but the words sounded hollow even to her own ears.

"You are alone and far from home and you are a prize of war," Noyon said, folding her arms. "I told you, you are most fortunate. Do you not see that?"

"I tell you, I'll kill myself first. I swear it."

Noyon shook her head in exasperation. She called out in Mongolian and a moment later the two female guardians came into the tent. Noyon spoke again and the women began searching the tent, occasionally pausing to collect something. Elaine realized they were confiscating anything she might use to kill herself. There wasn't much—a mirror, one or two sharp stones that had found their way inside. They also picked up the plate from last night's dinner and the knife that had been provided with it. Finally, they took Elaine's sling, but, after examining it for a moment, decided to leave the comb.

Elaine gathered herself and said with every ounce of dignity she had left, "I'm a princess of Tripoli and I have a right to return to my homeland. I meant what I said about killing myself. Somehow I'll find a way. Tell Chormaghun. Tell him!"

"You're behaving like a fool and you are offering a great insult to the General. Continue and you'll end up in the brothels with the other captured women, princess or no princess. Do you know what life is like for them? Being the wife of a Mongol general will be quite pleasant, once you learn to behave. You will have all you need and be treated with respect. As for Tripoli, put it out of your mind. You will never see Tripoli again."

After Noyon and the guards had gone, the hours dragged by slowly. Another meal was brought, this time without a knife.

Elaine ignored the food and drank sparingly of the water. The idea of becoming Chormaghun's wife was so repulsive that she couldn't bear it. And suppose he decided to come to her before they were married—this very night, for example? How would she defend herself?

But day turned into night again, and it seemed unlikely that Chormaghun would come. Yet this brought little comfort because Noyon's parting words lingered like a curse. *You will never see Tripoli again.*

How long had it been since she'd left the shelter of her castle? Nine weeks? Ten? She couldn't remember exactly. During that time she'd given little thought to Tripoli, but it had always been there, a backdrop to whatever else her mind was occupied with. It had never occurred to her that she might not see it again and the thought made her heart throb with pain. She remembered vividly the ocean breeze, the scent of orange blossoms, the way the Mediterranean sparkled in the sunshine, the sounds and pungent odor from the stables, the calm wisdom of Walter, the laughter of Matilda and her other ladies-in-waiting . . . was all that truly lost? Was she fated to spend the rest of her life as the wife of a barbarian she despised, in a culture and a country utterly alien to her?

Escape was impossible, and she wasn't sure she had the will to kill herself. She tried to imagine holding a knife to her breast—assuming she could get her hands on a knife—and pushing the point in far enough to reach her heart. Perhaps if she were truly desperate . . . perhaps not even then. Not to mention the fact that suicide was the ultimate sin—a direct path, if the priests were right, to eternal damnation. But to live as Chormaghun's wife, to suffer his attentions on their wedding night, and every night, as often as he chose . . .

Tears tried to come but she wouldn't let them. It was time to face unpleasant truths and she felt one coming, one that hadn't crossed her mind before but certainly should have. The thought of life without Tripoli was agonizing enough, but what of Tripoli without her? Who would rule the kingdom if she never returned? Not that she had done much ruling—Bernard, as Regent, had ruled in her name during her minority—but what would transpire in her absence? Bernard had no royal blood, and Elaine knew what happened when a country was left without a legitimate ruler—infighting and quite likely civil war, until someone, usually the most ruthless, emerged victorious.

All at once everything seemed upside down. Leaving Tripoli had not been courageous but reckless and selfish. True courage would have been to remain and carry out her duty—yes, duty, that word she so despised—to her country and her people, despite the threat of assassination and the pending marriage to Conrad. Instead she had deserted her kingdom and, so far as she could see, there was no way to set things right.

And that wasn't all. Conrad and Rashid might be dead—she stopped, again forcing herself to face the truth: they were dead, period. And she had as good as killed them by her insistence on meeting the Old Man. So not only Tripoli, but Antioch as well, was without a legitimate ruler—or would be, when Conrad's father, known to be in poor health, passed away.

Even this wasn't the worst of it. What had Chormaghun said when she'd mentioned Tripoli? *We know of it.* She recalled the expression on his face, smug and arrogant, as if the fate of Tripoli had already been decided. And indeed, once the Mongols had consolidated their conquest of Khwarazm, what would stop them from crossing the Zagros? They must already be planning the invasion—hence the presence of scouts and spies. Tripoli and Antioch had no idea of the danger that faced them—and with Elaine a prisoner, who would warn them? She had a sudden vision of a pyramid of skulls outside the ruined walls of Tripoli and she uttered a cry of despair. She had destroyed not only her own future and Conrad's, but very possibly the future of the last two Christian kingdoms in the Holy Land.

She was far from tears by this time. Her regret was much too bitter for that. Her own fate, dismal as it was, paled by comparison. She could never forgive herself for the damage she'd done. She wondered if she could be forgiven by God. Apart from a few fleeting moments during the recent battle she hadn't prayed once, not even for the souls of her parents, since the skulls outside Torgreh. Perhaps it was too late to start again now. Yet what else was there to do?

She knelt and closed her eyes. At first nothing came; she felt she wasn't worthy of forgiveness. So she prayed instead for the souls of Rashid and Conrad, and she prayed that the evil she foresaw for Tripoli and Antioch might by some miracle not come to pass. And then she asked that, whatever her own fate might be, she would find the strength to bear it.

Noyon had informed Chormaghun of Elaine's threat to kill herself, but he wasn't much troubled by it. She was emotionally volatile, as young girls tend to be, and she would be a woman soon enough. He would see to that personally, but not until after they were married. She was a princess and he would treat her as a princess should be treated.

The more he thought about his plan to make Elaine his wife, the better he liked it. She was young and strong and no doubt would be a pleasure to couple with. More important, what better wife could an ambitious general have than a princess? Not a Mongolian princess, true, but royalty nonetheless. Of course she wouldn't be his first wife; in fact, she would be his fourth. The other three were from good families, but they were not royalty. It was a happy thought—he would be so grand that his *fourth wife* would be a princess! It would elevate the status of his other wives, and his own status as well. Let the other generals consider that next time they were tempted to scoff at his stature or his limp! In addition to the political advantages, she would probably bear him many children, and if she did not, divorce was not difficult, especially if the wife was a foreigner. He had already instructed his servants to make plans for the wedding ceremony.

It would have to wait a few days, however, for the Khan was

planning a great feast and Chormaghun was in charge of security, ensuring the safety of all guests, Mongol and foreign alike. There was much to be done. It was to be a complicated affair, with hundreds of guests and a full day's travel on horseback, for the feast would take place on the shore of an enormous lake called the Caspian Sea.

◈ 33 ◈

The Khan fixed his ferocious glare on Conrad and, through Bataar, demanded an explanation for the attack on Chormaghun.

"What is the meaning of this?" he thundered in Mongolian. Bataar translated it into Frankish in a quavering voice that was comical by comparison, but nobody laughed. Conrad knew his life was at stake, as well as Elaine's future, so he spoke in simple words that were unlikely to be mistranslated.

"Your Majesty may remember that I spoke of a woman who was my betrothed and who I believed might be in your camp. This man has stolen her from me."

"He lies!" said Chormaghun. "I took the woman captive in battle and she belongs to me."

"She is mine," Conrad insisted.

"Then why were you not there to protect her?" sneered Chormaghun.

"Because I was fighting in the front lines while you were attacking women!" Conrad said. This provoked a burst of laughter when it was translated and Chormaghun had to be restrained from renewing the fight.

The Khan pretended to cough in order to hide his own smile.

He could not insult his General by showing amusement, but the Knight's answer had been a good one.

Chormaghun said, "This man has attacked a general of the Mongol army. He should be put to death at once."

This received murmurs of agreement but Conrad replied quickly, "I am an envoy from a country which is at peace with the Great King; to execute me would be contrary to your own laws." To some extent this silenced the murmurs.

The Khan did not reply, for both arguments were sound. Furthermore, his instincts told him that both men had spoken the truth, as they saw it, so there was no clear right or wrong concerning the woman. The Khan remained still as a stone and gradually the assembly fell silent, waiting to see how he would resolve this thorny problem.

On the one hand, Chormaghun, though prickly and unpopular, was a superb battlefield commander and the Khan did not want to humiliate him by siding with a foreigner. Moreover, the conventions of warfare dictated that the victor could claim the spoils of battle, including, or especially, any woman who caught his eye.

All that spoke for Chormaghun.

Yet the Khan could not deny a soft spot for the Frankish Knight who had once been enslaved, and who had the courage to admit fighting on the side of the Khwarazmians. And there was another reason why the Khan sympathized with Conrad, a reason wellknown among the Mongols but rarely spoken of. When he was a young man and just beginning his rise to power, the Khan had fallen passionately in love with a fiery beauty named Borte. He had married her and was taking her back to his own territory when they were set upon by a rival tribe that had taken Borte captive. The Khan had survived the attack, but it had been weeks before he'd been able to organize a raiding party of his own to recapture his bride, and during that time, as she had tearfully admitted, Borte had been raped by the rival chieftain.

The Khan had bedded her, too, on their wedding night before she'd been abducted. But, when a child was born shortly after her recapture, it was impossible to tell whether or not the boy was his. Nevertheless he had raised the child as his own and had given him a high position just as he had done for his other sons. And he had never spoken a word of reproach to Borte, for what had happened was no fault of hers.

So it was hard not to sympathize with the Frankish Knight, who, like the Khan himself, had once been enslaved and also had his woman stolen from him. On the other hand, Chormaghun was a Mongol general, and under Mongol law an attack on him was a capital offense.

The Khan became aware of the expectant faces all around him. For a time, silence could pass for wise deliberation, but at some point it would be revealed as indecision and he could feel that point approaching. He opened his mouth to see what words the Eternal Spirit would give him when much to his surprise someone else spoke instead.

It was the Frankish Knight's Arab companion. The Khan was so curious that he forgot to be angry at the interruption, and looked to a translator to find out what the Arab had said.

"They are warriors. Let them fight like warriors."

These words were greeted by a collective murmur of approval. Chormaghun's expression showed that he was eager to comply, and once the suggestion had been translated into Frankish, it was clear that Conrad felt the same. But the Khan shook his head "no" and the murmurs ceased at once. The Knight was no doubt a good swordsman and the Khan did not want to lose a general unnecessarily. He said, "Let them wrestle."

Immediately heads nodded and smiles appeared as men perceived the Khan's wisdom.

The Mongols had, from time immemorial, recognized Three Manly Skills—archery, horsemanship, and wrestling. Of these, wrestling was the most important. It was also the only one at which a non-Mongol might stand any chance of winning and therefore it was the fairest way to settle a dispute such as the present one. The Khan went on to impose certain conditions. Should the Frankish

Knight win the match, the woman would be given to him and they would be free to go. Should Chormaghun win, he would retain the woman . . . and the Knight would be executed, for he had attacked a Mongol general and that could not be completely overlooked.

It was a good solution and the Khan thanked the Eternal Blue Sky for putting the crude idea into the mind of the Arab so that it could be perfected by the Khan himself. He was already looking forward to the match.

"What have you found out?" asked Conrad.

Rashid, who had just returned to the tent, had been mingling with soldiers and camp followers, some of whom spoke Arabic, in the hope of learning a few things that might prove useful to Conrad.

"The rules are probably different than you're used to," Rashid said. "For one thing, you may not touch your opponent below the waist."

Conrad groaned. Some of his best throws involved gripping his opponent's knee or ankle. "Go on," he said.

"No biting," said Rashid.

"Go on."

"That's all," said Rashid.

"That's all?" Conrad said. "No biting, no hand below the waist, those are the only rules?"

"Apparently so."

"Eye gouging and knees to the groin are permitted?"

"Frowned upon, but permitted."

"What about scoring?" Conrad said.

"If any part of the body besides foot and hand touches the ground, it's a point for the opponent. Three points wins. One more thing. Chormaghun is a very good wrestler."

This was no surprise, for Chormaghun looked like a wrestler. Conrad himself was considered above average among his fellow knights—his tremendous strength guaranteed that much—but he was lacking in technique, for he spent most of his time with the sword.

"How's your shoulder?" Rashid asked.

Conrad flexed his arm a couple of times. "It's all right," he said.

The tent door opened and Bataar entered.

"I may have news," he said, "about the letter you seek."

Rashid jumped to his feet eagerly. Bataar continued, "The spoils of victory are distributed carefully and are easy to keep track of. This letter is a different matter if, as you claim, it was taken on the far side of the Zagros by one of our scouts."

"Different how?" said Rashid.

"All such items are remanded to the custody of the officer in charge of reconnaissance activities," Bataar intoned. "They will be translated by our scholars when we return—"

"Bataar, please come to the point! Where is the letter?"

"As I say, if we have it, then it is in the possession of the officer in charge of—"

"Yes, I understand! Who's the officer? Can we meet him?"

"You have already met him," said Bataar unhappily. "It is General Chormaghun."

This was followed by a long silence.

"Where is the letter?" Rashid asked finally.

"Most likely in the General's tent with other documents. But given the current circumstances, he will never grant either of you access and the Khan is unlikely to force him to do so." After a moment he added, "I am sorry to bring such distressing news," and then he left.

"So Chormaghun has Elaine and the letter, too," said Conrad, shaking his head. "We've had nothing but bad luck since we entered Mongol territory."

"We've had some good luck, too," said Rashid.

"Really? Like what?"

"We're alive. And so is Elaine. And at least we know where the letter is now."

"I suppose so," Conrad conceded. "But—"

"And maybe we can turn this latest piece of bad luck into good luck." Conrad gave him a quizzical look and Rashid continued, "They're building some sort of arena specially for the match. There will be many spectators. I think it will be a great distraction. . . ."

Conrad frowned. "You're not thinking of trying to sneak into Chormaghun's tent?"

"This will be my best chance—probably my only chance. The camp will be deserted or nearly so because of the match. But it means I won't be with you in the arena."

Conrad's reaction was immediate. "Once the match starts you could do nothing for me anyway. But be careful."

"I will," said Rashid. "After you defeat Chormaghun, you will have Elaine and I will have the letter and the three of us will meet back here and leave together."

Conrad smiled at the vote of confidence. "And if I lose?"

"You won't."

Conrad put his hand on Rashid's shoulder. "If you find the letter, leave as quickly as you can just to be safe. If I win, we'll catch up with you. If I lose, it won't matter anyway."

"God be with you," said Rashid.

"And you," Conrad said.

They did not ask, or even wonder, *Whose God?* as they lay down in the tent. They stared into the darkness, neither able to sleep but each taking comfort from the silent, steady presence of the other.

By the time Conrad awoke it was late morning, as he could see through the slits in the tent door. He relieved himself in the chamber pot and was beginning to wonder where Rashid was when the Arab came through the door with a plate of food.

"Good, you're up," said Rashid. "Eat this."

"I'm not hungry," said Conrad.

"Eat anyway, for strength."

Conrad took a piece of meat and forced himself to begin chewing.

"It's just as I thought," Rashid said. "Everyone is talking about the match. All eyes will be on it."

"You'll still need to be careful," said Conrad. "Don't get overconfident."

"I won't," said Rashid. "Eat some more."

"Yes, Mother," Conrad said.

"You'll thank me if the match is a long one," said Rashid.

"I plan to make it rather short."

"Don't you get overconfident, either."

They bantered in this vein for a time, to calm their nerves. A quarter hour before midday Bataar stepped inside the tent and said, "It's time."

The level of excitement struck Conrad like a blow when he stepped outside the tent. A great crowd of Mongols streaming toward the arena parted just enough to let Bataar, Conrad, and Rashid pass through. There was much shouting, mostly hostile, but Conrad was surprised to find that some of the shouting seemed aimed at encouraging him.

"Some of them must hate Chormaghun as much as you do," Rashid said.

"I doubt that," said Conrad.

A few moments later Rashid gripped Conrad's arm briefly in a gesture of farewell, then allowed himself to be absorbed into the crowd and Conrad continued on with Bataar.

The arena Rashid had spoken of was an enormous pit, fifty feet deep with gently sloping sides. This allowed each ring of spectators to stand a little higher than the ring in front, so the slopes formed an amphitheater, carved from earth rather than stone.

How many were in the crowd altogether was impossible to say, but Conrad was sure there were thousands. He'd fought in tournaments in front of what he'd thought were large audiences, but nothing like this. He resolved to put the crowd out of his mind— his fate, and Elaine's, depended on his staying focused. As Bataar led him down the slope to the bottom of the pit, Conrad saw spectators brandishing coins and jewels and he realized they were wagering on the outcome of the match. He wondered what the odds were, then decided it might be better not to know.

He reached the bottom of the pit. It was circular in shape, some thirty feet across, and the dirt had been thoroughly packed and leveled so that no uneven patches or stones of any size remained. Conrad caught a glimpse of the Great Khan himself, halfway up the opposite slope, his only badge of status a small awning to shield him from the sun. Conrad started to look away but was startled to see Elaine, in a place of honor near the Khan. So sure were the Mongols of Chormaghun's victory that she was already being treated as the wife of a Mongol general! Conrad's jaw tightened, and suddenly his eyes met Elaine's.

If such a thing were possible, her expression seemed to combine hope and despair in equal parts. He thought she'd never seemed more beautiful, more courageous, or more vulnerable. He nodded, trying to convey a reassurance he didn't entirely feel himself. She nodded in response and even seemed to smile very slightly, then he forced himself to tear his eyes away. Like the crowd, she had to be put out of his mind. How many times had Charles told him, *When you fight think of nothing but fighting,* and if ever there was a time to heed that advice it was now.

Bataar said, "Take off your shirt and shoes." As Conrad complied the crowd let out a cheer and Conrad saw that Chormaghun had arrived. The Mongol was already stripped to the waist. His chest was deeper than Conrad's and his shoulders broader, and the muscles bunched and knotted under his skin appeared rock-hard. Conrad wasn't intimidated. His own muscles were long and rangy by comparison, but that didn't mean they were weaker. There were many ways to win a wrestling match, just as there were many ways to win a sword fight.

A Mongol stepped into the ring carrying a baton of smooth wood capped with a small golden horse head. The man spoke to Chormaghun, who nodded, then said the same words to Conrad. "Are you ready?" Bataar translated, and Conrad nodded as well.

The arbiter stepped between them, holding his baton so that it pointed to the ground. Conrad looked at Chormaghun, who was looking back at him with a hatred that matched his own.

Then the arbiter raised the baton so that it pointed to the sky and stepped back and the air was shattered by the shouts of the crowd and the match began.

· 34 ·

After Rashid slipped away from Conrad he drifted unobtrusively against the grain until he had worked himself clear of the crowd. As he had anticipated, the rest of the camp was, if not quite deserted, far more sparsely populated than usual.

Nevertheless he had to be careful. He faced two major obstacles: The first was how to walk through the Mongol camp without being challenged. He had thought of trying to steal a Mongol uniform—the trousers, loose blouse, and felt cap would have been difficult to secure, but not impossible given his skills—but he was too tall and slender to make a convincing Mongol even at a distance.

Instead of stealing a uniform, he had stolen something else—a small leather pouch that he had seen couriers use when taking messages from one part of the camp to another. The couriers were not Mongol soldiers but usually servants or slaves. These wore no particular uniform, and a courier dressed as Rashid was—sandals, white linen trousers, and shirt—would attract no notice. Or so he hoped.

The second obstacle was locating Chormaghun's quarters. He couldn't ask because it would seem suspicious for a courier not to know, and in any event he spoke no Mongolian. But the highly organized nature of the Mongol army was a help, for every unit had an emblem; the emblem of Chormaghun's unit was a wooden stake with a crosspiece from which hung three horsetails, two white and one red. And he'd noticed some of Chormaghun's officers—he recognized them from the banquet—walking toward the northwest quadrant of the camp. His plan was to walk toward the northwest until he found Chormaghun's emblem.

The camp was enormous and Rashid walked for some time, passing a number of emblems but not Chormaghun's. Even depopulated, the camp still contained hundreds of Mongols repairing weapons, eating, or gathered in small groups and talking in the rough but comradely manner of soldiers everywhere. Most took no notice of him, but then a voice sounded behind him.

He ignored it, but it came again more sharply and he stopped and turned. A Mongol officer, lounging nearby with three others, seemed to be asking a question, but Rashid had no idea what it was. He gestured to his pouch—*As you see, I'm a courier.* A look of impatience crossed the officer's face and he started to speak again when the air was shattered by a distant roar, like a thunderclap. It came from the direction of the arena and Rashid realized the first point must have been scored in the match.

It distracted the officers—they began laughing and speculating and one of them trotted off to find out what had happened. Rashid moved along quickly, expecting to hear the officer's voice calling after him again, but it didn't come and he turned a corner and was safe for the moment.

Then he saw it—the crosspiece with two white horsetails and one red. In fact, there were a number of them, marking out the territory of Chormaghun's regiment, and as Rashid headed toward that territory he saw that it was almost completely deserted. *Of course!* Nearly all of Chormaghun's men were at the match watching their General in action.

Finding Chormaghun's tent was easy. It was larger than the rest and the entrance was flanked by two poles carrying his insignia and there was a lone guard at the entrance. There was another tent nearby, different from the rough tents the soldiers used, and Rashid realized it must be Elaine's. Rashid showed no apparent interest in either tent and walked well past them, then stopped and turned. This was the moment he'd been most concerned about, but there was not a soul to be seen and little apparent danger.

He moved to the back of the tent and drew his knife and cut a long slit just above ground level, then squeezed through it into the tent and waited. There was no reaction from the guard outside and he breathed again and stood up slowly and looked around. It was dark, but some light came through the slits in the entrance flap and Rashid had to hope it would be enough once his eyes adjusted. A second clap of thunder sounded from the arena. Either the match was tied at a point apiece, or one man was leading two points to none. He might already be running out of time.

His eyes adjusted to the semidarkness. Along one wall were four large wooden chests and Rashid stepped over to the first and lifted the lid. The chest was piled high with gold and silver coins and plates and cups and bowls, many inlaid with gems and jewels—a general's spoils of war. He took a few of the coins out—they would prove useful on his return journey—but not enough so they'd be missed. The second chest was full of weapons and armor and the third full of spare clothing. The fourth chest was locked.

Rashid drew his knife again and began using the point to pick the lock as he'd been trained to do. A third roar suddenly sounded from the arena, startling Rashid, for it came sooner on the heels of the second than he'd hoped. Three points had been scored— could the match already be over? No; when the match ended the roar would surely be particularly loud, but this one had been no louder than the first two, so most likely one of the contestants was leading two points to one and the match would continue. Good; that meant that Conrad—and Elaine—still had a chance.

He worked the point of his knife into the keyhole, felt the mechanism start to turn. Then it opened with an audible click. Rashid looked toward the tent door, but the guard didn't appear.

He opened the lid gently. Inside, neatly arranged, were hundreds of documents—maps, books, parchments, and scrolls.

A fourth thunderclap sounded from the arena.

No louder than the first three, he told himself. He still had time. *But not much.*

He forced himself not to panic. He was looking for a roll of parchment, he reminded himself, so he could ignore books and maps and anything flat. And the parchment would bear the Old Man's seal, an eagle pressed into soft wax. Working as rapidly as he could, he began removing the documents from the chest and placing them on the floor, one layer at a time. And then, suddenly, there it was: a roll of parchment, the Old Man's seal partially damaged but unmistakable. Rashid removed the letter and tucked it in his shirt next to his suddenly pounding heart. He willed his hands to stop trembling with excitement and carefully began replacing the things he'd taken out of the chest, hoping he remembered their original locations.

He was almost finished when he heard another sound from the arena—not a thunderclap, but more like a distant storm, rumbling and growing louder, then subsiding into a dull, confused murmur. He wondered if the match had ended in some strange or unexpected way, and felt a pang of guilt. Conrad's future was being decided—Elaine's as well—and here he was on the opposite side of the Mongol camp . . . useless! *But not really,* he reminded himself. As Conrad had said, there was nothing Rashid could do once the match started, and finding the letter would in the long run help all three of them.

Rashid finished repacking the chest and closed its lid, then slipped back under the slit in the tent and pulled the felt down and flattened it out to hide the slit. Then he hurried away from the tent to the nearest roads, still carrying the courier's pouch and feeling that his feet were at last set on a course for Paradise.

And how pleased Hasan would be, and of course the Old Man as well! He imagined their expressions when he took the letter from his shirt and held it out to them. The thought was a happy one, but on its heels came a less happy thought, one he hadn't expected: returning to the Eagle's Nest without either of his companions, even if he had the Old Man's letter, would be very sad indeed.

But then, perhaps Conrad had won and things would turn out well for everyone.

35

As soon as the arbiter raised his baton, Chormaghun lowered his head and extended his arms and bull-rushed Conrad, hoping to score a point in the first few seconds of the match. Conrad had expected this and stepped aside, avoiding Chormaghun's torso but taking a blow from his outstretched arm. The blow was powerful but Conrad kept his balance without much trouble. What he hadn't anticipated was the agility with which the Mongol stopped, wheeled, and charged again.

Conrad took a half step to the side and received the brunt of the charge on his left shoulder, the one that had been wounded in the battle. He managed to spin clear but Chormaghun turned and rushed him yet again and this time Conrad couldn't evade him.

Conrad knew that if it came to a bear hug he was doomed, so he bowed his back and braced his hands against the Mongol's chest to try to keep some distance between their bodies. Both men grunted with effort as Chormaghun tried to close that distance, his feet churning the dirt as he drove Conrad back, while the Knight tried to keep his own feet moving, now a step to the side, now a step back, but he could feel Chormaghun's superior body strength beginning to tell.

Every instinct told Conrad to drop down and grab one of

Chormaghun's legs, but it was forbidden by the rules. The Mongol's stocky body and short legs enabled him to stay low and use his leverage to keep pushing Conrad back until finally Conrad could no longer fend him off and found himself exactly where he didn't want to be—in a bear hug.

Chormaghun locked his hands behind Conrad's back and lifted him off the ground and began to squeeze with all his strength. That the Mongol would score the first point was a foregone conclusion— he merely had to throw Conrad to the ground like a sack of wheat— but first he wanted to crack Conrad's ribs and the Knight realized that in another few seconds he would succeed.

What was it Rashid had said about gouging—legal but frowned upon? Let them frown! Conrad wrapped one arm around Chormaghun's head to keep it still and dug his other thumb into the Mongol's right eye and tried to rip it out of its socket. The Mongol grunted and tried to twist his head, but Conrad pushed his thumb in deeper and with a roar of pain Chormaghun flung Conrad to one side. Conrad stumbled and slipped to one knee. He was back on his feet in an instant, but it was too late. A great shout went up from the crowd and the arbiter leveled his baton at Chormaghun to indicate a point scored.

Conrad became aware of pain in his wounded shoulder. He had thought it nearly healed but now it was beginning to ache. Chormaghun blinked his eye several times but otherwise seemed undisturbed by the gouge and with a growl he prepared to come at Conrad again. Conrad felt the beginnings of panic . . . the disadvantages were mounting—the rules, and now his shoulder. *Stop whining! What are your advantages?* Charles's voice seemed to sound in his ear as clearly as it had years ago when Charles was teaching him to wrestle. What were his advantages? He had longer limbs. He had to find a way to use them.

Chormaghun was bull-rushing again and Conrad stepped aside, but as he did he shifted his weight to his left leg and swept his right leg around in short, vicious arc and the Mongol stumbled badly and began to fall forward. He scrambled forward for several yards on his hands and feet, crablike, then, miraculously, came upright so that no point was scored.

But there was a trace of doubt in Chormaghun's eyes now, Conrad could see it, and he saw something else as well—Chormaghun's limp had become more pronounced as he circled. Perhaps Conrad's kick had aggravated it. Another advantage for Conrad.

Nevertheless the Mongol prepared to charge again and Conrad readied himself. What he had done once he could do again, and as Chormaghun approached, a bit more slowly than before, it seemed, Conrad stepped aside, to the right this time, and brought his left leg around . . . but Chormaghun's slowness had been deliberate and he stopped suddenly so that Conrad's sweep was mistimed and it was the Knight who was off balance. He saw what was coming but was helpless to prevent it; Chormaghun lashed out with his own leg and knocked Conrad's leg out from under him and the Knight tumbled ignominiously to the ground. The arbiter pointed his baton at Chormaghun as another great cheer rose from the crowd. The Mongol now led two points to none.

Conrad cursed himself as he rose to his feet. He should have recognized the slower charge as a ruse. He had been outmuscled once and outthought once and now there was no margin for error. And here came Chormaghun again, more confident than ever, almost smiling, if a face filled with hatred can smile.

Conrad could never explain what he did next; it might have been a technique he invented out of desperation or one he'd seen long ago and forgotten until now. Whatever the explanation Chormaghun couldn't have expected it because Conrad himself hadn't expected it. He dropped partly to ground, supporting his weight with one long arm, then kicked both legs straight out as hard as he could so that for a split second his entire body was parallel to the ground. The kick caught the Mongol squarely on one knee and spun him in the air like a windmill and he went sprawling in the dirt.

Conrad regained his footing and the arbiter pointed the baton at him and the crowd gave a spontaneous shout just as loud as the first two, for though most of them favored Chormaghun, all of them appreciated a fine wrestling move.

Chormaghun got up slowly and for the first time he looked shaken. His limp was worse and now he circled Conrad warily. But by now Conrad was beginning to understand his opponent. It was Chormaghun's nature to be the aggressor, he wouldn't be able to help himself, and if Conrad was patient the Mongol would charge again.

And so it proved. Chormaghun came on once more, but too slowly, and Conrad sensed a repeat of the ruse that had scored the Mongol's second point. Conrad started to drop to the ground as before, and the Mongol stopped, waiting for a leg kick that never came; instead, Conrad stayed on his feet and charged Chormaghun for the first time in the match.

The move caught Chormaghun flat-footed and Conrad grabbed him around the waist and hoisted him up and onto his shoulder and spun him around once and then threw him to the ground. It was another dazzling maneuver and it earned another appreciative outburst from the spectators, and the arbiter's baton pointed at Conrad. The match was tied at two points apiece.

But the effort had come at a terrible cost. Conrad's damaged shoulder had borne Chormaghun's weight and he felt something give way and the pain was excruciating. And it was not merely a matter of pain; Conrad realized the shoulder had been dislocated, for his left arm hung uselessly at his side. Chormaghun scrambled to his feet and turned to face him. The Mongol was panting heavily and caked with sweat and dirt and his lips were drawn back in a snarl. Conrad knew that he himself must look much the same. They were more like two wild beasts than men, but for the first time it was the Mongol who felt trapped and cornered, and fear and doubt were written on his face. And then he saw Conrad's arm, hanging limply from the shoulder.

Chormaghun paused to gather his strength, and to savor the victory he now knew would be his. There was no hurry. He would take his time, be careful, make certain of his prey.

Conrad tried desperately to conjure up some trick or subterfuge that would give him some chance of winning. He would have to find a way to use his longer legs and his one good arm, but nothing came to mind but the pain in his shoulder. He tried to block that out and braced himself as Chormaghun prepared to charge . . . and suddenly the arbiter stepped between them, with a sharp word that caused the Mongol to halt in his tracks. Conrad became aware of a commotion on the slope, a commotion that seemed to center around the Khan.

When Elaine had first heard that Conrad was alive, she'd been afraid to believe it. Then, when she'd learned of his pending match with Chormaghun, she had gone to the other extreme. It must be the answer to her prayer! Conrad would win, she would return to rule Tripoli and he to rule Antioch. She was surprised at how much confidence she felt in Conrad, and not only because of his physical strength. His heart was strong as well. She'd never known a more courageous man.

Then their eyes had met just after he'd come into the arena, and he'd nodded at her, and after that she felt even more confident. He was so calm, so sure of himself—he would not allow himself to be defeated. Watching him, she'd become aware of how fast her heart was beating—and not only with fear or worry.

Before she could fully reckon with the feeling, the match began. As she watched from her place near the Khan her mood veered wildly from hope to despair, then to hope again as Conrad began to gain the upper hand. Her heart almost leaped out of her breast when he flung Chormaghun to the ground, tying the match at two points apiece. Surely it would be over soon . . . and then she saw how Conrad's arm hung oddly at his side. She saw him try to raise his hand above his waist and fail; she saw him try to disguise the injury by letting his good arm dangle loosely like the other. But no one was fooled, least of all Chormaghun.

Elaine knew what must follow—Conrad thrown to the ground

and led away to his death. What had seemed impossible just moments ago was about to happen. She knew this would mean the end of any chance to warn Tripoli and Antioch, but at that moment it was as if a giant fist had closed around her heart and she had only one thought—*she couldn't let Conrad die.*

In that same moment she realized what she must do. She was the answer to her own prayer. She herself would provide the miracle! But she had to act quickly, before she had a chance to change her mind. She stepped toward the Khan and threw herself at his feet and called out loudly so as to be heard over the clamor of the crowd:

"Great Khan, stop the match. Stop it, I beg you!"

The Khan's eyes widened in surprise. He didn't understand the words but their import was plain and he raised his hand and on the floor of the arena the arbiter stepped between the combatants and stopped the match. Meanwhile Noyon had hurried to Elaine's side. "This is most improper!" she hissed angrily. "You must return to—"

"I have to speak to him. Tell him, please! Tell him!"

Again the Khan grasped her intent and nodded his permission. "Go on," Noyon said nervously. "I will translate." For the first time Elaine looked directly into the Khan's deep green eyes. They were intelligent, remote, mysterious, like those of a cat.

"Great Khan, I am the cause of this fight. For many, it is entertainment. For me, it is life and death. I have resisted marriage to General Chormaghun. Had I not done so, the Frankish Knight would not be fighting for me now. He has long been my friend and protector. I cannot bear to be the cause of his death. I ask you to stop the fight and spare him. I will marry General Chormaghun."

The Khan grunted. "You will marry him in any case," he said.

"I will marry him willingly. I will be a good wife, loyal and dutiful. I will be ever mindful of the great honor he bestows upon me by making me the wife of a general of the Great Khan. I will behave in all things as he wishes me to behave, and do so gladly.

And I will be your loyal and willing servant as well, and in your debt forever."

She paused. The Khan was at least listening. He glanced down at Conrad, and Elaine guessed he was thinking of Conrad's damaged arm. She continued quickly.

"What honor is there in killing a defenseless man? Show your strength in mercy, and let the Knight return to his kingdom, which he will rule wisely and well." *And do what he can to prepare for your invasion,* she thought, but strove to keep her expression free of guile.

The Khan shifted his gaze back to Elaine. "What you have said, about being a good and willing wife. You swear it?"

"I swear it," said Elaine.

There was another pause, then the Khan said, "I'm told you threatened suicide."

"It is true, Your Majesty."

"Do you now withdraw that threat?"

"I do withdraw it, Your Majesty. I will not need to commit suicide. If the Knight is killed on my account, I will die of shame and sorrow."

These words surprised Elaine even as she spoke them. She hadn't planned them, yet she felt they were the truest words she'd ever spoken. She saw a flicker of feeling in the Khan's eyes when he heard the translation. He continued looking at her for a long time and she returned his look steadily and then his impassive expression softened slightly. He inclined his great head once, in a nod of approval.

"Your request is granted," he said.

A stir went through the crowd as word of the Khan's decision spread. Many agreed with the decision, though some were disappointed; but of course no one raised any objection. For a moment Elaine felt relief at achieving her aim, but this was replaced by a feeling of numbness as Noyon took her arm and led her away from the Khan. Elaine turned for a last glimpse of Conrad and saw him looking back at her, confused. Well, he would find out the truth soon enough. She nodded at him, much as he had nodded at her at the beginning of the match, hoping he would understand that she freely accepted what was happening. It crossed her mind that this was the last time she would ever see him, but she didn't let herself dwell on the thought. She couldn't bear to, not yet. She turned and followed Noyon out of the arena.

What have I done? she thought. *What have I done?*

· 36 ·

As Rashid made his way back into the main portion of the camp, he passed a unit of auxiliary troops speaking excitedly in Arabic. He slowed down to listen.

". . . but for his injury he surely would have won . . ."

"I say he was mostly lucky."

". . . loved Chormaghun all along . . ."

"Nonsense! It was the only way to save her lover . . ."

There were many voices and the conversation was disjointed and he didn't want to attract attention by lingering. Nevertheless he heard enough to understand what must have happened in the match, and it left him stunned. Conrad had been badly injured and to save his life Elaine had agreed to be Chormaghun's loyal and obedient wife! Rashid was greatly relieved that Conrad was still alive, but he knew that the Knight himself would have chosen death rather than living with the knowledge that Elaine had disappeared forever into the tent of a Mongol general.

Nevertheless, Rashid told himself, his own course was clear. He had the Old Man's letter and he would do exactly as Conrad himself had advised. He would return it to the Old Man as quickly as possible. Conrad would join him soon and he, Rashid, would provide what comfort he could.

He walked to the stables, hoping that his horse was still in the same enclosure as when he'd first arrived in the Mongol camp. It was, and the saddle and supply sacks were nearby and he saddled the horse and secured the sacks, all the while protecting himself from unwanted inquiries by making sure the messenger's pouch was visible.

He rode unhurriedly away, ready to spur his mount instantly if he was challenged. But there was no reason for anyone to challenge him and it wasn't long before he was well clear of the camp. Then he stopped and waited for Conrad to appear.

An hour passed, then another. Absently he stroked the scar on his arm. It was flatter now; he realized it had been some time since he'd opened it. Perhaps he'd open it again tonight, when they camped. Yet another hour went by, and Rashid began to admit to himself what he already knew—what he had known ever since he left the Mongol camp: Conrad wasn't coming. And he knew why. Conrad was going to kill Chormaghun.

He closed his eyes tightly. *No!* he told himself. *I can't be weak again.* Not now, with success in his grasp. He'd had a moment of weakness in the stables at Tripoli and all his subsequent travails could be traced back to that moment, and he could not allow it to happen again. True, despite his best efforts and Conrad's as well, a friendship had grown between them, but what was that compared to his duty to the Old Man? He reminded himself how good it had felt, leaving Chormaghun's tent with the letter in his hand and imagining the Old Man's face, and Hasan's, when he handed it to them. Now was not the time to take further risks!

But it was no use. He thought of Conrad risking his life for Elaine, and her sacrificing her future for Conrad, while he, Rashid, rode away free and clear without lifting a finger to help either of them. He couldn't do it.

He had always been unworthy and always would be. Should the letter fail to reach the Old Man because of what he was about to do, he would never forgive himself. But he turned the horse's head around and headed back to the Mongol camp.

* * *

Conrad sat on the floor of his tent, still bare-chested and caked with blood and grime from the match. A Mongol physician had pushed his shoulder back in place. It still ached badly but he barely noticed. He knew he should spend his last night on earth trying to make peace with his Maker, but his mind was in too much turmoil to make peace with anything or anyone, even himself. Especially himself.

He should have beaten Chormaghun—and would have, if he hadn't given up the first two points so easily. He and Elaine should be far away by now, riding with Rashid toward the Zagros Mountains.

He had seen her talking with the Khan but couldn't hear the conversation over the noise of the crowd. But he should have guessed what she was saying. By the time he understood, it was too late. Chormaghun was surrounded by supporters and there was no way Conrad could renew the fight. He, Conrad, was sworn to protect Elaine, yet in the end she had thrown her life away to protect him. The political aspect didn't escape him—now he could warn Tripoli and Antioch about the Mongols—but the fact remained, he was safe while she would spend a lifetime in hell.

He remembered his last glimpse of Elaine as she was being led away. She'd glanced back at him, and her expression seemed to be trying to tell him that it was all right.

But it wasn't all right, and never would be. Most painful of all, at that moment, for the first time, he realized that he loved her. He knew she didn't love him, but that no longer mattered. He loved her. Not because she was his betrothed, or his right, or his duty, or a political necessity, but because . . . he loved her, that was all.

He must have loved her all along, from the first time he'd set eyes on her in Tripoli, and he had been too thickheaded, too unacquainted with his own heart, to realize it until now.

He thought of her eyes, her lips, her smile, her courage, her wit, her honesty. Even the things about her he thought he despised—her conceit and her sharp tongue—seemed now to be minor flaws, things that helped make her who she was and therefore had to be accepted. And how gladly he would accept them, given another chance. But that was not to be. And he'd been so sure he was finished with love after his affair with the Countess back in France. What a fool! The truth was he'd understood nothing at all of love until now—now that it was too late, too late even to tell Elaine how he felt.

He remembered something Chormaghun had said the night of the feast. *Why were you not there to protect her?* Chormaghun was a barbarian, but even he had seen that Conrad should have stayed with Elaine, protected her at all costs, rather than fighting in a battle that meant nothing to him. No doubt the Mongol General was pleased with himself at the thought that Elaine now belonged to him.

Well, Conrad had other ideas. His glance strayed to his sword, leaning against the wall of the tent. The sword was useless; he would never be allowed anywhere near Chormaghun wearing a sword. But a concealed dagger might be a different matter—not his best weapon, but it would have to do. He could approach the General on the pretext of offering a gift of some kind, a token of reconciliation—the Mongol could hardly refuse to accept it—then Conrad would use the dagger. Of course he himself would die within seconds, but that prospect did not disturb him in the least. He reflected that if Rashid were here he could offer some guidance on the proper use of a dagger, but by now the Arab would be many miles to the west.

At that moment the tent flap opened and Rashid stepped inside.

Conrad stared, mouth open, for a long moment. Rashid smiled slightly. "It's really me," he said.

"You didn't find the letter," Conrad managed finally.

"I found it," Rashid said, and took it from inside his shirt and held it out for Conrad to see. Then he put it back in his shirt.

Conrad said, "Then why are you here?"

"I heard what happened."

"You should have gone like I told you to."

"You're going to kill Chormaghun, aren't you," said Rashid.

"I'll have to use a knife. I was just thinking, you could give me some advice."

"My advice is, don't do it."

Conrad said nothing.

"Have you thought what they'll do to Elaine?" said Rashid.

"Give her to someone else, I suppose. But at least it won't be Chormaghun."

"They might give her to someone else, or they might give her to everyone else." Rashid let that sink in for a moment, then added, "They might even kill her."

"Maybe she'd prefer to die," said Conrad.

"Would you prefer that she die?"

Conrad sagged and closed his eyes and when he opened them they were filled with tears of frustration and rage. "I can't just stand by while—" The words caught in his throat.

"You can't throw your life away, either. It's not what she would want."

"I must do something."

"I was in Chormaghun's tent," Rashid said. "That's how I got the letter. I'm certain Elaine's tent is nearby."

"So?"

"So I know where it is, how to get in, and how to get out. Elaine is there now or soon will be. What I did once I can do again."

"That was during the match, when the camp was nearly deserted."

"That was also during the day. This time I'll go at night."

"It will have to be this very night," said Conrad. "The wedding is tomorrow."

"Then I'll go tonight."

Conrad sat up straighter, allowing himself the beginnings of hope. "Even if you get in, how will you get Elaine out?"

"We'll think of a way."

Conrad slumped back down and Rashid pressed his case. "At least it's a chance. If you kill Chormaghun . . ." He spread his hands as if to say, *All chances will cease.*

"What of the Old Man's letter?"

"We'll deliver it in due course," said Rashid. "All three of us."

"Rashid, you don't have to do this."

"Come, on your feet," said Rashid, as a plan continued to take shape in his mind. "We have things to do."

Like the Khwarazmians, the Mongol army had a baggage train consisting of cooks, blacksmiths, herders, armorers, and countless other tradesmen who supported the army's fighting wing. Conrad, acting on instructions from Rashid, went to the commissary, where the cooks plied their craft, looking for three items in particular. He found them without much trouble, paying with one of the coins Rashid had taken from Chormaghun's tent. The first item was opium, the brown powder that remained when the resin from poppy seeds was aged and dried. It was plentiful in the region to the east inhabited by a mysterious people called Afghans, and relatively inexpensive. The second and third items were even more common: a powder made from a daisy-like flower called chamomile, and the dried root of a valerian plant. Both were used as sedatives and were cheaper than opium and gave no cause for comment, since Conrad certainly looked like a man in need of a good rest. He also purchased, as Rashid had requested, a small clay pot, a narrow clay cylinder with a lid, and a leather thong.

A fourth substance was needed as well, but it was not something that could be asked for openly. Rashid took charge of finding it. He moved away from the baggage train and beyond the surrounding area, which had been picked clean by foragers. He walked for some time without finding what he was looking for, then came to a grove of cypress trees near a small stream. Growing on the ground near the cypress trunks was a modest spray of small white blossoms that despite their harmless appearance belonged to a flower known since ancient times to be a deadly poison. It was called hemlock.

Rashid picked the hemlock and met Conrad back at their tent. Rashid mixed the opium, chamomile, and valerian root together in the clay pot. Then he found two rocks and began to grind the hemlock between them.

This was the delicate part. The first three substances mixed together were certain to produce drowsiness, especially in a man as inebriated as Chormaghun would surely be on his wedding night; but they did not guarantee sleep. Thus the need for hemlock—but just the right amount, for too little might not induce sleep but too much might cause death, and while Chormaghun needed to be put to sleep, Rashid believed that killing him would be a mistake. He ground up the hemlock, enough to fill a small spoon, then mixed it into the rest of the powder and added enough water to form a thin paste. Then he poured the paste into the narrow clay cylinder, closed the lid, and fastened the cylinder to the leather thong.

The cypress grove where he'd found the hemlock was a mile from the camp and not far from the sector where Chormaghun's tent was located. This made it an excellent meeting place to wait with the horses. Rashid explained this to Conrad, and the last piece of the plan fell into place.

Their nerves taut as bowstrings, they sat back and waited for darkness to fall.

Elaine tossed and turned, haunted by the thought that the match might after all have been an answered prayer; that Conrad might have found a way to win even with his damaged arm; and that if she had simply held her peace she would have already left for home. To stay sane she reminded herself how severe Conrad's injury had seemed; that she had almost certainly saved his life; and that, contrary to her early opinion of him, he would make a fine king. He would rule Antioch well and might even find a way to unite Antioch with Tripoli. And, just maybe, he would find a way to fend off the Mongols. It was even conceivable that she could use her position as Chormaghun's wife to aid Tripoli in some fashion when the time came, if only to enter a plea for mercy, although she doubted such a plea would have much effect. Her fate was a strange one indeed. She'd come hundreds of miles from home in order to understand her duty to her country—only to find that duty required that she never see her country again. But she'd understood at last, and that would have to be her consolation.

But would all this be enough to sustain her for a lifetime as Chormaghun's "loyal and dutiful wife"? How could she have made such an abject pledge? To save Conrad, of course. But what if he hadn't really needed saving?

As Elaine agonized, outside her tent three torches cast their wavering shadows on the ground. The moon, just setting in the western sky, cast pale shadows of its own. Three sentinels made their rounds close by, never straying far from Elaine's tent or from each other. No person could hope to approach the tent without being seen.

But perhaps a shadow could. A shadow so careful and clever that it could hide within the changing patterns of the other shadows thrown by torches and the moon, and so still and disciplined that it could take an hour to travel ten feet in order to evade detection. . . .

Without warning a hand covered Elaine's mouth. She sat up with a start, or tried to, but the hand pressed her back down. She feared that Chormaghun had decided not to wait until their wedding night and, despite her promise to the Khan, began to struggle, but a familiar voice whispered, "It's Rashid! Be still!"

She stopped struggling. The hand was removed from her mouth.

"Rashid . . . ?"

"Yes. Be quiet!"

"But—"

"Shhhh! I can only stay a moment, so listen carefully. If you do as I say, by this time tomorrow you will be riding towards the mountains with me and Conrad. . . ."

· 37 ·

"You'll approach the platform from the east," Noyon was saying, "that is, from your left as you leave the tent . . ."

"I know," Elaine said wearily. "You've told me."

"But you must listen!" Noyon scolded. "You cannot make any mistakes, for an error would dishonor the General."

Elaine clenched her teeth and kept quiet. She was in her tent, surrounded by servant girls who dressed and perfumed her and arranged her hair while Noyon reiterated for the tenth time what she would be required to do during the ceremony.

They had dressed her in a garment of cotton and silk, the silk sky blue in color and embroidered in geometric patterns outlined in threads of silver and gold. Her hair had been carefully arranged, partly piled on top of her head and adorned with flowers, partly hanging down in braids, one of which had been separated from the rest and draped over her right shoulder.

By this time tomorrow you will be riding towards the mountains. Rashid's words helped steady her. She resisted the temptation to finger the thin cylinder hanging from the leather thong around her neck, hidden beneath her dress. This, too, was from Rashid and it was the key to her freedom.

The tent flap opened and one of the Mongol guards entered.

She inspected Elaine for a long moment while Noyon and the maidservants stood by anxiously. She made a slight adjustment in the long braid that lay over Elaine's right shoulder and straightened part of the dress that was already perfectly straight, then nodded as if, thanks to her, everything was now satisfactory.

She turned and left the tent and Noyon and the servant girls heaved a collective sigh of relief. Noyon said, "It is time," and pulled back the tent flap and Elaine stepped outside and the wedding began.

A wooden platform ten feet high had been constructed fifty yards from Elaine's tent. She approached it from the east, as instructed by Noyon, making her way slowly through a vast crowd of soldiers. Chormaghun's entire regiment, as well as many soldiers from other regiments, were present for the ceremony.

The soldiers watched her curiously, making occasional comments to one another but generally remaining silent, perhaps because they preferred listening to the music, of which there was a considerable amount. Some was produced by lutes of two or four strings, and some by strange-looking horsehair fiddles stroked by horsehair bows. There were dozens of musicians scattered throughout the crowd, apparently playing independently of one another, but the resulting sound was surprisingly coherent and unified, though the melodies themselves, which consisted of long, undulating phrases in minor keys, sounded strange to Elaine's ear.

Even stranger were the singers, placed at intervals along her path, and possessed of the astonishing ability to produce two separate tones simultaneously—a low, buzzing or humming note, accompanied by a melodic line an octave higher. The Mongols were particularly proud of such performers, called throat-singers, and Noyon had told Elaine to acknowledge them, for their skill was being displayed in her honor. So Elaine nodded and smiled whenever she passed a throat-singer, though she found the songs themselves, like the instrumental music, rather melancholy.

At the base of the platform was a wooden staircase, on each side of which lay a small pyre of wood and kindling. As Elaine approached the stairs she saw Chormaghun walking to meet her from the opposite direction. He, too, was dressed in a patterned robe of silk and cotton, though of a darker, midnight blue. His scalplock had been pulled to one side of his head and lay on his left shoulder.

Elaine met him at the foot of the platform and turned to face the stairs. A servant took the braid from her right shoulder and entwined it with the scalplock on Chormaghun's left shoulder, showing that they were now united. Then the servant used a torch to light the pyres on each side of the stairs. Chormaghun and Elaine walked together up the stairs between the flames, which both purified them and proved that they had the courage to rise above difficult times together as man and wife.

The symbolism had been explained to Elaine but she'd tried not to listen. She dared not consider that the ceremony might have meaning, that if Rashid's plan should fail for any reason, this would be the start of her new life as the wife—the fourth wife—of a Mongolian general.

She was well aware of the bitter irony of her situation. She'd fled from Tripoli in order to avoid a political marriage to Conrad, only to agree to a far more appalling political marriage in order to save Conrad's life! How different things would be if she'd simply done her duty as Bernard, and everyone else including Conrad himself, had advised.

But Conrad was alive, and so was Rashid, and they were working to free her. She would put her trust in them. It was the only way she could stay sane.

They reached the top of the stairs and stepped onto the platform, where a shaman was waiting. His face was covered by a brass mask with openings for his eyes and mouth, and he was dressed in a robe made from hundreds of brightly colored strips of cloth— cotton, linen, silk, and felt—interspersed with disks of dull brass that protected against evil spirits and polished brass that allowed the good spirits to be reflected. He stretched out his arms and began to speak.

Elaine didn't know what he was saying, but Chormaghun listened with rapt attention. The shaman spoke for several minutes, then reached out and unbraided Elaine's hair from Chormaghun's and turned the couple around to face the crowd and a cheer arose from the throats of the watching soldiers.

Elaine realized that the ceremony was over. In the eyes of the Mongols and the Spirit of the Eternal Blue Sky, she was now married to Chormaghun.

The wedding was over but the celebration was just beginning. Elaine and Chormaghun were taken to a large wooden table and seated at the head. Around the rest of the table sat the guests of honor, mostly senior officers in Chormaghun's regiment along with a few staff officers of the Khan's. The Khan himself, it was said, was coming later to confer his blessing on the happy couple.

The music and singing started up again, more enthusiastically than ever and, it seemed to Elaine, in a more cheerful vein. A number of shamans danced ecstatically, their strips of cloth flying wildly and the polished brass disks glinting in the sun, which was just beginning the last stage of its descent. Servants appeared with platters of meat and fruit and grains and bowls of *airag* and wines of every kind, and the guests, some seated at tables and some seated on the ground between tables, began eating and drinking with gusto.

Chormaghun had looked at Elaine several times since the end of the ceremony, but she could not bring herself to look back at him. This might be taken as a sign of the new bride's shyness, but she could sense his irritation. She had, after all, promised to be his dutiful wife. She forced herself to look at him and smile and this seemed to mollify him to a degree.

She ate a few mouthfuls of food and tried to look as cheerful as possible. But she drank sparingly of the wine, just enough to keep her mouth from becoming too dry. She knew that soon she would need to have a clearer mind and steadier nerves than she had ever had before in her life.

An hour passed, then another; dusk turned to darkness and torches were lit and the feasting and dancing and revelry continued unabated.

As promised, the Great Khan made an appearance, embracing Chormaghun and bestowing a benign smile on Elaine. He only stayed a few moments, then left so as not to distract attention from the bride and groom. Chormaghun became increasingly drunk, laughing and carousing with his fellow officers, occasionally throwing a leering glance Elaine's way and making remarks that provoked great merriment.

An hour before midnight Noyon appeared and signaled discreetly to Elaine that it was time to leave. The new bride must prepare for her first night in the conjugal bed. Elaine stood and bowed formally to Chormaghun, then she followed Noyon away from the table.

Noyon escorted her into Chormaghun's tent, which was lit by scented candles that surrounded a bed of silken sheets piled high with pillows. "I will call your servants to help you prepare for your husband," said Noyon.

"I don't need them," said Elaine.

"It is traditional for—"

"I don't need any servants tonight," Elaine said sharply.

Noyon stiffened, then said, "As you wish," in a disapproving tone.

"You may go as well," Elaine added, and Noyon bowed and walked out, leaving Elaine alone in the tent.

There were a number of trunks set against the wall across from the bed. Next to them was a small table, with a jug of wine and two double-handed cups of beaten gold. One of the cups was engraved with the image of two horses fighting, the other with that of a peacefully grazing flock of sheep; it was not hard to know which one Chormaghun would prefer to drink from.

Elaine took the cylinder off her neck. Her heart was pounding but her hand was steady as she poured the contents into the drinking cup engraved with fighting horses. Then she hid the empty cylinder behind the chest. Now there was nothing to do but wait.

◦ 38 ◦

An hour after sunset Conrad and Rashid arrived at the grove of cypress trees north of the camp. Their preparations had gone quite smoothly due, ironically, to the fact that Conrad had lost the wrestling match to Chormaghun. Everyone respected the hard fight he had put up, and no one resented him since he had lost in the end. He encountered friendly greetings wherever he went, and he and Rashid decided to be open, or partly open, about what they were doing and even enlisted the aid of Bataar, their translator, to get exactly what they wanted.

What they wanted was four good horses and enough supplies to see them across the Zagros Mountains. They were returning home, they said, planning to leave as early as they could the next morning, after paying their respects to the Great Khan. No one had reason to challenge this explanation and no one did.

They paid for the horses and supplies with money stolen from Chormaghun's tent, gave a coin to Bataar to thank him for his services, then rode out of the camp on the pretext of confirming the quality of the horses. Then they'd ridden around the perimeter of the camp to the cypress grove, where they were now.

That had been easy, but what followed was agonizingly hard:

waiting. The sounds of the bacchanalia floated toward them from the distant camp—shouts, laughter, music, and occasional snatches of an odd kind of singing that Conrad had never heard before. And all the while he had to imagine Elaine on display as the property of Chormaghun. *She's married to him!*

"I should have killed him." He didn't realize he'd spoken out loud until Rashid answered.

"It means nothing. Pagans celebrating—they may as well be baying at the moon. She'll be here soon and we'll be well away from here before they even know we're gone."

Conrad paced nervously as the sounds of the celebration grew louder, and Rashid, despite his soothing words, was just as tense. If any woman on earth could keep her nerve at such a time, Elaine was that woman. But he wondered if it would prove too much even for her.

Elaine looked at the gray concoction she'd poured into the wine cup. Did it need to be stirred? Rashid had said nothing about stirring so she left it alone. She suddenly wondered if the potion would really work. What if Rashid had made a mistake?

This thought made her heart start pounding and she glanced anxiously at the wine cups. She forced herself to stay calm, torn between the hope that Chormaghun would come soon so that the waiting would end, and the hope that he had already passed out from excess drink and would not come at all.

And suddenly she heard voices outside and the tent flap opened and he was there, inside the tent, not ten feet away, leering at her through eyes that gleamed with drunken desire. Knowing that her life depended on the next few seconds, Elaine suppressed every natural impulse and forced herself to look him in the eye and smile.

"Good evening, my lord," she said sweetly.

Chormaghun did not comprehend the words but he liked the attitude and smiled lecherously. Elaine went to the table and poured some wine into each golden cup, praying that the potion would dissolve enough to be inconspicuous yet still retain its potency—if it had any to begin with.

"A toast," she said, smiling again, and handing the cup engraved with horses to Chormaghun. She lifted her own cup and drank. Chormaghun drank as well. Then Elaine drank again, draining her cup in one go, and Chormaghun laughed and nodded and she could see him thinking, *At last, this is what I was promised!* He drained his cup in return and Elaine waited for him to stagger or frown or wince with pain or discomfort.

Instead he stepped away and began to take off his clothes.

After a moment he looked up and gestured for Elaine to do the same. She smiled faintly and began to unfasten the top stay of her dress, but she stopped and her smile faded. She couldn't force herself to go on, even for the sake of deceiving him. He glanced at her again, frowned, and again gestured at her to remove her dress. She tried to keep her true feelings from showing in her face but she failed. He began to realize she'd been putting on an act.

He took a step toward her. She tried to back away but he grabbed her wrist. She tried to pull free but he was far too strong and he flung her onto the bed. She got up immediately but he pushed her back down and began tearing at her dress. She knew screaming was pointless but she resolved to keep fighting to her last ounce of strength or, if necessary, her dying breath.

Then Chormaghun released her. He looked puzzled, then pained, then he grunted and put his hands on his stomach. He sank to his knees, his face contorted. He fell over, tried to rise, then fell back again. His breath came in shallow gasps and his back arched and he stared wide-eyed at the roof of the tent. Then his eyes slowly closed and he lay still.

Elaine hurried to the trunks and found one containing Chormaghun's clothing. He wasn't much taller than her, so the length wasn't bad but the width was ridiculous. Two of her could have fit comfortably into each blouse and each pair of pants. She did the best she could, folding over the excess material and tying it in place with strips of cloth from her wedding dress, then pulling a leather cap over her head to hide as much of her hair as possible. Finally, she took her mother's comb from her wedding dress, where she'd hidden it during the ceremony. Now she was ready.

She found the slit in the tent that Rashid had told her of and slipped through it into the night. She glanced around her and gasped in shock—the ground was strewn with bodies, and the horrible memory of the recent battle flashed through her mind. She quickly realized these bodies were drunk rather than dead or wounded. Even so it was a macabre sight in the flickering glow of those few torches that were still burning.

Any concern about her appearance vanished quickly. The few Mongols who remained upright were not nearby and in any case were in no condition to notice her or anything else, for they were too busy managing the difficult task of placing one foot in front of another. The throat-singers had fallen silent, but a few notes could be heard from a far-off lute and, occasionally, a shout or laugh sounded in the distance. But on the whole an atmosphere of serene, well-earned drunken satiation had descended on Chormaghun's portion of the camp. Elaine moved away from the tent.

With an occasional glance at the polestar to keep her oriented, Elaine walked due north as Rashid had instructed. She walked at a measured pace intended to convey purpose but not panic in case someone caught a glimpse of her. In a few minutes she had left the drunken bodies behind and moved into open ground. She was beginning to feel safe when a voice sounded sharply out of the darkness.

"Zogs!"

It was one of the few Mongolian words Elaine had come to recognize—stop. She hoped against hope it wasn't directed at her and kept walking.

"Zogs!" The command came again from a different voice, louder and, it seemed, a little closer.

She began running.

* * *

In the cypress grove Conrad had become so impatient that Rashid was afraid he would draw his sword and ride into the camp by himself.

"Maybe the potion didn't work," Conrad fretted.

"It worked," said Rashid.

"Then what's taking so long?"

"She'll be here."

"When?" Conrad was pacing like a caged tiger.

"Soon."

"She better be. It'll be daylight in a few hours."

They heard a voice in the distance calling out a single word: "*Zogs!*" They froze and listened; almost immediately the word was repeated by a different voice. Both men strained their eyes against the darkness.

They heard footsteps approaching—running footsteps—and they started to draw their weapons, but then a figure came into view and Conrad's heart leaped in his chest. Elaine! He stepped toward her, then realized by her expression that something was wrong.

"Someone's coming," she said.

Conrad lifted Elaine onto one of the horses and handed her the reins. "Go!" Then he and Rashid mounted up as well and all three began to ride.

Conrad let his own horse lag behind the other two. It would be better not to fight—a disturbance was the last thing he wanted—but on the other hand, if a rearguard action was necessary then he would provide it.

He heard the hiss of the arrow as it flew past the top of his head. Another followed a few seconds later. Conrad felt rage mingled with despair boil up inside him. To come so close to escaping! But he knew how far Mongol arrows could go and he couldn't allow the pursuers to fire any more than he could prevent. He would have to sell his life as dearly as possible and hope that Rashid and Elaine would get clear. He drew his sword and spurred his horse back toward the Mongol camp.

Conrad expected a squadron of guards but there were only two, some fifty paces away. He spurred his horse again.

The Mongols had heard him approaching and now they saw him. One took an arrow from his quiver and notched it. In one smooth motion he raised the bow and loosed the arrow. Conrad ducked his head and felt the arrow's feather brush his cheek. Then he was on the archer and swung his sword as hard as he ever had in his life. The blade split the bow in half and sliced through the Mongol's neck, sending his head spinning into the darkness.

Conrad wheeled around, expecting an arrow to bury itself in his chest, but the other Mongol was just drawing back his bowstring.

"*Zogs!*" a voice called out. Startled, the Mongol hesitated and looked toward the voice. In that instant there was a hissing sound as a knife flew through the air and buried itself in his throat. He made a gurgling sound and fell to the ground.

Conrad looked behind him—Elaine and Rashid had returned. Elaine had called out to distract the guard, and Rashid had thrown the knife.

"I told you to ride on!" said Conrad.

"Well, it's a good thing I didn't, isn't it?" Elaine said in her stubborn way, and Conrad felt the old familiar feeling. But at least now he knew what it was—a mixture of exasperation and helpless love.

"Make sure they're both dead," Elaine said in a tone harder and colder than Conrad had thought her capable of.

"They're dead," said Rashid. He'd retrieved his *shabriyah* and was already climbing back on his horse.

"For God's sake, ride!" Conrad said to them both.

Elaine and Rashid turned their horses and rode. Conrad took a last look toward the camp. The commotion had been quick and not terribly noisy, but it was possible someone had seen or heard something. A moment passed, then another . . . the camp remained still.

Conrad spurred his horse after the other two. He hoped the night would last long enough to cover their escape.

39

The Great Khan was not looking forward to the meeting with Chormaghun. The matter would require a degree of tact that would challenge even the Khan's considerable abilities.

Apparently Chormaghun had emerged from his tent a little after midday, looking very ill and demanding to know where his wife was. This had surprised his men, who'd thought she was with him. They had refrained from disturbing him under the assumption that he must be enjoying his new bride very much indeed.

But in fact she had disappeared into thin air after giving him a cup of wine that contained a poison of some kind. It developed that the Frankish Knight and his Arab companion were also gone, and the conclusion was obvious. Of course it made Chormaghun a laughingstock. There were many jokes circulating in the camp at his expense, the most common one being that Conrad had won the wrestling match after all, three points to two.

The General planned a thorough inquiry, but the first order of business was to recover Elaine. To that end he assembled a party of six of his best archers, with two ponies for each so that one would always be fresh. He had been on the point of riding out when the Khan had summoned him.

The Khan supposed that he should sympathize with a man

whose bride had vanished on his wedding night. But Chormaghun had already stolen the girl once; if he'd misplaced her so soon he had nobody to blame but himself. Of course, if Chormaghun had died it would have been a different matter. The assassination of a Mongol general would have been a tragedy of national import and the perpetrators would have been hunted down at all costs.

But as things stood the Khan did not intend to grant permission to give chase. The fugitives had a twelve-hour head start. No doubt they could be caught, but how long would it take? Two days, maybe three, and the same again to return. Meanwhile Chormaghun's regiment would be without its general because of his difficulties with a woman, and what kind of example would that set for the rest of the army?

In addition, in the next few days the Khan intended to move the army from its current location and so the decision was very clear. Chormaghun could not be allowed to leave. Yet the Khan knew that Chormaghun would have to be mollified in some way.

As for the Frankish Knight and his friends, the Khan was not sorry to be quit of them. He'd enjoyed the wrestling match and the girl had been interesting, but on balance they'd been more trouble than they were worth. Though he had to admit that at least they had not been boring.

Chormaghun came into the clearing and made a proper bow to the Khan, though his impatience to get moving was obvious. The Khan cleared his throat and spoke as tactfully as he could, using the formal language of the court.

"General Chormaghun, word has come to me of the terrible misfortune that has befallen you. Please accept my deepest sympathy. Normally I would support your intention to recover what is yours, and even lend some of my own staff to the effort, but military matters must take precedence and my plans call for the army to move out tomorrow morning. You cannot be absent during this time, you are far too valuable, so valuable, in fact, that I have decided to promote you. . . ."

* * *

Ten minutes later Chormaghun was on his way back to his quarters, barely able to contain his anger. Officers who been laughing behind his back cleared a path and avoided eye contact.

The Khan's decision had come as a shock to him and he was tempted to disobey it. But that would mean an end to his career and would also violate the oath of loyalty he, like all officers, had sworn to the Khan. Chormaghun took that oath seriously, for it had been sworn under the Eternal Blue Sky.

There was still some fighting to be done east of the mountains, but someday—not this fighting season, but perhaps the next—the Khan would lead the army westward over the mountains into the lands of the Arabs and the Christians. When that day came, he, Chormaghun, would be in the vanguard, commanding a division and not merely a regiment (at least the Khan had promoted him!). Then he would have his revenge.

He looked up at the Eternal Blue Sky and swore another oath. *One day the Christian and the Arab will die by my hand, and the woman will be mine again.*

Conrad, Rashid, and Elaine rode steadily through the remainder of the first night and for most of the following day, stopping only to feed and water the horses and then only briefly.

The terrain consisted mainly of barren, rolling hills with no peaks to speak of, so they had no vantage point from which to judge whether or not they were being pursued, and thus no choice but to push on. But toward evening Rashid said, "The horses need rest."

"The Mongols could be right behind us," said Conrad.

"If the horses give out, we're lost anyway," said Rashid, and Conrad agreed to stop.

They slept for four hours, taking turns keeping watch, then rode for another four hours, well past sunset, until they as well as the horses were too exhausted to continue. They made a skeleton camp and slept again. But they rose with the sun and pressed on.

The terrain gradually became more rugged, and in the afternoon they came to a hill that promised a wide view of the land behind and ahead. Rashid urged his horse up the side of the hill and when he reached the top he looked back. He stared for a long time while Conrad and Elaine watched him anxiously, then he gestured for them to join him, which they did.

"What do you see?" Conrad asked.

"Nothing," said Rashid, and indeed there was no sign of riders, even in the distance, nor any trace of a dust cloud such as a group of riders might be expected to raise.

Conrad looked in the opposite direction. "Maybe they're already ahead, cutting us off."

But in that direction, too, there was no sign of horsemen for many miles. Then Conrad noticed that Rashid was smiling at something. Shimmering in the distance above the horizon were the snow-capped peaks of the Zagros Mountains. Conrad and Elaine also smiled. It was like seeing an old friend.

There were still two hours of daylight remaining and no point in wasting it. The three friends urged their horses westward toward home.

PART SIX

PARADISE

◧ 40 ◨

The trip over the Zagros Mountains was uneventful while the weather held. In the weeks since the three friends had first crossed the mountains, thousands of refugees fleeing the Mongols had crossed them in the opposite direction, marking out a path that could be followed easily.

Furthermore, the mountain tribes along the path had set up stalls and carts to service the refugees, so food and supplies were readily available. Conrad scrutinized the tribesmen closely, looking for Sangar, the Kurdish guide who had stolen their gold, but he saw no face that looked familiar.

The three were comfortable together now, for a bond had been forged that would not easily be broken. But as their elation at escaping the Mongols faded, Conrad noticed that Elaine began to seem distracted and withdrawn. She was friendly toward him, even warm occasionally, and thanked him more than once for challenging Chormaghun and for helping her escape. But at the same time she was closed off in a way she had not been before.

Her eyes were sunken and she wasn't eating properly and most troubling of all was her hair, which had become matted and tangled. Once Conrad had considered her combing ritual an affectation, but as the nights passed and she did not resume the habit, he grew concerned.

He strongly suspected that her behavior was related to something she'd suffered at the hands of Chormaghun, and it wasn't hard to guess what that something might be. He gave the matter much thought, wondering what he might say to comfort her, but it was beyond him and he did not bring the subject up.

The first sign of the storm was a light mist, which rose from the ground one morning soon after they broke camp. By midday the mist had thickened and the temperature dropped sharply, then it began to rain and the wind rose and they decided to seek shelter. But they waited too long, for within minutes the rain turned to sleet and then snow, and the wind howling down the mountain passes shook the trees so violently it seemed they would be uprooted and flung through the air like twigs.

They struggled on, the wind driving the cold into their very bones, until they found a cave deep enough to accommodate them and the horses as well. They stumbled inside, dismounted, and began pulling the supply sacks from the backs of the horses.

"A fire!" said Conrad. Elaine gathered a few twigs and sticks from the floor of the cave and took out a flint, but her hands were shivering so badly she couldn't strike it. Conrad and Rashid finished unpacking the supply sacks and put blankets over the backs of the horses. It took bitter cold for a horse to freeze to death, but there was no sense in taking chances.

Elaine finally managed to strike a spark and the twigs caught. But it was obvious that the small flame would not last more than a few minutes.

"We need wood," said Rashid, yelling to be heard above the howling wind, and started to leave the cave.

Conrad grabbed his arm. "You'll never find your way back!"

"Don't worry, just keep the fire going." The Arab disappeared into the driving snow.

Conrad picked up a saddle and brought it over to the fire. It was made of wood and was still dry on the inside. He hacked it apart with his sword and stacked the smaller pieces on the fire. Then he took a blanket and wrapped it around Elaine. He pulled her close to him for warmth, but he could feel her tense up at his touch, so he sat back and removed his arm from her shoulders.

Rashid had never been in a blizzard but he had been in the desert many times and in at least one respect they were similar.

"When there are no landmarks," Hasan had told him, "people walk in a circle. One leg is stronger than the other and the stride therefore longer—only slightly longer, but enough so that you will begin to veer to one side and eventually end up back where you started."

Hasan stressed the importance of walking with precisely equal strides, and had drilled Rashid in that skill until he could stand in the desert a quarter mile from a palm tree and, blindfolded, walk in such a straight line that if he did not run into the tree head-on, he missed by less than an arm's length, touching it as he walked past.

Rashid relied on that training as he stepped into the blizzard. Except for an occasional break in the swirling snow he could only see a few feet in front of him, but he was confident that he was walking a straight path.

Of course there were differences between the desert and the mountains during a blizzard; one of them was the severe cold and another made itself plain when after twenty paces Rashid walked into a tree that he hadn't seen. But he wasn't discouraged—the tree could serve as a waymark on his return journey and he stepped around it and kept walking. In nineteen more paces he came to another tree and stepped around it the same way and twelve paces past that he literally stumbled upon exactly what he had hoped to find—a large tree limb lying on the ground.

He bent down and lifted one end of the limb. It appeared to have been on the ground for some time and was therefore not too green to burn. If it was not yet soaked through from the storm it should serve very well.

He turned around and began walking, hauling the limb behind him. For a few steps he was able to backtrack along his own footprints but the earlier ones had been obliterated by the falling snow, so he had to rely once more on his training. But he was confident he would be back in the cave very soon.

In the cave, Elaine stared vacantly at the fire. Conrad repositioned a piece of wood to catch more of the flame.

"Are you warm enough?" he said.

She gave a slight nod.

"There's another blanket in one of the saddlebags. . . ."

She didn't bother to answer.

"Elaine . . ."

"I'm fine."

"You're not fine. You're acting strangely."

"I'm sorry."

"No, that's not . . ." He stopped. He knew he might only make things worse, but he felt he had to do something before she disappeared inside herself for good. They would have to talk about something neither of them wanted to talk about.

"Did Chormaghun . . . were you . . . what I'm trying to say—"

"Did he violate me? No. He tried, but Rashid's poison worked just in time."

Conrad was greatly relieved, but also baffled. "Then I don't understand. What's wrong? And don't tell me you're fine."

She closed her eyes for a moment, then opened them and said, "Don't you see? I'm his wife!"

Conrad stared at her. "What on earth are you talking about?"

"I married him! There was a ceremony, a *wedding*. . . ."

"Not a real one."

"It was very real. There was music, and a priest, and witnesses . . . and Chormaghun believes I'm his loyal and obedient wife!"

"But you're *not* his loyal and obedient wife!"

"Why? Why am I not? I promised the Khan and then I went through the ceremony. . . ."

Conrad felt the waters rising—this was the kind of philosophical argument he always lost. But he could not afford to lose this one. He threw the blankets aside and grabbed Elaine by her arms and pulled her roughly to her feet. She stared at him, shocked.

"This ceremony," he said, "was it in Frankish?"

"No, Mongolian."

"Did you understand anything that was said?"

"No, I didn't."

"Did you yourself say anything?"

"No." She began to see what he was driving at.

"Not a single word?"

"No."

"Then you didn't consent. And it doesn't matter what the Khan thinks or Chormaghun thinks or a thousand witnesses think, if there was no consent there was no wedding and no marriage. There couldn't be."

"But the promise to the Khan—I swore an oath. . . ."

"You were a prisoner. A promise made under duress isn't binding, even the Church says so." His knightly training had taught him this, so he knew he was on solid ground.

"That's true," said Elaine. Despite the cold, some color had come back into her cheeks. But then she frowned. "But if . . ."

"If what?"

"I can't help feeling if people—people back home, I mean—knew about the wedding—"

"There was no wedding."

"If they knew what happened, they would think I was compromised, or unclean in some way, not fit. . . ."

"Not fit for what?"

"Not fit to marry anyone else. Ever."

A moment passed, then another, as they looked into each other's eyes. Elaine realized she was holding her breath.

Conrad said, slowly and carefully, "In the first place, no one is ever going to know what happened. In the second place, even if everyone did know, on my honor as a Knight I don't believe any person in Christendom would think that you're married, or compromised, or unfit in any way to marry anyone you please. And you shouldn't believe it either. *Don't you dare believe it!*"

He spoke with such vehemence that Elaine burst out in a short laugh that was also a sob of relief.

"You did what you had to do," Conrad continued more calmly. "You made the promise to the Khan in order to serve your country. And now the best way to serve your country is to go back and rule it. There's no shame and nothing to regret. It's the Mongols who should be ashamed for trying to force you into a marriage against your will."

"Yes, perhaps so," Elaine murmured.

"Not perhaps. It's the truth. The plain and simple truth. I tried to force you into marriage myself once. It was wrong and I regret it. And what Chormaghun did was just as wrong or worse, and no reflection whatsoever on you."

She nodded, letting his words soothe her like a balm.

"Perhaps you're right," she said.

"I am right," he said firmly. Then he blurted, "For once!"

She laughed a little at this, and Conrad laughed, too. Elaine sobbed once or twice, then laughed again more freely through her tears, and Conrad laughed along with her.

"All right?" he said after a moment, searching her eyes intently.

She nodded again. She knew it wouldn't be quite this easy—it would take time to let go of the memory—but a knot in her stomach began to unwind for the first time in days.

"Then we'll hear no more about it," Conrad said. "Agreed?"

"Agreed."

"Good." He squeezed her arms gently, then let go of them.

She felt something give way then—as if a river of ice were melting, or a dam breaking. She couldn't put it into words and she hoped Conrad would see it in her eyes, but he was already looking toward the mouth of the cave. "I wonder what's keeping Rashid?"

As he'd expected, Rashid got back to the cave quickly. Through the snow he could see Conrad and Elaine huddled together near the small fire. Rashid was about to enter when Conrad suddenly sprang to his feet and yanked Elaine up as well. Rashid stopped dead in his tracks.

Rashid had been well aware of the change in Elaine. He had wanted to help her, and also Conrad, whose distress was evident; they were his friends—the only two he'd ever had. But, like a war arrow, Rashid had been fashioned for one purpose only and he found the complexities of friendship difficult to navigate. But now, though he couldn't hear what they were saying, he sensed that friendship meant not interrupting. So he stayed where he was, hoping they'd stop talking before he froze solid.

At last Conrad turned away from Elaine and Rashid entered, dragging the tree limb behind him.

"Finally!" said Conrad.

Rashid dropped the limb on the floor of the cave, his hands shaking too badly to draw his dagger, and said, "Cut away the bark. Hurry!"

Conrad drew his knife and began to strip the bark from the tree and branches.

"What kept you?" said Conrad. "We were getting worried."

"It took longer than I thought," said Rashid, his teeth still chattering.

"You got lost, didn't you?"

"No, I didn't get lost," Rashid said irritably.

"You did, admit it," Conrad teased.

"Just for a minute," said Rashid. It was the quickest way to change the subject. He could see that Elaine was feeling better— she was adding the new wood to the fire, moving with something like her old energy. He wondered what Conrad had said to her. He'd ask later. Or perhaps a true friend wouldn't really need to know.

The newly cut wood gave off a white, acrid smoke, for some moisture had penetrated the bark, but it evaporated soon and the logs began to burn. Wrapped in blankets, the three leaned over the fire, letting it warm their faces and hands and waiting for the rest of their bodies to catch up.

Elaine was suddenly so exhausted she could barely keep her eyes open. She slumped to the side and soon she was leaning against Conrad, who put his arm around her and made sure the blanket remained in place. Just before she fell asleep she put her hand in the pocket of her dress and took hold of her ivory comb. She wasn't quite ready to use it yet, but she found comfort in its cool, smooth surface and for the first time in days her sleep was dreamless.

· 41 ·

Rashid felt almost at home as he walked through the marketplace of the small town. He was a long way from the Eagle's Nest, but at least he was out of the Zagros Mountains and in the foothills outside of Mosul, where the language was Arabic. For weeks he'd been swimming in an ocean of foreign tongues—Kurdish, Turkic, Persian, and Mongolian—and dependent on translators. He hadn't realized how much he'd missed his native language.

It was late afternoon and the market wasn't crowded, but there was enough activity so that Rashid could buy supplies and, more important, gather information about the current state of affairs in Mosul, the nearest place to cross the Tigris. What he heard was not encouraging.

"It's the damned refugees," said a tall, gaunt-faced man who sold woolen blankets out of a cart. Rashid had heard others say the same thing several times in the last hour.

He fingered one of the blankets casually, as if not really interested, though the blizzard had destroyed several blankets and he needed more. "Do the refugees not pay their own way?" Rashid asked.

"Some," said the tall man grudgingly. "But some beg or steal. Or flock to Mosul and ask for handouts from the Emir."

"How much for these," Rashid said, pointing to a stack of woolen blankets.

"A silver coin."

Rashid nodded thoughtfully. "How many are there at Mosul—refugees, I mean?"

"Who knows? Thousands. All wanting to cross the river. It's chaos."

"I suppose the magistrates will sort things out," Rashid remarked casually.

The tall merchant snorted. "The Emir has tripled the number of magistrates but it's done precious little good. Are you planning to cross?"

"No," Rashid lied, then added, stroking one of the blankets, "I'll give you a silver coin for two."

"For blankets such as these?" He clicked his tongue and tossed his head to one side dismissively.

"Two silver coins, then," said Rashid. "But for three, not two."

"You're as bad as the refugees!" the tall man said, but handed Rashid three blankets and took the two coins.

Conrad laid out the bedrolls while Elaine prepared the evening meal. Five days had passed since the blizzard. Rashid's tree limb had kept them alive through the night and the storm had exhausted itself the next day, after which the weather changed again, as if nature wanted to atone for the unseasonably harsh snowstorm with some unseasonably warm sunshine.

Conrad had kept a close eye on Elaine during the days that followed. She was clearly on the mend, joining more frequently in conversation and arguing with something like her old spirit. She'd bought a new sling and had begun practicing with it. When, two nights ago, she'd spent an hour combing her hair into a satisfactory condition, Conrad knew the worst was over.

She regarded him truly as a friend now, he was sure of it. She spoke freely and her occasional smile was frank and direct—not a lover's smile, but a warm one. His heart still ached when he looked at her, but perhaps the ache would lessen in time.

It didn't even bother him anymore when she deferred too quickly to Rashid's opinion, for Rashid, too, was his friend. In truth, Elaine and Rashid were the only friends he had ever had. He had been far too much in awe of Charles to truly regard him as a friend, and Gilbert had proved to be nearly worthless.

All this caused a dilemma that weighed upon Conrad heavily, centering on the Old Man's letter. He couldn't bear the thought of endangering his newly won friendships. Neither could he bear the thought of some harm coming to Elaine that he might have prevented. He decided to speak now, before Rashid returned from the market.

"Do you remember the Knight we found on the way to the Eagle's Nest, the one slain by a Mongol arrow?"

"Of course. Sir Raymond. I knew him well."

"Raymond, yes. Well, he was carrying the letter from the Old Man, the one Rashid has now. I think that letter was written to whoever hired the Old Man to assassinate you."

"Why do you think that?"

"The timing, for one thing. And Raymond's connection with Tripoli, and with you. It can't be a coincidence."

Of course. This made perfect sense, and Elaine couldn't believe she hadn't made the connection herself. But so much had happened since they'd come upon Raymond's body, beginning with the bandit attack a mere few hours later, that her thoughts had never circled back to wonder just what he had been doing so far east of Tripoli.

"You're probably right," she said. "But what can we do about it now?"

"We have to read the letter."

Elaine shook her head. "I swore an oath to the Old Man."

"An oath to a Muslim means nothing," Conrad said. "Everyone says so. Even priests."

Elaine shook her head more firmly. "I've already broken a

promise to the Khan and it's not a habit I want to get into. Besides, I swore this oath on the soul of my father."

"Yes, I remember," said Conrad. "But—"

"No. Besides, it would be a betrayal of Rashid."

"We'll have to talk to Rashid about it, of course," said Conrad. "But—"

"Talk to Rashid about what?" said a voice behind them.

They turned, startled. Rashid, as usual, had managed to appear without being seen or heard. Conrad came straight to the point. "I think Elaine should read the Old Man's letter. It might tell us who wants her dead."

"Or it might not," Rashid replied, so promptly that Conrad suspected the Arab had been thinking the matter over himself.

"We need to know for certain," said Conrad.

"Elaine is sworn not to read it, and I'm sworn to protect it," Rashid said evenly.

"I understand," Conrad said. "But suppose she doesn't read it and is killed as a result."

"The Old Man said he'd protect her," said Rashid.

"He'll try," said Conrad. "But he'll be in his castle and she'll be in Tripoli. What if he fails?"

Rashid hesitated. He'd already taken enough risks with the letter for the sake of Conrad and Elaine. To let Elaine read it seemed wrong—the Old Man had explicitly forbidden it. He understood Conrad's desire to protect Elaine; he wanted to protect her as well. But to betray the Old Man . . . He struggled to find an answer, but Elaine spoke first.

"That's not fair to Rashid," she said firmly. "Anyway, it's not up to him. I've sworn an oath on the soul of my father and I won't break it."

"Even if it costs your life," said Conrad.

"Even then," said Elaine.

Relieved, Rashid gave Elaine a look of thanks, and avoided meeting Conrad's gaze.

There was tension in the air and Conrad sensed that pressing the matter further would be futile. Reluctantly he held his tongue.

"We have another problem," said Rashid when the moment had passed. "We can't cross the Tigris at Mosul. They're turning many away at the landing and the city is crawling with magistrates."

"Will they still care about Jamal's murder?" said Conrad.

"They might—his father is a servant of the Emir's," Rashid pointed out. "We'll have to cross upriver. We should make an early start tomorrow."

The next morning they gave Mosul a wide berth and rode along the east bank of the Tigris for several miles until they came to a secondary landing where two ferries were operating. But even here there were a hundred travelers waiting to cross, and a dozen rough-looking men with scimitars and turbans bearing the blue and yellow cockade that marked them as magistrates. One of the magistrates glanced at them. Hands on hips, he watched while they pretended to be unaware of his scrutiny. They were past the landing and starting to relax when the magistrate shouted something at them.

"Ride," said Rashid.

They galloped for a mile, then trotted for a mile, then galloped again and maintained that rhythm for half an hour. Then Rashid performed his ritual of finding a high piece of ground and looking back, but he looked for only a moment before hurrying to rejoin his comrades.

"They're coming," he said. "Four of them."

"How far back?" Conrad asked.

"Not far."

Conrad shrugged. "Let's wait for them here," he said, fingering his sword.

"They'll just send others. And then others after them," said Rashid.

"So we keep running?" Conrad said.

"No," said Rashid. He looked at the river. "We cross." Rashid gave his horse a pat on the neck and headed him toward the Tigris.

"No!" said Conrad. He remembered all too well his last encounter with a river. He would fight all the magistrates Mosul could send before he'd plunge into another one.

Elaine moved her horse closer to his. "Horses are strong swimmers," she said.

"I'm not," said Conrad.

She leaned over and gave his arm an encouraging squeeze. "I can imagine what you're feeling. But you made it across then and you'll make it across this time as well. Just stay in the saddle and let the horse do the work. If anything goes wrong, Rashid and I will be there to pull you out, I promise." They held a look. There was no mockery in her eyes, just encouragement.

"All right," Conrad said.

"Good!" said Elaine, and spurred her horse toward the river. Conrad hesitated—despite Elaine's words he knew it was a desperate gamble. How strong was the current? What about whirlpools, or submerged branches? And were all three horses strong enough after the recent forced ride? If even one of them failed to cross before the magistrates arrived, the plan would fail.

But Rashid's horse was already up to his chest in water and Elaine's was not far behind. Conrad could still feel the touch of Elaine's hand on his arm as he took a deep breath and rode into the river.

The current wasn't overpowering, but it was strong enough so Conrad felt his horse struggling against it, and it was pushing them downstream, in the direction of the magistrates. This made it all the more critical to cross quickly, but the animal was already working as hard as it could.

At midriver he encountered a sandbar. The horse lurched onto the strip of earth and across it and plunged into the deep water on the other side and for one sickening moment Conrad felt the river start to lift him out of the saddle, but he managed to keep his seat. The horse, seeing the opposite shore so near, redoubled its efforts and soon Conrad, to his enormous relief, was on dry ground again.

Rashid and Elaine were already across and riding hard for a grove of trees two hundred yards from the riverbank and Conrad followed. All three reached the grove, using the trees to screen them, then turned and looked back.

In less than a minute four magistrates came into sight across the river, moving at a brisk trot. They kept moving upriver, not bothering to glance at the flowing water or at the grove of trees on the other side, and when they had ridden out of sight the three travelers breathed again.

"Shall we let the horses rest?" Conrad asked.

"Let's get away from the river first," Rashid said, and they began to walk the horses slowly out of the grove and onto the plain beyond. Only then did they notice a flock of sheep and a shepherd boy, twelve or thirteen years old, watching them curiously.

From where the boy stood he must have seen everything—their swim across the river, the dash for the trees, the passing of the magistrates on the other side. Conrad and Rashid looked at each other and Elaine knew what they were thinking. It would be well not to leave any witnesses behind.

She started to speak, but suddenly the shepherd boy raised his hand and gave them a friendly wave. They burst out laughing and rode on.

A half hour later they stopped near another grove, this one of elms whose broad leaves gave shade and rustled soothingly in the gentle breeze.

The horses weren't the only ones who needed rest. Conrad lay down with his back against one of the elms and closed his eyes. His mind went back to the Old Man's letter. Neither he nor Rashid was capable of reading it, and Elaine had refused to do so. Yet the letter had to be read.

Half-asleep, he wondered what Charles would do. As he drifted, he dreamt he heard Charles's voice, or perhaps it was his own voice saying what he imagined Charles would say if he were here. *You have a sword. Use it!*

Conrad shook his head drowsily. Yes, of course, use your advantages, use what you have. But how could a sword be used to read a letter? Then he realized the answer and sprang to his feet, suddenly wide-awake. "Elaine!"

Startled, she opened her eyes and stared at him.

"Does writing have to be any particular size?" he said.

"What are you talking about?"

"The letters, they can be made as big as you like?"

"I suppose so, but—"

"Rashid, come here!" Conrad said excitedly, and Rashid came over, his expression curious.

"I want you to show me the Old Man's letter. Do you object to that?"

"What's the point? You can't read it."

"No," said Conrad. "But I can copy it into the dirt with my sword. Then Elaine can read what's on the ground!" He'd feared it might sound stupid when he said it out loud, but he could tell by Elaine's expression that she didn't think it was stupid at all.

Rashid frowned. "How can you copy it if you can't read it?"

"I'll just be copying the marks," said Conrad. "I won't know what they mean but if I copy them accurately Elaine will. Won't you?" Again Elaine's expression confirmed his point.

He turned back to Rashid. "She won't be violating her oath because she won't be reading the letter. And you won't be breaking faith with the Old Man, because you won't be allowing anyone to read the letter."

Rashid's frown deepened. He'd hoped this matter had been laid to rest.

Conrad continued urgently, "Rashid! It harms no one, it violates no trust or oath, and it may save Elaine's life."

Rashid hesitated. "Elaine won't read the letter . . ."

"She won't even look at it," Conrad promised.

Rashid understood the logic. He also knew it was a trick, and that the Sheikh would be greatly disappointed if he went along with it. But Conrad was looking at him beseechingly, almost desperately, and now Elaine, too, seemed to be hoping he would agree. He knew Elaine's life, and therefore Conrad's future, might depend on what he did next. The choice was an impossible one. Whichever decision he made, he might end up regretting it bitterly.

Rashid reached into his shirt and took out the Old Man's letter and handed it to Conrad.

42

Conrad labored for an hour with the letter in one hand and his sword in the other, painstakingly scratching a precise, much enlarged copy of the markings into the soft dirt around the elm trees. When he was finished, Elaine read it aloud as Rashid and Conrad listened:

"To Bernard, most Gracious and Valiant Regent of Tripoli, Greetings and Salutations from ad-Din as-Sinan, Lord of the Eagle's Nest. Very soon the business for which you engaged me will be accomplished and you will be sole master of Tripoli. I congratulate you!"

Elaine stopped reading; she was stunned. The only "business" that would make Bernard sole master of Tripoli was her death. It had been Bernard who had hired the Old Man! She'd been certain, when Conrad began making his marks in the dirt, that it would prove to be Constable Delancey, or possibly Matilda's father, Basil.

"Bernard!" she said. "I can't believe it. I knew he had no great love for me, but I never dreamed . . . and Raymond. Raymond was my friend! He taught me how to use—" The words caught in her throat. After the Mongols, she'd thought nothing could ever shock her again, but she'd been mistaken.

"Raymond was your friend, but Bernard's vassal first," said Conrad. "Besides, it's quite possible he didn't know the contents of the messages he was carrying."

"That's true," said Elaine, and felt a little better. "But why did Bernard go to the trouble of arranging my marriage to you, if he was going to have me killed?"

"All the better to disguise his true purpose."

Elaine still found it hard to believe Bernard would have her murdered. On the other hand, he was certainly ambitious. And hiring the Old Man was clever, for without this letter the murder never would have been traced back to Bernard.

Conrad said, "Read the rest of it."

With an effort Elaine put aside her shock and resumed reading. *"God willing, you will soon be master of Antioch as well and the most powerful Christian ruler west of the Euphrates."*

"What?" Now it was Conrad's turn to be shocked. "My father is master in Antioch! Are you sure that's what it says?"

"I'm sure," Elaine said.

"Bernard must be planning to eliminate my father and myself as well," said Conrad, his face white with fury. "Go on."

Elaine continued: *"Despite our present dealings I know you regard me as an enemy and I confess that such has been my opinion of you. But I write to tell you of a different enemy, one that threatens your kingdom and mine as well. From reports I have received from beyond the Zagros Mountains, this enemy is so numerous and powerful that they have swept all before them, slaughtering believers and non-believers, my people and yours, alike."*

"The Mongols," Conrad said. "He's warning Bernard about the Mongols."

Elaine continued: *"The ruler is an arrogant dog who calls himself King of Kings and intends to lay waste to all lands east of the Great Sea. Though you and I are not of the same faith, does it not behoove us to join together against such a pagan enemy, who is an abomination in the sight of heaven? Are we not far more likely to prevail if we stand together, and do not permit this filthy cur to destroy us one by one? Will you not meet with me to discuss uniting our nations, and others as well,* both Christian and Muslim, in Holy War against him? Let us avoid the shame of being enslaved by this infidel heathen who is an offense to my God and to yours also! Tell me what conditions you require to ensure your safety but let us not delay our meeting, for this pig has already sent spies west of the Mountains and his army will surely follow in force, perhaps in the next fighting season. There is little time to lose."

Elaine stopped reading and looked up. "That's all," she said.

There was a moment of silence, then Conrad said, "The Old Man is trying to form a coalition to fight the Mongols. That's why he was so anxious to get the letter back."

Elaine nodded. "If the Khan saw this he'd pursue the Old Man to the ends of the earth."

Conrad could not help smiling. "Yes. I think the Khan would also object to being called an arrogant dog and a filthy cur."

"Also a pig and a heathen," said Rashid.

"An abomination in the sight of heaven," Elaine said.

They were laughing, but it was nervous laughter because, intemperate though the Old Man's language was, they knew he was right about the Khan's intentions.

Rashid realized there was another way in which the letter was dangerous to the Old Man. The Assassins were already regarded as renegades by the vast majority of Muslims, and if it became known that the Old Man had approached a Christian state about an alliance, the Assassins would be even more hated and despised than they already were.

Rashid held out his hand. Conrad handed him the letter and Rashid put it inside his shirt again, wondering if he'd done the right thing in allowing Conrad and Elaine to use it as they had. The sooner he placed it in the Old Man's hands the better he would feel. "You're finished with the markings?" he said.

"Yes," said Elaine. "We know what we need to know."

Rashid began rubbing out the marks in the dirt with his feet, and the other two joined in until there was no trace left of the work Conrad had done with his sword.

As they traveled on Elaine felt a reluctant admiration for the Old Man. His habit of murdering his enemies had alienated Christians and Muslims alike, yet he'd suspected what no one else west of the Zagros had: that before long Genghis Khan would lead his army over the Zagros and into the western lands, and the inhabitants of those lands would have two choices—death or submission. The only chance for the Muslims and Christians to survive as independent peoples would be to unite against the Mongols, just as the Old Man had said.

But she wondered if such an alliance was possible. Even leaving the Assassins aside, the infighting among the Muslims in the Holy Land was notorious, and was the only thing that allowed the Christians there to survive. Yet the Christians were no better—Bernard's plot against her and Conrad was proof of that. How much less could Christians and Muslims be expected to set aside their differences, even temporarily?

Yet Conrad and Rashid had once sworn to kill each other, and since that time they had risked their lives for one another repeatedly; and now they rode side by side, friends and companions. Perhaps the impossible was sometimes possible.

It was all very complicated. And of course, dealing with Bernard would be no simple matter either.

◈ 43 ◈

The last few months had not been pleasant for Bernard, Regent of Tripoli. First, the damned Assassin had unaccountably failed to kill Elaine; then he and the Princess had apparently vanished into thin air, and to top it off, Prince Conrad had mysteriously disappeared as well, and none of them had been seen since.

It was perplexing and also humiliating. As Regent he bore ultimate responsibility and he knew he was the subject of much criticism and even ridicule, which increased as time passed with no sign of any of the three renegades. Of course if the truth were known— that he himself had paid to have Elaine killed as part of a plan to make himself joint ruler of Tripoli and Antioch—ridicule would be the least of his problems. But exposure seemed highly unlikely, because whatever else the Old Man might be, he was always discreet. Secrecy was woven into the very fabric of his life.

So Bernard had believed; but now he could no longer be certain even of that. A month after Elaine had vanished, an iron strongbox had been given to the castle guards with instructions to pass it on to Bernard. Bernard had ordered it brought to his chamber, where he opened it in private; it held fifty gold coins—the advance payment he had sent to the Old Man for the murder of Elaine.

Why had the Old Man returned the money? Was he simply acknowledging his failure to carry out his part of their bargain? Or did it signify a change of heart—he was no longer willing to carry out his part? Bernard did not dare send a message to the Old Man to find out, for the only one of his servants with sufficient courage to carry one, Sir Raymond, had been discovered, slain by a strange arrow and buried in a shallow grave in the wilderness between Tripoli and the Eagle's Nest.

Everyone had wondered what Raymond was doing, alone, in such a deserted spot; only Bernard knew the answer, but of course he had pretended to be as puzzled as everyone else, and it was added to the list of inexplicable misfortunes that Tripoli had recently suffered.

Bernard had sent out envoys and spies by the dozen to make inquiries about the possible whereabouts of Conrad or Elaine or the Assassin. He got back hundreds of answers, mostly rumors, fabrications, or speculations that became more fantastical by the day. Yet by patiently sifting through and comparing the myriad reports, he was able to glean a few grains of wheat from the chaff, and he believed he had some idea of what had happened, if not why.

Three travelers, fitting the general descriptions of Elaine and the other two, had been seen together in various locations that suggested they had passed through the Old Man's territory and then crossed the Euphrates River at Ar-Raqqah. They had somehow become separated but had been reunited in Mosul, where they may or may not have been involved in a killing of some kind. Then they had gone over the Zagros Mountains into Khwarazm, which, according to various reports, was engaged in a war with some foreign power.

Why the three were traveling together, and what their purpose was, he couldn't guess. But the very fact that they were together damned Conrad and Elaine in the eyes of most Christians, and Bernard made sure that the results of his inquiries were made known throughout Tripoli and Antioch.

Discrediting the three was good, but it would be even better if they stayed away from Tripoli, preferably forever. But there were two problems. The first was the possibility that they had somehow discovered Bernard's treachery. The second problem was that they might come back. If they did return to Tripoli knowing the truth, his days were numbered.

Only one conclusion was possible: they must not return to Tripoli alive.

Walter, Sergeant-at-Arms and former Master of Horse at Tripoli, was also enduring a very difficult few months; in fact, he was thoroughly disgraced. He had been the one who'd hired Rashid in the first place, and he had also led the search party from which Conrad had vanished.

Walter and his men had remained in the field for many days, scouring the countryside for some trace of Elaine or the Assassin or Conrad, but had finally returned to the castle empty-handed, and very soon afterward Walter found himself a pariah and a laughingstock.

There had been some talk of exile, but he was spared that fate in view of his long years of faithful service to the kingdom. But he was removed from his position as Master of Horse; and his dream—one he had cherished secretly for many years—of one day being knighted, slim at best given his advanced age, was now an utter impossibility.

Since then he had lived a shadowy existence, formally part of the castle guard but without any real status, seemingly destined to live out his life in shame and obscurity. So when he received word that Bernard had sent for him he was not much perturbed, for he had little left to lose. When he appeared at the entrance to the throne room he was surprised to see that Bernard was alone, with no courtiers or advisers around him.

"Come in, Walter," the Regent said in a friendly tone, and Walter entered. Bernard closed the door behind him and said, "How are you, old friend?"

This was strange coming from the man who had been responsible for Walter's demotion, but Walter just said, "Well enough, m'lord."

"Perhaps you think it odd of me to call you friend?" said Bernard.

Very odd, thought Walter, but he said, "I hope we've always been on friendly terms, m'lord."

"I've been a better friend than you know," said Bernard. "You're aware that some wanted you exiled after the recent . . . unpleasantness?"

"I'd heard talk of it."

"Did you also know there were even some who thought you should be stripped of the right to bear arms?"

This was a shock. For a warrior such as Walter, death would have been far preferable.

"I would not permit it," Bernard said. "Unfortunately I was unable to preserve your station as Master of Horse, but I did what I could."

It seemed to Walter that Bernard, as ruler of Tripoli, could have done whatever he pleased, but he just said, "I thank you, m'lord."

"The fact is, Walter, you and I have both been victims of some extremely strange circumstances. Why did Elaine flee from the castle with the Assassin? Why did Conrad vanish as well? And why was Raymond slain? It's as if we were under a curse!"

"I confess the answer is beyond me," said Walter.

"It is a puzzle," Bernard agreed. "But I've been making inquiries and a few things have come to light."

He told Walter what he'd learned from his spies, most of which Walter had already heard through rumors, though he listened politely until Bernard had finished. Then Walter said, "They are beyond the Zagros, then."

"So it seems," said Bernard. "And once winter sets in they'll remain there at least until next year. But if they try to return sooner, say in the next few weeks, they will have to be stopped."

"Stopped, m'lord?"

"What possible good could result if they returned? The Assassin, by virtue of the very fact of what he is, should be killed on sight, and the Princess Elaine has become his whore."

Walter flinched at this, but the Regent pressed on. "What other explanation can there be? They've been together since the day they left Tripoli."

"Perhaps against her will."

"Not according to the reports I've received." Bernard paused to let this sink in.

Walter shook his head. "I can scarce believe it."

"Nor can I. But I ask again, what other explanation can there be?"

"None, I suppose."

"Exactly. Now, suppose she returns. What will she do? Move back into the castle with her lover the Assassin?"

"As you say, we'll kill the Assassin," said Walter.

"And what then?" said Bernard. "What future could there be for his former whore? Will anyone marry her? Will the citizens of Tripoli accept her as their ruler when she comes of age? She will be a shame and a disgrace to herself and to the nation. Can you deny it?"

Walter could not. In fact, everything Bernard was saying confirmed his worst fears—fears he had refused to articulate, even to himself. Bernard continued, "The truth—the very sad truth—is that Tripoli would be better off if she were dead. Her father, much as he loved her, would want her dead. Elaine herself would be better off dead! I know you were fond of her once. We all were. But she's betrayed us, all of us. And consider that every misfortune you yourself have suffered can be laid to her betrayal."

"You want her killed, along with the Assassin," Walter said carefully.

"It's not what I want," said Bernard. "It's what needs to be done. It's what *must* be done."

"And Prince Conrad?"

"His case is the most contemptible of all," said Bernard. "He is complicit in the unnatural union between his betrothed and an

Assassin. It was his duty to protect her virtue. Instead he became her whoremonger. And he a sworn Christian knight! Would you follow such a man into battle? Would you obey him as your prince?"

"No, m'lord."

"No. Nor would I, nor would any man. He, most of all, deserves to die."

Walter had no answer, and Bernard went on sorrowfully, as if proposing a sad necessity, "I want you to take a picked force of men—as many as you think fit. I'll pay generously but be sure they're the kind of men who will do their duty, however unpleasant. In addition I'll provide money to hire scouts and spies, as many as you need. If the three stay on the far side of the Zagros, well and good. But if they attempt to return to Tripoli you will kill them and bury them where they fall. Is that understood?"

"Yes, m'lord," said Walter.

"Good. If you succeed, I will see that you are justly rewarded."

"Might I hope to regain my old position as Master of Horse?" Walter asked.

Bernard paused dramatically. "I was thinking more in terms of a knighthood," he said. "Sir Walter of Tripoli. How does that strike you?"

Walter could hardly believe his ears. He swallowed hard. "It strikes me very nicely, m'lord," he said. "Very nicely indeed."

· 44 ·

After a month of patrolling the territory east of Tripoli, Walter thought there was very little chance that the three would return to the city before winter. There had been reports of a severe storm in the Zagros already, and few travelers would risk a crossing this late in the season. And despite the dozens of spies he had dispatched he had received no useful information whatsoever.

Then everything changed.

One of his spies had spoken with a shepherd boy on the west of the Tigris, upriver from Mosul. The boy claimed he had seen three riders, two men and a woman, fording the river just before a squadron of magistrates from Mosul had appeared riding along the opposite bank. The details—the riders were young, the woman and one of the men were Franks, the other man was an Arab—were too specific to be invented. Walter doubled the number of spies and told his men-at-arms to stay at the ready.

"At the ready" in this case meant sober, or at least reasonably so. Walter was not proud of the men he had brought with him. He would have preferred a more elite band, but there was still enough sympathy for the Princess in Tripoli so that most men of honor had refused the mission. So Walter had hired a disgraced knight, two sergeants-at-arms who had no fixed employment, and a dozen common soldiers who were little better than thugs. They were a motley group but they had two things in common: they would remain loyal to whoever paid them, and they were hardened killers.

Walter himself had no qualms about killing the Assassin and few about killing Conrad, whom he disliked heartily. But Elaine was a different matter. He had fond memories of her growing up in the castle, and whatever she may have done since, killing a woman was not fit work for a true soldier. He would leave that particular piece of business to the butchers he had hired.

One unexpected—and unwelcome—result of the new situation was the arrival of Bernard. As long as he'd thought the three were east of the Zagros, he'd been content to remain amid the comforts of Tripoli, but when word of the shepherd boy's report reached him he decided to take personal command of the search. He didn't interfere with the details—he had enough sense to leave military matters to Walter—but he was a bundle of nerves, always asking for "the latest information" and constantly scanning the horizon as if he expected the three to appear magically out of nowhere. What was he so anxious about? He had Walter and fifteen hardened soldiers for protection, and if that wasn't sufficient why had he left Tripoli at all?

"I have to be certain," was all he would say when Walter tactfully suggested that he return to the city. "I want to see them die."

"What's the difference between seeing them die and seeing their bodies after I've killed them?" Walter said.

"I have to be certain."

After the first few attempts Walter gave up trying to reason with him. The Regent was in charge and could do what he liked. But it was strange. What was the man afraid of?

Over the next few days scouts returned with various sightings. It seemed that the three had veered farther south than would have been the case if they were making for Tripoli. This wasn't surprising. It was likely, since the Assassin was with them, that they were going to the Eagle's Nest instead.

So Walter roused his soldiers and moved out, Bernard riding fretfully at his side. Walter knew exactly where to go. The three would be traveling through desert country and anyone who crossed it would be forced to stop at an oasis called Al-Khasa, some thirty miles from where Walter now was.

Walter and his men rode for the rest of that day, rested for a few hours, then rose early the next morning and started out again. They entered the desert, its rolling dunes broken only by the occasional scrubby bush that had managed to find a little moisture below the sand. They reached Al-Khasa at midmorning.

The oasis was crowded, for not only single travelers but whole caravans stopped there to replenish their stores of water and food. Most were Arab merchants, not heavily armed, and they cast nervous glances at the squadron of Frankish soldiers, but Walter, speaking Arabic, made it clear that he was seeking not plunder but information: had anyone encountered travelers fitting the description of the three?

Several of the merchants stepped forward and to Walter's amazement they all said the same thing: three such travelers had indeed been seen that very morning and had left not more than an hour ago, traveling westward.

"Impossible!" Walter snapped. "We've just come from the west. Why didn't we pass them?"

"I don't know," said the one of the merchants. "But that is the truth." Others nodded their heads in agreement.

Walter wondered if one of the caravans might be hiding the three for some reason, but it didn't seem likely. He cast a glance that encompassed all the merchants at once. "Very well, we'll ride west. But if we don't overtake them by noon we'll be back and not one of you will be left alive."

The merchants flinched at the words but did not change their story and Walter and his men headed westward at a brisk trot.

The rich soil and date groves of the oasis soon gave way to sand and Walter and his men were back in the desert again. They rode for an hour, spreading out to cover a wide path, but saw no sign of the three.

"The bastards lied to us," Bernard said.

"Patience, m'lord," Walter answered.

"I've been patient for a week now."

"Only a little longer, m'lord."

But after another hour passed Walter began to change his mind. Bernard was right: the merchants had lied. But why? Well, they'd regret it. Walter turned in the saddle to call his men in, then swore impatiently; one of the horses in the back of the line bore an empty saddle. Walter spurred toward it and saw the rider sprawled on his back in the sand fifty yards away, no doubt in a drunken stupor. Walter was half inclined to kill him on the spot as an object lesson to the others, but that proved to be unnecessary. For when Walter reached the man he saw that his throat was slit from ear to ear, the blood still flowing from the gaping wound.

Bernard had ridden along right behind Walter.

"My God, these fools are killing one another!" said Bernard.

"No, we'd have heard the clamor," Walter answered.

"Then what—" Bernard began, then he stopped and turned white. *"Assassins!"*

Walter was irritated at the panicked tone, but he had to admit Bernard was probably right. Assassins were famous for swift and silent murders, just like this one.

"I'm telling you," Bernard babbled, "this is the work of—"

"Silence!" Walter snapped, and Bernard was too frightened to object to the insult. Walter drew his sword and rose in his stirrups and looked intently around, and his soldiers, unnerved, did the same. Assassins were highly capable but they were flesh and blood and the killer couldn't have vanished into thin air. There had to be some trace, some sound.

But there was nothing to be heard but Bernard's ragged breathing, and nothing to be seen but sand.

After fording the Tigris, Conrad, Rashid, and Elaine had taken only ten days to cross the Al-Jazirah. But they had pushed too hard and Rashid's horse had gone lame, which delayed them a few days while it healed. Then they'd ferried across the Euphrates at Ar-Raqqah at almost the identical spot where Conrad had gone overboard, but the river was tame now and, apart from bad memories, there were no difficulties.

Now they were on the final stretch, perhaps a week from the Eagle's Nest, and Rashid thought it best to stay well to the south and avoid the large market town of Hama, where they might conceivably be recognized by sight or reputation, since it was only fifty miles from Tripoli.

"Where will we get provisions?" Conrad asked.

"There's an oasis called Al-Khasa," Rashid said.

So they swung southward, into the fringe of desert country, and reached Al-Khasa late in the evening. The next morning they purchased food and filled their waterskins, ignoring the curious stares of the merchants, and set off for the Eagle's Nest. They were just leaving the oasis when Rashid dismounted near a palm tree—the last, lonely one west of the oasis—and began clambering up its long, straight trunk, using his hands and bare feet for traction.

"What's wrong?" said Elaine.

Conrad smiled. "There's no hill for him to look out from so he's using the tree." Conrad wasn't concerned. After everything they'd been through it seemed inconceivable that disaster could befall them this close to their destination. But a few seconds later Rashid was back on the ground, his face tense.

"Riders from the west," he said.

"The west?" Conrad repeated. Anyone following them should be coming from the east, behind them.

"Franks," said Rashid. "The leader is Tripoli's Master of Horse."

"Walter?" Elaine said. "He's a friend."

"A friend with a small army of cutthroats," Rashid said.

"How many?" said Conrad.

"Seventeen."

"I don't understand," said Elaine. In fact she understood but didn't want to believe it.

"They're looking for us," said Conrad. "That's the only reason they'd be out here, which means they were probably sent by Bernard."

"I think Bernard is with them," said Rashid.

"Bernard never leaves the castle," said Elaine.

"I only saw him once, at the stables, but I'm almost certain he was riding just behind the Master of Horse."

"Either way they're coming for us, and they're not coming to chat," Conrad said. "How much time do we have?"

"None," said Rashid.

Rashid leaped into his saddle and they rode hard due north, at right angles to the line of approach that Walter was taking. Up one dune and down the far side, then over another and then a third and then they stopped. Conrad and Elaine remained hidden just on the far side of the dune's crest while Rashid, in the trough behind them, made sure the horses stayed silent.

Soon the Franks came in sight, led by Walter. As Rashid had said, Bernard was riding close behind him. The riders had spread out, but not quite widely enough; another hundred yards and they'd have stumbled across Conrad and Elaine. But they kept straight on, toward Al-Khasa.

Conrad and Elaine rejoined Rashid. A decision had to be made quickly, for they knew they'd been seen at the oasis and it would only be a half hour at most before Walter led his men back into the desert to pursue them.

They could continue north to Hama, but this risked being recognized. To the south was nothing but empty desert; and heading west in an attempt to outrun seventeen experienced riders was not a promising prospect either, especially since Rashid's horse had already gone lame once.

"Then we fight," said Elaine.

"I agree," said Conrad. "Let's stand our ground."

Rashid stooped down and picked up a handful of sand and let it trickle through his fingers. "Not ground, sand," he said, and quickly outlined his battle plan.

It wasn't hard to burrow into the desert and become invisible, at least for one who had been instructed by a master such as Hasan. Rashid lay quietly on his right side. The only part of him not covered in sand was his left eye, which he kept closed most of the time to eliminate even the slightest risk of detection. He only hoped that Walter and his men would return the same way they had come.

They did. Rashid waited, barely breathing, as the line of riders approached, looking everywhere for their prey except where he was: directly under their feet. When the riders had passed, Rashid rose from his burrow like a ghost from a grave and drew his knife and leaped on the back of the horse of the trailing rider and slit the man's throat from behind. The man fell silently to the ground and within a few seconds Rashid had returned to his burrow in the sand.

He heard the cries of alarm when the body was discovered, heard the soldiers gather, and knew they were searching for him in vain, though he lay within a few yards of where their horses stood stamping nervously at the scent of blood. It was time for the second part of the plan to take effect.

Elaine and Conrad had positioned themselves on the far side of an adjacent dune; now they made a sudden appearance on its crest. They did not make a formidable impression, a young woman on foot and a single mounted warrior holding a sword but wearing no armor. Those riders nearest the dune, seven in all, charged confidently up the slope.

Instantly a sling appeared in Elaine's hand. A stone flew through the air and struck the lead rider in the forehead, knocking him from his horse. Before he hit the ground Elaine had already seated another stone and the remaining riders attacked her, hoping to strike home before she could get off many more shots. She slung another stone that took out a second rider and by then Conrad was cutting across their path. He killed one man with a straight thrust of his blade and another with a backhand slash. When the other riders turned to face his attack, a third fell victim to Elaine's sling.

The remaining two soldiers, caught between Elaine on one side and Conrad on the other, hesitated, which was the worst thing they could have done, for Elaine picked off one with her sling and the other was no match for Conrad. Soon all seven attackers lay dead or wounded on the desert floor.

All this happened in less than a minute, while Walter and Bernard and the remaining soldiers gaped in astonishment. Then one of the soldiers gave a shrill cry and Walter turned and saw what the man had already seen—two more riderless horses. The Assassin had struck again, twice, while everyone had been watching the fight on the dune.

Stunned, Walter realized that ten of his fifteen men had been eliminated almost before he had realized the battle had been joined. He'd fallen into a trap and been outsmarted, but he'd be damned if he'd be outfought. He spurred his horse and headed straight for Conrad.

Conrad saw him coming and felt a surge of elation. Their dislike was mutual and now the reckoning was at hand. They met halfway up the dune.

Conrad knew at once that Walter was a far better swordsman than the men he had just defeated. Conrad was stronger and more agile, but there are only so many feints and parries and thrusts a man can make with a sword and Walter had seen them all a hundred times. He made no aggressive moves, but his defense was magnificent and Conrad knew the fight would be a long one. *If you can't beat them down, then wear them down*, Charles used to say, and that's what Conrad set out to do.

Walter sensed the Knight's frustration. *He's young, he thinks he knows how to be patient, but he'll make a mistake and then I'll strike.* And so the two men continued the struggle—their horses wheeled and counterwheeled, their blades rang and flashed wildly in the sun.

Besides Walter, five soldiers now remained. They were not cowards, but neither were they fools. To one side was the shadowy Assassin and his lethal dagger; to the other was a slinger whose missiles had proven just as effective; and in front of them their leader and paymaster was fighting a man who was at least his equal. If Walter died their chances of being paid died with him, and perhaps they would be able to enter into the service of the victors. They glanced at each other and, by unspoken mutual consent, did not pursue the battle further. All eyes turned to the struggle between Conrad and Walter.

Bernard, too, remained where he was. If Walter won the fight, all would yet be well. And Bernard had never seen Walter bested with the sword.

In the end the fight was decided by a fluke. Conrad's blade bit into the chain mail on Walter's left arm and became wedged in the tangle of broken links. Conrad could not pull it free. Walter swung his sword in a short, violent arc aimed at severing Conrad's hand at the wrist. At the last instant Conrad let go of his sword and yanked his hand back. Walter's sword missed his fingers by an inch.

Walter was off balance from the momentum of his stroke and Conrad's sword hung from the broken chain mail on his arm. Conrad grasped the hilt with both hands and jerked it free. When Walter tried to bring his sword up again, Conrad, still holding his own weapon with both hands, swung it viciously and sent Walter's sword flying. In an instant Conrad had the point of his sword at Walter's throat.

"Yield!"

"I will not," said Walter. "Slay me and be damned."

Conrad was about to oblige when Elaine's voice called out, "Wait!"

She spoke to Walter. "You would die for Bernard?"

"He is my liege lord," said Walter.

"He's also a traitor," said Elaine. "He's the one who tried to have me killed and I have proof of it. Whatever he told you about me was a lie."

Walter's eyes narrowed skeptically. "What proof?"

Elaine said, "I'll explain everything, but first tell your men to stand down."

"I'd say they're standing down already," Conrad observed drily, but a sudden shout caught his attention. It was Rashid who'd shouted, and the reason was quickly evident—a lone rider was fleeing the scene of the battle as fast as his horse would carry him.

"Bernard!" said Elaine. In the heat of the battle they'd all but forgotten him. "We have to stop him!"

Conrad reined his horse around to give chase. Elaine saw that Rashid had vaulted into the saddle of a nearby mount and was already pursuing Bernard. She turned to Walter.

"Wait here for us, please. Trust me, for the sake of our friendship and my father's memory."

Walter's lips curled with contempt. "You speak of friendship and your father's memory, but you fight alongside an Assassin!"

"I swear to you, I'll explain everything. Surely you trust me more than you trust Bernard?"

She thought she saw a flicker of response in his eyes, but she couldn't linger to find out for certain. She dug her heels into her horse and started after Conrad. At the moment catching Bernard was paramount. If he somehow managed to return safely to Tripoli he could still cause a great deal of trouble.

· 45 ·

Damn the girl and damn her sling. And damn that old fool Raymond for teaching her to use it! Bernard had forgotten how good she was. The band of hooligans Walter had assembled, repulsive as they were, might possibly have handled the Assassin and the Knight. Elaine and her sling had been the difference.

These reflections tumbled through Bernard's mind as he galloped westward over the dunes, but he knew he had to put them aside. There would be time for venting later. Now he had to think— which, fortunately for him, he was quite good at.

He knew everyone considered him a coward. Perhaps it was true, if being a coward meant refusing to run around with a sword, blustering and posturing and risking his life to no purpose. But he had a weapon sharper and more reliable than any blade—his brain. He'd always been a plotter and a schemer, and his schemes had always worked. Well, nearly always. He needed another one now, and quickly.

His pursuers were not far behind—the closest, the Assassin, was half a mile back, three-quarters at most, last time Bernard had looked. It was two days' hard ride to Tripoli and he knew he would never make it. The horse he was on, though swift enough, lacked the endurance for an extended chase. He would have to settle things here and now.

There were two things on his side: the sun was about to set, and the three pursuers were spread out, their horses moving at different speeds. But to use those advantages he needed more rugged terrain. He had to make it off this accursed sand before the three closed in on him.

Elaine was upset and she was worried—upset that she'd allowed Bernard to slip away, and very, very worried that he was going to make good his escape. She wasn't sure exactly where the desert ended and the rocky terrain began, but she didn't think it was more than a few miles—a distance a horse could cover in minutes. Once there, Bernard would be hard to follow and even harder to find if he broke visual contact for any length of time. Add the fact that darkness was coming and the problem became very serious indeed.

But the thing that bothered her most was that she, Conrad, and Rashid had become separated. Rashid had been the first to give chase, and Conrad next, followed by Elaine, who now regretted spending precious seconds talking to Walter. If there's one thing the three friends should have learned by now it was that they needed to work together. They should have stuck close and come up with a plan. Instead they were strung out over the desert by nearly a mile, with no way to communicate or coordinate their actions. She could see Conrad up ahead—he kept disappearing and reappearing as he crossed the rolling dunes. She kicked her horse's sides again, determined to gain as much ground as possible. At least she and Conrad might be able to join forces.

As for Rashid, she couldn't see him at all. She could only hope he hadn't lost sight of Bernard.

*　*　*

After what seemed to be an eternity but was probably no more than a quarter of an hour, Bernard began to emerge from the dunes into rockier country. He gave a satisfied grunt—now at least he had a fighting chance, or, more accurately, a thinking one. A few minutes later he saw what he'd been looking for—a narrow gap in the rocks, a natural passageway that any horseman on this course would have to travel through. He spurred his mount through the gap and into a small clearing surrounded by boulders and a few trees—they were scraggly but would have to do.

He dismounted quickly—he guessed he had at most a minute to work with—and scraped some dirt and pebbles into a small pile a few feet long. Then he stripped off his cloak and his pants and laid them on the ground over the pile; in the gathering dusk it might pass for a man lying on the ground, at least at first glance. Or so Bernard fervently hoped. Then he picked up a jagged, fist-sized rock from the ground and struck his horse on the left foreleg—not too hard, he might need the beast later—but hard enough to make the animal favor the leg for a few hours. Then he crouched down, concealed behind a boulder and one of the trees, and looked back at his handiwork.

Considering how little time he'd had, it wasn't terrible. The horse was searching out grass to graze on, limping, and the dirt and pebbles under the clothing provided a very rough approximation of a body—minus the head, of course, but you couldn't have everything. The implication was clear: a horse had gone lame and thrown its rider, who now lay unconscious or dead on the ground nearby. The subterfuge wouldn't fool anyone for long, but it didn't have to. A few seconds would be enough.

Bernard tensed at the sound of an approaching rider. It was the Assassin, entering the clearing. Bernard looked cautiously through the branches as the Assassin dismounted and drew his dagger, then glanced at the horse, who obligingly took a limping stride toward a tuft of grass. Then the Assassin cautiously approached the "body" lying prone on the ground. The Assassin was fooled only for a moment, but it was enough. Just as he realized something was wrong,

Bernard sprang from his hiding place. The Assassin whirled around and received a blow to the temple from the same rock Bernard had used on the horse. He grunted in pain, made a swipe with his dagger, but took another blow to the head, which Bernard delivered with all the strength that fear could provide. The Assassin crumpled to the ground.

The fearsome Assassins! So devious! So lethal! *But not quite as devious and lethal as I am!* Bernard tossed the rock aside and stooped down to pick up the Assassin's knife—what had Walter called the thing? A *shabriyah*? The knife had blood on it and Bernard became aware of a burning sensation in his side. He looked down—the infidel had wounded him, but it didn't appear too serious. Still, it would be a pleasure to finish the dog with his own knife, assuming he wasn't already dead. . . .

The Assassin's horse gave a loud whinny, which was answered at once by another whinny not fifty yards away on the other side of the rocky passageway. Bernard scrambled back to his hiding place.

It was Conrad. Bernard smiled. They were coming one at a time, like lambs to the slaughter. It was perfect—and this time there really was a body lying on the ground. The Knight dismounted, saw the Assassin's body, and didn't even glance at the fake.

"Rashid . . . Rashid!"

There was no mistaking the concern in his voice. So Conrad really had befriended the Assassin! *Disgusting.* He deserved what was coming to him. It was fitting that he would die by his companion's dagger.

The Knight hurried to the Assassin and knelt next to him, not even bothering to draw his sword. Slowly and quietly Bernard stepped out of hiding, raised the *shabriyah*, and plunged it into the Knight's unprotected back.

Or tried to. But just before he struck there was a loud thump, accompanied by the highly unpleasant feeling that his skull had split open. He had time for one very brief thought—*Damn the girl and damn her sling!*—before the world went dark.

◈ 46 ◈

It was up to Rashid to save Bernard's life. At least that was one way of looking at it, Elaine thought as she fashioned a rough bandage for the Assassin's bloody head.

Bernard had regained consciousness quickly, groggy but alive. Conrad stood over the terrified man with his sword at his throat.

"If he dies, you die."

"Please," Bernard whimpered.

"Be silent," Conrad said, and nudged the point of his sword into Bernard's neck enough to draw blood. Bernard closed his mouth, but voided his bladder.

Conrad wrinkled his nose in disgust, then glanced at Rashid. "How is he?"

"Alive, but the longer it takes him to wake up . . ." Elaine shook her head anxiously.

"There's a waterskin on his horse," said Conrad.

Elaine got the waterskin and let a stream of water trickle gently over Rashid's face. His eyes fluttered and his head turned slightly to one side.

"That's a good sign," Conrad said. Then after a moment he asked, "Do you think Walter trusts us?"

"No," said Elaine. "But he might reserve judgment until he sees us again."

"Then the sooner we rejoin him the better."

"It's nearly dark."

"Even so, we should leave as soon as Rashid's able to ride."

"Who knows when that will be?"

"Maybe I should go back with Bernard, while you stay here and—"

"No!" Elaine said sharply. "We stay together. All three of us."

"Yes, you're right. But if there's some way we can get Rashid on a horse . . ."

"I don't think it's wise to push him until—"

"I can get on a horse," Rashid said irritably.

Conrad and Elaine looked at each other and laughed with relief. "How long have you been awake?" asked Conrad.

"Long enough. Who can sleep with all this talking?" Rashid tried to sit up but groaned, holding his head, and lay down again.

"Just rest," said Elaine.

"We should get back to the Master of Horse," said Rashid.

"You're too weak. You can hardly talk, let alone—"

"I'll be all right. A few more minutes. Then we'll go."

Elaine shook her head, but she could tell that Rashid had made up his mind. Like Conrad, he'd rather die than admit weakness.

Conrad moved his sword from Bernard's throat. "Looks like you'll live. For a while, anyway." He reached down and dragged the cowering Regent up by his hair. "Now get moving. Thanks to you, we have a lot of ground to cover."

They rode slowly for Rashid's sake, though the darkness slowed them as well. Elaine covered Rashid in Bernard's cloak to keep out the chill and Conrad held his arm to help steady him in the saddle, but after a while Rashid shook him off.

"I'm fine now," he said. This wasn't entirely true—his head

ached abominably and he was seeing two of everything, but he was lucid and able to keep down some food and water and he could feel strength, very gradually, seeping back into his body. The physical discomfort was less painful than his embarrassment at falling for Bernard's crude trick—something Conrad would no doubt tease him about sooner or later. But then, he supposed he deserved it.

After two hours they saw the fire from what must surely be Walter's camp, and Elaine rode ahead to let him know they were coming in. Minutes later, while Rashid lay down by the fire to rest, Conrad and Elaine took Walter aside, and Bernard confessed everything. He was too demoralized to refuse, and his shame was so evident that Walter knew the confession was genuine and not coerced. The old soldier was shocked and angry—and then, after the truth had sunk in, nearly as ashamed as Bernard.

"I don't know what to say. I can hardly believe it."

"But you do believe it," Elaine said.

"Yes, I believe it. His guilt is written plain on his face. I should have seen through him. He was always a little too clever, too slippery."

"In hindsight, yes," Elaine said. "But I didn't see through him, either. No one did."

"I wonder the two of you don't strike me down on the spot for serving such a master," said Walter glumly.

"As far as I'm concerned it's over and done, let's speak no more of it," said Elaine.

Walter glanced hopefully at Conrad, who nodded his agreement.

"I'm greatly in debt to both of you," said Walter. "But tell me . . . you've been gone more than four months now! Where have you been, what have you been doing?"

Over the next hour, Elaine and Conrad told him the story of their journey—how they had come to travel together, how the Old Man had charged them with retrieving a certain letter he had written, how they had crossed the Al-Jazirah and its two great rivers and then crossed the Zagros Mountains and encountered the Great

King of the Mongols and had at last recovered the Old Man's letter. Only Conrad's slavery and their encounter with Chormaghun were omitted. As Walter listened he marveled at what he was hearing but didn't doubt it for a moment. This was no well-rehearsed tale but a plain statement of the truth.

Conrad glanced at the soldiers who had survived the fight. "These men—are they loyal to you or to Bernard?"

"To me, as long as I pay them."

"They'll be paid, double what they were promised. Make that clear to them."

"I'll see to it, Your Grace."

Elaine said, "What's the mood in Tripoli? Speak plainly."

Walter hesitated. "I don't wish to give offense."

Elaine said, "We need to know the truth, Walter. All of it."

"The mood in Tripoli is one of confusion, but Bernard has put it about that you and this Assassin are lovers, and that the Prince approves the arrangement. So opinion is against you both."

"The people will believe the truth when they hear it," said Elaine.

"I believe they will, Your Grace. Unless Bernard tries to muddy the waters by recanting his confession."

"You must persuade him not to do so," Conrad said.

"Never fear, I can be very persuasive," said Walter with a grim smile.

Recalling the dungeon at Tripoli, Elaine repressed a shudder, though if anyone deserved a stay in that terrible place it was Bernard.

"What's the news from Antioch?" Conrad said. "Is my father still alive?"

"Yes, Your Grace, but . . ." Walter hesitated.

"Go on."

"Much weakened, Your Grace, from what I'm told."

Conrad nodded somberly. Of course, his father had been in decline for some time; but now Conrad wondered if Bernard might have had something to do with it—slow poison, perhaps. Conrad would look into that as soon as he could. *I wonder what plans Bernard had for me,* he thought.

Aloud he said, "Rashid must rest for a day or two and you have some wounded men to attend to as well. In the meantime the Old Man should be informed that we're coming and that we have his letter. Send someone ahead with a flag of truce to deliver the message."

"How will he find the Old Man, Your Grace?"

"Tell him to ride due east and the Old Man will find him. You and the others stay here and serve as our escort. Then you'll take Bernard back to Tripoli and hold him until we arrive, which should be within the week."

"It will be done, Your Grace," said Walter, and started to leave. Then he turned back.

"Your Graces," he said, taking both Conrad and Elaine in with his glance.

"What is it?" said Elaine.

"Shall we make preparations for a wedding, as before?"

There was a momentary silence, then Conrad said, "There will be no wedding. Princess Elaine does not desire it." Elaine, surprised, glanced sharply at Conrad, who continued calmly, "She will rule in Tripoli and I in Antioch and our kingdoms will be allies."

"Yes, Your Grace," said Walter. "And, Your Graces, one more thing if I may. Bernard had promised me a knighthood. I do not ask for that, but I do ask, if I serve you faithfully, that you might restore me to my position as Master of Horse."

Conrad regarded him coldly. "Do you expect us to bargain like fishwives? Do your duty and we'll reward you as we see fit."

"Yes, Your Grace," Walter said, and beat a hasty retreat. But he was almost smiling as he walked away. He'd been dealing with Bernard for so long he'd forgotten what real royalty was like.

Conrad said, "I'm going to check on Rashid. He may be hungry."

Elaine watched him leave, and thought about what he'd said to Walter regarding the wedding. Conrad, at long last, had accepted the fact that they would never be married. That should have come as a great relief. But, strangely, she did not feel relieved at all.

The caravan broke camp the second day after Bernard's capture, heading toward the Eagle's Nest. Elaine, Rashid, and Conrad rode together, but Rashid was still recovering and said little, and Elaine's attempts to engage Conrad weren't very successful. He seemed preoccupied. When he spoke at all it was mainly to Walter concerning military matters such as where the outriders should be posted, or where an ambush was likely to come from.

Watching Walter obey Conrad's orders and defer to his opinions, Elaine could not help being impressed, for it was clearly not only Conrad's status as Prince that Walter respected, but Conrad himself. And the other men, hard-bitten and coarse though they were, evidenced a similar attitude whenever Conrad chanced to speak to them. Elaine had been aware of the change in Conrad for a while, but perhaps she hadn't fully appreciated it.

"What are you thinking?" she asked him finally.

"Nothing pleasant," he said.

"Tell me."

He took a breath. "What if Bernard didn't act alone?"

This hit Elaine like a thunderbolt. "I don't . . . I can't imagine . . ." she sputtered, then paused. "It didn't even occur to me. But you're right, of course."

"I'm not saying it's true, but we have to find out. You investigate in Tripoli—Walter will help you. I'll do the same in Antioch."

"You think Bernard might have included someone from Antioch in his plot?" Elaine said.

"I don't know, but best to be sure," said Conrad, thinking of his father's illness.

"We could investigate together," Elaine said hopefully.

"We will, of course. But it makes sense for you to concentrate on Tripoli, and me on Antioch."

"Yes, of course," she said. It did make sense for them to work separately, as Conrad had pointed out. So why was she so disappointed?

Two days later they entered territory that, according to Rashid, marked the eastern boundary of the Old Man's domain. Conrad sent Walter and his men south to Tripoli, with Bernard in tow.

"Send word if there's any trouble," Conrad said.

"I will, Your Grace," Walter replied. "But I doubt there will be once the truth is spread about. And I'll make sure that it is."

"Good. God be with you."

"And with you, Your Graces." Walter bowed to Elaine as well, and his men turned their mounts toward Tripoli.

In less than an hour a group of riders approached from the west. Conrad recognized their hawk-nosed leader and spurred his horse forward, flanked by Elaine and Rashid.

"Prince Conrad, Princess Elaine," Hasan greeted them courteously. He glanced at Rashid but didn't address him.

"Hasan," Conrad acknowledged.

"You have something for me," said Hasan, holding out his hand.

"We prefer to give the letter to the Old Man personally," Conrad said.

"He is properly called the Sheikh," said Hasan.

Rashid said quietly, "We prefer to give the letter personally to the Sheikh."

Hasan looked at him sharply. In situations such as this, young Assassins were expected to be seen, not heard.

"Hasan, I meant no offense," Conrad said. "But Rashid is right. We will give the letter personally to the Sheikh."

Hasan wasn't used to having his orders refused within the borders of the Old Man's territory. But now he became the most recent observer to note the change in Conrad. There was no conceit in the Knight's gaze, nor any of the old bravado, yet there was no hint of weakness either. And Rashid showed much the same demeanor. It was annoying, but it would be foolish to fight, now that the Old Man's objective was so nearly accomplished.

"We will be in the Eagle's Nest shortly," said Hasan, and turned his horse westward.

An hour later the massive wooden doors of the Eagle's Nest opened ponderously and the three friends followed Hasan into the court-yard and dismounted. The Old Man was waiting for them. He looked at the three friends for a moment as if he hardly dared believe they were really there, then murmured almost to himself, "Praise God, you have returned."

Rashid reached inside his shirt and took out the parchment and held it out to the Old Man, who unrolled it and looked at it briefly, then handed it to Hasan, who hurried off with it. The Old Man looked back at Rashid.

"You've done well," he said. "You all have. And I see you've paid a price for it," he added, looking at the bandages on Rashid's head.

"It's of no concern," Rashid said.

"We have much to discuss with you," said Conrad.

"Yes," said the Old Man. "But rest first, and partake of a good meal, and then it will be a better time to talk. Is it not so?"

Conrad looked at Elaine, who nodded; she thought the Old Man was right. "Very well," said Conrad.

"Good," said the Old Man. "My servants will show you both to your quarters and we will meet when you're ready."

Elaine and Conrad followed the respective servants indicated by the Old Man, but first they exchanged a quick, surreptitious look. They knew they were going to have to tell the Old Man something that was likely to make him very angry.

· 47 ·

"You swore not to read the letter. You swore on the soul of your father."

The Old Man had kept his temper but his voice was hard and Elaine could imagine what it might be like if he lost control. It wasn't a pleasant thing to contemplate.

"I did not read the letter," said Elaine.

"Then how did you come to know its contents?"

"A trick," Elaine said frankly, and explained how Conrad had used his sword to duplicate the letter in the dirt.

Conrad, Elaine, and Rashid had rested and eaten and then requested an audience with the Old Man, which had been promptly granted. They were alone with him now, and the meeting had barely begun when he realized they knew what was in the letter. When Elaine finished her explanation the Old Man looked at Rashid accusingly.

"And you permitted this?"

"I thought," mumbled Rashid, "that since the letter itself was not being read, at least not—"

"Enough," the Old Man said. His demeanor was hard to read, but it didn't seem that he intended to have them executed on the spot. "Well, you know what you know. And now?"

"Your letter was wise and true," said Elaine. "The Arrow-makers are everything you said and more. We know, for we have fought them in battle and lived in their camp and Conrad and Rashid were even granted an audience with their Great King."

At this the Old Man's eyes widened. "You spoke with him?" he said to Conrad.

"We did."

"What manner of man is he?"

"He's a great warrior, and leads a powerful army which fights with guile as well as with weapons and horses. As you predicted, he plans to cross the mountains soon and he'll sweep everything before him if he can."

"When do you think he will come?"

"I don't know," Conrad said. "This spring, or possibly the next."

"How large is his army?"

"Large enough."

There was a silence, then Conrad said, "You should not have sent your letter to Bernard. You should have sent it to my father or to me." His tone was direct and matter-of-fact. The Old Man answered the same way.

"I had no choice but Bernard. Your father was in failing health, and you had just returned from France and the reports I received concerning you . . ." He hesitated.

"Did not inspire confidence," Conrad finished for him.

The Old Man inclined his head tactfully.

"Those reports were wrong," Conrad said calmly. "Bernard will soon be in Tripoli's dungeon. Elaine will rule in Tripoli and I will rule in Antioch in my father's name, then in my own if and when he dies."

"You will not marry?" the Old Man said, sounding surprised.

"No," Conrad said. "Elaine does not wish it. But we'll form an alliance."

Conrad paused, then went on in a measured but firm tone, "I hope you'll forgive me for speaking plainly, but I know that most Muslims detest you Assassins almost as much as we Christians do.

Nevertheless, you must find some way to make peace with them—at least enough of a peace so that they will stand with you, and with us, against the Mongols."

The Old Man sighed. An alliance of Muslim with Muslim, Christian with Christian, and ultimately Christian with Muslim was what he himself had proposed. Yet, hearing it spoken aloud only made him realize what an immense undertaking it would be. There was too much hatred and mistrust—much of it, he knew, caused by his own activities—to overcome in too short a time.

"It will not be easy," he said.

"It may be impossible," Rashid spoke up suddenly. "But the alternative is just as impossible. We've seen it." And he described the pyramid of skulls outside the once prosperous town of Torgreh.

The Old Man studied Rashid as he talked. The Christians had changed, but so had Rashid. He was respectful, but not intimidated. His gaze was direct, his voice steady. He seemed capable of thinking for himself. He would require careful watching.

Elaine said, "Did you not mean the words you wrote in your letter?"

"I meant them," said the Old Man.

"Then why hesitate?" she asked. "Nothing we do will ensure success, but we're sure to fail if we do nothing. You will do what you can to reconcile with the Muslims in the region and prepare them for an alliance with us. And we will do everything possible in Antioch and Tripoli to make the Christians join that alliance. Rashid will serve as go-between—we trust him and so do you. He will be an honest messenger, loyal to you but truthful to us. Agreed?"

The Old Man was silent. His refusal to speak before he was ready reminded Conrad of the Khan. His eyes rested on each of them in turn, and finally he spoke a single word.

"Agreed."

After the three had left, the Old Man returned to his chamber to think things over.

He did not trust Conrad or Elaine completely—he never trusted anyone completely, especially Christians—but both had obviously grown a great deal during the course of their mission, and no doubt they would prove to be far more reliable allies than Bernard.

Then again, now that the letter had been retrieved, perhaps the Old Man should do an about-face and attempt to make an alliance with the Great King of the Arrow-makers instead of fighting against him. An intriguing notion, but the thought of kneeling before a pagan overlord was distasteful in the extreme.

There was another possibility, and that was to fall back on the weapon the Old Man had used so successfully for many years. He could send an Assassin to eliminate the Great King! Perhaps the empire of the Arrow-makers would disintegrate, as so many empires had done when deprived of their founder. Of course this was the riskiest option of all, for to fail was to incur the enmity of the Great King and his people forever.

The Old Man sighed, and began to consume his small repast of figs and water. The situation was complicated and fraught with danger on every side and it would take many nights of reflection and prayer to decide the best course of action. The life of a ruler was not an easy one despite what most men believed, for there was much to be thought on, and much to be done.

The three friends left the Old Man's room and walked down a staircase into the courtyard. Rashid said, "I have to go see Hasan."

"Are you still taking orders from him?" said Conrad.

"Not orders, exactly. But he wants to know everything that happened to us, for future reference."

"Oh. Well, tell him everything," said Conrad.

"Of course."

"Tell him about the Khan, and Chormaghun's tent, and the corpse . . ."

"The corpse?"

"You know, the one you found under Bernard's cloak, out in the desert . . ."

Elaine laughed and Rashid said, "Be quiet, infidel!" as he walked away, but they could see that he was smiling, too.

Elaine looked up, over the walls of the Eagle's Nest. The sun was just setting. The sky was a vivid blue and the gray-and-white spires of the surrounding mountain peaks stood out in stark contrast.

"It's lovely, isn't it?" said Elaine.

"What? Oh—yes, very. What do you think, will the Old Man cooperate with us?"

"I think he doesn't have a choice, if he wants to resist the Khan."

"I suppose so. I think the differences between Antioch and Tripoli are manageable, but what concerns me—"

"I want to talk about something else," Elaine said abruptly.

Conrad looked at her in surprise. "Go on."

"You've fallen into a rather unfortunate habit of late," she said.

Conrad frowned. "What habit is that?"

"Presuming to speak for me, instead of letting me speak for myself."

"I'm not aware of having done so," he said with something of his old stiffness.

"Well, you have, twice. A few days ago with Walter, and just now with the Old Man. You keep saying I don't wish to marry you."

"You can hardly fault me for that. You've said so yourself, many times."

This was a very fair point, which she decided to ignore.

"You have to admit that marriage would be the most logical way of making our two kingdoms into one," she said, as if he had been denying it. "Even the Old Man seemed to think so."

He regarded her warily. The familiar feeling that she was setting a trap came over him. "Perhaps so," he said carefully. "But I've come to believe that your opinion about marriage is a sound one. It should be an affair of the heart as well as of politics."

"I'm glad you agree," she said.

"Well, then," he said.

"Well, then what?"

"Well, then . . . I am merely telling people that you don't wish to marry me."

"And I am telling you, do not presume to speak for me." There was a hint of a smile in her eyes so that Conrad began to understand. But he dared not speak. Someone or something had cast a spell on her and he was afraid that a word from him might break it.

Elaine sighed. He was still a little slow sometimes. "I do believe that a marriage must be of the heart; and such shall this marriage be, at least on my part. That is, if you're still willing."

For a terrible moment Elaine feared her change of heart had come too late, but he was just making sure of her. They gazed at each other for a long time. They were not aware of willing it to happen, but they realized their hands were touching, and they pulled back instantly. There were various Assassins and castle officials passing through the courtyard, and in such circumstances it was unthinkable for two properly bred royals to make an overt display of affection.

But as every lover knows, it's possible to kiss with the eyes and that is what Conrad and Elaine did, just as the last rays of the setting sun cast a gentle glow on the spot where they stood.

Knowing that this would be their last night together, at least for a while, the three decided to spend it as they'd spent so many over the past months, by a fire under the open sky. They were outside the castle, sheltered by the walls but far enough away so they could imagine a world with only them in it. They spoke of all they had done and seen and all that still remained to be done, and Conrad and Elaine talked of their wedding plans, which made Rashid smile, and then Elaine, of course, combed her hair one hundred times, which made Conrad and Rashid smile. Then weariness overtook them and they settled under their blankets and into themselves.

Rashid had never seen so many stars, nor had they ever seemed so hard and bright. Perhaps because of them, or because of the look in Conrad's and Elaine's eyes as they'd talked of marriage, Rashid's thoughts turned to Paradise. For a long time, his visit there had been the most real thing that ever happened to him, but the events of the recent journey had eclipsed it; the memory had faded. He still believed in it, and wanted to return someday, but there no longer seemed any reason to hurry. There was a life to be lived first, and perhaps there were parts of that life—friendship, for example—that gave a hint of paradise right here on earth.

He knew Hasan would strongly disagree, but the Old Man . . . well, the Old Man had secrets in his eyes. What was it he had said that first day in the Eagle's Nest—that the mission was something that none of them could accomplish alone, but they might be able to accomplish together? Had he suspected all along that the three of them would end up as friends—that they would have to, if they were to survive? Perhaps one day the Old Man might find him worthy of sharing some of his secrets; and after all Rashid had been through, he might even know a thing or two worth sharing with the Old Man. He looked forward to their next meeting.

Conrad was also thinking of Paradise, though for him it took the form of the young woman lying a few feet away. He wondered if she was still awake. It was tempting to steal a kiss . . . but perhaps it was better to wait. It was all too new. Now he must give thought to becoming a ruler. He'd learned much since riding Tranquil through the gates of Tripoli, but he knew he had much still to learn. Of one thing he was certain: he would try to rule as the Khan did, from an inner strength, and not as the Khwarazmian Shah, who had depended on jewels and ceremony and the outward trappings of power. And that made Conrad think of something else—he needed a sword.

There was nothing wrong with the one he'd bought from the Kurds, but he wanted a new one. He would design it himself. It would be like Charles's sword in some ways, but different in others, for Conrad had seen and done things that Charles never had, and surely a ruler should have a sword all his own. He knew that Charles would approve of that, though he realized he no longer felt the need for Charles's approval. Then he reflected that Charles would approve of the fact that Conrad no longer needed his approval, and this thought brought with it a peaceful smile.

Like Rashid, Elaine was looking at the sky, particularly that long, white sprinkling of stars strewn across it like a milky pathway. It was a celestial reminder of the earthly journey she'd just taken and, she supposed, was still taking. She heard Conrad's deep, regular breathing and found it comforting. How wrong she'd been about him! If someone had told her that first day in Tripoli that she would fall in love with him—of course, he'd changed since that time; but then again, so had she. Neither of them alone was ready to rule, but together she thought they would be able to make a go of it. Above all, she would continue to trust her instincts, which had brought her through several varieties of hell (not without difficulties, true, and not without considerable help from her two companions); but from this point on her instincts would be placed at the service of her duty, which was to protect the countries and the people she and Conrad would rule together.

That night in her prayers she asked for blessings upon King Edmond, Queen Catherine, Conrad, and Rashid, and, for the first time, upon Tripoli and Antioch, the two kingdoms of which she would soon be Queen.

Though by different paths, the three converged on the same thought just before they drifted off to sleep. The future was uncertain—when was it not?—but it seemed they had already lived one lifetime together and there was no reason to fear the start of another. After all, they had each other and that, at least for the moment, was more than enough.

THE END

HISTORICAL NOTE

In 1095, 125 years before the events described in the novel, an army of Europeans, mainly from France and Germany, invaded what we now call the Middle East. This was the First Crusade, which resulted in the establishment of four "Crusader states," based, respectively, around the cities of Tripoli, Antioch, Jerusalem, and Edessa.

During the decades that followed there were other Crusades, as well as counterattacks by Muslim forces, and the fortunes of the Crusader states rose and fell, until by 1220 only two—Tripoli and Antioch—remained under Christian control. Both states underwent complex internal dynastic struggles over the years. Along the way, they sometimes squabbled with each other and sometimes made efforts to unite, always maintaining a precarious existence in a hostile and dangerous region. This is the world that Elaine, Rashid, and Conrad find themselves in as the novel begins; while they are fictional, the historical context is authentic, if somewhat simplified. (For example, Antioch was a principality, ruled by a prince, while Tripoli was a county, ruled by a count, and each state had its own hierarchy of titles, divided by gender. For the sake of simplicity I used the more familiar terminology of king, queen, prince, and princess for both Antioch and Tripoli.)

Three major figures in the novel are taken from history. The first is the mysterious character known to the Crusaders as the Old Man of the Mountain. Historically, the sect of the Assassins, also called the Nizaris, was larger than the novel implies. It originated in Persia in about 1090 and thereafter spread into what is now Syria, and occupied quite a few castles and fortresses at the peak of its power. The Old Man of the Mountain was the leader of the Syrian branch of the sect, and over the years there were a number of men who occupied that position. (The "Eagle's Nest" referred to the sect's headquarters in Persia, but I borrowed the name for the Old Man's castle in Syria. I have also borrowed the name of the most famous Old Man, Sheikh ad-Din as-Sinan, who actually lived a generation earlier than portrayed in the novel.) The unique method of motivating young Assassins by giving them a brief trip to "Paradise" is mentioned in several sources, though it has never been definitively proven.

Ala al-Din Muhammad II, the Khwarazmian Shah, is the second major historical figure to make an appearance. His empire, which included modern-day Iran, was extensive and his enormous army was considered invincible, until he made the mistake of offending Genghis Khan. After being defeated on the battlefield, he did flee from the Mongols disguised as a beggar but died on a small island in the Caspian Sea before he could be captured, and so was not executed as described in the novel. However, that method of execution—crushing prisoners under a banquet floor—really was inflicted by the Mongols on defeated monarchs to avoid shedding royal blood.

Finally, Genghis Khan was of course real, and one of the most striking figures in world history. The Mongol invasion and conquest of the Khwarazmian Empire was every bit as brutal as portrayed, though a bit more complicated. Four separate Mongol armies swept into the Empire from different directions. One of those armies did indeed chase the Shah to the western shores of the Caspian Sea, but the Khan himself was farther to the east, commanding an army that destroyed Nishapur (hometown of Gaspar the Persian); I took the liberty of reassigning the Khan to the western army so that our three travelers could meet him in person. "Torgreh" is a fictional town, conveniently located to serve the story, but the pyramid of skulls was a real Mongol tactic, designed to terrorize other cities into capitulating without a fight. Despite such atrocities, the Khan was a very able administrator who believed in the rule of law, forbade torture, conferred promotions based on merit rather than birth, and allowed his subjects (those that survived his conquests) complete religious freedom. Just as the Old Man of the Mountain feared, the Mongols eventually crossed the Zagros Mountains and invaded the Holy Land, though the Khan himself had died in a hunting accident by the time this occurred. But that is a subject for another book.

For those interested in more historical detail, there are many excellent books on the Crusades; a good start for the general reader is *The Dream and the Tomb: A History of the Crusades* by Robert Payne.

Storm from the East: From Genghis Khan to Khubilai Khan by Robert Marshall is a wonderful introduction to Genghis Khan and the Mongols.

For more information about the Old Man of the Mountain and his world, I recommend *The Assassins: A Radical Sect in Islam* by Bernard Lewis.

ACKNOWLEDGMENTS

First and foremost, a heartfelt thank-you to my wonderful wife, Laurie, who inspired me to write the novel, patiently read every draft, and always responded with enthusiasm, along with gentle but cogent observations and suggestions.

Thanks also to others in my family—Kelly, Sean, Logan, and Britta—for their encouragement, especially Kelly, who read the manuscript with close attention and provided many excellent suggestions.

Thanks to my agents, Steve Fisher and Lee Dinstman at APA, for their knowledge, guidance, persistence, and professionalism.

An enormous thank-you to Susan Chang, Tor's editor extraordinaire, who has an eagle eye for detail but never loses sight of the big picture. Her probing questions and insights helped bring the story into focus and made the book immeasurably better than it otherwise would have been.

Finally, I must thank the late Jack Repcheck, without whose enthusiasm and generosity of spirit this novel would most likely not exist. Jack, you are greatly missed.

ABOUT THE AUTHOR

ROBERT COCHRAN is an Emmy Award–winning executive producer and writer who cocreated the international television series phenomenon *24*. He also worked on a number of historical television projects, including the highly successful *Attila*, among many other popular shows. *The Sword and the Dagger* is his first novel. He lives in Monterey, California.